JONATHAN KELLERMAN

WHEN THE BOUGH BREAKS

headline

First published in Great Britain in 1985
as SHRUNKEN HEADS by Macdonald & Co (Publishers) Ltd

This edition published in 2008
by HEADLINE PUBLISHING GROUP

1

ISBN 978 0 7553 5924 0

Typeset in Fournier MT by Palimpsest Book Production Limited,
Grangemouth, Stirlingshire

Printed and bound in the UK by
CPI Mackays, Chatham ME5 8TD

Headline's policy is to use papers that are natural, renewable and recyclable products and
made from wood grown in sustainable forests. The logging and manufacturing processes are
expected to conform to the environmental regulations of the country of origin.

HEADLINE PUBLISHING GROUP
An Hachette Livre UK Company
338 Euston Road
London NW1 3BH

www.headline.co.uk

To Faye, Jesse and Rachel

1

IT WAS shaping up as a beautiful morning. The last thing I wanted to hear about was murder.

A cool Pacific current had swept its way across the coastline for two days running, propeling the pollution to Pasadena. My house is nestled in the foothills just north of Bel Air, situated atop an old bridle path that snakes its way around Beverly Glen, where opulence gives way to self-conscious funk. It's a neighborhood of Porsches and coyotes, bad sewers and sequestered streams.

The place itself is eighteen hundred square feet of silvered redwood, weathered shingles and tinted glass. In the suburbs it might be a shack; up here in the hills it's a rural retreat – nothing fancy, but lots of terraces, decks, pleasing angles and visual surprises. The house had been designed by and for a Hungarian artist who went broke trying to peddle oversized polychromatic triangles to the galleries on La Cienega. Art's loss had been my gain by way of LA probate court. On a good day – like today – the place came with an ocean view, a cerulean patch that peeked timidly above the Palisades.

I had slept alone with the the windows open – burglars and neo-Mansonites be damned – and awoke at ten, naked, covers thown to the floor in the midst of some forgotten dream.

Feeling lazy and sated, I propped myself on my elbows, drew up the covers and stared at the caramel layers of sunlight streaming through French doors. What finally got me up was the invasion of a housefly who alternated between searching my sheets for carrion and dive-bombing my head.

I shuffled to the bathroom and began filling a tub, then made my way to the kitchen to scavenge, taking the fly with me. I put up coffee, and the fly and I shared an onion bagel. Ten twenty on a Monday morning with nowhere to go and nothing to do. Oh, blessed decadence.

It had been almost half a year since my premature retirement and I was still amazed at how easy it was to make the transition from compulsive overachiever to self-indulgent bum. Obviously I'd had it in me from the beginning.

I returned to the bathroom, sat on the rim of the tub munching and drew up a vague plan for the day: A leisurely soak, a cursory scan of the morning paper, perhaps a jog down the canyon and back, a shower, a visit to—

The doorbell jarred me out of my reverie.

I tied a towel around my waist and walked to the front entry in time to see Milo let himself in.

'It was unlocked,' he said, closing the door hard and tossing the *Times* on the sofa. He stared at me and I drew the towel tighter.

'Good morning, nature boy.'

I motioned him in.

'You really should lock the door, my friend. I've got files at the station that illustrate nicely what happens to people who don't.'

'Good morning, Milo.'

I padded into the kitchen and poured two cups of coffee.

Milo followed me like a lumbering shadow, opened the refrigerator and took out a plate of cold pizza that I had no recollection of ever owning. He tailed me back to the living room, collapsed on my old leather sofa – an artifact of the abandoned office on Wilshire – balanced the plate on his thigh and stretched out his legs.

I turned off the bathwater and settled opposite him on a camelskin ottoman.

Milo is a big man – six-two, two-twenty – with a big man's way of going loose and dangly when he gets off his feet. This morning he looked like an oversized rag doll slumped against the cushions – a doll with a broad, pleasant face, almost boyish except for the acne pits that peppered the skin, and the tired eyes. The eyes were startlingly green and rimmed with red, topped by shaggy dark brows and a Kennedyesque shock of thick black hair. His nose was large and high-bridged, his lips full, childishly soft. Sideburns five years out of date trailed down the scarred cheeks.

As usual he wore ersatz Brooks Brothers: Olive-green gabardine suit, yellow button-down, mint and gold rep stripe tie, oxblood wing tips. The total effect was as preppy as W. C. Fields in red skivvies.

He ignored me and concentrated on the pizza.

'So glad you could make it for breakfast.'

When his plate was empty he asked, 'So, how are you doing, pal?'

'I *was* doing great. What can I do for you, Milo?'

'Who says I want you to do anything?' He brushed crumbs from his lap to the rug. 'Maybe this is a social call.'

'You waltzing in, unannounced, with that bloodhound look all over your face isn't a social call.'

3

'Such intuitive powers.' He ran his hands over his face, as if washing without water. 'I need a favor,' he said.

'Take the car. I won't be needing it until late afternoon.'

'No, it's not that this time. I need your professional services.'

That gave me pause.

'You're out of my age range,' I said. 'Besides, I'm out of the profession.'

'I'm not kidding, Alex. I've got one of your colleagues lying on a slab at the morgue. Fellow by the name of Morton Handler.'

I knew the name, not the face.

'Handler's a psychiatrist.'

'Psychiatrist, psychologist. Minor semantic distinction at this point. What he is, is dead. Throat slashed, a little bit of evisceration tossed in. Along with a lady friend – same treatment for her but worse – sexual mutilation, nose sliced off. The place where it happened – his place – was an abattoir.'

Abattoir. Milo's master's degree in American Lit asserting itself.

I put down my coffee cup.

'OK, Milo. I've lost my appetite. Now tell me what all of that has to do with me.'

He went on as if he hadn't heard me.

'I got called on it at five A.M. I've been knee-deep in blood and crud since then. It stunk in there – people smell bad when they die. I'm not talking decay, this is the stench that sets in before decay. I thought I was used to it. Every so often I catch another whiff and it gets me right here.' He poked himself in the belly. 'Five in the morning. I left an irritated lover in bed. My head feels ready to implode. Gobs of flesh at five in the morning. Jesus.'

He stood and looked out the window, gazing out over the tops of pines and eucalyptus. From where I sat I could see smoke rising in indolent swirls from a distant fireplace.

'It's really nice up here, Alex. Does it ever bore you, being in paradise with nothing to do?'

'Not a hint of ennui.'

'Yeah, I guess not. You don't want to hear any more about Handler and the girl.'

'Stop playing passive-aggressive, Milo, and spit it out.'

He turned and looked down at me. The big, ugly face showed new signs of fatigue.

'I'm depressed, Alex.' He held out his empty cup like some overgrown, slack-jawed Oliver Twist. 'Which is why I'll tolerate more of this disgusting swill.'

I took the cup and got him a refill. He gulped it audibly.

'We've got a possible witness. A kid who lives in the same building. She's pretty confused, not sure what she saw. I took one look at her and thought of you. You could talk to her, maybe try a little hypnosis to enhance her memory.'

'Don't you have Behavioral Sciences for that?'

He reached into his coat pocket and took out a handful of Polaroids. 'Look at the beauties.'

I gave the pictures a second's glance. What I saw turned my stomach. I returned them quickly.

'For God's sake, don't show me stuff like that!'

'Some mess, huh? Blood and crud.' He drained his cup, lifting it high to catch every last drop. 'Behavioral Science is cut down to one guy who's kept busy weeding weirdos out of the department. Next priority is counseling the weirdos who slip through. If I put in an application for this kind of thing I'll get a request to fill out another application form. They don't want to do it. On top of that, they don't know anything about kids. You do.'

'I don't know anything about homicide.'

'Forget homicide. That's my problem. Talk to a seven year old.'

I hesitated. He held out his hands. The palms were white, well scrubbed.

'Hey, I'm not expecting a total freebie. I'll buy you lunch. There's a fair-to-middling Italian place with surprisingly good gnocchi not far from the . . .'

'Not far from the abattoir?' I grimaced. 'No thanks. Anyway, I can't be bought for noodles.'

'So what can I offer you by way of a bribe – you've got everything – the house in the hills, the fancy car, the Ralph Lauren gear with jogging shoes to match. Christ, you've got retirement at thirty-three and a goddamn perpetual tan. Just talking about it is getting me pissed.'

'Yes, but am I happy?'

'I suspect so.'

'You're right.' I thought of the grisly photos. 'And I'm certainly not in need of a free pass to the Grand Guignol.'

'You know,' he said, 'I'll bet underneath all of that mellow is a bored young man.'

'Crap.'

'Crap nothing. How long has it been, six months?'

'Five and a half.'

'Five and a half, then. When I met you – correct that, soon *after* I met you, you were a vibrant guy, high energy,

6

lots of opinions. Your *mind* was working. Now all I hear about is hot tubs, how fast you run your goddamned mile, the different kinds of sunset you can see from your deck – to use your jargon, it's *regression*. Cutesy-poo short pants, roller-skating, water play. Like half the people in this city, you're functioning on a six-year-old level.'

I laughed.

'And you're making me this offer – to get involved in blood and crud – as a form of occupational therapy.'

'Alex, you can break your ass trying to achieve Nirvana Through Inertia, but it won't work. It's like that Woody Allen line – you mellow too much, you ripen and rot.'

I slapped my bare chest.

'No signs of decay yet.'

'It's internal, comes from within, breaks through when you're least expecting it.'

'Thank you, Doctor Sturgis.'

He gave me a disgusted look, went into the kitchen and returned with his mouth buried in a pear.

'S'good.'

'You're welcome.'

'All right, Alex, forget it. I've got this dead psychiatrist and this Gutierrez girl hacked up. I've got a seven year old who thinks she might have seen or heard something except she's too damned scared to make any sense of it. I ask you for two hours of your time – and time is one thing you've got plenty of – and I get bullshit.'

'Hold on. I didn't say I wouldn't do it. You have to give me time to assimilate this. I just woke up and you barge in and drop double homicide on me.'

He shot his wrist out from under his shirt cuff and peered

7

at his Timex. 'Ten thirty-seven. Poor baby.' He glared at me and chomped into the pear, getting juice on his chin.

'Anyway, you might recall that the last time I had anything to do with police business it was traumatic.'

'Hickle was a fluke. And you were a victim – of sorts. I'm not interested in getting you involved in this. Just an hour or two talking to a little kid. Like I said, hypnosis if it looks right. Then we eat gnocchi. I return to my place and try to reclaim my amour, you're free to go back to Spaceout Castle here. Finis. In a week we get together for a pure social time – a little sashimi down in Japtown. OK?'

'What did the kid actually see?' I asked and watched my relaxing day fly out the window.

'Shadows, voices, two guys, maybe three. But who really knows? She's a little kid, she's totally traumatized. The mother's just as scared and she impresses me as a lady who was no nuclear physicist in the first place. I didn't know how to approach her, Alex. I tried to be nice, go easy. It would have been helpful to have a juvie officer there, but there aren't too many of those any more. The department would rather keep three dozen pencil-pushing deputy chiefs around.'

He gnawed the pear down to the core.

'Shadows, voices. That's it. You're the *language specialist*, right? You know how to communicate with the little ones. If you can get her to open up, great. If she comes forth with anything resembling an ID, fantastic. If not, them's the breaks and at least we tried.'

Language specialist. It had been a while since I'd used the phrase – back in the aftermath of the Hickle affair, when I'd found myself suddenly spinning out of control, the faces of Stuart Hickle and all the kids he'd harmed marching through my head. Milo had taken me drinking. At about two in the morning he had wondered out loud why the kids had let it go on for so long.

'They didn't talk because nobody knew how to listen,' I'd said. 'They thought it was their fault, anyway.'

'Yeah?' He looked up, bleary-eyed, gripping his stein with both hands. 'I hear stuff like that from the juvie gals.'

'That's the way they think when they're little, egocentric. Like they're the center of the world. Mommy slips, breaks a leg, they blame themselves.'

'How long does it last?'

'In some people it never goes away. For the rest of us it's a gradual process. By eight or nine we see things more clearly – but at any age an adult can manipulate kids, convince them it's their fault.'

'Assholes,' muttered Milo. 'So how do you get their heads straight?'

'You have to know how kids think at different ages. Developmental stages. You talk their language – you become a language specialist.'

'That's what you do?'

'That's what I do.'

A few minutes later he asked: 'You think guilt is bad?'

'Not necessarily. It's part of what holds us together. Too much, though, can cripple.'

He nodded. 'Yeah, I like that. Shrinks always seem to be saying guilt is a no-no. Your approach I can buy. I tell you, we could use a lot more guilt – the world's full of fucked-up savages.'

At that moment he got no argument from me.

We talked a bit more. The alcohol tugged at our consciousness and we started to laugh, then cry. The bartender stopped polishing his glasses and stared.

It had been a low — a seriously low — period in my life and I remembered who'd been there to help me through it.

I watched Milo nibble at the last specks of pear with curiously small, sharp teeth.

'Two hours?' I asked.

'At the most.'

'Give me an hour or so to get ready, clear up some business.'

Having convinced me to help him didn't seem to cheer him up. He nodded and exhaled wearily.

'All right. I'll give a run down to the station and do my business.' Another consultation of the Timex. 'Noon?'

'Fine.'

He walked to the door, opened it, stepped out on the balcony and tossed the pear core over the railing and into the greenery below. Starting down the stairs he stopped mid-landing and looked up at me. The sun's glare hit his ravaged face and turned it into a pale mask. For a moment I was afraid he was going to get sentimental.

I needn't have worried.

'Listen, Alex, as long as you're staying here can I borrow the Caddy? That,' he pointed accusingly at the ancient Fiat, 'is giving out. Now it's the starter.'

'Bull, you just love my car.' I went into the house, got the spare keys and threw them at him.

He fielded them like Dusty Baker, unlocked the Seville

and squirmed in, adjusting the seat to accommodate his long legs. The engine started immediately, purring with vigor. Looking like a sixteen year old going to his first prom in Daddy's wheels, he cruised down the hill.

2

MY LIFE had been frantic ever since adolescence. A straight-A student, I started college at sixteen, worked my way through school free-lancing as a guitarist, and churned through the doctoral program in clinical psychology at UCLA, earning a PhD at twenty-four. I accepted an internship up north at the Langley Porter Institute, then returned to LA to complete a postdoctoral fellowship at Western Pediatric Medical Center: Once out of training I took a staff position at the hospital and a simultaneous professorship at the medical school affiliated with Western Peds. I saw lots of patients and published lots of papers.

By twenty-eight I was an associate professor of pediatrics and psychology and director of a support program for medically ill youngsters. I had a title too long for my secretaries to memorize and I kept publishing, constructing a paper tower within which I dwelled: Case studies, controlled experiments, surveys, monographs, textbook chapters and an esoteric volume of my own on the psychological effects of chronic disease in children.

The status was great, the pay less so. I began to moonlight, seeing private patients in an office rented from a Beverly Hills analyst. My patient load increased until I was putting in seventy hours a week and running between hospital and office like a deranged worker ant.

I entered the world of tax avoidance after discovering that without write-offs and shelters I'd be paying out to the IRS more than I used to consider a healthy yearly income. I hired and fired accountants, bought California real estate before the boom, sold at scandalous profits, bought more. I became an apartment-house manager – another five to ten hours a week. I supported a battalion of service personnel – gardeners, plumbers, painters and electricians. I received lots of calendars at Christmas.

By the age of thirty-two, I had a non-stop regimen of working to the point of exhaustion, grabbing a few hours of fitful sleep and getting up to work some more. When I remembered to eat, the food came out of hospital vending machines and I stuffed my mouth while zipping down the corridors, white coat flapping, notepad in hand, like some impassioned speed freak. I was a man with a mission, albeit a mindless one.

I was successful.

There was little time for romance in such a life. I engaged in occasional carnal liaisons, frenzied and meaningless, with nurses, female interns, graduate students and social workers. Not to forget the fortyish leggy blond secretary – not my type at all had I taken the time to think – who captivated me for twenty minutes of thrashing behind the chart-stuffed shelves of the medical records room.

By day it was committee meetings, paperwork, trying to quell petty staff bickering and more paperwork. By night it was facing the tide of parental complaints that the child therapist grows accustomed to, and providing comfort and support to the young ones caught in the crossfire.

In my spare time I received tenants' gripes, scanned the *Wall Street Journal* to measure my gains and losses, and sorted through mountains of mail, most of it, it seemed, from white-collared, white-toothed smoothies who had ways of making me instantly rich. I was nominated as an Outstanding Young Man by an outfit hoping to sell me their hundred-dollar, leather-bound directory of similarly honored individuals. In the middle of the day, there were times, suddenly, when I found it hard to breathe, but I brushed it off, too busy for introspection.

Into this maelstrom stepped Stuart Hickle.

Hickle was a quiet man, a retired lab technician. He looked the part of the kindly neighbor on a situation comedy – tall, stooped, fiftyish, fond of cardigans and old briar pipes. His tortoise-shell horn-rims perched atop a thin, pinched nose shielding kindly eyes the color of dishwater. He had a benign smile and avuncular mannerisms.

He also had an unhealthy appetite for fondling little children's privates.

When the police finally got him, they confiscated over five hundred color photographs of Hickle having his way with scores of two, three, four, and five year olds – boys and girls, white, black, Hispanic. In matters of gender and race he wasn't picky. Only age and helplessness concerned him.

When I saw the photos it wasn't the graphic starkness that got to me, though that was repulsive in its own right. It was the look in the kids' eyes – a terrified yet knowing vulnerability. It was a look that said *I know this is wrong. Why is this happening to me?* The look was in every snapshot, on the face of the youngest victim.

It personified violation.

It gave me nightmares.

Hickle had unique access to little children. His wife, a Korean orphan whom he'd met as a GI in Seoul, ran a successful day-care center in affluent Brentwood.

Kim's Korner had a solid reputation as one of the best places to leave your children when you had to work or play or just be alone. It had been in business for a decade when the scandal broke, and despite the evidence there were plenty of people who refused to believe that the school had served as a haven for one man's pedophilic rituals.

The school had been a cheerful-looking place, occupying a large, two-story house on a quiet residential street not far from UCLA. In its last year, it had cared for over forty children, most of them from affluent families. A large proportion of Kim Hickle's charges had been very young because she was one of the few day-care operators to accept children not yet toilet-trained.

The house had a basement – a rarity in earthquake country – and the police spent a considerable amount of time in that damp cavernous room. They found an old army cot, a refrigerator, a rusty sink and five thousand dollars' worth of photographic equipment. Particular scrutiny was given to the cot, for it served up a host of fascinating forensic details – hair, blood, sweat and semen.

The media latched on to the Hickle case with predictable vigor. This was a juicy one that played on everyone's primal fears, evoking memories of the Cosmic Bogeyman. The evening news featured Kim Hickle fleeing a mob of reporters, hands over face. She protested her ignorance. There was no evidence of her complicity so they closed the school down, took away her license and left it at that. She filed for divorce and departed for parts unknown.

I had my doubts about her innocence. I'd seen enough of these cases to know that the wives of child molesters often played a role, explicit or covert, in setting up the dirty deed. Usually these were women who found sex and physical intimacy abhorrent, and in order to get out of conjugal chores, they helped find substitute partners for their men. It could be a cold, cruel parody of a harem joke – I'd seen one case where the father had been bedding three of his daughters on a scheduled basis, with mom drawing up the schedule.

It was also hard to believe that Kim Hickle had been playing Legos with the kids while downstairs Stuart was molesting them. Nevertheless, they let her go.

Hickle himself was thrown to the wolves. The TV cameras didn't miss a shot. There were lots of instant mini-specials, filled with interviews with the more vocal of my colleagues, and several editorials about the rights of children.

The hoopla lasted two weeks, then the story lost its appeal and was replaced by reports of other atrocities. For there was no lack of nasty stories in LA. The city spawned ugliness like a predatory insect spewing out blood-hungry larvae.

I was consulted on the case three weeks after the arrest. It was a back-page story now and someone got to thinking about the victims.

The victims were going through hell.

The children woke up screaming in the middle of the night. Toddlers who'd been toilet-trained started to wet and soil themselves. Formerly quiet, well-behaved kids began to hit, kick and bite without provocation. There were lots of stomach aches and ambiguous physical symptoms reported, as well as the classic signs of depression – loss of appetite, listlessness, withdrawal, feelings of worthlessness.

The parents were racked with guilt and shame, seeing or imagining the accusing glances of family and friends. Husbands and wives turned on each other. Some of them spoiled the victimized children, increasing the youngsters' insecurity and infuriating the siblings. Later, several brothers and sisters were able to admit that they'd wished they'd been molested in order to be eligible for special treatment. Then they'd felt guilty about those thoughts.

Entire families were coming apart, much of their suffering obscured by the public blood lust for Hickle's head. The families might have been permanently shunted to obscurity, saddled with their confusion, guilt and fear but for the fact that the great aunt of one of the victims was a philanthropic member of the board of Western Pediatric Medical Center. She wondered out loud why the hell the hospital wasn't doing anything, and where was the institution's sense of public service, anyway. The chairman of the board salaamed and simultaneously saw the chance to grab some good press. The last story about Western Peds had exposed salmonella in the cafeteria's coleslaw, so positive PR was mighty welcome.

The medical director issued a press release announcing a psychological rehabilitation program for the victims of Stuart Hickle, with me as therapist. My first inkling of being appointed was reading about it in the *Times*.

When I got to his office the next morning I was ushered in immediately. The director, a pediatric surgeon who hadn't operated in twenty years and had acquired the smugness of a well-fed bureaucrat, sat behind a gleaming desk the size of a hockey field and smiled.

'What's going on, Henry?' I held up the newspaper.

'Sit down, Alex. I was just about to call you. The board decided you'd be perfect – pluperfect – for the job. Some urgency was called for.'

'I'm flattered.'

'The board remembered the beautiful work you did with the Brownings.'

'Brownells.'

'Yes, whatever.'

The five Brownell youngsters had survived a light plane crash in the Sierras that had killed their parents. They'd been physically and psychologically traumatized – overexposed, half starved, amnesiac, mute. I'd worked with them for two months and the papers had picked up on it.

'You know, Alex,' the director was saying, 'sometimes in the midst of trying to synthesize the high technology and heroics that comprise so much of modern medicine, one loses sight of the human factor.'

It was a great little speech. I hoped he'd remember it when budget time rolled around next year.

He went on stroking me, talking about the need for the hospital to be in the 'forefront of humanitarian endeavors,' then smiled and leaned forward.

'Also, I imagine there'd be significant research potential in all of this – at least two or three publications by June.'

June was when I came up for full professorship. The director was on the tenure committee at the medical school.

'Henry, I believe you're appealing to my baser instincts.'

'Perish the thought.' He winked slyly. 'Our main interest

18

is helping those poor, poor children.' He shook his head. 'A truly repugnant affair. The man should be castrated.'

A surgeon's justice.

I threw myself, with customary monomania, into designing the treatment program. I received permission to run the therapy sessions in my private office after promising that Western Peds would get all the credit.

My goals were to help the families express the feelings that had been locked inside since Hickle's subterranean rites had been exposed, and to help them share those feelings with each other in order to see that they weren't alone. The therapy was designed as an intensive, six-week program, using groups – the kids, parents, siblings and multiple families – as well as individual sessions as needed. Eighty per cent of the families signed up and no one dropped out. We met at night in my suite on Wilshire, when the building was quiet and empty.

There were nights when I left the sessions physically and emotionally drained after hearing the anguish pour out like blood from a gaping wound. Don't let anyone ever tell you different: Psychotherapy is one of the most taxing endeavors known to mankind. I've done all sorts of work, from picking carrots in the scorching sun to sitting on national committees in paneled boardrooms, and there's nothing that compares to confronting human misery, hour after hour, and bearing the responsibility for easing that misery using only one's mind and mouth. At its best it's tremendously uplifting, as you watch the patient open up, breathe, let go of the pain. At its worst it's like surfing in a cesspool, struggling for balance while being slapped with wave after putrid wave.

The treatment worked. Sparkle returned to the kids' eyes. The families reached out and helped each other. Gradually, my role diminished to that of silent observer.

A few days before the last session I received a call from a reporter for *National Medical News* – a throwaway for physicians. His name was Bill Roberts, he was in town and wanted to interview me. The piece would be for practising pediatricians, to alert them to the issue of child molestation. It sounded like a worthy project and I agreed to meet him.

It was seven thirty in the evening when I nosed my car out of the hospital parking lot and headed westward. Traffic was light and I reached the black-granite-and-glass tower that housed my office by eight. I parked in the subterranean garage, walked through double glass doors into a lobby that was silent save for Muzak and rode the elevator to the sixth floor. The doors slid open, I made my way down the corridor, turned a corner and stopped.

There was nobody waiting for me, which was unusual because I'd always found reporters to be punctual.

I approached my office door and saw a stiletto of light slashed diagonally across the floor. The door was ajar, perhaps an inch. I wondered if the night cleaning crew had let Roberts in. If so I'd have a talk with the building manager over the breach of security.

When I reached the door I knew something was wrong. There were scratch marks around the knob, metal filings in the rug. Yet, as if working from a script, I entered.

'Mr Roberts?'

The waiting room was empty. I went into the consultation office. The man on my sofa wasn't Bill Roberts. I'd never met him but I knew him very well.

Stuart Hickle slumped in the soft cotton cushions. His head – what was left of it – was propped against the wall, the eyes staring vacantly at the ceiling. His legs splayed out spastically. One hand rested near a wet spot on his groin. He had an erection. The veins in his neck stood out in bas relief. His other hand lay limply across his chest. One finger hooked around the trigger of an ugly little blue steel pistol. The gun dangled, butt downward, the muzzle an inch from Hickle's open mouth. There were bits of brain, blood and bone on the wall behind the head. A crimson splotch decorated the soft-green print of the wallpaper like a child's fingerpainting. More crimson ran out of the nose, the ears and the mouth. The room smelled of firecrackers and human waste.

I dialed the phone.

The coroner's verdict was death by suicide. The final version went something like this: Hickle had been profoundly depressed since his arrest and, unable to bear the public humiliation of a trial, he'd taken the Samurai way out. It was he, as Bill Roberts, who'd set up the appointment with me, he who'd picked the lock and blown his brains out. When the police played me tapes of his confession the voice did sound similar to that of 'Roberts' – at least similar enough to prevent my saying it wasn't a match.

As for why he'd chosen my office for his swan song, the supporting cast of shrinks had an easy answer: Because of my role as the victims' therapist, I was a symbolic father figure, undoing the damage he'd perpetrated. His death was an equally symbolic gesture of repentance.

Finis.

But even suicides – especially those connected with

felonies – must be investigated, the loose ends tied up, and there began a buck-passing contest between the Beverly Hills Police Department and LAPD Beverly Hills acknowledged the suicide had taken place on their turf but claimed that it was an extension of the original crimes – which had occurred in West LA Division territory. Punt. West LA would have liked to kick it back but the case was still in the papers and the last thing the department wanted was a dereliction-of-duties story.

So West LA got stuck with it. Specifically, Homicide Detective Milo Bernard Sturgis got stuck with it.

I didn't start to have problems until a week after finding Hickle's body, a normal delay, because I was denying the whole thing and was more than a little numb. Since, as a psychologist, I was presumed able to handle such things, no one thought to inquire after my welfare.

I held myself in check when facing the children and their families, creating a façade that was calm, knowledgeable and accepting. I looked *in control*. In therapy we talked about Hickle's death, with an emphasis upon *them*, upon how *they* were coping.

The last session was a party during which the families thanked me, hugged me and gave me a framed print of Braggs' *The Psychologist*. It was a good party, lots of laughter and mess on the carpet, as they rejoiced at getting better, and, in part, at the death of their tormentor.

I got home close to midnight and crawled between the covers feeling hollow, cold and helpless, like an orphaned child on an empty road. The next morning the symptoms began.

I grew fidgety and had trouble concentrating. The episodes of labored breathing increased and intensified. I became unaccountably anxious, had a constantly queasy feeling in my gut, and suffered from premonitions of death.

Patients began asking me if I was all right. At that point I must have been noticeably troubled because it takes a lot to shift a patient's focus away from himself.

I had enough education to know what was going on but not enough insight to make sense of it.

It wasn't finding the body, for I was used to shocking events, but the discovery of Hickle's corpse was a catalyst that plunged me into a full-fledged crisis. Looking back now I can see that treating his victims had allowed me to step off the treadmill for six weeks, and that the end of treatment had left me with time to engage in the dangerous pastime of self-evaluation. I didn't like what I learned.

I was alone, isolated, without a single real friend in the world. For almost a decade the only humans I'd related to had been patients, and patients by definition were takers, not givers.

The feelings of loneliness grew painful. I turned further inward and became profoundly depressed. I called in sick to the hospital, canceled my private patients and spent days in bed watching soap operas.

The sound and lights of the TV washed over me like some vile paralytic drug, deadening but not healing.

I ate little and slept too much, felt heavy, weak and useless. I kept the phone off the hook and never left the house except to shove the junk mail inside the door and retreat to solitude.

On the eighth day of this funereal existence Milo appeared

at the door wanting to ask me questions. He held a notepad in his hands, just like an analyst. Only he didn't look like an analyst: A big, droopy, shaggy-haired fellow in slept-in clothes.

'Dr Alex Delaware?' He held up his badge.

'Yes.'

He introduced himself and stared at me. I was dressed in a ratty yellow bathrobe. My untrimmed beard had reached rabbinic proportions and my hair looked like electrified Brillo. Despite thirteen hours of sleep I looked and felt drowsy.

'I hope I'm not disturbing you, Doctor. Your office referred me to your home number, which was out of order.'

I let him in and he sat down, scanning the place. Foot-high stacks of unopened mail littered the dining-room table. The house was dark, drapes drawn, and smelled stale. *Days of Our Lives* flickered on the tube.

He rested his notepad on one knee and told me the interview was a formality for the coroner's inquest. Then he had me rehash the night I'd found the body, interrupting to clarify a point, scratching and jotting and staring. It was tediously procedural and my mind wandered often, so that he had to repeat his questions. Sometimes I talked so softly he asked me to repeat my answers.

After twenty minutes he asked:

'Doctor, are you all right?'

'I'm fine.' Unconvincingly.

'Oka-ay.' He shook his head, asked a few more questions, then put his pencil down and laughed nervously.

'You know, I feel kind of funny asking a doctor how he feels.'

'Don't worry about it.'

He resumed questioning me and, even through the haze, I could see he had a curious technique. He'd skip from topic to topic with no apparent line of inquiry. It threw me off balance and made me more alert.

'You're an assistant professor at the medical school?'

'Associate.'

'Pretty young to be an associate professor, aren't you?'

'I'm thirty-two. I started young.'

'Uh-huh. How many kids in the treatment program?'

'About thirty.'

'Parents?'

'Maybe ten, eleven couples, half a dozen single parents.'

'Any talk about Mr Hickle in treatment?'

'That's confidential.'

'Of course, sir.'

'You ran the treatment as part of your job at—' he consulted his notes – 'Western Pediatric Hospital.'

'It was volunteer work associated with the hospital.'

'You didn't get paid for it?'

'I continued to receive my salary and the hospital relieved me of other duties.'

'There were fathers in the treatment groups, too.'

'Yes.' I thought I'd mentioned couples.

'Some of those guys were pretty mad at Mr Hickle, I guess.'

Mr Hickle. Only a policeman could be so artificially polite as to call a dead pervert *sir*. Between themselves they used other terms, I supposed. Insufferable etiquette was a way of keeping the barrier between cop and civilian.

'That's confidential, Detective.'

He grinned as if to say *Can't blame a fella for trying*, and scribbled in his notepad.

'Why so many questions about a suicide?'

'Just routine.' He answered automatically without looking up. 'I like to be thorough.'

He stared at me absently, then asked:

'Did you have any help running the groups?'

'I encouraged the families to participate – to help themselves. I was the only professional.'

'Peer counseling?'

'Exactly.'

'We've got it in the department now.' Noncommittal. 'So they kind of took over.'

'Gradually. I was always there.'

'Did any of them have a key to your office?'

Aha.

'Absolutely not. You're thinking one of those people killed Hickle and faked it to look like suicide?' Of course he was. The same suspicion had occurred to me.

'I'm not drawing conclusions. Just investigating.' This guy was elusive enough to *be* an analyst.

'I see.'

Abruptly he stood, closed his pad and put his pencil away.

I rose to walk him to the door, teetered and blacked out.

The first thing I saw when things came back into focus was his big ugly face looming over me. I felt damp and cold. He was holding a washcloth and dripped water on to my face.

'You fainted. How do you feel?'

'Fine.' The last thing I felt was *fine*.

'You don't look wonderful. Maybe I should call a doctor, Doctor.'

'No.'

'You sure?'

'No. It's nothing, I've had the flu for a few days. I just need to get something in my stomach.'

He went into the kitchen and came back with a glass of orange juice. I sipped slowly and started to feel stronger.

I sat up and held the glass myself.

'Thank you,' I said.

'To protect and serve.'

'I'm really fine now. If you don't have any more questions . . .'

'No. Nothing more at this time.' He got up and opened some windows; the light hurt my eyes. He turned off the TV.

'Want something to eat before I go?'

What a strange, motherly man.

'I'll be fine.'

'OK, Doctor. You take care now.'

I was eager to see him go. But when the sound of his car engine was no longer audible I felt disoriented. Not depressed, like before, but agitated, restless, without peace. I tried watching *As the World Turns* but couldn't concentrate. Now the inane dialog annoyed me. I picked up a book but the words wouldn't come into focus. I took a swallow of orange juice and it left a bad taste in my mouth and a stabbing pain in my throat.

I went out on the patio and looked up at the sky until luminescent disks danced in front of my eyes. My skin itched. Bird songs irritated me. I couldn't sit still.

It went on that way the entire afternoon. Miserable.

At four thirty he called.

'Dr Delaware? This is Milo Sturgis. Detective Sturgis.'

'What can I do for you, Detective?'

'How are you feeling?'

'Much better, thank you.'

'That's good.'

There was silence.

'Uh, Doctor, I'm kind of on shaky ground here . . .'

'What's on your mind?'

'You know, I was in the Medical Corps in Vietnam. We used to see a lot of something called acute stress reaction. I was wondering if . . .'

'You think that's what I've got?'

'Well . . .'

'What was the prescribed treatment in Vietnam?'

'We got them back into action as quickly as possible. The more they avoided combat the worse they got.'

'Do you think that's what I should do? Jump back into the swing of things?'

'I can't say, Doctor. I'm no psychologist.'

'You'll diagnose but you won't treat.'

'OK, Doctor. Just wanted to see if—'

'No. Wait. I'm sorry. I appreciate your calling.' I was confused, wondering what ulterior motive he could possibly have.

'Yeah, sure. No problem.'

'Thanks, really. You'd make a hell of a shrink, Detective.'

He laughed.

'That's sometimes part of the job, sir.'

After he hung up I felt better than I'd felt in days. The

next morning I called him at the West LA Division head-quarters and offered to buy him a drink.

We met at Angela's, across from the West LA station on Santa Monica Boulevard. It was a coffee shop with a smoky cocktail lounge in the back populated by several groupings of large, solemn men. I noticed that few of them acknowledged Milo, which seemed unusual. I had always thought cops did a lot of backslapping and good-natured cussing after hours. These men took their drinking seriously. And quietly.

He had great potential as a therapist. He sipped Chivas, sat back, and let me talk. No more interrogation now. He listened and I spilled my guts.

By the end of the evening, though, he was talking too.

Over the next couple of weeks Milo and I found out that we had a lot in common. We were about the same age – he was ten months older – and had been born into working-class families in medium-sized towns. His father had been a steelworker, mine an electrical assembler. He too had been a good student, graduating with honors from Purdue and with an MA in literature from Indiana U, Bloomington. He'd planned to be a teacher when he was drafted. Two years in Vietnam had somehow turned him into a policeman.

Not that he considered his job at odds with his intellectual pursuits. Homicide detectives, he informed me, were the intellectuals of any police department. Investigating murder requires little physical activity and lots of brain-work. Veteran homicide men sometimes violate regulations and don't carry a weapon. Just lots of pens and pencils.

Milo packed his .38 but confessed that he really didn't need it.

'It's very white collar, Alex, with lots of paperwork, decision-making, attention to detail.'

He liked being a cop, enjoyed catching bad guys. Sometimes he thought he might like to try something else, but exactly what that something else was, wasn't clear.

We had other interests in common. We'd both done some martial arts training. Milo had taken a mixed bag of self-defense courses while in the army. I'd learned fencing and karate while in graduate school. We were miserably out of shape but deluded ourselves that it would all come back if we needed it. Both of us appreciated good food, good music and the virtues of solitude.

The rapport between us developed quickly.

About three weeks after we'd known each other he told me he was homosexual. I was taken by surprise and had nothing to say.

'I'm telling you now because I don't want you to think I've been trying to put the make on you.'

Suddenly I was ashamed, because that had been my initial thought, exactly.

It was hard to accept, at first, his being gay, despite all my supposed psychological sophistication. I know all the facts. That *they* make up 5 to 10 per cent of virtually any human grouping. That most of *them* look just like me and you. That *they* could be anybody – the butcher, the baker, the local homicide dick. That most of *them* are reasonably well adjusted.

And yet the stereotypes adhere to the brain. You expect them to be mincing, screaming, nelly fairies; leather-armored shaven-skull demons; oh-so-preppy mustachioed young things in Izod shirts and khaki trousers; or hiking-booted bulldykes.

Milo didn't look homosexual.

But he was and had been comfortable with it for several years. He wasn't in the closet, neither did he flaunt it.

I asked him if the department knew about it.

'Uh-huh. Not in the sense of filing an official report. It's just something that's known.'

'How do they treat you?'

'Disapproval from a distance – cold looks. But basically it's live and let live. They're short-staffed and I'm good. What do they want? To drag in the ACLU and lose a good detective in the bargain? Ed Davis was a homophobe. He's gone and it's not so bad.'

'What about the other detectives?'

He shrugged.

'They leave me alone. We talk business. We don't double-date.'

Now the lack of recognition by the men at Angela's made sense.

Some of Milo's initial altruism, his reaching out to help me, was a little more understandable, too. He knew what it was like to be alone. A gay cop was a person in limbo. You could never be one of the gang back at the station, no matter how well you did your job. And the homosexual community was bound to be suspicious of someone who looked, acted like and *was* a cop.

'I figured I should tell you, since we seem to be getting friendly.'

'It's no big deal, Milo.'

'No?'

31

'No.' I wasn't really all that comfortable with it. But I was damn well going to work on it.

A month after Stuart Hickle stuck a .22 in his mouth and blasted his brains all over my wallpaper, I made some major changes in my life.

I resigned my job at Western Pediatric and closed down my practice. I referred all my patients to a former student, a first-rate therapist who was starting out in practice and needed the business. I had taken very few new referrals since starting the groups for the Kim's Korner families, so there was less separation anxiety than would normally be expected.

I sold an apartment building in Malibu, forty units that I'd purchased seven years before, for a large profit. I also let go of a duplex in Santa Monica. Part of the money – the portion that would eventually go to taxes – I put in a high-yield money market. The rest went into tax-free municipals. It wasn't the kind of investing that would make me richer, but it would provide financial stability. I figured I could live off the interest for two or three years as long as I didn't get too extravagant.

I sold my old Chevy Two and bought a Seville, a seventy-nine, the last year they looked good. It was forest-green with a saddle-colored leather interior that was cushy and quiet. With the amount of driving I'd be doing, the lousy mileage wouldn't make much difference. I threw away most of my old clothes and got new stuff – mostly soft fabrics – knits, cords, rubber-soled shoes, cashmere sweaters, robes, shorts, and pullovers.

I had the pipes cleaned out on the hot tub that I'd never used since I bought the house. I started to buy food and drink milk. I pulled my old Martin out of its case and strummed it on the balcony. I listened to records. I read for pleasure for the first time since high school. I got a tan. I shaved off my beard and discovered I had a face, and not a bad one at that.

I dated good women. I met Robin and things really started to get better.

Be-kind-to-Alex time. Early retirement six months before my thirty-third birthday.

It was fun while it lasted.

3

MORTON HANDLER's last residence — if you didn't count the morgue — had been a luxury apartment complex off Sunset Boulevard in Pacific Palisades. It had been built into a hillside and designed to give a honeycomb effect: A loosely connected chain of individual units linked by corridors that had been placed at seemingly random locations, the apartments staggered to give each one a full view of the ocean. The motif was bastard Spanish: Blindingly white textured stucco walls, red tile roofs, window accents of black wrought iron. Plantings of azalea and hibiscus filled in occasional patches of earth. There were lots of potted plants sunk in large terracotta containers: Coconut palms, rubber plants, sun ferns, temporary-looking, as if someone planned on moving them all out in the middle of the night.

Handler's unit was on an intermediate level. The front door was sealed, with an LAPD sticker taped across it. Lots of footprints dirtied the terrazzo walkway near the entrance.

Milo led me across a terrace filled with polished stones and succulents to a unit cater-cornered from the murder scene. Adhesive letters spelling out the word MAN GER were affixed to the door. Bad jokes about Baby Jesus flashed through my mind.

34

Milo knocked.

I realized then that the place was amazingly silent. There must have been at least fifty units but there wasn't a soul in sight. No evidence of human habitation.

We waited a few minutes. He raised his fist to knock again just before the door opened.

'Sorry, I was washin' my hair.'

The woman could have been anywhere from twenty-five to forty. She had pale skin with the kind of texture that looked as if a pinch would crumble it. Large brown eyes topped by plucked brows. Thin lips. A slight under-bite. Her hair was wrapped in an orange towel and the little that peeked out was medium brown. She wore a faded cotton shirt of ocher-and-orange print over rust-colored stretch pants. Dark blue tennis shoes on her feet. Her eyes darted from Milo to me. She looked like someone who'd been knocked around plenty and refused to believe that it wasn't going to happen again at any moment.

'Mrs Quinn? This is Dr Alex Delaware. He's the psychologist I told you about.'

'Pleased to meet you, Doctor.'

Her hand was thin and cold and moist and she pulled away as quickly as she could.

'Melody's watchin' TV in her room. Out of school, with all that's been goin' on. I let her watch to keep her mind off it.'

We followed her into the apartment.

Apartment was a charitable word. What it was, really, was a couple of oversized closets stuck together. An architect's postscript. Hey, Ed, we've got an extra four hundred square feet of corner in back of terrace number 142. Why don't we throw a roof over it, nail up some drywall and call it a manager's unit? Get some poor soul to do scutwork for the privilege of living in Pacific Palisades ...

The living room was filled with one floral sofa, a masonite end table and a television. A framed painting of Mount Rainier that looked as if it came from a Savings and Loan calendar and a few yellowed photographs hung on the wall. The photos were of hardened, unhappy-looking people and appeared to date from the Gold Rush.

'My grandparents,' she said.

A cubicle of a kitchen was visible and from it came the smell of frying bacon. A large bag of sour-cream-and-onion-flavored potato chips and a six pack of Dr Pepper sat on the counter.

'Very nice.'

'They came here in 1902. From Oklahoma.' She made it sound like an apology.

There was an unfinished wooden door and from behind it came the sound of sudden laughter and applause, bells and buzzers. A game show.

'She's watchin' back there.'

'That's just fine, Mrs Quinn. We'll let her be until we're ready for her.'

The woman nodded her head in assent.

'She don't get much chance to watch the daytime shows, bein' in school. So she's watchin' 'em now.'

'May we sit down, ma'am?'

'Oh yes, yes.' She flitted around the room like a mayfly, tugging at the towel on her head. She brought in an ashtray and set it down on the end table. Milo and I sat on the sofa and she dragged in a tubular aluminum-and-Naugahyde chair from the kitchen for herself. Despite the fact that she was thin her haunches settled and spread. She took out a pack of cigarettes, lit one up and sucked in the smoke until her cheeks hollowed. Milo spoke.

'How old is your daughter, Mrs Quinn?'

'Bonita. Call me Bonita. Melody's the girl. She's just seven this past month.' Talking about her daughter seemed to make her especially nervous. She inhaled greedily on her cigarette and blew a little smoke out. Her free hand clenched and unclenched in rapid cadence.

'Melody may be our only witness to what happened here last night.' Milo looked at me with a disgusted frown.

I knew what he was thinking. An apartment complex with seventy to one hundred residents and the only possible witness a child.

'I'm scared for her, Detective Sturgis, if someone else finds out.' Bonita Quinn stared at the floor as if doing it long enough would reveal the mystic secret of the Orient.

'I assure you, Mrs Quinn, that no one will find out. Dr Delaware has served as a special consultant to the police many times.' He lied shamelessly and glibly, 'He understands the importance of keeping things secret. Besides—' he reached over to pat her shoulder reassuringly. I thought she'd go through the ceiling – 'all psychologists demand confidentiality when working with their patients. Isn't that so, Dr Delaware?'

'Absolutely.' We wouldn't get into the whole muddy issue of children's rights to privacy.

Bonita Quinn made a strange, squeaking noise that was impossible to interpret. The closest thing to it that I could remember was the noise laboratory frogs used to make in

Physiological Psych right before we pithed them by plunging a needle down into the tops of their skulls.

'What's all this hypnotism gonna do to her?'

I lapsed into my shrink's voice – the calm, soothing tones that had become so natural over the years that they switched on automatically. I explained to her that hypnosis wasn't magic, simply a combination of focused concentration and deep relaxation, that people tended to remember things more clearly when they were relaxed and that was why the police used it for witnesses. That children were better at going into hypnosis than were adults because they were less inhibited and enjoyed fantasy. That it didn't hurt, and was actually pleasant for most youngsters and that you couldn't get stuck in it or do anything against your will while hypnotized.

'All hypnosis,' I ended, 'is self-hypnosis. My role is simply to help your daughter do something that comes natural to her.'

She probably understood about ten per cent of it, but it seemed to calm her down.

'You can say that again, natural. She daydreams all the time.'

'Exactly. Hypnosis is like that.'

'Teachers complain all the time, say she's driftin' off, not doing her work.'

She was talking as if she expected me to do something about it.

Milo broke in.

'Has Melody told you anything more about what she saw, Mrs Quinn?'

'No, no.' An emphatic shake of the head. 'We haven't been talkin' about it.'

Milo pulled out his notepad and flipped through a few pages.

'What I have on record is that Melody couldn't sleep and was sitting in the living room – in this room at around one in the morning.'

'Must've been. I got in by eleven thirty and I got up once for a cigarette at twenty after twelve. She was asleep then and I didn't hear her for the while it took me to fall off. I'd a' heard her. We share the room.'

'Uh-huh. And she saw two men – here it says "I saw big men." The officer's question was "How many, Melody?" and she answered, "Two, maybe three." When he asked her what did they look like, all she could say was that they were dark.' He was talking to me now. 'We asked her black, Latino. Nothing. Only *dark*.'

'That could mean shadows. Could mean anything to a seven year old,' I said.

'I know.'

'Which could mean two men, or one guy with a shadow, or—'

'Don't say it.'

Or nothing at all.

'She don't always tell the truth about everything.'

We both turned to look at Bonita Quinn who had used the few seconds we had ignored her to put out her cigarette and light a new one.

'I'm not sayin' she's a bad kid. But she don't always tell the truth. I don't know why you want to depend on her.'

I asked, 'Do you have problems with her chronically lying about things that don't make much sense – or does she do to avoid getting in trouble?'

'The second. When she don't want me to paddle her an
I know somethin's broken, it's got to be her. She tells m
no, mama, not me. And I paddle her double.' She looked t
me for disapproval. 'For not tellin' the truth.'

'Do you have other problems with her?' I asked gently

'She's a good girl, Doctor. Only the daydreams, and th
concentration problems.'

'Oh?' I needed to understand this child if I was going t
be able to do hypnosis with her.

'The concentratin' – it's hard for her.'

No wonder, in this tiny, television-saturated cell. N
doubt the apartments were Adults Only and Melody Quin
was required to keep a low profile. There's a large segmer
of the population of Southern California that views th
sight of anyone too young or too old as offensive. It's a
if nobody wants to be reminded from whence they can
or to where they will certainly go. That kind of denia
coupled with face lifts and hair transplants and makeu
creates a comfortable little delusion of immortality. For
short while.

I was willing to bet that Melody Quinn spent most of h
time indoors despite the fact that the complex boasted thre
swimming pools and a totally equipped gym. Not to mentic
the ocean a half-mile away. Those playthings were mear
for the grownups.

'I took her to the doctor when the teachers kept sendi
home these notes sayin' she can't sit still, her mind wander
He said she was overactive. Somethin' in the brain.'

'Hyperactive?'

'That's right. Wouldn't surprise me. Her dad wasn't a
together right up there.' She tapped her forehead. 'Used tl

40

illegal drugs and the wine until he—' she stopped cold, looking at Milo with sudden fear.

'Don't worry, Mrs Quinn, we're not interested in that kind of thing. We only want to find out who killed Dr Handler and Ms Gutierrez.'

'Yeah, the headshrinker—' she stopped again, this time staring at me. 'Can't seem to say anything' right, today.' She forced a weak smile.

I nodded reassurance, smiled understandingly.

'He was a nice guy, that doctor.' Some of my best friends are psychotherapists. 'Used to joke with me a lot and I'd kid him, ask him if he had any shrunken heads in there.' She laughed, a strange giggle, and showed a mouthful of teeth badly in need of repair. By now I had narrowed her age to middle thirties. In ten years she'd look truly elderly. 'Terrible about what happened to him.'

'And Ms Gutierrez.'

'Yeah, her too. Only her I wasn't so crazy about. She was Mexican, you know, but uppity Mexican. Where I come from they did the stoop labor and the cleanup. This one had the fancy dresses and the little sports car. And her a teacher, too.' It wasn't easy for Bonita Quinn, brought up to think of all Mexicans as beasts of burden, to see that in the big city, away from the lettuce fields, some of them looked just like real people. While she did the donkey work.

'She was always carryin' herself like she was too good for you. You'd say hello to her and she'd be lookin' off into the distance, like she had no time for you.'

She took another drag on her cigarette and smiled slyly.

'This time I'm OK,' she said.

We both looked at her.

'Neither of you gents is a Mex. I didn't put my foot in it again.'

She was extremely pleased with herself and I took advantage of her lifted spirits to ask her a few more questions.

'Mrs Quinn, is your daughter on any sort of medication for her hyperactivity?'

'Oh yeah, sure. The doc gave me pills to give her.'

'Do you have the prescription slip handy?'

'I got the bottle.' She got up and returned with an amber vial half full of tablets.

I took it and read the label. Ritalin. Methylphenidate hydrochloride. A super-amphetamine that speeds up adults but slows down kids, it's one of the most commonly prescribed drugs for American youngsters. Ritalin is addictive and potent and has a host of side effects, one of the most common of which is insomnia. Which might explain why Melody Quinn was sitting, staring out the window of a dark room at one in the morning.

Ritalin is a sweetheart drug when it comes to controlling children. It improves concentration and reduces the frequency of problem-behaviors in hyperactive kids – which sounds great, except that the symptoms of hyperactivity are hard to differentiate from those of anxiety, depression, acute stress reaction, or simple boredom at school. I've seen kids who were too bright for their classroom look hyper. Ditto for little ones going through the horrors of divorce or any other significant trauma.

A doctor who's doing his job correctly will require comprehensive psychological and social evaluation of a child before prescribing Ritalin or any other behavior-modifying drug. And there are plenty of good doctors. But some physicians take the easy way out, using the pills as the first step. If it's not malpractice it's dangerously close.

I opened the vial and shook some pills onto my palm. They were amber, the 20-milligram kind. I examined the label. One tablet three times daily. Sixty mg was the maximum recommended dosage. Strong stuff for a seven year old.

'You give her these three times a day?'

'Uh-huh. That's what it says, don't it?'

'Yes, it does. Did your doctor start off with something smaller – white or blue pills?'

'Oh yeah. We had her takin' three of the blue ones at first. Worked pretty good but I still got the complaints from the school, so he said it was OK to try these.'

'And this dosage works well for Melody?'

'Works real fine for me. If it's gonna be a rough day with lots of visitors comin' over – she don't do real good with lots of people, lots of commotion – I give her an extra one.'

Now we were talking overdose.

Bonita Quinn must have seen the look of surprise and disapproval that I tried unsuccessfully to conceal, for she spoke up with indignation in her voice.

'The doc says it was OK. He's an important man. You know, this place don't allow kids and I get to stay here only on account as she's a quiet kid. M and M Properties – they own the place – told me any time there's complaints about kids, that's it.'

No doubt that did wonders for Melody's social life. Chances are she had never had a friend over.

There was cruel irony to the idea of a seven year old imprisoned amidst single-swingle splendor, tucked away in a slum pocket on an eyrie high above the high Pacific, and dosed up with Ritalin to appease the combined wishes of the Los Angeles school system, a dim-witted mother and M and M Properties.

I examined the label on the vial to find out the name of the prescribing physician. When I found it, things began to fall into place.

L.W. Towle. Lionel Willard Towle, MD. One of the most established and respected pediatricians on the West Side. I had never met him but knew him by reputation. He was on the senior staff of Western Pediatric and a half dozen other Westside hospitals. A big shot in the Academy of Pediatrics. A guest speaker, highly in demand, at seminars on learning disabilities and behavior problems.

Dr Towle was also a paid consultant to three major pharmaceutical concerns. Translate: Pusher. He had a reputation, especially among the younger doctors who were generally more conservative about drugs, as easy with the prescription pad. No one said it too loudly, because Towle had been around a long time and had lots of important patients and plenty of connections, but the whispered consensus was that he was a Dr Feelgood for tots. I wondered how someone like Bonita Quinn had ended up in his practice. But there was no easy way to ask without appearing unduly nosy.

I handed the vial back to her and turned to Milo, who'd been sitting through the exchange in silence.

'Let me talk to you,' I said.

'Just one moment, ma'am.'

Outside the apartment I told him, 'I can't hypnotize this kid. She's drugged to the gills. It would be a risk to work with her, and besides, there's little chance of getting anything worthwhile out of her.'

Milo digested this.

'Shit.' He scratched his head. 'What if we take her off the pills for a few days.'

'That's a medical decision. We get into that and we're way out of bounds. We need the physician's permission. Which blows confidentiality.'

'Who's the doc?'

I told him about Towle.

'Wonderful. But maybe he'll agree to let her off for a few days.'

'Maybe, but there's no guarantee she'll give us anything. This kid's been on stimulants for a year. And what about Mrs Q? She's scared plenty as is. Take her darling off the pills and first thing she'll do is lock the kid inside twelve hours a day. They like it quiet here.'

The complex was still silent as a mausoleum. At one forty-five in the afternoon.

'Can you at least look at the kid? Maybe she's not that doped.'

Across the way the door to the Handler apartment was open. I caught a glimpse of elegance in disarray – oriental rugs, antiques, and severe acrylic furniture broken and upended, blood-spattered white walls. The police lab men worked silently, like moles.

'By now she's had her second dose, Milo.'

'Shit.' He punched his fist into his palm. 'Just meet the kid. Give me your impression. Maybe she'll be alert.'

She wasn't. Her mother led her into the living room and then left with Milo. She stared off into the distance, sucking her thumb. She was a small child. If I hadn't known her age I would have guessed it at five, maybe five-and-a-half. She had a long, grave face with oversized brown eyes. Her straight blond hair hung to her shoulders, held in place by twin plastic barrettes. She wore blue jeans and a blue-green-and-white-striped T-shirt. Her feet were dirty and bare.

I led her to a chair and sat opposite her on the couch.

'Hello, Melody. I'm Dr Delaware. I'm a psychologist. Do you know what that is?'

No response.

'I'm the kind of doctor who doesn't give shots. What I do is talk and draw and play with kids. I try to help kids who are sad, or angry, or scared.'

At the word *scared* she looked up for a second. Then she resumed staring past me and sucked her thumb.

'Do you know why I'm talking to you?'

A shake of the head.

'It's not because you're sick or because you've done anything wrong. We know you're a good girl.'

Her eyes moved around the room, avoiding me.

'I'm here because you may have seen something last night that's important. When you couldn't sleep and were looking out the window.'

She didn't answer. I continued.

'Melody, what kind of things do you like to do?'

Nothing.

'Do you like to play?'

She nodded.

'I like to play too. And I like to skate. Do you skate?'

'Uh-uh.' Of course not, skates make noise.

'And I like to watch movies. Do you watch movies?'

She mumbled something. I bent closer.

'What's that, hon?'

46

'On TV.' Her voice was thin and quivering, a trembling breathy sound like the breeze through dry leaves.

'Uh-huh. On TV. I watch TV, too. What shows do you like to watch?'

'Scooby-Doo.'

'Scooby-Doo. That's a good show. Any other shows?'

'My mama watches the soap operas.'

'Do you like the soap operas?'

She shook her head.

'Pretty boring, huh?'

A hint of a smile, around the thumb.

'Do you have toys, Melody?'

'In my room.'

'Could you show them to me?'

The room she shared with her mother was neither adult nor childlike in character. It was no more than ten foot square, low-ceilinged with a solitary window set high in the wall, which gave it the ambience of a dungeon. Melody and Bonita shared one twin bed unadorned by a headboard. It was half unmade, the thin chenille spread folded back to reveal rumpled sheets. On one side of the bed was a nightstand filled with bottles and jars of cold cream, hand lotion, brushes, combs and a piece of cardboard onto which a score of bobby pins were clasped. On the other side was a huge, moth-eaten stuffed walrus, made of fuzzy material and colored an atrocious turquoise blue. A baby picture was the sole adornment on the wall. A sagging bureau made of unfinished pine and covered with a crocheted doily, and the TV, were the only other pieces of furniture in the room.

In one corner was a small pile of toys.

Melody led me over to it, hesitantly. She picked up a grimy, naked plastic baby doll.

'Amanda,' she said.

'She's beautiful.'

The child clutched the doll to her chest and rocked back and forth.

'You must really take good care of her.'

'I do.' It was said defensively. This was a child who was not used to praise.

'I know you do,' I said gently. I looked over to the walrus. 'Who's he?'

'Fatso. My daddy gave him to me.'

'He's cute.'

She walked over to the animal, which was as tall as she, and stroked it purposefully.

'Mama wants me to throw him out 'cause he's too big. But I won't let her.'

'Fatso's really important to you.'

'Uh-huh.'

'Daddy gave him to you.'

She nodded, emphatically, and smiled. I'd passed some kind of test.

For the next twenty-five minutes we sat on the floor and played.

When Milo and the mother returned, Melody and I were in fine spirits. We'd built and destroyed several worlds.

'Well, you're sure lookin' frisky,' said Bonita.

'We're having a good time, Mrs Quinn. Melody's been a very good girl.'

'That's good.' She went over to her daughter and placed a hand on her head. 'That's good, hon.'

There was unexpected tenderness in her eyes, then it was gone. She turned to me and asked:

'How'd it go with the hypnotism?'

She asked it the same way she might inquire, how's my kid doing in arithmetic.

'We haven't done any hypnosis yet. Melody and I are just getting to know each other.'

I drew her aside.

'Mrs Quinn, hypnosis requires trust on the part of the child. I usually spend a little time with children beforehand. Melody was very cooperative.'

'She didn't tell you nothin'?' She reached into the breast pocket of her shirt and pulled out another cigarette. I lit it for her and the gesture surprised her.

'Nothing of importance. With your permission I'd like to come over some time tomorrow and spend a little more time with Melody.'

She eyed me suspiciously, chewed on the cigarette, then shrugged.

'You're the doctor.'

We rejoined Milo and the child. He was kneeling on one leg and showing her his detective's badge. Her eyes were wide.

'Melody, if it's OK with you, I'd like to come by tomorrow and play with you some more.'

She looked up at her mother and began sucking her thumb again.

'It's fine with me,' Bonita Quinn said curtly. 'Now run along.'

Melody sprang for her room. She stopped in the doorway and gave me a tentative look. I waved, she waved back and then she disappeared. A second later the TV began blaring.

'One more thing, Mrs Quinn. I'll need to talk to Dr Towle before I do any hypnosis with Melody.'

'That's OK.'

'I'll need your permission to talk with Dr Towle about the case. You realize he's professionally bound to keep this confidential, just as I am.'

'That's OK. I trust Dr Towle.'

'And I may ask him to take her off her medicine for a couple of days.'

'Oh all right, all right.' She waved her hand, exasperated.

'Thank you, Mrs Quinn.'

We left her standing in front of her apartment, smoking frantically, taking the towel off her head and shaking her hair loose in the midday sun.

I took the wheel of the Seville and drove slowly up towards Sunset.

'Stop smirking, Milo.'

'What's that?' He was looking out the passenger window, his hair flapping like duck wings.

'You know you've got me hooked, don't you? A kid like that, those big eyes like something out of a Keene painting.'

'If you want to quit right now, it wouldn't make me happy, Alex. But I wouldn't stop you. There's still time for gnocchi.'

'The hell with gnocchi. Let's talk with Dr Towle.'

The Seville was consuming fuel with customary gluttony. I pulled into a Chevron self-serve at Bundy. While Milo pumped gas I got Towle's number from information and dialed it. I used my title and got through to the doctor in a half-minute. I gave him a brief explanation of why I needed to talk with him and told him we could chat now over the phone.

'No,' he said. 'I've got an office full of kids.' His voice was smooth and reassuring, the kind of voice a parent would want to hear at two in the morning when the baby was turning blue.

'When would be a good time to call you?'

He didn't answer. I could hear the bustle of activity in the background, then muffled voices. He came back on the line.

'How about dropping by at four thirty? I've got a lull around then.'

'I appreciate your time, Doctor.'

'No bother.' And he hung up.

I left the phone booth. Milo was removing the nozzle from the rear of the Seville, holding it at arm's length to avoid getting gasoline on his suit.

I settled in the driver's seat and stuck my head out the window.

'Catch the windshield for me, son.'

He made a gargoyle face – not much of an effort – and gave me the finger. Then he went to work with paper towels.

It was two forty and we were only fifteen minutes from Towle's office. That left over an hour to kill. Neither of us was in a good enough mood to want first-rate food, so we drove back to West LA and went to Angela's.

Milo ordered something called a San Francisco Deluxe Omelet. It turned out to be a bright yellow horror stuffed with spinach, tomatoes, ground beef, chilies, onions and marinated eggplant. He dug into it with relish while I contented myself with a steak sandwich and a Coors. In between bites he talked about the Handler murder.

'It's a puzzler, Alex. You've got all the signs of a psychotic thrill killer – both of them trussed up in the bedroom, like animals ready for the slaughter. And stuck about five dozen times. The girl looked like she ran into Jack the Ripper with her—'

'Spare me.' I pointed to my food.

'Sorry. I forget when I'm talking to a civilian. You get used to it after wading in it for a few years. You can't stop living, so you learn to eat and drink and fart through all of it.' He wiped his face with his napkin and took a long, deep swallow of his beer. 'Anyway, despite the craziness, there's no sign of forced entry. The front door was open. Normally that would be very puzzling. Except in this case with the victim being a psychiatrist, it might make sense, his knowing the bad guy and letting him in.'

'You think it was one of his patients?'

'It's a good possibility. Psychiatrists have been known to deal with crazies.'

'I'd be surprised if it turned out that way, Milo. Ten to one Handler had a typical West Side practice – depressed middle-aged women, disillusioned executives, and a few adolescent identity crises thrown in for good measure.'

'Do I detect a note of cynicism?'

I shrugged.

'That's just the way it is in most cases. High-priced friendship – not that it's not valuable, mind you. But there's very little real mental illness in what most of us –

52

psychiatrists, psychologists – see in practice. The real crazies, the really disturbed ones, are hospitalized.'

'Handler worked at a hospital before he went out on his own. Encino Oaks.'

'Maybe you'll dig up something there,' I said doubtfully. I was tired of being the wet blanket so I didn't tell him that Encino Oaks Hospital was a repository for the suicidal progeny of the rich. Very little sexual psychopathy, there.

He pushed his empty plate away and motioned for the waitress.

'Bettijean, a nice slab of that green apple pie, please.'

'A la mode, Milo?'

He patted his gut and pondered.

'What the hell, why not. Vanilla.'

'And you, sir?'

'Just coffee, please.'

When she had gone he continued, thinking out loud more than talking to me.

'Anyway, it appears as if Dr Handler let someone into his place sometime between midnight and one and got ripped up for his efforts.'

'And the Gutierrez woman?'

'Your quintessential innocent bystander. Being in the wrong place at the wrong time.'

'She was Handler's girlfriend?'

He nodded.

'For about six months. From the little we've learned she started out as a patient and ended up going from couch to bed.'

A not uncommon story.

'The irony of it was that she was hacked up worse than

he was. Handler got his throat slit and probably died relatively quickly. There were a few other holes in him but nothing lethal. It looks as if the killer took his time with her. Makes sense if it's a sexual crazy.'

I could feel my digestive process come to a halt. I changed the subject.

'Who's your new love?'

The pie came. Milo smiled at the waitress and attacked the pastry. I noticed that the filling was indeed green, a bright, almost luminescent green. Someone in the kitchen was fooling around with food dyes. I shuddered to think what they could do with something really challenging, like a pizza. It would probably end up looking like a mad artist's palette.

'A doctor. A nice Jewish doctor.' He looked heavenward. 'Every mother's dream.'

'What happened to Larry?'

'He's gone off to find his fortunes in San Francisco.'

Larry was a black stage manager with whom Milo had conducted an on-again, off-again relationship for two years. Their last half-year had been grimly platonic.

'He's hooked up with some show sponsored by an anonymous corporation. Something racy for educational television, along the lines of "Our Agricultural Heritage: Your Friend the Plow." Hot stuff.'

'Bitchy, bitchy.'

'No, really, I do wish the boy well. Behind that neurotic exterior was genuine talent.'

'How did you meet your doctor?'

'He works the Emergency Room at Cedars. A surgeon, no less. I was following up an assault that turned into manslaughter, he was commandeering the catheters, and our eyes locked. The rest is history.'

I laughed so hard the coffee almost went up my nose.

'He's been out of the closet for about two years. Marriage in medical school, messy divorce, excommunication by family. The whole bit. Fantastic guy, you'll have to meet him.'

'I'd like to.'

'Give me a few days to slog through Morton Handler's life history and we'll double.'

'It's a deal.'

It was five to four. I let the Los Angeles Police Department pay for my lunch. In the best tradition of policemen the world over, Milo left an enormous tip. He patted Bettijean's fanny on the way out and her laughter followed us out on to the street.

Santa Monica Boulevard was beginning to choke up with traffic and the air had started to foul. I closed the Seville's windows and turned on the air-conditioning. I slipped a tape of Joe Pass and Stephane Grappelli into the deck. The sound of 'Only a Paper Moon,' delivered hot forties style, filled the car. The music made me feel good. Milo took a cat nap, snoring deeply. I eased the Seville into the traffic and headed back to Brentwood.

4

TOWLE'S OFFICE was on a side street off San Vicente, not far from the Brentwood Country Mart – one of the few neighborhoods where movie stars could shop without being harassed. It was in a building designed during the early fifties, when tan brick, low-slung roofs and wall inserts of glass cubes were in vogue. Plantings of asparagus fern and climbing bougainvillaea did something to relieve the starkness, but it still looked pretty severe.

Towle was the building's sole occupant and his name was stenciled in gold leaf on the glass front door. The parking lot was a haven for wood-sided station wagons. We pulled in next to a blue Lincoln with a SPEAK UP FOR CHILDREN bumper sticker that I figured belonged to the good doctor himself.

Inside, the decor was something else. It was as if some interior decorator had tried to make up for the harshness of the building by cramming the waiting room full of mush. The furniture was colonial maple with nubby seat cushions. The walls were covered with needlepoint homilies and cutesy-poo prints of little boys fishing and little girls preening themselves in front of mirrors, wearing mommy's hat and shoes. The room was full of children and harried-looking mothers. Magazines, books and toys cluttered the floor. There was an odor of dirty diapers in the air. If this was Towle's lull I didn't want to be there during his busy period.

When we walked in, two childless males, we drew stares from the women. We had agreed beforehand that Towle would relate better doctor to doctor, so Milo found a seat sandwiched in between two five year olds and I walked to the reception window. The girl on the other side was a sweet young thing with Farah Fawcett hair and a face almost as pretty as that of her role model. She was dressed in white and her name tag proclaimed her to be Sandi.

'Hi. I'm Dr Delaware. I've got an appointment with Dr Towle.'

I got a smile fronted by lots of nice, white teeth.

'Appointments don't mean much this afternoon. But come right in. He'll be with you in just a minute.'

I walked through the door with several pairs of maternal eyes boring into my back. Some of them had probably been waiting for over an hour. I wondered why Towle didn't hire an associate.

Sandi showed me into the doctor's consultation office, a dark-paneled room about twelve by twelve.

'It's about the Quinn child, isn't it?'

'That's right.'

'I'll pull the chart.' She came back with a manila folder and placed it on Towle's desk. There was a red tag on the cover. She saw me looking at it.

'The reds are the hypers. We code them. Yellow for chronically ill ones. Blue for specialty consults.'

'Very efficient.'

'Oh, you have no idea!' She giggled and placed one hand on a shapely hip. 'You know,' she said, leaning a bit closer and letting me have a whiff of something fragrant, 'between you and me that poor child has it rough growing up with a mother like that.'

'I know what you mean.' I nodded, not knowing what she meant at all but hoping she'd tell me. People usually do when you don't seem to care.

'I mean, she's such a scatterbrain – the mother. Every time she comes here she forgets something, or loses something. One time it was her purse. The other time she locked her keys in the car. She really doesn't have it together.'

I clucked sympathetically.

'No that she hasn't had it rough, growing up doing farm work and then marrying that guy who ended up in pris—'

'Sandi.'

We both turned to see a short, sixtyish woman with hair cut in an iron-gray helmet, standing in the doorway, arms folded across her bosom. Her eyeglasses hung suspended from a chain around her neck. She, too, was dressed in white, but on her it looked like a uniform. *Her* name tag proclaimed her to be Edna.

I knew her right away. The doctor's right hand gal. She'd probably been working for him since he hung out his shingle and was making about the same amount of money she'd started out with. But no matter, lucre wasn't what she was after. She was secretly in love with the Great Man. I was willing to bet a handful of blue chip stock that she called him *Doctor*. No name after it. Just Doctor. As if he were the only one in the world.

'There are some charts that need filing,' she said.

'OK, Edna.' Sandi turned to me, gave a conspiratorial

look that said *Isn't this old witch a drag?* and sashayed down the hall.

'Can I do anything for you?' Edna asked me, still keeping her arms crossed.

'No, thank you.'

'Well, then, Doctor will be right with you.'

'Thank you.' Kill 'em with courtesy.

Her glance let me know that she didn't approve of my presence. No doubt anything that upset Doctor's routine was viewed as an intrusion upon Paradise. But she finally left me alone in the office.

I took a look around the room. The desk was mahogany and battered. It was piled high with charts, medical journals, books, mail, drug samples, and a jar full of paper clips. The desk chairs and the easy chair in which I sat were once classy items – burnished leather – now both aged and cracked.

Two of the walls were covered with diplomas, many of which hung askew and at odds with one another. It looked like a room that had just been nudged by a minor earthquake – nothing broken, just shaken up a bit.

I casually examined the diplomas. Lionel W. Towle had amassed an impressive collection of paper over the years. Degrees, certificates of internship and residency, a walnut plaque with gavel commemorating his chairmanship of some medical task force, honorary membership in this and that, specialty board certification, commendations for public service on the Good Ship Hope, consultant to the California Senate subcommittee on child welfare. And on and on.

The other wall displayed photographs. Most were of Towle. Towle in fisherman's garb, knee-deep in some river holding aloft a clutch of steelhead. Towle with a marlin the size of a Buick. Towle with the mayor and some little squat guy with Peter Lorre eyes – everyone smiling, shaking hands.

There was one exception to this seeming self-obsession. In the center of the wall hung a color photograph of a young woman holding a small child. The colors were faded and from the style of clothing worn by the subjects, the picture looked three decades old. There was some of the tell-tale fuzziness of an enlarged snapshot. The hues were misty, almost pastel.

The woman was pretty, fresh-faced, with a sprinkle of freckles across her nose, dark eyes and medium-length brown hair with a natural wave. She wore a filmy-looking, short-sleeved dress of dotted swiss cotton, and her arms were slender and graceful. They wrapped around the child – a boy – who looked around two or younger. He was beautiful. Rosy-cheeked, blond, with cupid's-bow lips and green eyes. He was dressed in a white sailor suit and sat beaming in his mother's embrace. The mountains and lake in the distance looked real.

'It's a lovely picture, isn't it?' said the voice I'd heard over the phone.

He was tall, at least six-three, and lean, with the kind of features bad novels label as chiseled. He was one of the most handsome middle-aged men I had ever seen. His face was noble – a strong chin bisected by a perfect cleft, the nose of a Roman senator, and twinkling eyes the color of a clear sky. His thick, snow-white hair hung down over his forehead, Carl Sandburg style. His eyebrows were twin white clouds.

He wore a short white coat over a blue oxford shirt, burgundy print tie, and dark gray trousers of a subtle check.

His shoes were black calfskin loafers. Very proper, very tasteful. But clothes didn't make the man. He would have looked patrician in doubleknits.

'Dr Delaware? Will Towle.'

'Alex.'

I stood and we shook hands. His grip was firm and dry. The fingers that clasped mine were enormous and I was conscious of abundant strength behind them.

'Please, sit.'

He took his place behind the desk, swiveled back and threw his feet up on top, resting on a year's back issues of the *Journal of Pediatrics*.

I responded to his question.

'It is a beautiful shot. Somewhere in the Pacific Northwest?'

'Washington state. Olympic National Forest. We were vacationing there in fifty-one. I was a resident. That was my wife and son. I lost them a month later. In a car crash.'

'I'm sorry.'

'Yes.' A distant, sleepy look came on his face; it was a moment before he shook himself out of it and came back into focus.

'I know you by reputation, Alex, so it's a pleasure to get to meet you.'

'Same here.'

'I've followed your work, because I have a strong interest in behavioral pediatrics. I was particularly interested in your work with those children who'd been victimized by Stuart Hickle. Several of them were in the practice. The parents spoke highly of your work.'

'Thank you.' I felt as if I was expected to say more but

that was one subject that was closed. 'I do remember sending consent forms to you.'

'Yes, yes. Delighted to cooperate.'

Neither of us spoke, then we both spoke at the same time.

'What I'd like to—' I said.

'What can I do for—' he said.

It came out a garbled mess. We laughed, good old boys at the University Club. I deferred to him. Despite the graciousness I sensed an enormous ego lurking behind that white forelock.

'You're here about the Quinn child. What can I do for you?'

I filled him in on as few details as possible, stressing the importance of Melody Quinn as a witness and the benign nature of the hypnotic intervention. I ended by requesting that he allow her to go off Ritalin for one week.

'You really think this child will be able to give you information of substance?'

'I don't know. I've asked the same question. But she's all the police have got.'

'And your role in all of this?'

I thought up a quicky title.

'I'm a special consultant. They call me in sometimes when there are children involved.'

'I see.'

He played with his hands, constructing ten-legged spiders and killing them.

'I don't know, Alex. When we start to remove a patient from what has been determined to be an optimal dosage we sometimes upset the entire pattern of biochemical response.'

'You think she needs to be on medication constantly.'

'Of course I do. Why else would I prescribe it for her?'
He wasn't angry or defensive. He smiled calmly and with
great forbearance. The message was clear: Only an idiot
would doubt him.

'There'd be no way to reduce the dosage?'

'Oh, that's certainly possible, but it creates the same type
of problem. I don't like to tamper with a winning combination.'

'I see.' I hesitated, then continued. 'She must have posed
quite a problem to merit sixty mgs.'

Towle placed a pair of reading glasses low on his nose,
picked up the chart and flipped through it.

'Let me see. Ah, yes. Hmm. "Mother complains of severe
behavioral problems."' After thumbing through a few more
pages: '"Teachers report failure to complete school assign-
ments. Difficulty in maintaining attention span for more than
brief periods." Ah – here's a later notation – "Child struck
mother during argument about keeping room clean." And
here's a note of mine: "Poor peer relations, few friends."'

I was certain that the argument had something to do with
giving away the giant walrus, Fatso. The gift from Daddy.
And as for friends – it was easy to see that M and M Properties
wouldn't truck with that kind of nonsense.

'That sounds pretty severe to me, don't you think?'

What I thought was that it was horseshit. There'd been
nothing resembling a thorough psychological evaluation.
Nothing beyond taking the mother at her word. I looked at
Towle and saw a quack. A nice-looking, white-haired quack
with lots of connections and the right pieces of paper on his
wall. I longed to tell him so, but that would do nobody –
Melody, Milo – any good.

So I hedged.

'I can't say. You're her doc.' Faking the comradely grin was an exercise in moral self-control.

'That's right, Alex. I am.' He leaned back in his chair and placed his hands behind his head. 'I know what you're thinking. Will Towle is a pill pusher. Stimulants are just another form of child abuse.'

'I wouldn't say that.'

He waved away my objection.

'No, no, I know. And I don't hold it against you. Your training is behavioral and you see things behaviorally. We all do it, settle into professional tunnel vision. The surgeons want to cut everything out. We prescribe and you fellows like to analyse it to death.'

It was starting to sound like a lecture.

'Granted, drugs have risks. But it's a matter of cost-risk analysis. Let's consider a child like the little Quinn girl. What does she start out with? Inferior genes – both parents somewhat *limited* intellectually.' He made the word *limited* sound very cruel. 'Lousy genes and poverty, and a broken marriage. Absent father – although in some of these cases the children are better off without the kind of role models the fathers provide. Bad genes, bad environment. The child's got two strikes against her before she leaves the womb.

'Is it any wonder then that soon we're seeing all the tell-tale signs – antisocial behavior, noncompliance, poor school performance, unsatisfactory impulse control?'

I felt a sudden urge to defend little Melody. Her genial doctor was describing her as some kind of total misfit. I kept silent.

'Now a child like this—' he took off his glasses and put down the chart – 'is going to have to do moderately well in school in order to achieve some semblance of a decent life for herself. Otherwise it's another generation of PPP.'

Piss-poor protoplasm. One of the quaint expressions dreamed up by the medical profession to describe especially unfortunate patients.

Playing straight man to Towle wasn't my idea of a fun afternoon. But I had a hunch it was some kind of ritual, that if I held out and let him smilingly browbeat me he might give me what I came for.

'But there is no way a child like this *can* achieve with her genes and her environment working against her. Not without help. And that's where stimulant medication comes in. Those pills allow her to sit still long enough and pay attention long enough to be able to learn something. They control her behavior to the point where she no longer alienates everyone around her.'

'I got the impression that the mother was using the medication in a haphazard way – giving her an extra pill on days when there were lots of visitors at the apartment complex.'

'I'll have to check that.' He didn't sound concerned. 'You have to remember, Alex, that this child does not exist in a vacuum. There's a social context here. If there's nowhere for her mother and her to live, that isn't exactly therapeutic, is it?'

I listened, certain there was more. Sure enough: 'Now you may ask, what about psychotherapy? What about behavior modification? My answer is: What about them? There is no chance of this particular mother developing the capacity for insight to successfully benefit from psychotherapy. And she lacks the ability to even comply with a stable system of rules and regulations necessary for behavior mod. What she *can* deal with is administering three pills a day to her child. Pills that work. And I don't mind telling you, I don't feel a damn bit guilty about prescribing them, because I think they're this child's only hope.'

It was a great ending. No doubt it made a big hit at the Western Pediatric Ladies Auxiliary Tea. But basically it was all crap. Pseudo-scientific gibberish mixed in with a lot of condescending fascism. Dope up the *Untermenschen* to make them good citizens.

He had worked himself up a bit. But now he was perfectly composed, as handsome and in control as ever.

'I haven't convinced you, have I?' He smiled.

'It's not a matter of that. You raise some interesting points. I'll have to think about it.'

'That's always a good idea, thinking things over.' He rubbed his hands together. 'Now, back to what you came for – and please forgive my little diatribe. You really think that taking this child off stimulants will make her more susceptible to hypnosis.'

'I do.'

'Despite the fact that her concentration will be poorer?'

'Despite that. I've got inductions that are especially suited for children with short attention spans.'

The snowy eyebrows rose.

'Oh, really? I'll have to find out about those. You know, I did some hypnosis, too. In the Army, for pain control. I know it works.'

'I can send you some recent publications.'

'Thank you, Alex.' He rose and it was clear that my time was up.

'Pleasure to meet you, Alex.' Another handshake.

'The pleasure is mine, Will.' This was getting sickening.

The unasked question hung in the air. Towle snagged it.

'I'll tell you what I'm going to do,' he said, smiling ever so faintly.

'Yes?'

'I'm going to *think* about it.'

'I see.'

'Yes, I'll think it over. Call me in a couple of days.'

'I'll do that, Will.' And may your hair and teeth fall out overnight, you sanctimonious bastard.

On the way out Edna glared and Sandi smiled at me. I ignored them both and rescued Milo from the trio of munchkins that were climbing over him as if he were playground equipment. We made our way through the now-boiling mob of children and mothers and reached the car safely.

5

I TOLD Milo about the encounter with Towle as we drove back to my place.

'Power play.' His forehead creased and cherry-sized lumps appeared just above his jawline.

'That and something else that I can't quite figure. He's a strange guy. Comes across very courtly – almost obsequious – then you realize he's playing games.'

'Why'd he have you come all the way out there for something like that?'

'I don't know.' It was a puzzle, his taking time out from a frantic afternoon to deliver a leisurely lecture. Our entire conversation could have been handled in a five-minute phone call. 'Maybe it's his idea of recreation. One-upping another professional.'

'Hell of a hobby for a busy man.'

'Yeah, but the ego comes first. I've met guys like Towle before, obsessed with being in control, with being the boss. Lots of them end up as department heads, deans and chairmen of committees.'

'And captains and inspectors and police chiefs.'

'Right . . .'

'You going to call him like he said?' He sounded defeated.

'Sure, for what it's worth.'
'Yeah.'

Milo reclaimed his Fiat and after a few moments of prayer and pumping it started up. He leaned out of the window and looked at me wearily.

'Thanks, Alex. I'm going to go home and crash. This no-sleep routine is catching up with me . . .'

'You want to take a nap here and then head out?'

'No thanks. I'll make it if this pile of junk will.' He slapped the dented door. 'Thanks anyway.'

'I'll follow up with Melody.'

'Great. I'll call you tomorrow.' He drove away until I stopped him with my shout. He backed up.

'What?'

'It's probably not important, but I thought I'd mention it. The nurse in Towle's office told me Melody's dad's in prison.'

He nodded somnambulantly.

'So's half the country. It's that way when the economy goes bad. Thanks.'

Then he was off.

It was six fifteen and already dark. I lay down on my bed for a few minutes and when I awoke it was after nine. I got up, washed my face, and called Robin. No one answered.

I took a quick shave, threw on a windbreaker and drove down to Hakata in Santa Monica. I drank sake and ate sushi for an hour, and bantered with the chef, who, as it turned out, had a master's degree in psychology from the University of Tokyo.

I got home, stripped naked, and took a hot bath, trying

to erase all thoughts of Morton Handler, Melody Quinn and L. W. Towle, MD, from my mind. I used self-hypnosis, imagining Robin and myself making love on top of a mountain in the middle of a rain forest. Flushed with passion I got out of the tub and called her again. After ten rings, she answered, mumbling and confused and half-asleep.

I apologized for waking her, told her I loved her and hung up.

Half a minute later she called back.

'Was that you, Alex?' She sounded as if she was dreaming.

'Yes, hon. I'm sorry to wake you.'

'No, that's OK – what time is it?'

'Eleven thirty.'

'Oh, I must have conked out. How are you, sweetie?'

'Fine. I called you around nine.'

'I was out all day buying wood. There's an old violin-maker out in Simi Valley who's retiring. I spent six hours choosing tools and picking out maple and ebony. I'm sorry I missed you.'

She sounded exhausted.

'I'm sorry too, but go back to bed. Get some sleep and I'll call you tomorrow.'

'If you want to come over, you can.'

I thought about it. But I was too restless to be good company.

'No, doll. You rest. How about dinner tomorrow? You pick the place.'

'OK, darling.' She yawned – a soft, sweet sound. 'I love you.'

'Love you too.'

* * *

70

It took me a while to fall asleep and when I finally did, it was restless slumber, punctuated by black-and-white dreams with lots of frantic movement in them. I don't remember what they were about, but the dialog was sluggish and labored, as if everyone were talking with paralysed lips and mouths filled with wet sand.

In the middle of the night I got up to check that the doors and windows were locked.

6

I WOKE UP at six the next morning, filled with random energy. I hadn't felt that way for over five months. The tension wasn't all bad, for with it came a sense of purpose, but by seven it had built up some, so that I paced around the house like a jaguar on the prowl.

At seven thirty I decided it was late enough. I dialed Bonita Quinn's number. She was wide-awake and she sounded as if she'd been expecting my call.

'Morning, Doctor.'

'Good morning. I thought I'd drop by and spend a few hours with Melody.'

'Why not? She's not doin' anything. You know—' she lowered her voice – 'I think she liked you. She talked about how you played with her.'

'That's good. We'll do some more today. I'll be there in half an hour.'

When I arrived she was all dressed and ready to go. Her mother had put her in a pale yellow sundress that exposed bony white shoulders and pipe-stem arms. Her hair was tied back in a ponytail, fastened by a yellow ribbon. She clutched a tiny patent-leather purse. I had thought we'd spend some time in her room and then perhaps go out for lunch, but it was clear she was primed for an outing.

'Hi, Melody.'

She averted her gaze and sucked her thumb.

'You look very pretty this morning.'

She smiled shyly.

'I thought we'd take a drive, go to a park. How does that sound?'

'OK.' The shaky voice.

'Great.' I peeked my head into the apartment. Bonita Quinn was pushing around a vacuum cleaner as if it were a wagonload of sins. She wore a blue bandanna on her head and a cigarette dangled from her lips. The television was tuned in to a gospel show, but snow obscured the picture and the choir was drowned out by the sound of the vacuum.

I touched her shoulder. She jumped.

'I'm taking her now, OK?' I yelled over the din.

'Sure.' When she spoke the cigarette bobbled like a trout lure in a rushing brook.

She resumed her chore, stooping over the roaring machine and plowing it forward.

I rejoined Melody.

'Let's go.'

She walked alongside me. Midway to the parking lot a small hand slipped into mine.

Through a series of hilltop turns and lucky detours, I connected to Ocean Avenue. I drove south, toward Santa Monica, until we reached the park at the top of the cliff overlooking Pacific Coast Highway. It was eight thirty in the morning. The sky was clear, pebbled only with a handful of clouds that might have been as distant as Hawaii. I found a parking space on the street, directly in front of the Camera Obscura and the Senior Citizens' Recreation Center.

Even that early in the morning the place was bustling. Old people packed the benches and the shuffleboard court. Some of them jabbered nonstop to each other, or themselves. Others stared out at the boulevard in mute trance. Leggy girls in skimpy tops and satin shorts that covered a tenth of their gluteal regions skated by, transforming the walkways between the palms into fleshy freeways. Some of them wore stereo headsets – speeding spacewomen, with glazed, beatific expressions on their California-perfect faces.

Japanese tourists snapped pictures, nudged each other, pointed and laughed. Shabby bums loitered against the guardrail that separated the crumbling bluff from sheer space. They smoked behind cupped hands and regarded the world with distrust and fear. A surprising number of them were young men. They all looked as if they'd crawled out of some deep, dark, unproductive mine.

There were students reading, couples sprawled on the grass, small boys darting between the trees and a few furtive encounters that looked suspiciously like dope deals.

Melody and I walked along the outer rim of the park, hand in hand, talking little. I offered to buy her a hot pretzel from a street vendor, but she said she wasn't hungry. I remembered that loss of appetite was another side effect of Ritalin. Or maybe she'd just had a big breakfast.

We came to the walkway that led to the pier.

'Have you ever been on a merry-go-round?' I asked her.

'Once. We went on a school trip to Magic Mountain. The fast rides scared me but I liked the merry-go-round.'

'C'mon.' I pointed out toward the pier. 'There's one here. We'll take a ride.'

In contrast to the park, the pier was nearly deserted. There were a few men fishing here and there, mostly old blacks and Asians, but their expressions were pessimistic, their buckets empty. Dried fish scales were embedded in the aged wooden planks of the walkway, giving it a sequined effect in the morning sun. There were cracks in several of the weathered boards, and as we walked I caught glimpses of the water below slapping against the pilings and retreating with a hissed warning. In the shadow of the pier's under-belly the water looked greenish black. There was a strong smell of creosote and salt in the air, a ripe, raw fragrance of loneliness and wasted hours.

The pool hall where I used to hide while playing hookey had been closed down. In its place was an arcade full of elec-tric video games. A solitary Mexican boy intently pulled the joystick on one of the garishly painted robots. Computer noise emerged in blips and dreeps.

The merry-go-round was housed in a cavernous barn of a building that looked as if it would collapse with the next high tide. The operator was a tiny man with a potbelly the size of a cantaloupe and flaky skin around his ears. He was sitting on a stool reading a racing form and trying to pretend we weren't there.

'We'd like to ride the merry-go-round.'

He looked up, gave us the once-over. Melody was staring at the ancient posters on the wall. Buffalo Bill Victorian Love.

'Quarter a spin.'

I handed him a couple of bills.

'Keep it going for a while.'

'Sure.'

I lifted her up onto a large white-and-gilded horse with a pink plume for a tail. The brass rod upon which it was impaled had diagonal stripes running across it. A sure bet to go up and down. I stood next to her.

The tiny man was buried in his reading. He reached out a hand, pushed a button on a rusty console, pulled a lever and a rheumy rendition of the 'Blue Danube Waltz' piped out of a dozen hidden speakers. The carousel started off slowly, and then it began to turn; horses, monkeys, chariots coming to life, moving in vertical counter-point to the revolution of the machine.

Melody's hands tightened around the neck of her steed; she stared straight ahead. Gradually, she relaxed her grip and allowed herself to look around. By the twentieth revolution, she was swaying with the music, eyes closed, mouth open in silent laughter.

When the music finally stopped I helped her down and she stepped dizzily onto the dirty concrete floor. She was giggling and swinging her purse in joyful rhythm, in time with the now dissipated waltz.

We left the barn and ventured to the end of the pier. She was fascinated by the enormous bait tanks teeming with squirming anchovies, amazed at the bin of fresh rockfish that was being brought up by a trio of muscled, bearded fishermen. The reddish fish lay dead in a heap. The quick ascent from the bottom of the ocean had caused the air bladders on several of them to explode and extrude from their open mouths. Crabs the size of bees crawled in and around the motionless bodies. Gulls swooped down to plunder and were waved off by the horned brown hands of the fisher-men.

One of the fishermen, a boy of no more than eighteen, saw her staring.

'Pretty gross, huh?'

'Yeah.'

'Tell your daddy to take you to prettier places on his day off.' He laughed.

Melody smiled. She didn't try to correct him.

Someone was deep-frying shrimp. I saw her nose wrinkle.

'You hungry?'

'Kind of.' She looked uneasy.

'Anything wrong?'

'Mama told me not to be too grabby.'

'Don't you worry. I'm going to tell your mom what a good girl you've been. Have you had breakfast?'

'Kind of.'

'What'd you have?'

'Some juice. A piece of donut. The white powdery kind.'

'That's it?'

'Uh-huh.' She looked up at me as if expecting to be punished. I softened my tone.

'I guess you weren't hungry at breakfast time.'

'Uh-huh.' So much for the big-breakfast theory.

'Well, *I'm* pretty hungry.' It was true. All I'd had was coffee. 'What do you say we both get something?'

'Thank you, Doctor Del—' she stumbled over my name.

'Call me Alex.'

'Thank you, Alex.'

We located the source of the cooking smells at a shabby dinerette sandwiched between a souvenir shop and a bait and tackle stand. The woman behind the counter was pasty white and obese. Steam and smoke rose in billows around her moon face, creating a shimmering halo. Deep fryers crackled in the background.

I bought a large greasy bag full of goodies: Foil-wrapped servings of shrimp and fried cod, a basket of French fries the size of billy clubs, plastic covered tubs of tartar sauce and ketchup, fluted paper tubes of salt, two cans of an off-brand of cola.

'Don't forget these, sir.'

The fat woman held out a handful of napkins.

'Thanks.'

'You know kids.' She looked down at Melody. 'You enjoy yourself now, hon.'

We carried the food off the pier and found a quiet spot on the beach, not far from the Pritikin Longevity Center. We ate our greasy fare watching middle-aged men attempt to jog around the block, fueled by whatever heartless menu the center was serving nowadays.

She ate like a trucker. It was getting close to noon, which meant that normally she'd be ready for her second dose of amphetamine. Her mother hadn't offered the medication to me, and I hadn't thought – or wanted – to ask.

The change in her behavior became evident halfway through lunch, and grew more obvious each minute.

She began to move more. She was more alert. Her face became more animated. She fidgeted, as if waking from a long, confusing sleep. She looked around, newly in touch with her environment.

'Look at them.' She pointed to a covey of wet-suited surfers riding waves in the distance.

'They look like seals, don't they?'

She giggled.

'Could I go in the water, Alex?'

'Take your shoes off and wade near the shoreline — where the water touches the sand. Try not to get your dress wet.'

I popped shrimp in my mouth, leaned back and watched her run along the tideline, skinny legs kicking up the water. Once she turned in my direction and waved.

I watched her play that way for twenty minutes or so, and then I rolled up my pants legs, took off my shoes and socks and joined her.

We ran together. Her legs worked better with every passing moment; soon she was a gazelle. She whooped and splashed and kept going until we were both out of breath. We walked back to our picnic site and collapsed on the sand. Her hair was a mess so I loosened the barrettes and re-fastened them for her. Her small chest heaved. Her feet were crusted with grit from the ankle down. When she finally caught her breath she asked me:

'I — I've been a good girl, haven't I?'

'You've been great.'

She looked unsure.

'Don't you think so, Melody?'

'I don't know. Sometimes I think I am and Mama gets mad or Mrs Brookhouse says I'm bad.'

'You're always a good girl. Even if someone thinks you've done something wrong. Do you understand that?'

'I guess so.'

'Not sure, huh?'

'I — I get mixed up.'

79

'Everyone gets mixed up. Kids and moms and dads. And doctors.'

'Dr Towle, too?'

'Even Dr Towle.'

She digested that for a while. The large, dark eyes darted around, moving from the water, to my face, to the sky, and back to me.

'Mama said you were going to hypnotize me.' She pronounced it hip-mo-tize.

'Only if you want me to. Do you understand why we think it might be helpful?'

'Sort of. To make me think better?'

'No. You think just fine. This—' I patted her head – 'works fine. We want to try hypnosis – hypnotizing – so that you can do us a favor. So that you can remember something.'

'About when the other doctor was hurt.'

I hesitated. My habit was to be honest with children, but if she hadn't been told about Handler and Gutierrez being dead I wasn't going to be the one to break the news. Not without the chance to be around to help pick up the pieces.

'Yes. About that.'

'I told the policeman I didn't remember anything. It was all dark and everything.'

'Sometimes people remember better after being hypnotized.'

She looked at me, frightened.

'Are you scared of being hypnotized?'

'Uh-huh.'

'That's OK. It's OK to be scared of new things. But there really isn't anything scary about hypnotizing. It's really kind of fun. Have you ever seen anyone hypnotized before?'

'Nope.'

'Never? Even in a cartoon?'

She lit up. 'Yeah, when the guy in the pointy hat hypnotized Popeye and the waves came out his hands and Popeye walked out of the window into the air and he didn't fall.'

'Right. I've seen that one too. The guy in the pointy hat made Popeye do all sorts of weird things.'

'Yeah.'

'Well that's great for cartoons, but real hypnotizing isn't anything like that.' I gave her a child's version of the lecture I'd delivered to her mother. She seemed to believe me, because fascination took the place of fear.

'Can we do it now?'

I hesitated. The beach was empty; there was plenty of privacy. And the moment was right. To hell with Towle . . .

'I don't see why not. First, let's get real comfortable.'

I had her fix her eyes upon a smooth shiny pebble as she held it in her hand. Within moments she was blinking in response to suggestion. Her breathing slowed and became regular. I told her to close her eyes and listen to the sound of the waves slapping against the shore. Then I instructed her to imagine herself descending a flight of stairs and passing through a beautiful door to a favorite place.

'I don't know where it is, or what's in it, but it's a special place for you. You can tell me or keep it secret, but being there makes you feel so comfortable, so happy, so in control . . .'

A bit more of that and she was in a deep hypnotic state.

'Now you can hear the sound of my voice without having to listen. Just continue to enjoy your favorite place, and have a real good time.'

I let her go for five more minutes. There was a peaceful, angelic expression on her thin little face. A soft wind rustled the loose strands of her hair. She looked tiny, sitting in the sand, hands resting in her lap.

I gave her a suggestion to go back in time, brought her back to the night of the murder. She tensed momentarily, then resumed the deep, regular breathing.

'You're still feeling totally relaxed, Melody. So comfortable and in control. But now you can watch yourself, just as if you were a star on TV. You see yourself getting out of bed ...'

Her lips parted, she ran the tip of her tongue over them.

'And you go to the window and sit there, just looking out. What do you see?'

'Dark.' The word was barely audible.

'Yes, it's dark. And is there anything else?'

'No.'

'OK. Let's sit there a while longer.'

A few minutes later:

'Can you see anything else in the dark, Melody?'

'Uh-uh. Dark.'

I tried a few more times, and then gave up. Either she had seen nothing, and the talk of two or three dark men had been confabulation, or she was blocking. In either event I wasn't going to get anything from her.

I let her enjoy her favorite place, gave her suggestions for mastery, control, and feeling refreshed and happy, and brought her gently out of hypnosis. She came out smiling.

'That was fun!'

'I'm glad you liked it. You seemed to have a real good favorite place.'

'You said I don't have to tell you!'

'That's true. You don't.'

'Well what if I want to?' she pouted.

'Then you can.'

'Hmm.' She savored her power for a moment. 'I want to tell you. It was riding around on the merry-go-round. Going round and round, faster and faster.'

'That's a great choice.'

'Each time I went around I felt happier and happier. Can we go again some time?'

'Sure.' Now you've done it, Alex. Gotten yourself into something that won't be easy to pull out of. Instant daddy, just add guilt.

Back in the car she turned to me.

'Alex, you said hypnotizing makes you remember better?'

'It can.'

'Could I use it to remember my daddy?'

'When's the last time you saw him?'

'Never. He left when I was a little baby. He and Mama don't live together any more.'

'Does he visit?'

'No. He lives far away. Once he called me, before Christmas, but I was sleeping, so Mama didn't wake me up. That made me mad.'

'I can understand that.'

'I hit her.'

'You must have been really mad.'

'Yeah.' She bit her lip. 'Sometimes he sends me stuff.'

'Like Fatso?'

'Yeah, and other stuff.' She dug in her purse and pulled

out what looked to be a large dried pit, or seed. It had been carved to resemble a face – a snarling face – with rhinestone eyes, and strands of black acrylic hair glued to the top. A head, a shrunken head. The kind of hideous trash you can pick up at any Tijuana tourist stall. From the way she held it, it could have been the Crown Jewel of Kwarshiorkor.

'Very nice.' I handled the knobby thing and gave it back to her.

'I'd like to see him but Mama says she doesn't know where he is. Can hypnotizing help remember him?'

'It would be hard, Melody, because you haven't seen him in a long time. But we could try. Do you have anything to remember him by – any picture of him?'

'Yeah.' She searched in her purse again and came up with a spindled and mutilated snapshot. It had probably been fingered like a rosary. I thought of the photograph on Towle's wall. This was the week for celluloid memories. Mr Eastman, if you only knew how your little black box can be used to preserve the past like a stillborn fetus in a jar of formalin.

It was a faded color photograph of a man and woman. The woman was Bonita Quinn in younger, but not much prettier, days. Even in her twenties she had possessed a sad mask of a face that foreshadowed a merciless future. She wore a dress that exposed too much undernourished thigh. Her hair was long and straight and parted in the middle. She and her companion were in front of what looked like a rural bar, the kind of watering place you find peeking out around sudden highway curves. The walls of the building were rough-hewn logs. There was a Budweiser sign in the window. Her arm was around the waist of the man, who had placed his arm around her shoulder. He wore a T-shirt, jeans and Wellington boots. The rump of a motorcycle was visible next to him.

He was a strange-looking bird. One side of him – the left – sagged and there was more than a hint of atrophy running all the way down from face to foot. He looked crooked, like a piece of fruit that had been sliced and then put back together with less than full precision. When you got past the asymmetry he wasn't bad-looking – tall, slender, with shoulder-length shaggy blond hair and a thick mustache.

He had a wise-guy expression on his face that contrasted with Bonita's solemnity. It was the kind of look you see on the face of the local yokels when you walk into a small-town tavern in a strange place, just wanting a cold drink and some solitude. The kind of look you go out of your way to avoid, because it means trouble, and nothing else.

I wasn't surprised its owner had ended up behind bars.

'Here you go.' I handed the photo back to her and she carefully put it back in her purse.

'Want to take another run?'

'Naw. I'm kinda tired.'

'Want to go home?'

'Yeah.'

During the ride back to the apartment complex she was very quiet, as if she'd been doped up again. I had the uneasy feeling that I hadn't done right by this child, that I had over-stimulated her, only to return her to a dreary routine.

Was I prepared to play the rescuing good guy on a regular basis?

I thought of the parting lecture one of the senior

professors in graduate school had given our graduating class of aspiring psychotherapists.

'When you choose to earn your living by helping people who are in emotional pain, you're also making a choice to carry them on your back for a while. To hell with all that talk of taking responsibility, assertiveness. That's crap. You're going to be coming up against helplessness every day of your lives. Your patients will imprint you, like goslings who latch on to the first creature they see when they stick their heads out of the egg shell. If you can't handle it, become an accountant.'

Right now a ledger book full of numbers would have been a welcome sight.

I DROVE OUT to Robin's studio at half-past seven. It had been several days since I'd seen her and I missed her. When she opened the door she was wearing a gauzy white dress that accentuated the olive tint of her skin. Her hair hung loose and she wore gold hoops in her ears.

She held out her arms to me and we embraced for a long while. We walked inside, still clinging together.

Her place is an old store on Pacific Avenue in Venice. Like lots of other studios nearby, it's unmarked, the windows painted over in opaque white.

She led me past the front part, the work area full of power tools – table saw, band saw, drill press – piles of wood, instrument molds, chisels, gages and templates. As usual the room smelled of sawdust and glue. The floor was covered with shavings.

She pushed open swinging double doors and we were in her living quarters: Sitting room, kitchen, sleeping loft with bath, small office. Unlike the shop, her personal space was uncluttered. She had made most of the furniture herself, and it was solid hardwood, simple and elegant.

She sat me down on a soft cotton couch. There was coffee and pie set out on a ceramic tray, napkins, plates and forks.

She sidled next to me. I took her face in my hands and kissed her.

'Hello, darling.' She put her arms around me. I could feel the firmness of her back through the thin fabric, firmness couched in yielding, curving softness. She worked with her hands and it always amazed me to find in her that special combination of muscles and distinctly female lushness. When she moved, whether manipulating a hunk of rosewood around the rapacious jaws of a band saw or simply walking, it was with confidence and grace. Meeting her was the best thing that had ever happened to me. It alone had been worth dropping out for.

I'd been browsing at McCabe's, the guitar shop in Santa Monica, looking through the old sheet music, trying out the instruments that hung on the walls. I'd spied one particularly attractive guitar, like my Martin but even better made. I admired the craftsmanship – it was a hand-made instrument – and ran my fingers over the strings, which vibrated with perfect balance and sustain. Taking it off the wall I played it and it sounded as good as it looked, ringing like a bell.

'Like it?'

The voice was feminine and belonged to a gorgeous creature in her mid-twenties. She stood close to me – how long she'd been there I wasn't sure; I'd been lost in the music. She had a heart-shaped face topped by a luxuriant mop of auburn curls. Her eyes were almond shaped, wide set, the color of antique mahogany. She was small, not more than five-two, with slender wrists leading to delicate hands and long tapering fingers. When she smiled, her upper two incisors, larger than the rest of her teeth, flashed ivory.

'Yes. I think it's terrific.'

'It's not that good.' She put her hands on her hips – very definite hips. She had the kind of figure, small-waisted, busty and gently concave, that couldn't be camouflaged by the overalls she'd thrown on over her turtleneck.

'Oh, really?'

'Oh, really.' She took the guitar from me. 'There's a spot right here—' she tapped the soundboard '– where it's been sanded too thin. And the balance between head-stock and box could be better.' She strummed a few chords. 'All in all I'd give it an eight on a scale of one to ten.'

'You seem to be quite an expert on it.'

'I should be. I made it.'

She took me to her shop that afternoon and showed me the instrument she was working on. 'This one's going to be a ten. The other was one of my first. You learn as you go along.'

Some weeks later she admitted it had been her way of picking me up, her version of *Come up and see my etchings*.

'I liked the way you played. Such sensitivity.'

We saw each other regularly after that. I learned that she had been an only child, the special daughter of a skilled cabinetmaker who had taught her everything he knew about how to transform raw wood into objects of beauty. She had tried college, majoring in design, but the regimentation had angered her, as had the fact that her dad had known more about form and function intuitively than all the teachers and books combined. After he died, she dropped out, took the money he left her and invested in a shop in San Luis Obispo. She got to know some local musicians, who brought her their instruments to fix. At first it was a sideline, for she was trying to make a living designing and manufacturing custom furniture. Then she began to take a greater interest in the guitars, banjos and mandolins that found their way to her workbench. She read a few books on instrument-making, found she had all the requisite skills and made her first guitar. It sounded great and she sold it for five hundred dollars. She was hooked. Two weeks later she moved to LA, where the musicians were, and set up shop.

When I met her she was making two instruments a month as well as handling repairs. She'd been written up in trade magazines and was back-ordered for four months. She was starting to make a living.

I probably loved her the first day I met her but it took me a couple of weeks to realize it.

After three months we started to talk about living together, but it didn't happen. There was no philosophical objection on either side, but her place was too small for two people and my house couldn't accommodate her shop. It sounds unromantic, letting mundane matters like space and comfort get in the way, but we were having such a good time with each other while maintaining our privacy, that the incentive to make a change wasn't there. Often she would spend the night with me, other times I'd collapse in her loft. Some evenings we'd go our separate ways.

It wasn't a bad arrangement.

I sipped coffee and eyed the pie.

'Have some, babe.'

'I don't want to pork out before dinner.'

'Maybe we won't go out for dinner.' She stroked the back of my neck. 'Ooh, such tension.' She began to knead the muscles of my upper back. 'You haven't felt this way in a long time.'

'There's good reason for it.' And I told her about Milo's morning visit, the murder, Melody, Towle.

When I was through she placed her hands on my shoulders.

'Alex, do you really want to get into something like this?'

'Do I have a choice? I see that kid's eyes in my sleep. I was a fool for getting sucked in, but now I'm stuck.'

She looked at me. The corners of her mouth lifted in a smile.

'You are such a pushover. And so sweet.'

She nuzzled me under my chin. I held her to me and buried my face in her hair. It smelled of lemon and honey and rosewood.

'I really love you.'

'I love you, too, Alex.'

We undressed each other and when we were totally naked, I lifted her in my arms and carried her up the stairs to the loft. Not wanting to be apart from her for one second I kept my mouth fastened upon hers while I maneuvered myself on top of her. She clung to me, her arms and legs like tendrils. We connected, and I was home.

8

WE SLEPT until 10 P.M., then awoke famished. I went down to the kitchen and made sandwiches of Italian salami and Swiss cheese on rye, found a jug of burgundy and toted it all back upstairs for a late supper in bed. We shared garlicky kisses, got crumbs in the bed, hugged each other and fell back asleep.

We were jolted awake by the telephone.

Robin answered it.

'Yes, Milo, he's here. No, that's all right. Here he is.'

She handed me the receiver and buried herself under the covers.

'Hello, Milo. What time is it?'

'Three A.M.'

I sat up and rubbed my eyes. Through the skylight the heavens were black.

'What's going on?'

'It's the kid – Melody Quinn. She's freaked out – woke up screaming. Bonita called Towle who called me. Demanded you get over there. He sounds pissed.'

'Screw him. I'm not his errand boy.'

'You want me to tell him that? He's right here.'

'You're over there now? At her place?'

'Certainly. Neither rain nor hail nor darkness stays this trusted civil servant and all that shit. We're having a little party.

The doctor, Bonita, me. The kid's sleeping. Towle gave her a shot of something.'

'Figures.'

'The kid spilled to her mom about the hypnosis. He wants you there if she wakes up again – to rehypnotize or something.'

'That asshole. The hypnosis didn't cause this. The kid's got sleep problems because of all the dope he's been shoving into her system.'

But I was far from certain of that. She *had* been troubled after the session on the beach.

'I'm sure you're right, Alex. I just wanted to give you the option to come down here, to know what was going on. If you want me to tell Towle to forget it, I will.'

'Hold on a minute.' I shook my head, trying to clear it. 'Did she say anything when she woke up – anything coherent?'

'I just caught the tail end of it. They said it was the fourth time tonight. She was screaming for her daddy: "Oh Daddy. Daddy, Daddy" – like that, but very loud. It looked and sounded pretty bad, Alex.'

'I'll be down there as soon as I can.'

I gave the sleeping mummy next to me a kiss on the fanny, got up, and threw on my clothes.

I sped along Pacific, heading north. The streets were empty and slick with marine mist. The guide lights at the end of the pier were distant pinpoints. A few trawlers sat on the horizon. At this hour the sharks and other nocturnal predators would be prowling the bottom of the ocean floor. I wondered how much carnage was hidden by the glossy black outer skin of the water; and how many of the night-hunters lurked on dry land, hiding in alleys, behind trash bins, concealed among the leaves and twigs of suburban shrubbery, wild eyed, breathing hard.

As I drove I developed a new theory of evolution. Evil had its own metamorphic intelligence: The sharks and the razor-toothed serpents, the slimy, venomous things that hid in the silt, hadn't given way in an orderly progression to amphibian, reptile, bird and mammal. A single quantum leap had taken evil from water to land. From shark to rapist, eel to throat-slasher, poison slug to skullcrusher, with bloodlust at the core of the helix.

The darkness seemed to press against me, insistent, fetid. I pushed down harder on the accelerator and forced my way through it.

When I got to the apartment complex, Milo met me at the door.

'She's just started again.'

I could hear it before I got to the bedroom.

The light was dim. Melody sat upright in her bed, her body rigid, eyes wide open but unfocused. Bonita sat next to her. Towle, in sports clothes, stood on the other side.

The child was sobbing, a wounded animal sound. She wailed and moaned and rocked back and forth. Then the moan picked up volume, gradually, like a siren, until she was screaming, her thin voice a piercing, shrieking assault upon the silence.

'Daddy! Daddy! Daddy!'

Her hair was plastered against her face, slick with sweat. Bonita tried to hold her but she flailed and struck out. The mother was helpless.

The screaming continued for what seemed like forever, then it stopped and she began moaning again.

'Oh, Doctor,' Bonita pleaded, 'she's going at it again. Do something.'

Towle spotted me.

'Maybe Dr Delaware can help.' His tone of voice was nasty.

'No, no, I don't want *him* near her! He caused all of this!'

Towle didn't argue with her. I could have sworn he looked smug.

'Mrs Quinn—' I began.

'No. You stay away! Get out!'

Her screaming set Melody off, and she began calling for her father again.

'Stop it!'

Bonita went for her, putting her hand over the child's mouth. Shaking her.

Towle and I moved at the same time. We pulled her off. He took her aside and said something that quieted her down.

I moved next to Melody. She was breathing hard. Her pupils were dilated. I touched her. She stiffened.

'Melody,' I whispered. 'It's Alex. You're OK. You're safe.'

As I talked she calmed down. I blabbed on, knowing that what I said was less important than how I said it. I maintained a low, rhythmic pattern of speech, easy-going, reassuring. Hypnotic.

Soon she had slipped lower in the bed. I helped her lie down. Her hands unfolded. I kept talking to her soothingly. Her muscles began to relax and her breathing became slow and regular. I told her to close her eyes and she did. I stroked her shoulder, continued to talk to her, to tell her everything was all right, that she was safe.

She snuggled into a fetal position, drew the covers over her, and placed her thumb in her mouth.

'Turn off the light,' I said. The room became dark. 'Let's leave her alone.' The three of them left.

'Now you're going to continue sleeping, Melody, and you'll have a very peaceful, restful night, with good dreams. When you wake up in the morning you'll feel very good, very rested.'

I could hear her snoring ever so slightly.

'Good night, Melody.' I leaned over and gave her a light kiss on the cheek.

She mumbled one word.

'Da-da.'

I closed the door to her room. Bonita was in the kitchen, wringing her hands, She wore a frayed man's terrycloth robe. Her hair had been pulled back in a bun and covered with a scarf. She looked paler than I remembered as she busied herself cleaning up.

Towle bent over his black bag. He clicked it shut, stood and ran his fingers through his hair. Seeing me he raised himself up to his full height and glared down, ready to give another lecture.

'I hope you're happy,' he said.

'Don't start,' I warned him. 'No I-told-you-so's.'

'You can see why I was reluctant to tamper with this child's mind.'

'Nobody tampered with anything.' I could feel tension rising in my gut. He was every hypocritical authority figure I'd detested.

He shook his head condescendingly.

'Obviously your memory needs some polishing.'

'Obviously you're a sanctimonious prick.'

The blue eyes flashed. He tightened his lips.

'What if I bring you up before the ethics committee of the State Medical Board?'

96

'You do that, Doctor.'

'I'm seriously considering it.' He looked like a Calvinist preacher, all stern and tight and self-righteous.

'You do it and we'll get into a little discussion on the proper use of stimulant medication with children.'

He smiled.

'It will take more than you to tarnish my reputation.'

'I'm sure it will.' My fists were clenched. 'You've got legions of loyal followers. Like that woman in there.' I pointed toward the kitchen. 'They bring their kids to you, human jalopies, and you tinker with them, give 'em a quick tune-up and a pill; you fix them to their specifications. Make them nice and quiet, compliant, and obedient. Drowsy little zombies. You're a goddamn hero.'

'I don't have to listen to this.' He moved forward.

'No you don't, hero. But why don't you go in there and tell her what you really think of her? Piss-poor protoplasm, and let's see — bad genes, no insight.'

He stopped in his tracks.

'Easy, Alex.' Milo spoke from the corner, cautiously.

Bonita came in from the kitchen.

'What's going on?' she wanted to know. Towle and I were facing each other like boxers after the bell.

He changed his manner and smiled at her charmingly. 'Nothing, my dear. Just a professional discussion. Doctor Delaware and I were trying to decide what was best for Melody.'

'What's best is no more hypnotizing. You told me that.'

'Yes.' Towle tapped his foot, tried not to look uncomfortable. 'That was my professional opinion.' He loved that word, professional. 'And it still is.'

'Well, you tell *him* that.' She pointed at me.

'That's what we were discussing, dear.'

He must have been just a little too smooth, because her face got tight and her voice lowered suspiciously.

'What's to discuss? I don't want him or him—' the second jab was at Milo – 'around here no more.' She turned to us. 'You try and be a good Samaritan and help the cops and you get the shaft! Now my baby's got the seizures and she's screamin' and I'm gonna lose my place. I know I'm gonna lose it!'

Her face crumpled. She buried it in her hands and began to cry. Towle moved in like a Beverly Hills gigolo, putting his arms around her, consoling her, saying now, now.

He guided her to the couch and sat her down, standing over her, patting her shoulder.

'I'm gonna lose my place,' she said into her hands. 'They don't like noise here.' She uncovered her face and looked wet-eyed up at Towle.

'Now, now, it's going to be all right. I'll see to that.'

'But what about the seizures!?'

'I'll see to that, too.' He gave me a sharp look, full of hostility and, I was sure, a bit of fear.

She sniffled and wiped her nose on her sleeve.

'I don't understand why she has to wake up screaming Daddy Daddy! That bastard's never been around to lift a finger or give me a cent of child support! He has no love for her! Why does she cry out for *him*, Doctor Towle?' She looked up at him, a novitiate beseeching the pope.

'Now, now.'

'He's a crazy man, that Ronnie Lee is. Look at this!' She tore the scarf from her head, shook her hair loose and lowered her head exposing the top of it. Giving a whimper she parted the strands at the center of her crown. 'Look at this!'

It was ugly. A thick, raw red scar the size of a fat worm. A worm that had burrowed under her scalp and settled there. The skin around it was livid and lumpy, showing the results of bad surgery, devoid of hair.

'Now you know why I cover it!' she cried. '*He* did that to me! With a *chain*! Ronnie Lee Quinn.' She spat out the name. 'A crazy, evil bastard. That's the Daddy Daddy she's cryin' out for! That scum!'

'Now, now,' said Towle. He turned to us. 'Do you gentlemen have anything more to discuss with Mrs Quinn?'

'No, Doctor,' said Milo and turned to leave. He took hold of my arm to guide me out. But I had something to say.

'Tell her, Doctor. Tell her those were not seizures. They were night terrors and they'll go away by themselves if you keep her calm. Tell her there'll be no need for phenobarbitol or Dilantin or Tofranil.'

Towle continued to pat her shoulder.

'Thank you for your professional opinion, Doctor. I'll manage this case as I see fit.'

I stood there rooted.

'Come on, Alex.' Milo eased me out of the door.

The parking lot of the apartment complex was crammed full of Mercedes, Porsches, Alfa Romeos and Datsun Zs. Milo's Fiat, parked in front of a hydrant, looked sadly out of place, like a cripple at a track meet. We sat in it, glum.

'What a mess,' he said.

'The bastard.'

'For a minute I thought you were going to hit him.' He chuckled.

'It was tempting. The bastard.'

'It looked like he was baiting you. I thought you guys got along.'

'On his terms. On an intellectual level we were good old boys. When things fell apart he had to find a scapegoat. He's an egomaniac. *Doctor* is omnipotent. *Doctor* can fix anything. Did you see how she worshiped him, the goddamned Great White Father? Probably slit the kid's wrists if he told her to.'

'You're worried about the kid, aren't you?'

'You're damn right I am. You know exactly what he's going to do, don't you – more dope. She'll be a total space cadet in two days.'

Milo chewed on his lip. After a few minutes he said:

'Well, there's nothing we can do about it. I'm sorry I pulled you into it in the first place.'

'Forget it. It wasn't your fault.'

'Nah, it was. I've been lazy, trying for an instant miracle on this Handler mess. Been avoiding the old wear-down-the-shoe leather routine. Question Handler's associates, get the list of known bad guys with razor-happy fingers from the computer and plod through it. Go through Handler's files. The whole thing was iffy in the first place, a seven-year-old kid.'

'She could have turned out to be a good witness.'

'Is it ever that easy?' He started up the engine, after three attempts. 'Sorry for ruining your night.'

'You didn't. He did.'

'Forget him, Alex. Assholes are like weeds – a bitch to get rid of and when you do, another one grows back in the same place. That's what I've been doing for eight years – pouring weed-killer and watching them grow back faster than I can clear them away.'

He sounded weary and looked old.

I got out of the car and leaned in through the window.

'See you tomorrow.'

'What?'

'The files. We have to go through Handler's files. I'll be able to tell faster than you will which ones were dangerous.'

'You're kidding.'

'Nope. I'm carrying around a huge Zeigarnik.'

'A what?'

'Zeigarnik. She was a Russian psychologist who discovered that people develop tension for unfinished business. They named it after her. The Zeigarnik effect. Like most overachievers I've got a big one.'

He looked at me like I was talking nonsense.

'Uh-huh. Right, And this Zeigarnik is big enough for you to let it intrude upon the mellow life?'

'What the hell, life was getting boring.' I slapped him on the back.

'Suit yourself.' He shrugged. 'Regards to Robin.'

'You give regards to your doctor.'

'If he's still there when I get back. This middle-of-the-night stuff is testing that relationship.' He scratched at the corner of his eye and scowled.

'I'm sure he'll put up with it, Milo.'

'Oh yeah? Why's that?'

'If he's crazy enough to go for you in the first place, he's crazy enough to stick with you.'

'That's very reassuring, pal.' He ground the Fiat into first and sped away.

9

AT THE TIME of his murder, Morton Handler had been in practice as a psychiatrist for a little under fifteen years. During that period he had consulted on or treated over two thousand patients. The records of these individuals were stored in manila folders and packed, one hundred and fifty to a box, in cardboard cartons that were taped shut and stamped with the LAPD seal.

Milo brought these boxes to my house, assisted by a slight, balding, black detective named Delano Hardy. Huffing and wheezing, they loaded the cartons in my dining room. Soon it looked as if I was either moving in or moving out.

'It's not as bad as it seems,' Milo assured me. 'You won't have to go through all of them. Right, Del?'

Hardy lit a cigarette and nodded assent.

'We've done some preliminary screening,' he said 'We eliminated anyone known to be deceased. We figured they'd be low probability suspects.'

The two of them laughed. Dark detective laughs.

'And the coroner's report,' he continued, 'says Handler and the girl were cut by someone with a lot of muscle. The throat wound on him went clear back to the spine on the first try.'

'Which means,' I interrupted, 'a man.'

'Could be one hell of a tough lady,' laughed Hardy, 'but we're betting on a male.'

'There are six hundred male patients,' added Milo. 'Those four boxes over there.'

'Also,' said Hardy, 'we brought you a little present.'

He gave me a small package wrapped in green and red Christmas paper with a bugle and holly wreath pattern on it. It was tied with red ribbon.

'Couldn't find any other paper,' Hardy explained.

'We hope you like it,' added Milo. I began to feel as if I were the audience for a salt-and-pepper comedy team. A curious transformation had come over Milo. In the presence of another detective he had distanced himself from me and adopted the tough-wiseacre banter of the veteran cop.

I unwrapped the box and opened it. Inside, on a bed of cotton, was a plastic-coated LAPD identification badge. It bore a picture of me like the one on my driver's license, with that strange, frozen look that all official photos seem to have. Under the picture was my signature, also from my license, my name printed out, my degree and the title 'Special Consultant.' Life imitates art . . .

'I'm touched.'

'Put it on,' said Milo. 'Make it official.'

The badge wasn't unlike the one I had worn at Western Pediatric. It came with a clasp. I affixed it to my shirt collar.

'Very attractive,' said Hardy. 'That and ten cents might get you a local phone call.' He reached into his jacket and drew out a folded piece of paper. 'Now, if you'll just read and sign this.' He held out a pen.

I read it, all small print.

'This says you don't have to pay me.'

'Right,' said Hardy with mock sadness. 'And if you get a paper cut looking over the files you can't sue the department.'

'It makes the brass happy, Alex,' said Milo.

I shrugged and signed.

'Now,' said Hardy, 'you're an *o*-fficial consultant to the Los Angeles Police Department.' He folded the paper and slipped it back in his pocket. 'Just like the rooster who was jumping the bones of all the hens in the henhouse. So they castrated him and turned him into a consultant.'

'That's very flattering, Del.'

'Any friend of Milo and all that.'

Milo, meanwhile, was opening the sealed cartons with a Swiss Army knife. He took out files in dozens and made neat little piles that covered the dining-room table.

'These are alphabetized, Alex. You can go through them and pull out the weird ones.'

He finished setting things up and he and Hardy got ready to go.

'Del and I will be talking to bad guys off the NCIC printout.'

'We've got our work cut out for us,' said Hardy. He cracked his knuckles and looked for a place to put out his cigarette, which was smoked down to the filter.

'Toss it in the sink.'

He left to do so.

When we were alone Milo said: 'I really appreciate this, Alex. Don't drive yourself — don't try to get it all done today.'

'I'll do as many as I can before the eyes start to blur.'

'Right. We'll call you a couple of times today. To see if you've got anything we can pick up while we're on the road.'

Hardy came back straightening his tie. He was dapper in a three-piece navy worsted suit, white shirt, blood-red tie, shiny black calfskin loafers. Next to him Milo looked more shopworn than ever in his sagging trousers and lifeless tweed sport coat.

'You ready, my man?' Hardy asked.

'Ready.'

'Onward.'

When they were gone I put a Linda Ronstadt record on the turntable. To the accompaniment of 'Poor, Poor Pitiful Me,' I started to consult.

Eighty per cent of the male patients in the files fell into two categories: Affluent executive types referred by their internists due to a variety of stress-related symptoms – angina, impotence, abdominal pain, chronic headaches, insomnia, skin rashes of unknown origins – and depressed men of all ages. I reviewed these and put aside the remaining twenty per cent for more detailed perusal.

I knew nothing about what kind of psychiatrist Morton Handler had been when I started, but after several hours of reviewing his charts I began to build an image of him – one that was far from saintly.

His therapy session notes were sketchy, careless, and so ambiguous as to be meaningless. It was impossible to know from reading them what he had done during those count-less forty-five-minute hours. There was scant mention of treatment plans, prognoses, stress histories – anything that could be considered medically or psychologically relevant.

This shoddiness was most evident in notes taken during the last five or six years of his life.

His financial records, on the other hand, were meticulous and detailed. His fees were high, his form letters to debtors strongly worded.

Though during the last few years he had done less talking and more prescribing, the rate at which he ordered medication wasn't unusual. Unlike Towle, he didn't appear to be a pusher. But he wasn't much of a therapist, either.

What really bothered me was his tendency, again more common during later years, to inject snide comments into the notes. These, which he didn't even bother to couch in jargon, were nothing more than sarcastic put-downs of his patients. 'Likes to alternately whimper and simper' was the description of one older man with a mood disorder. 'Unlikely to be capable of anything constructive' was his pronouncement on another. 'Wants therapy as camouflage for a boring, meaningless life.' 'A real washout.' And so on.

By late afternoon my psychological autopsy of Handler was complete. He was a burnout, one of the legions of worker ants who had grown to hate his chosen profession. He might have cared at one time – the early files were decent, if not inspired – but he hadn't by the end. Nevertheless, he had kept it up, day after day, session after session, unwilling to give up the six-figure income and the perquisites of prosperity.

I wondered how he had occupied his time as his patients poured out their inner turmoil. Did he daydream? Engage in fantasies (sexual? financial? sadistic?)? Plan the evening's dinner menu? Do mental arithmetic? Count sheep? Compute how many manic depressives could dance on the head of a pin?

Whatever it had been, it hadn't included really listening to the human beings who sat before him believing he cared.

It made me think of the old joke, the one about the two shrinks who meet on the elevator at the end of the day. One of them is young, a novice, and he is clearly bedraggled – tie askew, hair messed, fraught with fatigue. He turns and notices that the other, a seasoned veteran, is totally composed – tan, fit, every hair in place, a fresh carnation stuck jauntily in his lapel.

'Doctor,' beseeches the young one, 'please tell me how you do it?'

'Do what, my son?'

'Sit, hour after hour, day after day, listening to people's problems without letting it get to you.'

'Who listens?' replies the guru.

Funny. Unless you were shelling out ninety bucks a session to Morton Handler and getting a covert assessment as a simpering whimperer for your money.

Had one of the subjects of his nasty prose somehow discovered the sham and murdered him? It was difficult to imagine someone engaging in the kind of butchery that had been visited upon Handler and his girlfriend in order to avenge a peeve of that kind. But you never knew. Rage was a tricky thing; sometimes it lay dormant for years, only to be triggered by a seemingly trivial stimulus. People had been ripped apart over a nudged car bumper.

Still I found it hard to believe that the depressives and psychosomaticizers whose files I had reviewed were the stuff of which midnight skulkers were fashioned. What I really didn't want to believe was that there were two thousand potential suspects to deal with.

It was close to five. I pulled a Coors out of the refrigerator, took it out to the balcony and lay down on a lounger, my feet propped up on the guardrail. I drank and watched the sun dip beneath the tops of the trees. Someone in the neighborhood was playing punk rock. Strangely enough it didn't seem discordant.

At five thirty Robin called.

'Hi, hon. You want to come over? *Key Largo*'s on tonight.'

'Sure,' I said. 'Should I pick up anything to eat?'

She thought a moment.

'How about chili dogs? And beer?'

'I've got a head start on the beer.' Three squashed Coors empties sat on the kitchen counter.

'Give me time to catch up, love. See you around seven.'

I hadn't heard from Milo since one thirty. He'd called in from Bellflower, just about to interrogate a guy who'd assaulted seven women with a screwdriver. Very little similarity to the Handler case but you had to work with what you had.

I phoned West LA Division and left the message for him that I'd be out for the evening.

Then I called Bonita Quinn's number. I waited for five rings and when nobody answered, hung up.

Humphrey and Lauren were great, as usual. The chili dogs left us belching, but satisfied. We held each other and listened to Tal Farlow and Wes Montgomery for a while. Then I picked up one of the guitars she had lying around the studio and played for her. She listened, eyes closed, a faint smile on her lips, then gently removed my hands from the instrument and pulled me to her.

I had planned to stay the night but at eleven I grew restless.

'Is anything the matter, Alex?'

'No.' Just my Zeigarnik tugging at me.

'It's the case, isn't it?'

I said nothing.

'I'm starting to worry about you, sweetie.' She put her head on my chest, a welcome burden. 'You've been so edgy since Milo got you into all of this. I never knew you before, but from what you told me it sounds like the old days.'

'The old Alex wasn't such a bad guy,' I reacted defensively.

She was wisely silent.

'No,' I corrected myself. 'The old Alex was a bore. I promise not to bring him back, OK?'

'OK.' She kissed the tip of my chin.

'Just give me a little time to get through this.'

'All right.'

But as I dressed she looked at me with a combination of worry, hurt, and confusion. When I started to say something, she turned away. I sat down on the edge of the bed and took her in my arms. I rocked her until her arms slid around my neck.

'I love you,' I said. 'Give me a little time.'

She made a warm sound and held me tighter.

When I left she was sleeping, her eyelids fluttering in the throes of the first dream of the night.

* * *

I tore into the one hundred and twenty files I had set aside, working until the early morning hours. Most of these turned out also to be rather mundane documents. Ninety-one of the patients were physically ill men whom Handler had seen as a consultant when he was still working at Cedars-Sinai as part of the liaison psychiatry team. Another twenty had been diagnosed schizophrenic, but they turned out to be senile (median age, seventy-six) patients at a convalescent hospital where he'd worked for a year.

The remaining nine men were of interest. Handler had diagnosed them all as psychopathic character disorders. Of course those diagnoses were suspect, as I had little faith in his judgment. Nevertheless the files were worth examining more closely.

They were all between the ages of sixteen and thirty-two. Most had been referred by agencies – the Probation Department, the California Youth Authority, local churches. A couple had experienced several scrapes with the law. At least three were judged violent. Of these, one had beaten up his father, another had stabbed a fellow high school student, and the third had used an automobile to run down someone with whom he'd exchanged angry words.

A bunch of real sweethearts.

None of them had been involved in therapy for very long, which was not surprising. Psychotherapy hasn't much to offer the person with no conscience, no morals, and, quite often, no desire to change. In fact, the psychopath by his very nature is an affront to modern psychology, with its egalitarian and optimistic philosophical underpinnings.

Therapists become therapists because down deep they feel that people are really good and have the capacity to change

110

for the better. The notion that there exist individuals who are simply evil – bad people – and that such evil cannot be explained by any existing combination of nature or nurture is an assault upon a therapist's sensitivities. The psychopath is to the psychologist and the psychiatrist what the terminal cancer patient is to the physician: Walking, breathing evidence of hopelessness and failure.

I knew such evil people existed. I had seen a mercifully small number of them, mostly adolescents, but some children. I remember one boy, in particular, not yet twelve years old, but possessed of a cynical, hardened, cruelly grinning face that would have done a San Quentin lifer proud. He'd handed me his business card – a bright rectangle of shocking pink paper with his name on it, followed by the single word *Enterprises*.

And an enterprising young man he had been. Buttressed by my assurances of confidentiality, he had told me proudly of the dozens of bicycles he had stolen, of the burglaries he had pulled off, of the teenage girls he had seduced. He was so pleased with himself.

He had lost his parents in a plane crash at the age of four and had been brought up by a baffled grandmother who tried to assure everyone – and herself – that down deep he was a good boy. But he wasn't. He was a *bad* boy. When I asked him if he remembered his mother, he leered and told me she looked like a real piece of ass in the pictures he had seen. It wasn't defensive posturing. It was really him.

The more time I spent with him, the more discouraged I grew. It was like peeling an onion and finding each layer more rotten than the last. He was a bad boy, irredeemably so. Most likely, he would get worse.

111

And there was nothing I could do. There was little doubt he would end up establishing an anti-social career. If society was lucky, it would be limited to con games. If not, a lot of blood would be shed. Logic dictated that he should be locked up, kept out of harm's way, incarcerated for the protection of the rest of us. But democracy said otherwise, and, on balance, I had to admit it shouldn't be any other way.

Still, there were nights when I thought of that eleven year old and wondered if I'd be seeing his name in the papers one day.

I set the nine files aside.

Milo would have more of his work cut out for him.

10

THREE DAYS of the old wear-down-the-shoe-leather routine had worn Milo down.

'The computer was a total bust,' he lamented, flopping down on my leather sofa. 'All of those bastards are either back in the joint, dead, or alibied. The coroner's report has no forensic magic for us. Just six and a half pages of gory details telling us what we knew the first time we saw the bodies: Handler and Gutierrez were hacked up like sausage filler.'

I brought him a beer, which he drained in two long gulps. I brought him another.

'What about Handler? Anything on him?' I asked.

'Oh yeah, you were definitely right in your initial impression. The guy was no Mr Ethical. But it doesn't lead anywhere.'

'What do you mean?'

'Six years ago, when he was doing hospital consultations, there was a bit of a stink — insurance fraud. Handler and some others were running a little scam. They'd peek their heads in for a second, say hello to a patient, and bill it as a full visit, which I take it is supposed to be forty-five or fifty minutes long. Then they'd make a note in the chart, bill for another visit, talk to the nurse, another visit, talk to the doctor, etc., etc. It was big bucks — one guy could put in for thirty, forty visits a day, at seventy, eighty bucks a visit. Figure it out.'

'No surprise. It's done all the time.'

'I'm sure. Anyway, it blew wide open because one of the patients had a son who was a doctor, and he started to get suspicious, reading the chart, seeing all these psychiatric visits. Especially 'cause the old man had been unconscious for three months. He griped to the medical director, who called Handler and the others in on the carpet. They kept it quiet, on the condition that the crooked shrinks leave.'

Six years ago. Just before Handler's notes had started to get slipshod and sarcastic. It must have been hard going from four hundred grand a year to a measly one hundred. And having to actually work for it. A man could get bitter . . .

'And you don't see an angle in that?'

'What? Revenge? From whom? It was insurance companies that were getting bilked. That's how they kept it going so long. They never billed the patients, just billed insurance.' He took a swig of beer. 'I've heard bad things about insurance companies, pal, but I can't see them sending around Jack the Ripper to avenge their honor.'

'I see what you mean.'

He got up and paced the room.

'This goddamn case sucks. It's been a week and I've got absolutely zilch. The captain sees it as a dead end. He's pulled Del off and left me with the whole stinking mess. Tough breaks for the faggot.'

'Another beer?' I held one out for him.

'Yeah, goddammit, why not? Drown it all in suds.' He wheeled around. 'I tell you, Alex, I should have been a schoolteacher. Vietnam left me with this big psychic hole, you know? All that death for nothing. I thought becoming a cop would help me fill that hole, catch bad guys, make some sense out of it all. Jesus, was I wrong!'

He grabbed the Coors out of my hand, tilted it over his mouth, and let some of the foam dribble down his chin.

'The things that I see – the monstrous things that we supposed humans do to each other. The shit I've become inured to. Sometimes it makes me want to puke.'

He drank silently for a few minutes.

'You're a goddamn good listener, Alex. All that training wasn't for naught.'

'One good turn, my friend.'

'Yeah, right. Now that you mention it, Hickle was another shitty case. I never convinced myself that was suicide. It stunk to high heaven.'

'You never told me.'

'What's to tell? I've no evidence. Just a gut feeling. I've got lots of gut feelings. Some of them gnaw at me and keep me up at night. To paraphrase Del, my gut feelings and ten cents.'

He crushed the empty can between his thumb and fore-finger, with the ease of someone pulverizing a gnat.

'Hickle stunk to high heaven, but I had no evidence. So I wrote it off. Like a bad debt. No one argued, no one gave a shit, just like no one'll give a shit when we write off Handler and the Gutierrez girl. Keep the records tidy, wrap it up, seal it, and kiss it goodbye.'

Seven more beers, another half-hour of ranting and punishing himself, and he was stoned drunk. He crashed on the leather sofa, going down like a B-52 with a bellyful of shrapnel.

I slipped his shoes off and placed them on the floor beside him. I was about to leave him that way, when I realized it had turned dark.

I called his home number. A deep, rich male voice answered.

'Hello.'

'Hello, this is Alex Delaware, Milo's friend.'

'Yes?' Wariness.

'The psychologist.'

'Yes, Milo's spoken of you. I'm Rick Silverman.'

The doctor, the mother's dream, now had a name.

'I just called to let you know that Milo stopped by here after work to discuss a case and he got kind of – intoxicated.'

'I see.'

I felt an absurd urge to explain to the man at the other end that there was really nothing going on between Milo and me, that we were just good friends. I suppressed it.

'Actually, he got stoned. Had eleven beers. He's sleeping it off now. I just wanted you to know.'

'That's very considerate of you,' Silverman said, acidly.

'I'll wake him, if you'd like.'

'No, that's quite all right. Milo's a big boy. He's free to do as he pleases. No need to check in.'

I wanted to tell him, listen you insecure, spoiled brat, I just called to do you a favor, to set your mind at ease. Don't hand me any of your delicate indignation. Instead, I tried flattery.

'OK, just thought I'd call you to let you know, Rick. I know how important you are to Milo, and I thought he'd want me to.'

'Uh, thanks. I really appreciate it.' Bingo. 'Please excuse me. I've just come off a twenty-four-hour shift myself.'

'No problem.' I'd probably woken the poor devil. 'Listen, how about if we get something together some time – you and Milo and my girlfriend and myself?'

'I'd like that, Alex. Sure. Send the big slob home when he sobers up and we'll work out the details.'

'Will do. Good talking to you.'

'Likewise.' He sighed. 'Good night.'

At nine thirty Milo awoke with a wretched look on his face. He started to moan, turning his head from side to side. I mixed tomato juice, a raw egg, black pepper, and Tabasco in a tall glass, propped him up and poured it down his throat. He gagged, sputtered, and opened his eyes suddenly, as if a bolt of lightning had zapped him in the tailbone.

Forty minutes later he looked every bit as wretched but he was painfully sober.

I got him to the door and stuck the files of the nine psychopaths under his arm.

'Bedtime reading, Milo.'

He tripped down the stairs, swearing, made his way to the Fiat, groped at its door handle and threw himself in with a single lurching movement. With the aid of a rolling start, he got it ignited.

Alone at last, I got into bed, read the *Times*, watched TV – but damned if I could tell you what I saw, other than that it had lots of flat punch lines and jiggling boobs and cops who looked like male models. I enjoyed the solitude for a couple of hours, only pausing to think of murder and greed and twisted evil minds a few times before drifting off to sleep.

11

'ALL RIGHT,' said Milo. We were sitting in an interrogation room at West LA Division. The walls were pea-green paint and one-way mirrors. A microphone hung from the ceiling. The furniture consisted of a gray metal table and three metal folding chairs. There was a stale odor of sweat and falsehood and fear in the air, the stink of diminished human dignity.

He had fanned out the folders on the table and picked up the first one with a flourish.

'Here's the way your nine bad guys shape up. Number one, Rex Allen Camblin, incarcerated at Soledad, assault and battery.' He let the folder drop.

'Number two, Peter Lewis Jefferson, working on a ranch in Wyoming. Presence verified.'

'Pity the poor cattle.'

'That's a fact – he looked like a likely one. Number three, Darwin Ward – you'll never believe this – attending law school, Pennsylvania State University.'

'A psychopathic attorney – not all that amazing, really.'

Milo chuckled and picked up the next folder.

'Número cuatro – uh – Leonard Jay Helsinger, working construction on the Alaska pipeline. Location likewise confirmed by Juneau PD Five, Michael Penn, student at Cal State Northridge. Him we talk to.' He put Penn's file aside.

'Six, Lance Arthur Shattuck, short-order cook on the Cunard Line luxury cruiser *Helena*, verified by the Coast Guard to have been floating around in the middle of the Aegean Sea somewhere for the past six weeks. Seven, Maurice Bruno, sales representative for Presto Instant Print in Burbank – another interviewee.' Bruno's file went on top of Penn's.

'Eight, Roy Longstreth, pharmacist for Thrifty's Drug chain, Beverly Hills branch. Another one. And – last but not least – Gerard Paul Mendenhall, Corporal, United States Army, Tyler, Texas, presence verified.'

Beverly Hills was closer than either Northridge or Burbank, so we headed for Thrifty's. The Beverly Hills branch turned out to be a brick-and-glass cube on Canon Drive just north of Wilshire. It shared a block with trendy boutiques and a Häagen Dazs ice-cream parlor.

Milo showed his badge surreptitiously to the girl behind the liquor counter and got the manager, a light-skinned middle-aged black, in seconds flat. The manager got nervous and wanted to know if Longstreth had done anything wrong. In classic cop style, Milo hedged.

'We just want to ask him a few questions.'

I had trouble keeping a straight face through that one, but the cliché seemed to satisfy the manager.

'He's not here now. He comes on at two thirty, works the night shift.'

'We'll be back. Please don't tell him we were here.'

Milo gave him his card. When we left he was studying it like a map to buried treasure.

The ride to Northridge was a half-hour cruise on the Venture Freeway West. When we got to the Cal State campus, we headed straight for the registrar's office. Milo obtained a copy of Michael Penn's class schedule. Armed with that and his mug shot, we located him in twenty minutes, walking across a wide, grassy triangle accompanied by a girl.

'Mr Penn?'

'Yes?' He was a good-looking fellow, medium height, with broad shoulders and long legs. His light brown hair was cut preppy short. He wore a light blue Izod shirt and blue jeans, penny loafers with no socks. I knew from his file that he was twenty-six but he looked five years younger. He had a pleasant, unlined face, a real All-American type. He didn't look like the kind of guy who'd try to run someone down with a Pontiac Firebird.

'Police.' Again, the badge. 'We'd like to talk to you for a few moments.'

'What about?' The hazel eyes narrowed and the mouth got tight.

'We'd prefer to talk to you in private.'

Penn looked at the girl. She was young, no more than nineteen, short, dark, with a Dorothy Hamill wedge cut.

'Give me a minute, Julie.' He chucked her under the chin.

'Mike . . . ?'

'Just a minute.'

We left her standing there and walked to a concrete area furnished with stone tables and benches. Students moved by as if on a treadmill. There was little standing around. This was a commuter campus. Many of the students worked part-time jobs and squeezed classes in during their spare time. It was a good place to get your BA in computer science or business, a teaching credential or a master's in accounting. If you wanted fun or leisurely intellectual debates in the shade of an ivy-encrusted oak, forget it.

Michael Penn looked furious but he was working hard at concealing it.

'What do you want?'

'When's the last time you saw Dr Morton Handler?'

Penn threw back his head and laughed. It was a disturbingly hollow sound.

'That asshole? I read about his death. No loss.'

'When did you see him last?'

Penn was smirking now.

'Years ago, *officer*.' He made the title sound like an insult. 'When I was in *therapy*.'

'I take it you didn't think much of him.'

'Handler? He was a shrink.' As if that explained it.

'You don't think much of psychiatrists.'

Penn held out his hands, palms up.

'Hey listen. That whole thing was a big mistake. I lost control of my car and some paranoid idiot claimed I tried to kill him with it. They busted me, railroaded me and then they offered me probation if I saw a shrink. Gave me all those garbage tests.'

Those garbage tests included the Minnesota Multiphasic Personality Inventory and a handful of projectives. Though far from perfect, they were reliable enough when it came to someone like Penn. I had read his MMPI profile and psychopathy oozed from every index.

'You didn't like Dr Handler?'

'Don't put words in my mouth.' Penn lowered his voice. He moved his eyes back and forth, restless, jumpy. Behind the handsome face was something dark and dangerous. Handler hadn't misdiagnosed this one.

'You did like him.' Milo played with him like a gaffed stingray.

'I didn't like him or dislike him. I had no use for him. I'm not crazy. And I didn't kill him.'

'You can account for your whereabouts the night he was murdered?'

'When was that?'

Milo gave him the date and time.

Penn cracked his knuckles and looked through us as if zeroing in on a distant target.

'Sure. That entire night I was with my girl.'

'Julie?'

Penn laughed.

'Her? No. I've got a mature woman, officer. A woman of means.' His brow creased and his expression changed from smug to sour. 'You're going to have to talk to her, aren't you?'

Milo nodded his head.

'That'll screw things up for me.'

'Gee, Mike, that's really too bad.'

Penn threw him a hateful look, then changed it to bland innocence. He could play his face like a deck of cards, shuffling, palming from the bottom, coming up with a new number every second.

'Listen, officer, that whole incident is behind me. I'm holding down a job, going to school – I'm getting my degree in six months. I don't want to get messed up because my name's in Handler's files.'

He sounded like Wally on *Leave It To Beaver* – all earnest innocence. Gosh, Beave . . .

'We'll have to verify your alibi, Mike.'

'OK, OK, do it. Just don't tell her too much, OK? Keep it general.'

Keep it general so I can fabricate something. You could see the gears spinning behind the high, tan forehead.

'Sure, Mike.' Milo took his pencil out and tapped it on his lips.

'Sonya Magary. She owns the Puff 'n' Stuff Children's Boutique in the Plaza de Oro in Encino.'

'Have you got the number handy?' Milo asked pleasantly.

Penn clenched his jaws and gave it to him.

'We'll call her, Mike. Don't you call her first, OK? We treasure spontaneity.' Milo put away his pencil and closed his notepad. 'Have a nice day, now.'

Penn looked from me to Milo, then back to me, as if seeking an ally. Then he got up and walked away in long, muscular strides.

'Oh, Mike!' Milo called.

Penn turned around.

'What are you getting your degree in?'

'Marketing.'

As we left the campus we could see him walking with Julie. Her head was on his shoulder, his arm around her waist. He was smiling down on her and talking very fast.

'What do you think?' Milo asked as he settled behind the wheel.

'I think he's innocent as far as this case goes, but I'll bet you he's got some kind of dirty deal going on. He was really relieved when he found out what we were there for.'

Milo nodded.

'I agree. But what the hell — that's someone else's headache.'

We got back on the freeway, heading east. We exited in Sherman Oaks, found a little French place on Ventura near Woodman and had lunch. Milo used the pay phone to call Sonya Magary. He came back to the table, shaking his head.

'She loves him. "That dear boy, that sweet boy, I hope he's not in trouble."' He imitated a thick Hungarian accent. 'She verifies he was with her on the fateful night. Sounds proud of it. I expected her to tell me about their sex life — in Technicolor.'

He shook his head and buried his face in a plate of steamed mussels.

We caught up with Roy Longstreth as he got out of his Toyota in the Thrifty's parking lot. He was short and frail-looking, with watery blue eyes and an undernourished chin. Prematurely bald, what little hair he did have was on the sides; he had left it long, hanging down over his ears, so that the general effect was of a friar who'd been meditating too long and had neglected his personal grooming. A mousy brown mustache snuck across his upper lip. He had none of Penn's bravado but there was that same jumpiness in the eyes.

'Yes, what do you want?' He piped up in a squeaky voice after Milo gave him the badge routine. He looked at his watch.

When Milo told him, he looked as if he were going to cry. Uncharacteristic anxiety for a supposed psychopath. Unless the whole thing was an act. You never knew the tricks those types could come up with when they had to.

'When I read about it I just knew you'd come after me.' The insignificant mustache trembled like a twig in a storm.

'Why's that, Roy?'

'Because of the things he said about me. He told my mother I was a psychopath. Told her not to trust me. I'm probably on some whacko list, right?'

'Can you account for your whereabouts the night he was killed?'

'Yes. That's the first thing I thought of when I read about it – they're going to come and ask me questions about it. I made sure I knew. I even wrote it down. Wrote a note to myself. Roy, you were at church that night. So when they come and ask you, you'll know where you were—'

He could have gone on that way for a couple of days but Milo cut him off.

'Church? You're a religious man, Roy?'

Longstreth gave a laugh that was choked with panic.

'No, no. Not praying. The Westside Singles group at Bel Air Presbyterian – it's the same place Ronald Reagan used to go to.'

'The singles group?'

'No, no, no. The church. He used to worship there before he was elected and—'

'OK, Ron. You were at the Westside Singles group from when to when?'

The sight of Milo taking notes made him even more nervous. He began bouncing up and down, a marionette at the hands of a palsied puppeteer.

'From nine to one thirty – I stayed to the end. I helped clean up. I can tell you what they served. It was guacamole and nachos and there was Gallo jug wine and shrimp dip and—'

'Of course there'll be lots of people who saw you there.'

'Sure,' he said, then stopped. 'I – I didn't really mingle much. I helped out, tending bar. I saw lots of people but I don't know if any of them will – remember me.' His voice had quieted to a whisper.

'That could be a problem, Roy.'

'Unless – no – yes – Mrs Heatherington. She's an older woman. She volunteers at church functions. She was cleaning up, too. And serving. I spent a lot of time talking to her – I can even tell you what we talked about, It was about collectables – she collects Norman Rockwells and I collect Icarts.'

'Icarts?'

'You know, the Art Deco prints.'

The works of Louis Icart went for high prices these days. I wondered how a pharmacist could afford them.

'Mother gave me one when I was sixteen and they—' he searched for the right word – 'captivated me. She gives them to me on my birthday and I pick up a few myself. Dr Handler collected them, too, you know. That—' he let his words trail off.

'Oh, really? Did he show you his collection?

Longstreth shook his head energetically.

'No. He had one in his office. I noticed it and we started talking. But he used it against me later on.'

'How's that?'

'After the evaluation – you know I was sent to him by the court after I was caught—' he looked nervously at the Thrifty's building – 'shoplifting.' Tears filled his eyes. 'For God's sake, I took a tube of rubber cement at Sears and they caught me! I thought Mother would die from the shame. And I worried the School of Pharmacy would find out – it was horrible!'

'How did he use the fact that you collected Icarts against you?' asked Milo patiently.

'He kind of implied, never came out and said it, but phrased it so you knew what he meant but he couldn't be pinned down.'

'Implied what, Roy?'

'That he could be bought off. That if I bribed him with an Icart or two – he even mentioned the ones he liked – he would write a favorable report.'

'Did you?'

'What? Bribe him? Not on your life. That would be dishonest!'

'And did he press the issue?'

Longstreth picked at his fingernails.

'Like I said, not so you could pin him down. He just said that I was a borderline case – psychopathic personality, or something less stigmatizing – anxiety reaction or something like that – that I could go either way. In the end he told Mother I was a psychopath.'

The wan face screwed up with rage.

'I'm glad he's dead! There, I've said it! It's what I thought the first time I read about it in the paper.'

'But you didn't do it.'

'Of course not. I couldn't. I run from evil, I don't embrace it!'

'We'll talk to Mrs Heatherington, Roy.'

'Yes, ask her about the nachos and the wine – I believe it was Gallo Hearty Burgundy. And there was fruit punch with slices of orange floating in it, too. In a cut glass bowl. And one of the women got sick on the floor at the end. I helped mop it up—'

'Thanks, Roy. You can go now.'

'Yes. I will.'

He turned around like a robot, a thin figure in a short blue druggist's smock, and walked into Thrifty's.

'He's dispensing drugs?' I asked, incredulous.

'If he's not in some whacko file he should be.' Milo pocketed his notepad and we walked to the car. 'He look like a psychopath to you?'

'Not unless he's the best actor on the face of the earth. Schizoid, withdrawn. Pre-schizophrenic, if anything.'

'Dangerous?'

'Who knows? Put him up against enough stress and he might blow. But I'd judge him more likely to go the hermit route – curl up in bed, play with himself, wither, stay that way for a decade or two while Mommy propped his pillows.'

'If that story about the Icarts is true it sheds some light on our beloved victim.'

'Handler? A real Dr Schweitzer.'

'Yeah.' said Milo. 'The kind of guy someone might want dead.'

We got on Coldwater Canyon before it clogged with the cars of commuters returning to their homes in the Valley, and made it to Burbank by half past four.

Presto Instant Print was one of scores of gray concrete edifices that filled the industrial park near the Burbank airport like so many oversized tombstones. The air smelled toxic and the flatulent roar of jets shattered the sky at regular intervals. I wondered about the life expectancy of those who spent their daylight hours here.

Maurice Bruno had come up in the world since his file

had been compiled. He was now a vice-president, in charge of sales. He was also unavailable, we were told by his secretary, a lissome brunette with arched eyebrows and a mouth meant for saying no.

'Then give me his boss,' barked Milo. He shoved his badge under her nose. We were both hot and tired and discouraged. The last place we wanted to be stalled was Burbank.

'That would be Mr Gershman,' she said as if discovering some new insight.

'Then that would be who I want to talk to.'

'Just one second.'

She wiggled off and came back with her clone in a blond wig.

'I'm Mr Gershman's secretary,' the clone announced.

It must be the poison in the air, I decided. It caused brain damage, eroded the cerebral cortex to the point where simple facts took on an aura of profundity.

Milo took a deep breath.

'We'd like to talk with Mr Gershman.'

'May I inquire what it's about?'

'No, you may not. Bring us to Gershman now.'

'Yes, sir.' The two secretaries looked at each other. Then the brunette pushed a buzzer and the blonde led us through double glass doors into an enormous production area filled with machines that chomped, stamped, bit, snarled, and smeared. A few people hung around the periphery of the rabid steel monsters, dull-eyed, loose-jawed, breathing in fumes that reeked of alcohol and acetone. The noise, alone, was enough to kill you.

She made a sudden left, probably hoping to lose us to the

maws of one of the behemoths, but we hung on, following the movement of her swaying butt until we came to another set of double doors. These she pushed and let go, forcing Milo to fall forward to catch them. A short corridor, another set of doors, and we were confronted by silence so complete as to be overwhelming.

The executive suite at Presto Instant Print might have been on another planet. Plush, plum-colored carpets that you had to bargain with in order to reclaim your ankles, walls paneled in real walnut. Large doors of walnut burl with names made of brass letters tastefully centered on the wood. And silence.

The blonde stopped at the end of the hall, in front of an especially large door with especially tasteful gold letters that said Arthur M. Gershman, President. She let us into a waiting room the size of an average house, motioned us to sit in chairs that looked and felt like unbaked bread dough. Settling behind her desk, a contraption of plexiglass and rosewood that afforded the world a perfect view of her legs, she pushed a button on a console that belonged at NASA Control Center, moved her lips a bit, nodded, and stood up again.

'Mr Gershman will see you, now.'

The inner sanctum was as expected – the size of a cathedral, decorated like something conceived in the pages of *Architectural Digest*, softly lit and comfortable but hard-edged enough to keep you awake – but the man behind the desk was a complete surprise.

He wore khaki pants and a short-sleeved white shirt that needed ironing. His feet were clad in Hush Puppies and since they were on the desk the holes in their soles were obvious. He was in his mid-seventies, bald, bespectacled, with one of the sidepieces of his glasses held together with masking tape, and potbellied.

He was talking on the phone when we came in.

'Hold the wire, Lenny.' He looked up. 'Thanks, Denise.' The blonde disappeared. To us: 'One second. Sit down, fix something.' He pointed to a fully stocked bar that covered half of one wall.

'OK, Lenny, I got cops here, gotta go. Yeah, cops. I don't know, you wanna ask 'em? Ha ha. Yeah, I'll tell 'em that for sure, you *momzer*. I'll tell 'em what *you* did in Palm Springs the last time we were there. Yeah. OK, the Sahara job in lots of three hundred thousand with coasters and matchbooks — not boxes, books. I got it. I give you delivery in two weeks. What? Forget it.' He winked at us. 'Go ahead, go to someone local, see if I care. I got maybe one, two more months before I drop dead from this business — you think I care if an order drops dead? It's all gonna go to Uncle Sam and Shirley and my prince of a son who drives a German car. Nah, Nah. A BMW. With my money. Yeah. What can you do, it's out of control. Ten days?' He made a masturbating motion with his free hand and beamed at us. 'You're jerking off, Lenny. At least close the door, no one will see. Twelve days, tops. OK? Twelve it is. Right. Gotta go, these cossacks are going to drag me away any minute. Goodbye.'

The phone slammed down, the man shot up like an uncoiled spring.

'Artie Gershman.'

He held out an ink-stained hand. Milo shook it, then I did. It was as hard as granite and horned with callus.

He sat down again, threw his feet back up on the desk.

'Sorry for the delay.' He had the joviality of someone

who was surrounded by enough automatons like Denise to ensure his privacy. 'You deal with casinos they think they got a right to instant everything. That's the mob, you know – but what the hell am I telling you that, you're cops, you know that, right? Now, what can I do for you, officers? The parking situation I know is a problem. If it's that bastard at Chemco next door complaining, all I want to say is he can go straight to hell in a handbasket, because his Mexican ladies park in my lot all the time – you should also check how many of them are legal – if he wants to get really nasty, I can play that game too.'

He paused to catch his breath.

'It's not about parking.'

'No? What then?'

'We want to talk to Maurice Bruno.'

'Morry? Morry's in Vegas. We do a lot of our business there, with the casinos, the motels and hotels. Here.' He opened a drawer of the desk and tossed a handful of match-books at us. Most of the big names were represented.

Milo pocketed a few.

'When will he be back?'

'In a few days. He went on a selling trip two weeks ago, first to Tahoe, then Reno, end up in Vegas – probably playing around a bit on company time, not to mention the expense account – but who cares, he's a terrific salesman.'

'I thought he was a vice-president.'

'Vice-president in charge of sales. It's a salesman with a fancy title, a bigger salary, a nicer office – what do you think of this place – looks like some fag fixed it up, right?'

I searched Milo's face for a reaction, found none.

'My wife. She did this herself. This place used to be nice.

There were papers all over the place, a couple of chairs, white walls – normal walls so you could hear the noise from the plant, know something was going on. This feels like death, you know. That's what I get for taking a second wife. A first wife leaves you alone, a second one wants to make you into a new person.'

'Are you sure Mr Bruno's in Las Vegas?'

'Why shouldn't I be sure? Where else would he go?'

'How long has Mr Bruno been working for you, Mr Gershman?'

'Hey, what's this – this isn't child support or something like that?'

'No. We just want to talk to him about a homicide investigation we're conducting.'

'Homicide?' Gershman shot out of his chair. 'Murder? Morry Bruno? You got to be kidding. He's a gem of a guy!'

A gem who had been excellent at passing rubber checks.

'How long has he been working for you, sir?'

'Let me see – a year and a half, maybe two.'

'And you've had no problem with him?'

'Problem? I tell you he's a gem. Knew nothing about the business, but I hired him on hunch. Hell of a salesman. Outsold all the other guys – even the old-timers – by the fourth month. Reliable, friendly, never a problem.'

'You mentioned child support. Mr Bruno's divorced?'

'Divorced,' said Gershman sadly. 'Like everyone. Including my son. They give up too easily nowadays.'

'Does he have family here in Los Angeles?'

'Nah. The wife, kids – three of 'em, I think – they moved back east. Pittsburg, or Cleveland, some place with no ocean.

133

He missed 'em, talked about it. That's why he volunteered at the Casa.'

'Casa?'

'That kids' place, up in Malibu. Morry used to spend his weekends there, volunteering with the kids. He got a certificate. C'mon I'll show you.'

Bruno's office was a quarter the size of Gershman's, but decked out in the same eclectically elegant style. The place was neat as a pin, not surprising, since Bruno spent most of his time on the road. Gershman pointed to a framed plaque that shared wall space with a half-dozen Number One Salesman commendations.

'You see – "awarded to Maurice Bruno in recognition of voluntary service to the homeless children of La Casa de los Niños" blah blah blah. I told you he was a gem.'

The certificate was signed by the Mayor, as honorary witness, and by the director of the children's home, a Reverend Augustus J. McCaffrey. It was all calligraphy and floral intaglio. Very impressive.

'Very nice,' said Milo. 'Do you know what hotel Mr Bruno was staying at?'

'He used to stay at the MGM, but after the fire, I don't know. Let's go back to the office and find out.'

Back in Office Beautiful, Gershman picked up the telephone, punched the intercom and barked into the receiver.

'Denise, where's Morry staying in Vegas? Do that.'

A half-minute later the intercom buzzed.

'Yeah? Good. Thanks, darling.' He turned to us. 'The Palace.'

'Caesar's Palace?'

'Yeah. You want me to call there, you can talk to him?'

'If you don't mind, sir. We'll charge it to the Police Department.'

'Nah!' Gershman waved his hand. 'On me. Denise, call Caesar's Palace, get Morry on the phone. He's not there, leave him a message to call—'

'Detective Sturgis. West LA Division.'

Gershman completed the instructions.

'You're not thinking about Morry as a suspect, are you?' he asked when he got off the phone. 'This is a witness thing, right?'

'We really can't say anything about it, Mr Gershman.' Milo paid lip service to discretion.

'I can't believe it!' Gershman slapped his head with his hand. 'You think Morry's a murderer! A guy who works with kids on the weekend – a guy who never had a cross word with anybody here – go ask around, I give you permission. You find someone who has a bad word to say about Morry Bruno, I'll eat this desk!'

He was interrupted by the intercom buzzer.

'Yes, Denise. What's that? You're sure? Maybe it was a mistake. Check again. And then call the Aladdin, the Sands, maybe he changed his mind.'

The old man's face was solemn when he hung up.

'He's not at the Palace.' He said it with the sadness and fear of someone about to be torn from the comforting warmth of his preconceptions.

Maurice Bruno wasn't at the Aladdin or the Sands or any other major hotel in Las Vegas. Additional calls from Gershman's office revealed the fact that none of the airlines had a record of him flying from LA to Vegas.

'I'd like his home address and phone number, please.'

'Denise will give it to you,' said Gershman. We left him sitting alone in his big office, grizzled chin resting in his hands, frowning like a battered old bison who'd spent too many years at the zoo.

Bruno lived in Glendale, normally a ten-minute drive from the Presto plant, but it was 6 P.M., there had been an accident just west of the Hollywood-Golden State interchange, and the freeway was stagnant all the way from Burbank to Pasadena. By the time we exited on Brand, it was dark and both of us were in foul moods.

Milo turned north and headed toward the mountains. Bruno's house was on Armelita, a side street half a mile from where the boulevard ended. It was situated at the end of a cul-de-sac, a small, one-story mock Tudor, fronted by a neat, square lawn, yew hedges and sprigs of juniper stuffed in the empty spaces. Two large arborvitae bushes guarded the entrance. It wasn't the kind of place I would have imagined for a Vegas-haunting bachelor. Then I remembered what Gershman had said about the divorce. No doubt this was the homestead left behind by the fleeing wife and children.

Milo rang the doorbell a couple of times, then he knocked hard. When no one answered he went to the car and called the Glendale police. Ten minutes later a squad car pulled up and two uniformed officers got out. Both were tall, beefy and sandy-haired and wore bushy, bristly, strawlike mustaches under their noses. They came over with that swagger unique to cops and drunks trying hard to look sober, and conferred with Milo. Then they got on their radio.

The street was quiet and devoid of visible human habitation. It stayed that way as the three additional squad cars and the unmarked Dodge drove up and parked. There was a brief conference that resembled a football huddle and then guns were drawn. Milo rang the bell again, waited a minute and then kicked the door in. The assault was on.

I stayed outside, watching, waiting. Soon the sound of gagging and retching could be heard. Then cops began running out of the house, spilling out on the lawn, their hands to their noses, an action sequence in reverse. One particularly stalwart patrolman busied himself puking into the junipers. When it appeared that they'd all retreated, Milo came to the door, a handkerchief held over his nose and mouth. His eyes were visible and they made contact with me. They gave me a choice.

Against my better judgment I pulled out my own handkerchief, masked the lower part of my face and went in.

The thin cotton was scant defense against the hot stench that rose up against me as I stepped across the threshold. It was as if raw sewage and swamp gas had blended into a bubbling, swirling soup, then vaporized and sprayed into the air.

My eyes watering, I fought the urge to vomit, and followed Milo's advancing silhouette into the kitchen.

He was sitting there at a Formica table. The bottom part of him, the part in clothing, still looked human. The sky-blue salesman's suit, the maize-colored button-down shirt with blue silk foulard. The dandy's touches – the breast pocket hankie, the shoes with tiny tassels, the gold bracelet that hung around a wrist teeming with maggots.

From the neck up he was something the pathologists threw out. It looked as if he'd been worked over with a crowbar – the entire front part of what used to be his face was caved

137

in – but it was really impossible to know what the swollen bloody lump attached to his shoulders had been subjected to, so advanced was the state of decay.

Milo began throwing open windows and I realized that the house felt as hot as a blast furnace, fueled by the hydrocarbons emitted by decomposing organic matter. A quick answer to the energy crisis: Save kilowatts, kill a friend . . .

I couldn't take any more. I ran for the door, gasping and flung away the handkerchief when I reached the out doors. I gulped hungrily at the cool night air. My hand shook.

There was lots of excitement on the block now. Neighbors – men, women and children – had come out of their castles, pausing in the middle of the evening news, interrupting their defrosted feasts to gawk at the blinking crimson lights and listen to the stuttering radio static of the squad car, staring at the coroner's van that had pulled up to the curb with the cold authority of a parading despot. A few kids rode their bikes up and down the street. Mumbling voices took on the sound of ravaging locusts. A dog barked. Welcome to suburbia.

I wondered where they'd all been when someone had gotten into Bruno's house, battered him into jelly, closed all the windows and left him to rot.

Milo finally came out, looking green. He sat on the front steps and hung his head between his knees. Then he got up and called the attendants from the coroner's office over. They had come prepared, with gas masks and rubber gloves. They went in with an empty stretcher and came out carrying something wrapped in a black plastic sheath.

'Ugh. Gross,' said a teenage girl to her friend.

It was as eloquent a way to put it as any.

12

THREE MORNINGS after we discovered the butchery of Bruno, Milo wanted to come over to review the salesman's psychiatric file in detail. I postponed it until the afternoon. Motivated by instincts that were unclear to me, I called André Jaroslav at his studio in West Hollywood and asked him if he had time to help me refresh my karate skills.

'Doctor,' he said, the accent as thick as goulash, 'such a long time since I see you.'

'I know, André. Too long. I've let myself go. But I hope you can help me.'

He laughed.

'Tsk, tsk. I have intermediate group at eleven and private lessons at twelve. Then I am going to Hawaii, Doctor. To choreograph fight scenes for new television pilot. Girl policeperson who knows judo and catches rapists. What do you think?'

'Very original.'

'Ya. I get to work with the redheaded chickie – this Shandra Layne. To teach her how to throw around large men. Like Wonder Woman, ya?'

'Ya. Do you have any time before eleven?'

'For you, Doctor – certainly. We get you in shape. Come at nine and I give you two hours.'

* * *

The Institute of Martial Arts was located on Santa Monica at Doheny, next to the Troubador nightclub. It was an LA institution, predating the Kung Fu craze by fifteen years. Jaroslav was a bandy-legged Czech Jew who'd escaped during the fifties. He had a high, squeaky voice that he attributed to having been shot in the throat by the Nazis. The truth was that he'd been born with the vocal register of a hysterical capon. It hadn't been easy, being a squeaky-voiced Jew in postwar Prague. Jaroslav had developed his own way of coping. Starting as a boy he taught himself physical culture, weight-lifting and the arts of self-defense. By the time he was in his twenties he had total command of every martial arts doctrine from saberfencing to hopkaido, and a lot of bullies received painful surprises.

He greeted me at the door, naked from the waist up, a spray of daffodils in his hand. The sidewalk was filled with anorectic individuals of ambiguous gender, hugging guitar cases as if they were life preservers, dragging deeply on cigarettes and regarding the passing traffic with spaced-out apprehension.

'Audition,' he squeaked, pointing a finger at the door to the Troubador and glancing at them scornfully. 'The artisans of a new age, Doctor.'

We went into the studio, which was empty. He placed the flowers in a vase. The practice room was an expanse of polished oak floor bordered by whitewashed walls. Autographed photographs of stars and near-stars hung in clusters. I went into a dressing room with the set of stiff white garments he gave me and emerged looking like an extra in a Bruce Lee movie.

Jaroslav was silent, letting his body and his hands talk. He positioned me in the center of the studio and stood facing me. He smiled faintly, we bowed to each other and he led me through a series of warm-up exercises that made my joints creak. It had been a long time.

When the introductory *katas* were through, we bowed again. He smiled, then proceeded to wipe the floor with me. At the end of one hour I felt as if I'd been stuffed down a garbage disposal. Every muscle fiber ached, every synapse quivered in exquisite agony.

He kept it up, smiling and bowing, sometimes letting out a perfectly controlled, high-pitched scream, tossing me around like a bean bag. By the end of the second hour, pain had ceased to be obtrusive – it had become a way of life, a state of consciousness. But when we stopped I was starting to feel in command of my body once again. I was breathing hard, stretching, blinking. My eyes burned as the perspiration dripped into them. Jaroslav looked as if he'd just finished reading the morning paper.

'You take a hot bath, Doctor, get some chickie to massage you, use a little witch hazel. And remember: Practice, practice, practice.'

'I will, André.'

'You call me when I get back, in a week. I tell you about Shandra Layne and check if you've been practising.' He poked a finger in my gut, playfully.

'It's a deal.'

He held out his hand. I reached out to take it, then tensed, wondering if he was going to throw me again.

'Ya, good,' he said. Then he laughed and let me go.

* * *

The throbbing agony made me feel righteous and ascetic. I had lunch at a restaurant run by one of the dozens of quasi-Hindu cults that seem to prefer Los Angeles to Calcutta. A vacant-eyed, perpetually smiling girl swaddled in white robes and burnoose took my order. She had a rich kid's face coupled with the mannerisms of a nun and managed to smile while she talked, smile as she wrote, smile as she walked away. I wondered if it hurt.

I finished a plate heaped with chopped lettuce, sprouts, refried soya beans and melted goat cheese on *chapati* bread – a sacred tostada – and washed it down with two glasses of pineapple-coconut-guava nectar imported from the holy desert of Mojave. The bill came to ten dollars and thirty-nine cents. That explained the smiles.

I made it back to the house just as Milo pulled up in an unmarked bronze Matador.

'The Fiat finally died,' he explained. 'I'm having it cremated and scattering the ashes over the offshore rigs in Long Beach.'

'My condolences.' I picked up Bruno's file.

'Contributions to the down payment on my next lemon will be accepted in lieu of flowers.'

'Get Dr Silverman to buy you one.'

'I'm working on it.'

He let me read for a few minutes then asked, 'So what do you think?'

'No profound insights. Bruno was referred to Handler by the Probation Department after the bad-check bust. Handler saw him a dozen times over a four-month period. When the probationary period was over so was the treatment. One thing I did notice was that Handler's notes on him are relatively benign. Bruno was one of the more recently acquired patients. At the time he started therapy, Handler was at his nastiest, yet there are no vicious comments about him. Here, in the beginning Handler calls him a "slick con man."' I flipped some pages. 'A couple of weeks later he makes a crack about Bruno's "Cheshire grin." But after that, nothing.'

'As if they became buddies?'

'Why do you say that?'

Milo handed me a piece of paper. 'Here,' he said, 'Look at this.'

It was a printout from the phone company.

'This,' he pointed to a circled seven-digit code, 'is Handler's number – his home number, not the office. And this one is Bruno's.'

Lines had been drawn between the two, like lacing on a high-topped shoe. There'd been lots of connections over the last six months.

'Interesting, huh?'

'Very.'

'Here's something else. Officially the coroner says it's impossible to fix a time of death for Bruno. The heat inside the house screwed up the decomposition tables – with the flack they've been getting they're not willing to go out on a limb and take the chance of being wrong. But I got one of the young guys to give me an off-the-record guess and he came up with ten to twelve days.'

'Right around the time Handler and Gutierrez were murdered.'

'Either right before or right after.'

'But what about the differing MOs?'

'Who says people are consistent, Alex? Frankly there are

143

other differences between the two cases besides m.o. In Bruno's case it looks like forced entry. We found broken bushes under a rear window and chisel marks on the pane – used to be a kid's room. Glendale PD also thinks they've got two sets of heelprints.'

'Two? Maybe Melody really saw something.' *Dark men. Two or three.*

'Maybe. But I've abandoned that line of attack. The kid will never be a reliable witness. In any event, despite the discrepancies, it looks like we might be on to something – what, I don't know. Patient and doctor, concrete proof that they maintained some kind of contact after treatment was over, both ripped off around the same time. It's too cute for coincidence.'

He studied his notes, looking scholarly. I thought about Handler and Bruno and then it hit me.

'Milo, we've been held back in our thinking by social roles.'

'What the hell are you talking about?'

'Roles. Social roles – prescribed sets of behaviors. Like doctor and patient. Psychiatrist and psychopath. What are the characteristics of a psychopath?'

'Lack of conscience.'

'Right. And an inability to relate to other people except by exploiting them. The good ones have a glib, smooth façade, often they're good-looking. Usually above-average intelligence. Sexually manipulative. A predilection to engage in cons, blackmail, frauds.'

Milo's eyes opened wide.

'Handler.'

'Of course. We've been thinking of him as the doctor in

the case and assuming psychological normalcy – he's been protected, in our eyes, by his role. But take a closer look. What do we know about him? He was involved in insurance fraud. He tried to blackmail Roy Longstreth, using his power as a psychiatrist. He seduced at least one patient – Elaine Gutierrez – and who knows how many more? And those putdowns in the margins of his notes – at first I thought they were evidence of burnout, but now I don't know. That was cold, pretending to listen to people, taking their money, insulting them. His notes were confidential – he never expected anyone else to read them. He could hang it all out, show his true colors. Milo, I tell you the guy comes across like your classic psychopath.'

'The evil doctor.'

'Not exactly a *rara avis*, is it? If there can be a Mengele, why not scores of Morton Handlers? What better façade for an intelligent psychopath than the title of Doctor – it yields instant prestige and credibility.'

'Psychopathic doctor and psychopathic patient.' He mulled it over.

'Not buddies, but partners in crime.'

'Sure. Psychopaths don't have buddies. Only victims and accomplices. Bruno must have been Handler's dream come true if he was plotting something and needed one of his own kind for help. I'll bet you those first sessions were incredible, the two of them hungry hyenas, checking each other out, looking over their shoulders, sniffing the ground.'

'Why Bruno, in particular? Handler treated other psychopaths.'

'They were too crude. Short-order cooks, cowboys, construction workers. Handler needed a smooth type.

Besides, how do we know how many of those guys were deliberately misdiagnosed like Longstreth?'

'Just to play devil's advocate for one second – one of those jokers was in law school.'

I thought about it for a minute.

'Too young. In Handler's eyes a callow punk. In a few years, with degree in hand and a veneer of sophistication, maybe. Handler needed a businessman type for what he wanted to pull off. Someone really slick. And Bruno appears to have fit that bill. He fooled Gershman, who's no idiot.'

Milo got up and paced the room, running his fingers through his hair, creating a bird's nest.

'It's definitely appealing. Shrinker and shrinkee pulling off a scam.' He seemed amused.

'It's not the first time, Milo. There was a guy back East a few years ago – very good credentials. Married into a rich family and started a clinic for juvenile delinquents – back when they still called them that. He used his in-laws' social connections to organize fund-raising soirées for the clinic. While the champagne flowed, the JDs were busy burglarizing the partygoers' townhouses. They finally caught him with a warehouse full of silver and crystal, furs and rugs. He didn't even need the stuff. He was doing it for the challenge. They sent him away to one of those discreet institutions in the rolling hills of southern Maryland – for all I know he's running the place by now. It never hit the papers. I found out about it through the professional grapevine. Convention gossip.'

Milo pulled out his pencil. He started writing, thinking out loud.

'To the marble corridors of high finance. Bank records,

brokerage statements, businesses filed under fictitious names. See what's left in the safe-deposit boxes after the IRS has done its dirty work. County assessor for info on property ventures. Insurance claims out of Handler's office.' He stopped. 'I hope this gets me somewhere, Alex. This goddamn case hasn't helped my status in the department. The captain is aiming for promotion and he wants to show more arrests. Handler and Gutierrez weren't ghetto types he can afford to let fade away. And he's running scared that Glendale will solve Bruno first and make us look like shmucks. You remember Bianchi.'

I nodded. A small-town police chief in Bellingham, Washington, had caught the Hillside Strangler – something the LAPD war machine hadn't been able to do.

He got up, went into the kitchen and ate half of a cold chicken standing over the sink. He washed it down with a quart of orange juice and came back wiping his mouth.

'I don't know why I'm fighting not to laugh, up to my ass in dead bodies and no apparent progress, but it seems so funny, Handler and Bruno. You send a guy to a shrink to get his head straight and the doc is as fucked-up as the patient and *systematically* puts the warp on him.'

Put that way it didn't *sound* funny. He laughed anyway.

'What about the girl?' he asked.

'Gutierrez? What about her?'

'Well, I was thinking about those social roles. We've been looking at her as the innocent bystander. If Handler could connive with one patient, why not with two?'

'It's not impossible. But we know Bruno was psychopathic. Any of that kind of evidence about her?'

'No,' he admitted. 'We looked for Handler's file on her

and couldn't find it. Maybe he shredded it when their relationship changed. Do you guys do that?'

'I wouldn't know. I never slept with my patients – or their mothers.'

'Don't be touchy. I tried to interview her family. The old, plump *mamacita*, two brothers, one of 'em with those angry, macho eyes. There's no father – he died ten years ago. The three of them live in a tiny place in Echo Park. When I got there they were in the middle of mourning. The place was full of the girl's pictures, in shrines. Lots of candles, baskets of food, weeping neighbors. The brothers were sullen. Mama barely spoke English. I made a serious attempt to be sensitive, culturally aware and all that. I borrowed Sanchez from Ramparts Division to translate. We brought food, kept a low profile. I got *nada*. Hear no evil, speak no evil. I honestly don't think they knew much about Elena's life. To them West LA's as distant as Atlantis. But even if they did they sure as hell weren't going to tell me.'

'Even,' I asked, 'if it would help find her murderer.'

He looked at me wearily.

'Alex, people like that don't think the police can help them. To them *la policía* are the bastards who roust their *cholos* and insult their home girls and are never around when the low riders cruise the neighborhood at night with their lights off and pop shotgun shells through bedroom windows. Which reminds me – I interviewed a friend of the girl. Her roommate, also a teacher. This one was outwardly hostile. Made it clear she wanted nothing to do with me. Her brother had been killed five years ago in a gang shootout and the police did nothing for her and her family then, so to hell with me now.'

He got up and padded around the room like a tired lion.

'In summation, Elaine Gutierrez is a cipher. But there's nothing to indicate she wasn't as pure as the freshly driven snow.'

He looked miserable, plagued with self-doubt.

'It's a tough case, Milo. Don't be so hard on yourself.'

'It's funny you should say that. That's what my mother used to tell me. Go easy, Milo Bernard. Don't be such a *profectionist* – that was the way she pronounced it. The whole family had a tradition of low personal expectations. Drop out of school in tenth grade, go to work at the foundry, lay out a life for yourself of plastic dishes, TV, church picnics, and steel splinter that stuck in your skin. After thirty years enough pension and disability to give you a weekend in the Ozarks once in a while, if you're lucky. My Dad did it, his dad, and both of my brothers. The Sturgis game plan. But not the *profectionist*. For one, the game plan worked best if you got married and I'd been liking boys since I was nine. And second – this was more important – I figured I was too smart to do what the rest of those peasants were doing. So I broke the mold, shocked them all. And the hotshot who everyone thought was going to become a lawyer or a professor or at least some kind of accountant goes and ends up as a member of *la policía*. Ain't that something for a guy who wrote a goddamn thesis on transcendentalism in the poetry of Walt Whitman?'

He turned away from me and stared at the wall. He had worked himself into a funk. I had seen it before. The most therapeutic thing to say was nothing. I ignored him and did some calisthenics.

'Goddam Jack La Lanne,' he muttered.

It took him ten minutes to come out of it, ten minutes of clenching and unclenching his big fists. Then came the tentative raising of the eyes, the inevitable sheepish grin.

'How much for the therapy, Doctor?'

I thought a minute.

'Dinner. At a good place. No crap.'

He stood up and stretched, growled like a bear.

'How about sushi? I'm goddamn barbaric tonight. I'll eat those fish alive.'

We drove to Oomasa, in Little Tokyo. The restaurant was crowded, mostly with Japanese. This was no trendy hotspot decked out in shoji-screen elegance and waxed pine counters. The decor was red Naugahyde, stiff-backed chairs and plain white walls decorated only by a few Nikon calendars. The solitary concession to style was a large aquarium, in full view of the sushi bar, in which fancy goldfish struggled to propel themselves through bubbling, icy clear water. They gasped and bobbed, mutations ill-suited for survival in any but the most rarefied captivity, the products of hundreds of years of careful Oriental tinkering with nature – lionheads with faces obscured by glossy, raspberry growths, bug-eyed black moors, celestials with eyes forced perpetually heavenward, *ryukins* so overloaded with finnage that they could barely move. We stared at them and drank Chivas.

'That girl,' Milo said, 'the roommate. I felt she could help me. That she knew something about Elaine's lifestyle, maybe something about her and Handler. She was nailed tight, goddamn her.'

He finished his drink and motioned for another. It came and he gulped down half.

A waitress skittered over on geisha feet and handed us

hot towels. We wiped our hands and face. I felt my pores open, hungry for air.

'You should be pretty good at talking to teachers, right? Probably did a lot of it back in the days when you were earning an honest living.'

'Sometimes teachers hate psychologists, Milo. They see us as dilettantes dropping theoretical pearls of wisdom on them while they do the dirty work.'

'Hmm.' The rest of the Scotch disappeared.

'But no matter. I'll talk to her for you. Where can I find her?'

'Same school Gutierrez taught at. In West LA, not far from you.' He wrote the address on a napkin and gave it to me. 'Her name's Raquel Ochoa.' He spelled it, his voice thickening, slurring the words. 'Use your badge.' He slapped me on the back.

There was a grating sound above our heads. We looked up to find the sushi chef smiling and sharpening his knives.

We ordered. The fish was fresh, the rice just slightly sweet. The *wasabe* horseradish cleared my sinuses. We ate in silence, against a backdrop of *samisen* music and foreign chatter.

13

I AWOKE as stiff as if I'd been spray-starched; a full-fledged charley horse had taken hold of my muscles, a souvenir of my dance with Jaroslav. I fought it by taking a two-mile run down the canyon and back. Then I practiced karate moves out on the rear deck, to the amused comments of a pair of mockingbirds who interrupted their domestic quarrel long enough to look me over, then delivered what had to be the avian equivalent of a raspberry.

'Fly down here, you little bastards,' I grunted, 'and I'll show you who's tough.' They responded with hilarious screeching.

The day was shaping up as a lung-buster, grimy fingers of pollution reaching over the mountains to strangle the sky. The ocean was obscured by a sulfurous sheath of airborne garbage. My chest ached in harmony with the stiffness in my joints, and by ten I was ready to quit.

I planned to time my visit to the school where Raquel Ochoa taught for the noon break, hoping to find her free. That left enough time for a long, hot bath, a cold shower, and a carefully assembled breakfast of eggs with mushrooms, sourdough toast, grilled tomatoes and coffee.

I dressed casually in dark brown slacks, tan corduroy sport

coat, checked shirt and brown-knit tie. Before I left I dialed a now-familiar number. Bonita Quinn answered.

'Yes?'

'Mrs Quinn, Dr Delaware. I just wanted to call to find out how Melody's been doing.'

'She's fine.' Her tone would have frosted a beer mug. 'Fine.'

Before I could say more she hung up.

The school was in a middle-class part of town, but it could have been anywhere. It was the old familiar layout of citadels of learning throughout the city: Flesh-colored buildings arranged in classic penitentiary style, surrounded by a desert of black asphalt and secured by ten-foot-high chain-link fencing. Someone had tried to brighten it up by painting a mural of children playing along the side of one of the buildings but it was scant redemption. What helped a bit more were the sight and sound of real children playing – running, jumping, tumbling, chasing each other, screaming like banshees, throwing balls, crying out with the fervor of the truly persecuted ('Teacher, he *hit* me!'), sitting in circles, reaching for the sky. A small group of bored-looking teachers watched from the sidelines.

I climbed the front stairs and found the main office with little trouble. The internal floor plan of schools was as predictable as the drab exterior.

I used to wonder why all the schools I knew were so hopelessly ugly, so predictably oppressive, then I dated a nurse whose father was one of the chief architects for the firm that had been building schools for the state for the past fifty years. She had unresolved feelings about him, and talked a lot about him: A drunken, melancholic man who hated his wife and despised his children more, who saw the world in terms of minimally varying shades of disappointment. A real Frank Lloyd Wright.

The office reeked of mimeographing fluid. Its sole occupant was a stern, black woman in her forties, ensconced in a fortress of scarred golden oak. I showed her my badge, which didn't interest her, and asked for Raquel Ochoa. The name didn't seem to interest her either.

'She's a teacher here. Fourth grade,' I added.

'It's lunchtime. Try the teachers' dining room.'

The dining room turned out to be an airless place, twenty feet by fifteen, into which folding tables and chairs had been crammed. A dozen men and women sat hunched over sack lunches and coffee, laughing, smoking, chewing. When I entered the room all activity ceased.

'I'm looking for Ms Ochoa.'

'You won't find her here, honey,' said a stout woman with platinum hair.

Several of the teachers laughed. They let me stand there for a while and then a fellow with a young face and old eyes said:

'Room 304. Probably.'

'Thanks.'

I left. I was halfway down the hall before they started talking again.

The door to 304 was half-open. I went in. Rows of unoccupied school desks filled every square inch of space, with the exception of a few feet at the front that had been cleared for the teacher's desk, a boxy metal rectangle behind which sat a woman busy at work. If she had heard me enter she gave no indication, as she continued to read, make check-marks, cross out errors. An unopened brown bag sat at her elbow. Light streamed in through dusty windows in beams that were suffused with dancing, suspended particles. The Vermeer softness was at odds with the utilitarian severity of the room: Stark walls, a blackboard veneered with chalky residue, a soiled American flag.

'Ms Ochoa?'

The face that looked up was out of a mural by Rivera. Reddish-brown skin stretched tightly over sharply defined but delicately constructed bones; liquid lips and melting black eyes gabled by full, dark brows. Her hair was long and sleek, parted in the middle, hanging down her back. Part Aztec, part Spanish, part unknown.

'Yes?' Her voice was soft in volume but the timbre was defensively hard. Some of the hostility Milo had described was immediately apparent. I wondered if she was one of those people who had turned psychological vigilance into a fine art.

I walked over to her, introduced myself and showed her the badge. She inspected it.

'PhD, in what?'

'Psychology.'

She looked at me with disdain.

'The police don't get satisfaction, so they send in the shrinks?'

'It's not that simple.'

'Spare me the details.' She returned her eyes to her paper-work.

'I just want to talk to you for a few minutes. About your friend.'

'I told that big detective everything I know.'

'This is just a double-check.'

'How thorough.' She picked up her red pencil and began slashing at the paper. I felt sorry for the students whose work was coming under scrutiny at this particular moment.

'This isn't a psychological interview, if that's what you're worried about. It's—'

'I'm not worried about anything. I told him everything.'

'He doesn't think so.'

She slammed the pencil down. The point broke.

'Are you calling me a liar, Mr PhD?' Her speech was crisp and articulate but it still bore a Latin tinge.

I shrugged.

'Labels aren't important. What is, is finding out as much as possible about Elaine Gutierrez.'

'*Elena*,' she snapped. 'There's nothing to tell. Let the police do their job and stop sending their scientific snoopers around harassing people who are busy.'

'Too busy to help find the murderer of your best friend?'

The head shot up. She brushed furiously at a loose strand of hair.

'Please leave,' she said between clenched jaws. 'I have work to do.'

'Yes, I know. You don't even eat lunch with the rest of the teachers. You're very dedicated and serious – that's what it took to get out of the *barrio* – and that puts you above the laws of common courtesy.'

She stood up, all five feet of her. For a moment I thought

she was going to slap me, as she drew her hand back. But she stopped herself, and stared.

I could feel the acid heat coming my way but I held my gaze. Jaroslav would have been proud.

'I'm busy,' she finally said, but there was a pleading quality to the statement, as if she was trying to convince herself.

'I don't want to take you on a cruise. I just want to ask a few questions about Elena.'

She sat down.

'What kind of psychologist are you? You don't talk like one.'

I gave her a capsulized, deliberately vague history of my involvement in the case. She listened and I thought I saw her soften.

'A child psychologist. We could use you around here.'

I looked around the classroom, counted forty-six desks in a space meant for twenty-eight.

'I don't know what I could do – help you tie them down?'

She laughed, then realized what she was doing and cut it off, like a bad connection.

'It's no use talking about Elena,' she said. 'She only got – into trouble because of being involved with that . . .' She trailed off.

'I know Handler was a creep. Detective Sturgis – the big guy – knows. And you're probably right. She was an innocent victim. But let's make sure, OK?'

'You do this a lot. Work for the police?' She evaded me.

'No. I'm retired.'

She looked at me with disbelief. 'At your age?'

'Post-burnout.'

That hit home. She dropped her mask a notch and a bit of humanity peeked through.

'I wish I could afford it. Retirement.'

'I know what you mean. It must be crazy working with this kind of bureaucracy.' I threw out the lure of empathy – administrators were the object of every teacher's ire. If she didn't go for it I wasn't sure what I'd do to gain rapport.

She looked at me suspiciously, searching for a sign that I was patronizing her.

'You don't work at all?' she asked.

'I do some freelance investing. It keeps me busy enough.'

We chatted for a while about the vagaries of the school system. She carefully avoided mention of anything personal, keeping it all in the realm of pop sociology – how rotten things were when parents weren't willing to get emotionally and intellectually involved with their children, how difficult it was to teach when half the kids came from broken homes and were so upset they could barely concentrate, the frustration of dealing with administrators who'd given up on life and stuck around only for their pensions, anger at the fact that a teacher's starting salary was less than that of a trash collector. She was twenty-nine and she'd lost any shred of idealism that had survived the transition from East LA to the world of Anglo bourgeoisie.

She could really talk when she got going, the dark eyes flashing, the hands gesticulating – flying through the air like two brown sparrows.

I sat like the teacher's pet and listened, giving her what everyone wants when they're unloading – empathy, an understanding gesture. Part of it was calculated – I wanted to break through to her in order to find out more about

Elena Gutierrez – but some of it was my old therapeutic persona, thoroughly genuine.

I was starting to think I'd gotten through when the bell rang. She became a teacher again, the arbiter of right and wrong.

'You must go now. The children will be coming back.'

I stood up and leaned on her desk.

'Can we talk later? About Elena?'

She hesitated, biting her lip. The sound of a stampede began as a faint rumble and grew thunderous. Highpitched voices wailed their way closer.

'All right. I'm off at two thirty.'

An offer to buy her a drink would have been a mistake. Keep it businesslike, Alex.

'Thank you. I'll meet you at the gate.'

'No. Meet me in the teachers' parking lot. At the south side of the building.' Away from prying eyes.

Her car was a dusty white Vega. She walked toward it carrying a stack of books and papers that reached up to her chin.

'Can I help you?'

She gave me the load, which must have weighed at least twenty pounds, and took a minute to find her keys. I noticed that she'd put on makeup – eye shadow that accentuated the depth of her orbs. She looked around eighteen.

'I haven't eaten yet,' she said. It was less an angling for an invitation than a complaint.

'No brown bag.'

'I threw it out. I make a lousy lunch. On a day like today it's too lousy to take. There's a chop house on Wilshire.'

'Can I drive you?'

She looked at the Vega.

'Sure, why not? I'm low on gas, anyway. Toss those on the front seat.' I put the books down and she locked the car. 'But I'll pay for my own lunch.'

We left the school grounds. I led her to the Seville. When she saw it her eyebrows rose.

'You must be a good investor.'

'I get lucky from time to time.'

She sank back in the soft leather and let out a breath. I got behind the wheel and started up the engine.

'I've changed my mind,' she said. 'You pay for the lunch.'

She ate meticulously, cutting her steak into tiny pieces, spearing each morsel individually and slipping it into her mouth, and wiping her mouth with her napkin every third bite. I was willing to bet she was a tough grader.

'She was my best friend,' she said, putting down her fork and picking up her water glass. 'We grew up together in East LA Rafael and Andy – her brothers – played with Miguel.' At the mention of her dead brother her eyes misted then grew hard as obsidian. She pushed her plate away. She'd eaten a quarter of her food. 'When we moved to Echo Park the Gutierrezes moved with us. The boys were always getting into trouble – minor mischief, pranks. Elena and I were good girls. Goody-goodies, actually. The nuns loved us.' She smiled.

'We were as close as sisters. And like sisters there was a lot of competition between us. She was always better-looking.'

She read the doubt in my face.

'Really. I was a scrawny kid. I developed late. Elena was – voluptuous, soft. The boys followed her around with their tongues hanging out. Even when she was eleven and twelve. Here.' She reached into her purse and took out a snapshot. More photographic memories.

'This is Elena and me. In high school.'

Two girls leaned against a graffiti-filled wall. They wore Catholic school uniforms – short-sleeved white blouses, gray skirts, white socks and saddle shoes. One was tiny, thin and dark. The other a head taller, had curves the uniform couldn't conceal and a complexion that was surprisingly fair.

'Was she a blonde?'

'Surprising, isn't it? Some German rapist way back, no doubt. Later she lightened it even more, to be really all-American. She got sophisticated, changed her name to Elaine, spent lots of money on clothes, her car.' She realized she was criticizing the dead girl and quickly changed her tune. 'But she was a person of substance underneath all of that. She was a truly gifted teacher – there aren't many like that. She taught EH, you know.'

Educationally Handicapped classes were for children who weren't retarded but still had difficulties learning. The category could include everything from bright kids with specific perceptual problems to youngsters whose emotional conflicts got in the way of their learning to read and write. Teaching EH was tough. It could be constant frustration or a stimulating challenge, depending on a teacher's motivation, energy and talent.

'Elena had a real gift for drawing them out – the kids no one else could work with. She had patience. You wouldn't have thought it to look at her. She was – flashy. She used lots of makeup, dressed to show herself off. Sometimes she looked like a party girl. But she wasn't afraid to get down on the floor with the children, didn't mind getting her hands dirty. She got into their heads – she dedicated herself to them. The children loved her. Look.'

Another photograph. Elena Gutierrez surrounded by a group of smiling children. She was kneeling and the kids were climbing on her, tugging at the hem of her skirt, putting their heads in her lap. A tall, well-built young woman, pretty rather than beautiful, with an earthy, open look, the yellow hair a styled, thick shag framing an oval face, and contrasting dramatically with the Hispanic features. Except for those features she was the classic California girl. The kind who should have been lying face down in the Malibu sand, bikini top undone, smooth brown back exposed to the sun. A girl for cola commercials and custom van shows and running down to the market in halter and shorts for a six-pack. She shouldn't have ended up as savaged, lifeless flesh in a refrigerated drawer downtown.

Raquel Ochoa took the picture out of my hands and I thought I saw jealousy in her face.

'She's dead,' she said, putting it back in her purse, frowning, as if I'd committed some kind of heresy.

'It looked like they adored her,' I said.

'They did. Now they've brought in some old bag who doesn't give a damn about teaching. Now that Elena's – gone.'

She started to cry, using her napkin to shield her face from my eyes. Her thin shoulders shook. She sank lower in the booth, trying to disappear, sobbing.

I got up, moved to her side and put my arms around her. She felt as frail as a cobweb.

'No, no. I'm all right.' But she moved closer to me, burying herself in the folds of my jacket, burrowing in for the long, cold winter.

As I held her I realized that she felt good. She smelled good. This was a surprisingly soft, feminine person in my arms. I fantasized swooping her up, featherweight and vulnerable, carrying her to bed where I'd still her painful cries with that ultimate panacea: Orgasm. A stupid fantasy because it would take more than a fuck and a hug to solve her problems. Stupid because that wasn't what this encounter was all about. I felt an annoying heat and tension in my groin. Tumescence rearing its ugly head when least appropriate. Still, I held her until her sobbing slowed and her breathing became regular. Thinking of Robin, I finally let her go and moved back to my side.

She avoided my eyes, took out her compact and fixed her face.

'That was really dumb.'

'No it wasn't. That's what eulogies are for.'

She thought for a moment then managed a faint smile.

'Yes, I suppose you're right.' She reached across the table and placed a small hand on mine. 'Thank you. I miss her so much.'

'I understand.'

'Do you?' She drew her hand away, suddenly cross.

'No, I guess not. I've never lost anyone to whom I was that close. Will you accept a serious attempt at empathy?'

'I'm sorry. I've been rude – from the moment you walked in. It's been so hard. All of these feelings – sadness, and

163

emptiness and anger at the monster who did it – it had to be a monster, didn't it?'

'Yes.'

'Will you catch him? Will that big detective catch him?'

'He's a very capable guy, Raquel. In his own way, quite gifted. But he's got little to go on.'

'Yes. I suppose I should help you, shouldn't I?'

'It would be nice.'

She found a cigarette in her purse and lit it with trembling hands. She took a deep drag and let it out.

'What do you want to know?'

'For starts, how about the old cliché – did she have any enemies?'

'The clichéd answer: No. She was popular, well liked. And besides, whoever did this to her was no acquaintance – we didn't know anyone like that.' She shuddered, confronting her own vulnerability.

'Did she go out with a lot of men?'

'The same questions.' She sighed. 'She dated a few guys before she met *him*. Then it was the two of them all the way.'

'When did she begin seeing him?'

'She started as a patient almost a year ago. It's hard to know when she began sleeping with him. She didn't talk to me about that kind of thing.'

I could imagine sexuality being a taboo topic for the two best friends. With their upbringing there was bound to be lots of conflict. And given what I had seen of Raquel and heard about Elena it was almost certain they had gone about resolving those conflicts in different ways: One, the party girl, a man's woman; the other, attractive but perceiving herself in pitched battle with the world. I looked across the table at the dark, serious face and knew her bed would be ringed with thorns.

'Did she tell you they were having an affair?'

'An affair? That sounds so light and breezy. He violated his professional ethics and she fell for it.' She puffed on her cigarette. 'She giggled about it for a week or so then came out and told me what a wonderful guy he was. I put two and two together. A month later he picked her up at our place. It was out in the open.'

'What was he like?'

'Like you said before – a creep. Too well dressed – velvet jackets, tailored pants, sunlamp tan, shirt unbuttoned to show lots of chest hair – curly gray chest hair. He smiled a lot and got familiar with me. Shook my hand and held on too long. Lingered with a goodbye kiss – nothing you could pin him on.' The words were almost identical to Roy Longstreth's.

'Slick?'

'Exactly. Slippery. She's gone for that type before. I couldn't understand it – she was such a good person, so real. I figured it had something to do with losing her dad at a young age. She had no good male role model. Does that sound plausible?'

'Sure.' Life was never as simple as the psych texts but it made people feel good to find solutions.

'He was a bad influence on her. When she started going with him was when she dyed her hair and changed her name and bought all those clothes. She even went out and bought a new car – one of those Datsun-Z turbos.'

'How did she afford it?' The car cost more than most teachers made in a year.

'If you're thinking he paid for it, forget it. She bought it on payments. That was another thing about Elena. She had no conception of money. Just let it pass through her fingers. She always joked how she was going to have to marry a rich guy to accommodate her tastes.'

'How often did they see each other?'

'At first once or twice a week. By the end she might as well have moved in with him. I rarely saw her. She'd drop in to pick up a few things, invite me to go out with them.'

'Did you?'

She was surprised at the question.

'Are you kidding? I couldn't stand to be around him. And I have a life of my own. I had no need to be the odd one out.'

A life, I suspected, of grading papers until ten and then retiring, nightgown buttoned high, with a gothic novel and a cup of hot cocoa.

'Did they have friends, other couples with whom they associated?'

'I have no idea. I'm trying to tell you – I kept out of it.' An edge crept into her voice and I retreated.

'She started out as his patient. Do you have any idea why she went to a psychiatrist in the first place?'

'She said she was depressed.'

'You don't think she was?'

'It's hard to tell with some people. When I get depressed everyone knows about it. I withdraw, don't want anything to do with anybody. It's like I shrink, crawl into myself. With Elena, who knows? It's not like she had trouble eating or sleeping. She would just get a little quiet.'

'But she said she was depressed?'

'Not until after she told me she was seeing Handler — after I asked her why. She said she was feeling down, the work was getting to her. I tried to help but she said she needed more. I was never a big fan of psychiatrists and psychologists.' She smiled apologetically. 'If you have friends and family you should be able to work it out.'

'If that's enough, great. Sometimes it's like she said, Raquel. You need more.'

She put out her cigarette.

'Well, I suppose it's fortunate for you that many people agree with that.'

'I suppose so.'

There was an awkward silence. I broke it.

'Did he prescribe any medication for her?'

'Not as far as I know. Just talked to her. She went to see him weekly, and then twice a week after one of her students died. Then she was obviously depressed — cried for days.'

'When was this?'

'Let me see, it was pretty soon after she started going to Handler, maybe after they were already dating — I don't know. About eight months ago.'

'How did it happen?'

'Accident. Hit-and-run. The kid was walking along a dark road at night and a car hit him. It destroyed her. She'd been working with him for months. He was one of her miracles. Everyone thought he was mute. Elena got him to talk.' She shook her head. 'A miracle. And then to have it all go down the drain like that. So meaningless.'

'The parents must have been shattered.'

'No. There were no parents. He was an orphan. He came from La Casa.'

'La Casa de los Niños? In Malibu Canyon?'

'Sure. Why the surprise? They contract with us to provide special education to some of their kids. They do it with several of the local schools. It's part of a state-funded project or something. To mainstream children without families into the community.'

'No surprise,' I lied. 'It just seems so sad for something like that to happen to an orphan.'

'Yes. Life is unfair.' The declaration seemed to give her satisfaction.

She looked at her watch.

'Anything more? I've got to get back.'

'Just one. Do you recall the name of the child who died?'

'Nemeth. Cary or Corey. Something like that.'

'Thanks for your time. You've been helpful.'

'Have I? I don't see how. But I'm glad if it brings you closer to that monster.'

She had a concrete vision of the murderer that Milo would have envied.

We drove back to the school and I walked her to her car.

'OK,' she said.

'Thanks again.'

'You're welcome. If you have more questions you can come back.' It was as forward as she was going to get – for her the equivalent of asking me over to her place. It made me sad, knowing there was nothing I could do for her.

'I will.'

She smiled and held out her hand. I took it, careful not to hold on for too long.

14

I'VE NEVER BEEN a big believer in coincidence. I suppose it's because the notion of life being governed by the random collision of molecules in space cuts at the heart of my professional identity. After all, why spend all those years learning how to help people change when deliberate change is just an illusion? But even if I had been willing to give the fates their due, it would have been hard to see as coincidence the fact that Cary or Corey Nemeth (deceased), a student of Elena Gutierrez (deceased), had been a resident of the same institution where Maurice Bruno (deceased) had volunteered.

It was time to learn more about La Casa de los Niños.

I went home and searched through the cardboard boxes I had stored in the garage since dropping out, until I found my old office Rolodex. I located Olivia Brickerman's number at the Department of Social Services and dialed it. A social worker for thirty years, Olivia knew more about agencies than anyone in the city.

A recording answered the phone and told me DPSS's number had been changed. I dialed the new number and another recording told me to wait. A tape of Barry Manilow came on the line. I wondered if the city paid him royalties. Music to wait for your caseworker by.

'DPSS.'

'Mrs Brickerman, please.'

'One moment, sir.' Two more minutes of Manilow. Then: 'She's no longer with this office.'

'Can you please tell me where I can locate her?'

'One moment.' I was informed, once again, who wrote the music that made the whole world sing. 'Mrs Brickerman is now at the Santa Monica Psychiatric Medical Group.'

So Olivia had finally left the public domain.

'Do you have that number?'

'One moment, sir.'

'Thanks anyway.' I hung up and consulted the Yellow Pages under Mental Health Services. The number belonged to an address on Broadway where Santa Monica approached Venice, not far from Robin's studio. I called it.

'SMPMG.'

'Mrs Olivia Brickerman, please.'

'Who shall I say is calling?'

'Dr Delaware.'

'One moment.' The line was silent. Apparently the utility of phonehold Muzak hadn't become apparent to SMPMG.

'Alex! How are you?'

'Fine, Olivia, and you?'

'Wonderful, wonderful. I thought you were somewhere in the Himalayas.'

'Why's that?'

'Isn't that where people go when they want to find themselves – somewhere cold with no oxygen and a little old man with a beard sitting on top of a mountain munching on twigs and reading *People* magazine?'

'That was the sixties, Olivia. In the eighties you stay home and soak in hot water.'

'Ha!'

'How's Al?'

'His usual extroverted self. He was hunched over the board when I left this morning, muttering something about the Pakistani defense or some such *naarishkeit*.'

Her husband, Albert D. Brickerman, was the chess editor for the *Times*. In the five years I'd known him I hadn't heard him utter a dozen words in a row. It was difficult to imagine what he and Olivia, Miss Sociability of 1930 through '80, had in common. But they'd been married thirty-seven years, had raised four children, and seemed content with each other.

'So you finally left DPSS.'

'Yes, can you believe it? Even barnacles can be dislodged!'

'What led to such an impulsive move?'

'I tell you, Alex, I would have stayed. Sure the system stank – what system doesn't? But I was used to it, like a wart. I like to think I was still doing a good job – though I tell you, the stories got sadder and longer. Such misery. And with cuts in funding the people would get less and less – and madder and madder. They took it out on the case-workers. We had a girl stabbed in the downtown office. Now there're armed guards in every office. But what the hell, I was brought up in New York. Then my nephew, my sister's boy, Steve, he finished medical school and decided to become a psychiatrist – can you believe that, another mental health person in the family? His father's a surgeon and that was the safest way for him to rebel. Anyway, he's always been very close to me and it's been a running joke that when he went into practice he was going to rescue Aunt Livvy from

DPSS and take her into his office. And would you believe he took me up on it? Writes me a letter, tells me he's coming out to California and joining a group, and they need a social worker for intakes and short-term counseling, would I like to do it? So here I am, with a view of the beach, working for little Stevie – of course I don't call him that in front of other people.'

'That's great, Olivia. You sound happy.'

'I am. I go down to the beach for lunch, read a book, get a tan. After twenty-two years I finally feel like I'm living in California. Maybe I'll take up roller-skating, huh?'

The image of Olivia, who was built somewhat like Alfred Hitchcock, whizzing by on skates, made me laugh.

'Ah, you scoff now. Just wait!' She chuckled. 'Now, enough autobiography. Whan can I do for you?'

'I need some information on a place called La Casa de los Niños, in Malibu.'

'McCaffrey's place? You thinking of sending someone there?'

'No. It's a long story.'

'Listen, if it's that long why don't you give me a chance to dig in my files? Come over to the house tonight and I'll give it to you in person. I'll be baking and Albert will be meditating over the board. We haven't seen you in a long time.'

'What are you baking?'

'Strudel, pirogis, fudge brownies.'

'I'll be over. What time?'

'Eightish. You remember the place?'

'It hasn't been that long, Olivia.'

'It's been twice as long. Listen, I don't want to be a yenta, but if you don't have a girlfriend there's a young lady – also a psychologist – who just came to work here. Very cute. The two of you would have brilliant children.'

'Thanks, but I've got someone.'

'Terrific. Bring her along.'

The Brickermans lived on Hayworth, not far from the Fairfax district, in a small beige stucco house with Spanish tile roof. Olivia's mammoth Chrysler was parked in the driveway.

'What am I doing here, Alex?' Robin asked as we approached the front door.

'Do you like chess?'

'Don't know how to play.'

'Don't worry about it. This is one house where you don't have to be concerned about what to say. You'll be lucky if you get a chance to talk. Eat brownies. Enjoy yourself.'

I gave her a kiss and rang the doorbell.

Olivia answered it. She looked the same – maybe a few pounds heavier – her hair a hennaed frizz, her face rosy-cheeked and open. She was wearing a shift, a Hawaiian print, and ripples went through it as she laughed. She spread her hands and hugged me to a bosom the size and consistency of a small sofa.

'Alex!' She released me and held me at arm's length. 'No more beard – you used to resemble D.H. Lawrence. Now you look like a graduate student.' She turned and smiled at Robin. I introduced them.

'Pleased to meet you. You're very lucky, he's a darling boy.'

Robin blushed.

'Come in.'

The house was redolent with good, sweet baking smells.

Al Brickerman, a prophet with white hair and beard, sat hunched over an ebony-and-maple chessboard in the living room. He was surrounded by clutter – books in shelves and on the floor, bric-a-brac, photographs of children and grand-children, menorahs, souvenirs, overstuffed furniture, an old robe and slippers.

'Al, Alex and his friend are here.'

'Hmm.' He grunted and raised his hand, never averting his eyes from the pieces on the board.

'Nice to see you again, Al.'

'Hmm.'

'He's a real schizoid,' Olivia confided to Robin, 'but he's dynamite in bed.'

She ushered us into the kitchen. The room was the same as it had been when the house had been built forty years ago: Yellow tile with maroon borders, narrow porcelain sink, window sills filled with potted plants. The refriger-ator and stove were vintage Kenmore. A ceramic sign hung over the doorway leading out to the service porch: *How Can You Soar Like An Eagle When You're Surrounded By Turkeys?*

Olivia saw me looking at it.

'My going-away present when I left DPSS. To myself from myself.' She brought over a plate of brownies, still warm.

'Here, have some before I eat them. Look at this – I'm growing obese.' She patted her rear.

'More to love,' I told her and she pinched my cheek.

'Mmm. These are great,' Robin said.

'A woman with taste. Here, sit down.'

We pulled up chairs around the kitchen table, the plate

set down before us. Olivia checked the oven and then she joined us. 'In about ten minutes you'll have strudel. Apples, raisins and figs. The latter an improvisation for Albert.' She crooked a thumb toward the living room. 'The system gets clogged, from time to time. Now then you want to know about Casa de los Niños. Not that it's any of my business, but could you tell my why?'

'It has to do with some work I'm doing for the police department.'

'The police? You.'

I told her about the case, leaving out the gory details. She had met Milo before – they'd hit it off marvelously – but hadn't been aware of the extent of our friendship.

'He's a nice boy. You should find him a nice woman like you found for yourself.' She smiled at Robin and handed her another brownie.

'I don't think that would work, Olivia. He's gay.'

It didn't stop her, only slowed her down. 'So? Find him a nice young man.'

'He's got one.'

'Good. Forgive me, Robin, I tend to run off at the mouth. It's all those hours I spend with clients listening and nodding and saying uh-huh. Then I get home and you can imagine the depth of conversational interplay I get with Prince Albert. Anyway, Alex, these questions about La Casa, Milo asked you to ask them?'

'Not exactly. I'm following my own leads.'

She looked at Robin.

'Philip Marlowe here?'

Robin gave her a helpless look.

'Is this dangerous, Alex?'

'No. I just want to look into a few things.'

'You be careful, you understand?' She squeezed my bicep. She had a grip like a bouncer. 'Make sure he's careful, darling.'

'I try, Olivia. I can't control him.'

'I know. These psychologists, they get so used to being in a position of authority they can't take advice. Let me tell you about this handsome fellow. I first met him when he was an intern assigned for three weeks to DPSS to teach him what life was like for people without money. He started out as a wise guy but I could tell he was special. He was the smartest thing on two feet. And he had compassion. His big problem was he was too hard on himself, he drove himself. He was doing twice as much work as anyone else and he thought he was doing nothing. I wasn't surprised when he took off like a missile, the fancy title and the books and all that. But I was worried he was going to burn himself out.'

'You were right, Olivia,' I admitted.

'I thought he went to the Himalayas, or something,' she laughed, continuing to address Robin. 'To get frozen so he could come back and appreciate California. Have more, both of you.'

'I'm stuffed.' Robin touched her flat tummy.

'You're probably right – keep the figure, if you have it. Me, I started out like a barrel, nothing to maintain. Tell me darling, do you love him?'

Robin looked at me. She put her arm around my neck.

'I do.'

'Fine, I pronounce you husband and wife. Who cares what he says?'

She got up and went to the oven, peering through the glass window.

'Still a few more minutes. I think the figs take longer to bake.'

'Olivia, about La Casa de los Niños?'

She sighed and her bosom sighed along with her. 'OK. You're obviously serious about playing policeman.' She sat down. 'After you called I went into my old files and pulled out what I could find. You want coffee?'

'Please,' said Robin.

'I'll have some too.'

She came back with three steaming mugs, cream and sugar on a porcelain tray upon which had been silk-screened a panorama of Yellowstone Park.

'This is delicious, Olivia,' Robin said, sipping.

'Kona. From Hawaii. This dress is from there, too. My younger son, Gabriel, he's there. He's in import-export. Does very well.'

'Olivia—'

'Yes, yes, OK. La Casa de los Niños. The Children's Home. Started in 1974 by the Reverend Augustus McCaffrey, as a place of refuge for children with no home. That's right off the brochure.'

'Do you have the brochure with you?'

'No, it's at the office. You want me to mail you a copy?'

'Don't bother. What kind of kids stay there?'

'Abused and neglected children, orphans, some status offenders – you know, runaways. They used to put them in jail or the CYA but those places got too crowded with fourteen-year-old murderers and rapists and robbers, so now they try to find foster placement for them or a place like La

Casa. In general these institutions get the kids nobody wants, the ones they can't find foster placement or adoptive homes for. Lots of them have physical and psychological problems – spastic, blind, deaf, retarded. Or they're too old to be attractive adoptees. There are also the children of women in prison – mostly junkies and alcoholics. We tried to place them with individual families, but often nobody wanted them. To sum up, dear: Chronic wards of the Dependency Court.'

'How's a place like that funded?'

'Alex, the way the state and federal systems are set up, an operator can pull in over a thousand dollars a month per child if he knows how to bill it right. Kids with disabilities bring in more – you get paid for all the special services. On top of that I hear McCaffrey's terrific at bringing in private donations. He's got connections – the land the place is on is an example. Twenty acres in Malibu, used to belong to the government. They interned the Japanese there during World War II. Then it was used as a labor camp for first offenders – embezzlers, politicians, that type. He got the county to give it to him on long-term lease. Ninety-nine years with token rent.'

'He must be a good talker.'

'He is. A good old boy. Used to be a missionary down in Mexico. I hear he ran a similar place there.'

'Why'd he move back up?'

'Who knows? Maybe he got tired of not drinking the water? Maybe he longed for Kentucky Fried Chicken – although I hear they've got it down there now.'

'What about the place? Is it a good one?'

'None of those places is utopia, Alex. The ideal would be a little house in suburbia with a picket fence around it, gingham curtains and a green lawn, Mommy and Daddy and Rover the Dog. The reality is that there are over seventeen thousand kids on the Dependency Court docket in LA county alone. Seventeen thousand unwanted children! And they're piling into the system faster than they can be – here's a terrible word – processed.'

'That's unbelievable,' said Robin. She had a troubled look on her face.

'We've turned into a society of child-haters, darling. More and more abuse and neglect. People have kids and then change their minds. Parents don't want to take responsibility for them so they shunt them over to the government – how's that from an old Socialist, Alex? And abortion – I hope this doesn't offend you, because I'm for liberation as much if not more than the next woman. I was screaming for equal pay before Gloria Steinem went through puberty. But let's face it, this wholesale abortion we've got is just another form of birth control, another way out for people to avoid their responsibility. And it's killing kids, at least in some sense, isn't it? Maybe it's better than having them and then trying to get rid of them – I don't know.' She wiped the sweat from her forehead and dabbed at her upper lip with a paper napkin. 'Excuse me, that was a tedious polemic.'

She stood up and smoothed down her dress.

'Let me check the strudel.'

She came back with a steaming platter. 'Blow on it, it's hot.'

Robin and I looked at each other.

'You look so serious, I ruined your appetite with my polemic, didn't I?'

'No, Olivia.' I took a slab of strudel and ate a bite. 'It's delicious and I agree with you.'

Robin looked grave. We'd discussed the abortion issue many times, never resolving anything.

'In answer to your question, is it a good place, I can only say that we had no complaints when I was with DPSS. They offer the basics, it looked clean, the area is certainly nice – most of those kids never saw a mountain except on TV. They bus the kids to the public schools when they have special needs. Otherwise they've got in-house teaching. I doubt if anyone helps them with their homework – it's certainly not "Father Knows Best" over there, but McCaffrey keeps the place up, pushes for lots of community involvement. That means public exposure. Why do you want to know so much about it, you think that kid's death was suspicious?'

'No. There's no reason to suspect anything.' I thought about her question. 'I guess I'm just fishing.'

'Well don't go fishing for minnows and come up with a shark, darling.'

We nibbled at the strudel. Olivia called into the living room:

'Al, you want some strudel – with the figs?'

There was no answer I could hear, but she put some pastry on a plate nonetheless and brought it into him.

'She's a nice lady,' said Robin.

'One in a million. And very tough.'

'And smart. You should listen to her when she says to be careful. Alex, please leave the detecting to Milo.'

'I'll take care of myself, don't worry.' I took her hand but she pulled away. I was about to say something but Olivia returned to the kitchen.

'The dead man — the salesman, you said he volunteered at La Casa?'

'Yes. He had a certificate in his office.'

'He was probably a member of the Gentlemen's Brigade. It's something dreamed up by McCaffrey to get the business community involved with the place. He gets corporations to get their executives to volunteer weekend time with the kids. How much of it is voluntary on the part of the "Gentlemen" and how much is the result of pressure from the boss I don't know. McCaffrey give them blazers and lapel pins and certificates signed by the mayor. They also get brownie points with their bosses. Hopefully the kids get something out of it too.'

I thought of Bruno, the psychopath, working with homeless children.

'Is there any sort of screening?'

'The usual. Interviews, some paper-and-pencil tests. You know, dear boy, what that kind of thing is worth.'

I nodded.

'Still, like I said, we never got any complaints. I'd have to give the place a B-minus, Alex. The major problem is that it's too big of an operation for the kids to get any personalized attention. A good foster home would definitely be preferable to having four to five hundred kids in one place at the same time — that's how many he's got. Aside from that, La Casa is as good as any.'

'That's good to hear.' But in some perverse way I was disappointed. It would have been nice to find out that the place was a hellhole. Anything to connect it with the three murders. Of course that meant misery for four hundred children. Was I becoming just another member of the child-hating society Olivia had described? Suddenly the strudel tasted like sugar-coated paper and the kitchen seemed oppressively hot.

'So, is there anything else you want to know?'

'No. Thanks.'

'Now, darling.' She turned to Robin. 'Tell about yourself and how you met this impetuous fellow . . .'

We left an hour later. I put my arm around Robin. She let it lay there but was unresponsive. We walked to the car in silence as uncomfortable as a stranger's shoes.

Inside, I asked her:

'What's wrong?'

'Why did you bring me here tonight?'

'I just thought it would be nice . . .'

'Nice talking about murder and child abuse? Alex, that was no social call.'

I had nothing to say so I started the car and pulled away from the curb.

'I'm worried sick about you,' she said. 'The things you were describing in there were hideous. What she said about sharks is true. You're like a little boy adrift on a raft in the middle of the ocean. Oblivious to what's going on around you.'

'I know what I'm doing.'

'Right.' She looked out the window.

'What's wrong with my wanting to get involved in something other than hot tubs and jogging?'

'Nothing. But why can't it be something a little less hazardous than playing Sherlock Holmes? Something you know something about?'

'I'm a fast learner.'

She ignored me. We cruised through darkened empty streets. A light drizzle speckled the windshield.

'I don't enjoy hearing about people getting their faces bashed in. Or children run down by hit-run drivers,' she said.

'That's part of what's out there.' I motioned toward the blackness of the night.

'Well, I don't want any part of it!'

'What you're saying is you'll go along for the ride as long as it's pretty.'

'Oh, Alex! Stop being so damned melodramatic – that's right out of a soap opera.'

'It's true, though, isn't it?'

'No, it's not – and don't try to put me on the defensive. I want the man I first met – someone who was satisfied with himself and not so full of insecurity that he had to run around trying to prove himself. That was what attracted me to you. Now you're like a – a man possessed. Since you've gotten involved in your little intrigues you haven't been there for me. I talk and your mind is somewhere else. It's like I told you before – you're going back to the bad old days.'

There was something to that. The last few mornings had found me waking up early with a taut sense of urgency in my gut, the old obsessive drive to take care of business. Funny thing was, I didn't want to let go of it.

'I promise you,' I told her, 'I'll be careful.'

She shook her head in frustration, leaned forward and switched on the radio. Loud.

When we got to her door she gave me a chaste peck on the cheek.

'Can I come in?'

She stared at me for a long moment and gave a resigned smile.

'Oh, hell, why not?'

Upstairs in the loft I watched her undress in the meager share of moonbeam admitted by the skylight. She stood on one foot, undoing her sandal, and her breasts swung low. A diagonal stroke of illumination turned her white, then gray as she pivoted, then invisible as the slipped under the covers. I reached out for her, aroused, and pulled her hand down toward me. She touched me for a second, then removed her fingers, moved them upward, let them settle around my neck. I buried myself in the sanctuary between her shoulder and the arching sweetness under her chin.

We fell asleep that way.

In the morning her side of the bed was empty. I heard rumbling and grinding and knew she was downstairs in the shop.

I got dressed, descended the narrow stairs and joined her. She was wearing bib overalls and a man's work shirt. Her mouth was covered with a bandanna, her eyes goggled.

The air was full of wood dust.

'I'll call you later,' I shouted over the din of the table saw.

She stopped for a moment, waved, then resumed working. I left her surrounded by her tools, her machines, her art.

15

I CALLED MILO at the station and gave him a full report of my interview with Raquel Ochoa and the Casa de los Niños connection, including the information given to me by Olivia.

'I'm impressed,' he said. 'You missed your calling.'

'So what do you think? Shouldn't this McCaffrey be looked into?'

'Wait a minute, friend. The man takes care of four hundred kids and one of them is killed in an accident. That's not evidence of major mayhem.'

'But that kid happened to be a student of Elena Gutierrez. Which means she probably discussed him with Handler. Not long after his death Bruno began volunteering at the place. A coincidence?'

'Probably not. But you don't understand the way things work around here. I am in the toilet with this case. So far those bank records are showing nothing – everything in both the accounts looks kosher. I've got more work to do on it, but singlehanded it takes time. Every day the captain looks me up and down with that *No-progress, Sturgis?* stare. I feel like a kid who hasn't done his homework. I expect him to pull me off the case any day and stick me on some garbage detail.'

'If things are so screwed up I'd expect you to jump for joy at the prospect of a new lead.'

'That's right. A lead. Not conjecture or a string of flimsy associations.'

'They don't look that damned flimsy to me.'

'Look at it this way – I start snooping around about McCaffrey, who's got connections from Downtown all the way to Malibu. He places a few strategic phone calls – no one can accuse him of obstructing justice because I've got no legitimate reason to be investigating him – and I'm yanked off the case faster than you can spit.'

'All right,' I conceded, 'but what about the Mexican thing? The guy was down there for years. Then all of a sudden he leaves, surfaces in LA, and becomes a hotshot.'

'Upward mobility is no felony, and sometimes a cigar is a cigar, Dr Freud.'

'Shit. I can't stand it when you get overly cute.'

'Alex, please. My life is far from rosy. I don't need crap from you on top of it all.'

I seemed to be developing a talent for alienating those close to me. I had yet to call Robin, to find out where last night's dreams had led her.

'I'm sorry. I guess I'm over-involved.'

He didn't argue.

'You've done good work. Been a big help. Sometimes things don't fall into place just because you do a good job.'

'So what are you going to do? Drop it?'

'No. I'll look into McCaffrey's background – quietly. Especially the Mexican bit. I'm going to continue sifting through Handler and Bruno's financial records and I'll add Gutierrez's to that. I'm even going to call the Malibu Sheriff Station and get copies of the accident report on that kid. What did you say his name was?'

'Nemeth.'

'Fine. That should be easy enough.'

'Is there anything else you want from me?'

'What? Oh. No, nothing. You've done a great job, Alex. I want you to know I really mean that. I'll take it from here. Why don't you take it easy for a while?'

'OK,' I said without enthusiasm. 'But keep me posted.'

'I will,' he promised. 'Bye.'

The voice on the other end was female and very professional. It greeted me with the sing-song lilt of a detergent jingle, an isn't-life-wonderful buoyancy that bordered on the obscene.

'Good morning! La Casa!'

'Good morning. I'd like to speak to someone about becoming a member of the Gentlemen's Brigade.'

'Just one moment, sir!'

In twenty seconds a male voice came on the line.

'Tim Kruger. Can I help you?'

'I'd like to talk about joining the Gentlemen's Brigade.'

'Yes, sir. And what corporation do you represent?'

'None. I'm inquiring as an individual.'

'Oh. I see.' The voice lost a touch of its friendliness. Disruption of routine did that to some people – threw them off, made them wary.

'And your name, please.'

'Dr Alexander Delaware.'

It must have been the title that did it because he shifted gears again, immediately.

'Good morning, Doctor. How are you today?'

'Just fine, thank you.'

'Terrific. And what kind of doctor are you, if I might ask?'

You might.

'Child psychologist. Retired.'

'Excellent. We don't get many mental health professionals volunteering. I'm an MFCC myself, in charge of screening and counseling at La Casa.'

'I'd imagine most of them would consider it too much like work,' I said. 'Being away from the field for a while, the idea of working with children again appeals to me.'

'Wonderful. And what led you to La Casa?'

'Your reputation. I've heard you do good work. And you're well organized.'

'Well, thank you, Doctor. We *do* try to do well by our kids!'

'I'm sure you do.'

'We give group tours for prospective Gentlemen. The next one is scheduled a week from this Friday.'

'Let me check my calendar.' I left the phone, looked out the window, did a half-dozen knee bends, and came back. 'I'm sorry, Mr Kruger. That's a bad day for me. When's the next one?'

'Three weeks later.'

'That's such a long way off. I was hoping to get going sooner.' I tried to sound wistful and just a little impatient.

'Hmm. Well, Doctor, if you don't mind something a bit more impromptu than the group orientation, I can give you a personalized tour. There'll be no way to assemble the video show in time, but as a psychologist you know a lot of that stuff, anyway.'

'That sounds just fine.'

'In fact, if you're free this afternoon, I could arrange it for then. Reverend Gus is here today – he likes to meet all potential Gentlemen – and that's not always the case, what with his travel schedule. He's taping Merv Griffin this week, then flying to New York for an "A.M. America."'

He imparted the news of McCaffrey's television activities with the solemnity of a crusader unveiling the Holy Grail.

'Today would be perfect.'

'Excellent. Around three?'

'Three it is.'

'Do you know where we are?'

'Not exactly. In Malibu?'

'In Malibu Canyon.' He gave me directions, then added: 'While you're there you can fill out our screening questionnaires. It would be a formality in a case such as yours, Doctor, but we do have to go through the motions. Though I don't imagine psychological tests would be very valid for screening a psychologist, would they?'

'I don't imagine so. We write 'em, we can subvert 'em.'

He laughed, straining to be collegial.

'Any other questions?'

'I don't think so.'

'Terrific. I'll see you at three.'

Malibu is as much an image as it is a place. The image is beamed into the living rooms of America on TV, splashed across the movie screen, etched into the grooves of LPs and emblazoned on the covers of trashy paperbacks. The image is one of endless stretches of sand; oiled, naked brown bodies; volleyball on the beach; sun-bleached hair; making love under a blanket with coital cadence timed to match the in-and-out of the tide; million-dollar shacks that teeter on pilings sunken into terra that isn't firma and, in fact, does the hula after a hard rain; Corvettes, seaweed and cocaine.

All of that is valid. But limited.

There's another Malibu, a Malibu that encompasses the canyons and dirt roads that struggle through the Santa Monica mountain range. This Malibu has no ocean. What little water it does possess comes in the form of streams that trickle through shaded gullies and disappear when the temperature rises. There are some houses in this Malibu, situated near the main canyon road, but there remain miles of wilderness. There are still mountain lions roaming the more remote regions of this Malibu, and packs of coyotes that prowl at night, making off with a chicken, a possum, a fat toad. There are shady groves where the tree frogs breed so abundantly that you step into them thinking your foot is resting on soft, gray earth. Until it moves. There are lots of snakes – kings, garters and rattlers – in this Malibu. And secluded ranches where people live under the illusion that the latter half of the twentieth century never occurred. Bridle trails punctuated by steaming mounds of horse droppings. Goats. Tarantulas.

There are also lots of rumors surrounding the second, beachless Malibu. Of ritual murders carried out by Satanic cults. Of bodies that will never – can never be found. Of people lost while hiking and never heard from again. Horror stories, but perhaps just as valid as Beach Blanket Bingo.

I turned off Pacific Coast Highway, up Rambla Pacifica, and traversed the boundary from one Malibu to the other. The Seville climbed the steep grade with ease. I had Django Reinhardt on the tape deck and the music of the Gipsy was in synch with the emptiness that unfolded before my windshield – the serpentine ribbon of highway, assaulted by the relentless Pacific sun one moment and shaded by giant eucalyptus the next. A dehydrated ravine to one side, a sheer drop into space on the other. A road that urged the weary traveler to keep going, that offered promises it could never keep.

I had slept fitfully the night before, thinking of Robin and myself, seeing the faces of children – Melody Quinn, the countless patients I had treated over the last ten years, the remains of a boy named Nemeth, who had died just a few miles up this same road. What had been his last vision, I wondered, what impulse had crossed a crucial synapse at the last possible moment before a giant machine-monster roared down on him from nowhere . . . And what had led him to walk this lonesome stretch of road in the dead of night?

Now, fatigue, nursed by the monotony of the journey, was tracing a slow but inexorable passage along my spine, so that I had to fight to remain alert. I turned the music louder and opened all the windows in the car. The air smelled clean, but tinged with the odor of something burning – a distant bridge?

So occupied was I in the struggle for clarity of consciousness that I almost missed the sign the county had erected announcing the exit for La Casa de los Niños in two miles.

The turnoff itself was easy to miss, only a few hundred yards past a hairpin bend in the road. The road was narrow, barely wide enough for two vehicles to pass in opposite directions, and heavily shadowed by trees. It rose a half-mile at an unrelenting incline, steep enough to discourage any but the most purposeful foot traveler. Clearly the site had never been meant to attract the walkin trade. Perfect for a labor camp, work farm, detention center, or any nexus of activity not meant for the prying eyes of strangers.

The access road ended at a twelve-foot-high-barrier of chain link. Four-foot-high letters spelled out La Casa de los Niños in polished aluminum. A hand-painted sign of two huge hands holding four children – white, black, brown and yellow – rose to the right. A guardhouse was ten feet on the other side of the fence. The uniformed man inside took note of me, then spoke to me through a squawk box attached to the gate.

'Can I help you?' The voice came out steely and mechanical, like human utterance pureed into bytes, fed into a computer and regurgitated.

'Dr Delaware. Here for a three o'clock appointment with Mr Kruger.'

The gate slid open.

The Seville was allowed a brief roll until it was stopped by an orange and white striped mechanical arm.

'Good afternoon, Doctor.'

The guard was young, mustachioed, solemn. His uniform was dark gray, matching his stare. The sudden smile didn't fool me. He was looking me over.

'You'll be meeting Tim at the administration building. That's straight up this way and take the road to the left. You can park in the visitors' lot.'

'Thank you.'

'You're quite welcome, Doctor.'

He pushed a button and the striped arm rose in salute.

* * *

The administration building looked like it had once served a similar purpose during the days of Japanese internment. It had the low-slung, angry look of military architecture, but there was no doubt that the paint job — a mural of a baby blue sky filled with cotton candy clouds — was a contemporary creation.

The front office was paneled in cheap imitation oak and occupied by a grandmotherly type in a colorless cotton smock.

I announced myself and received a grandmotherly smile for my efforts.

'Tim will be right with you. Won't you please sit down and make yourself comfortable.'

There was little of interest to look at. The prints on the walls looked as if they'd been purloined from a motel. There was a window but it afforded a view of the parking lot. In the distance was a thick growth of forest — eucalyptus, cypress, and cedar — but from where I sat only the bottoms of the trees were visible, an uninterrupted stretch of gray-brown. I tried to busy myself with a two-year-old copy of *California Highways*.

It wasn't much of a wait.

A minute after I'd sat down the door opened and a young man came out.

'Dr Delaware?'

I stood.

'Tim Kruger.' We shook hands.

He was short, mid-to-late twenties, and built like a wrestler, all hard and knobby and endowed with just that extra bit of muscle in all the strategic places. He had a face that was well formed, but overly stolid, like a Ken doll that hadn't been allowed to bake sufficiently. Strong chin, small ears, prominent straight nose of a shape that foreshadowed bulbousness in middle age, an outdoorsman's tan, yellowish-brown eyes under heavy brows, a low forehead almost totally hidden by a thick wave of sandy hair. He wore wheat-colored slacks, a light blue short-sleeved shirt and a blue-and-brown tie. Clipped to the corner of his collar was a badge that said T. Kruger, MA, MFCC, Director, Counseling.

'I was expecting someone quite a bit older, Doctor. You told me you were retired.'

'I am. I believe in taking it early, when I can enjoy it.'

He laughed heartily.

'There's something to be said for that. I trust you had no trouble finding us?'

'No. Your directions were excellent.'

'Great. We can begin the tour, if you'd like. Reverend Gus is on the grounds somewhere. He should be back to meet you by four.'

He held the door for me.

We crossed the parking lot and stepped onto a walkway of crushed gravel.

'La Casa,' he began, 'is situated on twenty-seven acres. If we stop right here, we can get a pretty good view of the entire layout.'

We were at the top of a rise, looking down on buildings, a playground, spiraling trails, a curtain of mountains in the background.

'Out of those twenty-seven, only five are actually fully developed. The rest is wide-open space, which we believe is great for the kids, many of whom come from the inner city.' I could make out the shapes of children, walking in groups, playing ball, sitting alone on the grass. 'To the north' – he pointed to an expanse of open fields – 'is what we call the Meadow. It's mostly alfalfa and weeds right now, but there are plans to begin a vegetable garden this summer. To the south is the Grove.' He indicated the forest I'd seen from the office. 'It's protected timberland, perfect for nature hikes. There's a surprising abundance of wildlife out there. I'm from the Northwest, myself, and before I got here I used to think the wildest life in LA was all on the Sunset Strip.'

I smiled.

'Those buildings over there are the dorms.'

He swiveled around and pointed to a group of ten large quonset huts. Like the administration building, they'd been gone at with the freewheeling paint brush, the corrugated iron sides festooned with rainbow-hued patterns, the effect bizarrely optimistic.

He turned again and I let my gaze follow his arm.

'That's our Olympic-sized pool. Donated by Majestic Oil.' The pool shimmered green, a hole in the earth filled with lime jello. A solitary swimmer sliced through the water, cutting a foamy pathway. 'And over there are the infirmary and the school.'

I noticed a grouping of cinder-block buildings at the far end of the campus where the perimeter of the central hub met the edge of the 'Grove.' He didn't say what they were.

'Let's take a look at the dorms.'

I followed him down the hill, taking in the idyllic panorama. The grounds were well tended, the place bustling with activity but seemingly well organized.

Kruger walked with long, muscular strides, chin to the

wind, rattling off facts and figures, describing the philosophy of the institution as one that combined 'structure and the reassurance of routine with a creative environment that encourages healthy development,' He was resolutely positive – about La Casa, his job, the Reverend Gus, and the children. The sole exception was a grave lament about the difficulties of coordinating 'optimal care' with running the financial affairs of the institution on a day-to-day basis. Even this was followed, however, by a statement stressing his understanding of economic realities in the eighties and a few upbeat paeans to the free-enterprise system.

He was well trained.

The interior of the bright pink quonset hut was cold, flat white over a dark plank floor. The dorm was empty and our footsteps echoed. There was a metallic smell in the air. The children's beds were iron double bunks arranged, barracks style, perpendicular to the walls, accompanied by foot lockers and bracket shelves bolted to the metal siding. There was an attempt at decoration – some of the children had hung up pictures of comic book superheroes, athletes, *Sesame Street* characters – but the absence of family pictures or other evidence of recent, intimate human connection was striking.

I counted sleeping space for fifty children.

'How do you keep that many kids organized?'

'It's a challenge,' he admitted, 'but we've been pretty successful. We use volunteer counselors from UCLA, Northridge, and other colleges. They get intro psych credit, we get free help. We'd love a full time professional staff but it's fiscally impossible. We've got it staffed two counselors to a dorm, and we train them to use behavior mod – I hope you're not opposed to that.'

'Not if it's used properly.'

'Oh, very definitely. I couldn't agree with you more. We minimize heavy aversives, use token economies, lots of positive reinforcements. It requires supervision – that's where I come in.'

'You seem to have a good handle on things.'

'I try.' He gave an aw, shucks grin. 'I wanted to go for a doctorate but I didn't have the bucks.'

'Where were you studying?'

'U. of Oregon. I got an MA there – in counseling ed. Before that, a BA in psych from Jedson College.'

'I thought everyone at Jedson was rich.' The small college outside of Seattle had a reputation as a haven for the offspring of the wealthy.

'That's almost true,' he grinned. 'The place was a country club. I got in on an athletic scholarship. Track and baseball. In my junior year I tore a ligament and suddenly I was *persona non grata*.' His eyes darkened momentarily, smoldering with the memory of almost-buried injustice. 'Anyway, I like what I'm doing – plenty of responsibility and decision-making.'

There was a rustling sound at the far end of the room. We both turned toward it and saw movement beneath the blankets of one of the lower bunks.

'Is that you, Rodney?'

Kruger walked to the bunk and tapped a wriggling lump. A boy sat up, holding the covers up to his chin. He was chubby, black and looked around twelve, but his exact age was impossible to gage, for his face bore the telltale stigmata of Down's syndrome: Elongated cranium, flattened features, deep-set eyes spaced close together, sloping brow, low-set ears, protruding tongue. And an expression of bafflement so typical of the retarded.

'Hello, Rodney.' Kruger spoke softly. 'What's the matter?'

I had followed him and the boy looked at me questioningly.

'It's all right, Rodney. He's a friend. Now tell me what's the matter.'

'Rodney sick.' The words were slurred.

'What kind of sickness?'

'Tummy hurt.'

'Hmm. We'll have to have the doctor look at you when he makes his visit.'

'No!' the boy screamed. 'No docka!'

'Now, Rodney!' Kruger was patient. 'If you're sick you're going to have to get a checkup.'

'No docka!'

'All right, Rodney, all right.' Kruger spoke soothingly. He reached out and touched the boy softly on the top of the head. Rodney went hysterical. His eyes popped out and his chin trembled. He cried out and lurched backward so quickly that he hit the rear of his head on the metal bedpost. He yanked the covers over his face, uttering an unintelligible wail of protest.

Kruger turned to me and sighed. He waited until the boy calmed down and then spoke to him again.

'We'll discuss the doctor later, Rodney. Now where are you supposed to be? Where's your group right now?'

'Snack.'

'Aren't you hungry?'

The boy shook his head.

'Tummy hurts.'

'Well you can't just lie here by yourself. Either come to the infirmary and we'll call someone to have a look at you or get up and join your group for snack.'

'No docka.'

'OK. No doctor. Now get up.'

The boy crawled out of bed, away from us. I could see now that he was older than I'd thought. Sixteen at least, with the beginning of beard growth dotting his chin. He stared at me, eyes wide in fright.

'This is a friend, Rodney. Mr Delaware.'

'Hello, Rodney.' I held out my hand. He looked at it and shook his head.

'Be friendly, Rodney. That's how we earn our goodie points, remember?'

A shake of the head.

'Come on, Rodney, shake hands.'

But the retarded boy was resolute. When Kruger took a step forward he retreated, holding his hands in front of his face.

It went on that way for several moments, a flat-out contest of wills. Finally Kruger gave in.

'OK, Rodney,' he said softly, 'we'll forget social skills for today because you're ill. Now run along and join your group.'

The boy backed away from us, circling the bed in a wide arc. Still shaking his head and holding his arms in front of him like a punchy fighter, he moved away. When he was close to the door he turned, bolted and half ran, half waddled out, disappearing into the sun's glare.

Kruger turned to me and smiled weakly.

'He's one of our more difficult ones. Seventeen and functioning like a three year old.'

'He seems to be really afraid of doctors.'

'He's afraid of lots of things. Like most Downs kids he's had plenty of medical problems – cardiac, infections, dental complications. Add that to the distorted thinking going on in that little head and it builds up. Have you had much experience with MRs?'

'Some.'

'I've worked with hundreds of them and I can't remember one who didn't have serious emotional problems. You know, the public thinks they're just like any other kids, but slower. It ain't so.'

A trace of irritation had crept into his voice. I put it down to the humiliation of losing at psychic poker to the retarded boy.

'Rodney's come a long way,' he said. 'When he first got here he wasn't even toilet-trained. After thirteen foster homes.' He shook his head. 'It's really pathetic. Some of the people the county gives kids to aren't fit to raise dogs, let alone children.'

He looked ready to launch into a speech, but stopped and slipped his smile back on quickly. 'Many of the kids we get are low-probability adoption cases – MR, defective, mixed race, in and out of foster homes, or thrown on the trash heap by their families. When they come here they have no conception of socially appropriate behavior, hygiene, or basic day-to-day living skills. Quite often we're starting from ground zero. But we're pleased at our progress. One of the students is publishing a study on our results.'

'That's a great way to collect data.'

'Yes. And quite frankly, it helps us raise money, which is often the bottom line, Doctor, when you want to keep a great place like La Casa going. Come on.' He took my arm. 'Let's see the rest of the grounds.'

We headed toward the pool.

'From what I hear,' I said, 'Reverend McCaffrey is an excellent fund-raiser.'

Kruger gave me a sidelong glance, evaluating the intent of my words.

'He is. He's a marvelous person and it comes across. And it takes most of his time. But it's still difficult. You know, he ran another children's home in Mexico, but he had to close it down. There was no government support and the attitude of the private sector there was let the peasants starve.'

We were poolside now. The water reflected the forest, green-black dappled with streaks of emerald. There was a strong odor of chlorine mixed with sweat. The lone swimmer was still in the water doing laps – using a butterfly stroke with a lot of muscle behind it.

'Hey, Jimbo!' Kruger called.

The swimmer reached the far end, raised his head out of the water and saw the counselor's wave. He glided effortlessly toward us and pulled himself waist-high out of the water. He was in his early forties, bearded and sinewy. His sun-baked body was covered with wet, matted hair.

'Hey, Tim.'

'Dr Delaware, this is Jim Halstead, our head coach. Jim, Dr Alexander Delaware.'

'Actually your only coach.' Halstead spoke in a deep voice that emerged from his abdomen. 'I'd shake your hand, but mine's kinda clammy.'

'That's fine.' I smiled.

'Dr Delaware's a child psychologist, Jim, He's touring La Casa as a prospective Gentleman.'

'Great to meet you, Doc, and I hope you join us. It's beautiful out here, isn't it?' He extended a long, brown arm to the Malibu sky.

'Gorgeous.'

'Jim used to work in the inner city,' said Kruger. 'At Manual Arts High. Then he got smart.'

Halstead laughed.

'It took me too long. I'm an easy-going guy but when an ape with a knife threatened me after I asked him to do pushups, that was it.'

'I'm sure you don't get that here,' I said.

'No way,' he rumbled. 'The little guys are great.'

'Which reminds me, Jim,' interrupted Kruger, 'I've got to talk to you about working out a program for Rodney Broussard. Something to build up his confidence.'

'You bet.'

'Check you later, Jim.'

'Right on. Come back again, Doc.'

The hirsute body entered the water, a sleek torpedo, and swam otterlike along the bottom of the pool.

We took a quarter-mile walk around the periphery of the institution. Kruger showed me the infirmary, a spotlessly white, smallish room with an examining table and a cot, sparkling of chrome and reeking of antiseptic. It was empty.

'We have a half-time RN who works mornings. For obvious reasons we can't afford a doctor.'

I wondered why Majestic Oil or some other benefactor couldn't donate a part-time physician's salary.

'But we're lucky to have a roster of volunteer docs, some of the finest in the community, who rotate through.'

As we walked, groups of youngsters and counselors passed us. Kruger waved, the counsellors returned the greeting. More often than not the children were unresponsive. As Olivia had predicted and Kruger had confirmed, most had obvious physical or mental handicaps. Boys seemed to outnumber girls by about three to one and the majority of the kids were black or Hispanic.

Kruger ushered me into the cafeteria, which was high-ceilinged, stucco-walled and meticulously clean. Unspeaking Mexican women waited impassively behind a glass partition, serving tongs in hand. The food was typical institutional fare – stew, creative use of ground meat, jello, overcooked vegetables in thick sauce.

We sat down at a picnic-type table and Kruger went behind the food counter to a back room. He emerged with a tray of Danish pastries and coffee. The baked goods looked high-quality. I hadn't seen anything like them behind the glass.

Across the room a group of children sat at a table eating and drinking under the watchful eyes of two student counselors. Actually, attempting to eat was more accurate. Even from a distance I could see that they suffered from cerebral palsy, some of them spastically rigid, others jerking in involuntary movements of head and limb, and had to struggle to get the food from table to mouth. The counselors watched and sometimes offered verbal encouragement. But they didn't help physically and lots of custard and jello was ending up on the floor.

Kruger bit with gusto into a chocolate Danish. I took a

cinnamon roll and played with it. He poured us coffee and asked me if I had any questions.

'No. Everything looks very impressive.'

'Great. Then let met tell you about the Gentlemen's Brigade.'

He gave me a canned history of the volunteer group, stressing the wisdom of the Reverend Gus in enlisting the participation of local corporations.

'The Gentlemen are mature, successful individuals. They represent the only chance most of these kids have of being exposed to a stable male role model. They're accomplished, the cream of our society and as such give the children a rare glimpse of success. It teaches them that it's indeed possible to be successful. They spend time with the kids here, at La Casa, and take them off-campus – to sporting events, movies, plays, Disneyland. And to their homes for family dinners. It gives the children access to a lifestyle they've never known. And it's fulfilling for the men, as well. We ask for a six-month commitment and sixty per cent sign up for second and third hitches.'

'Can't it be frustrating, for the kids,' I asked, 'to get a taste of the good life that's so far out of their grasp?'

He was ready for that one.

'Good question, Doctor. But we don't emphasize *anything* being out of our kids' reach. We want them to feel that the only thing limiting them is their own lack of motivation. That they must take responsibility for themselves. That they can reach the sky – that's the name of a book written for children by Reverend Gus. *Touch the Sky*. It's got cartoons, games, coloring pages. It teaches them a positive message.'

It was Norman Vincent Peale spiced up with humanistic

psychological jargon. I looked over and saw the palsied children battling with their food. No amount of exposure to the members of the privileged class was going to bring them membership in the Yacht Club, an invitation to the Blue Ribbon Upper Crust Debutante Ball of San Marino, or a Mercedes in the garage.

There were limits to the power of positive thinking.

But Kruger had his script and he stuck to it. He was damned good. I had to admit, he'd read all the right journals and could quote statistics like a Rand Corporation whiz kid. It was the kind of spiel designed to get you reaching for your wallet.

'Can I get you anything else?' he asked after finishing a second pastry. I hadn't touched my first.

'No thanks.'

'Let's head back, then. It's almost four.'

We passed through the rest of the place quickly. There was a chicken coop where two dozen hens pecked at the bars like Skinnerian pigeons, a goat at the end of a long leash eating trash, hamsters treading endlessly on plastic wheels and a basset hound who bayed half-heartedly at the darkening sky. The schoolroom had once been a barracks, the gym a World War II storage depot, I was informed. Both had been remodeled artfully and creatively on a budget, by someone with a good feel for camouflage. I complimented the designer.

'That's the work of Reverend Gus. His mark is on every square inch of this place. A remarkable man.'

As we headed toward McCaffrey's office I saw, once again, the cinder-block buildings at the edge of the forest. From up close I could see there were four structures, roofed in concrete, windowless, and half-submerged in earth, like bunkers, with tunnel-like ramps sloping down to iron doors. Kruger showed no indication of explaining what they were, so I asked him.

He looked over his shoulder.

'Storage,' he said casually. 'Come on. Let's get back.'

We'd come full circle, back to the cumulus-covered administration building. Kruger escorted me in, shook my hand, told me he hoped to hear from me again and that he'd be dropping off the screening materials while I talked to the Reverend. Then he handed me over to the good graces of Grandma, the receptionist, who tore herself away from her Olivetti and bade me sweetly to wait just a few moments for The Great Man.

I picked up a copy of *Fortune* and worked hard at building an interest in a feature on the future of microprocessors in the tool-and-die industry, but the words blurred and turned into gelatinous gray blobs. Futurespeak did that to me.

I'd barely had a chance to uncross my legs when the door opened. They were big on punctuality here. I'd started to feel like a hunk of raw material – what kind didn't really matter – being whisked along on an assembly line trough, melted, molded, tinkered with, tightened, and inspected.

'Reverend Gus will see you now.' said Grandma.

The time had come, I supposed, for the final polishing.

16

IF WE'D been standing outdoors he would have blocked the sun.

He was six-and-a-half feet tall and weighed well over three hundred pounds, a pear-shaped mountain of pale flesh in a fawn-colored suit, white shirt, and black silk tie the breadth of a hotel hand towel. His tan oxfords were the size of small sailboats, his hands, twin sandbags. He filled the doorway. Black horn-rimmed glasses perched atop a meaty nose that bisected a face as lumpy as tapioca pudding. Wens, moles and enlarged pores trekked their way across the sagging cheeks. There was a hint of Africa in the flatness of his nose, the full lips as dark and moist as raw liver, and the tightly kinked hair the color of rusty pipes. His eyes were pale, almost without color. I'd seen eyes like that before. On mullet, packed in ice.

'Dr Delaware, I'm Augustus McCaffrey.'

His hand devoured mine then released it. His voice was strangely gentle. From the size of him I'd expected something along the lines of a tug horn. What came out was surprisingly lyrical, barely baritone, softened by the lazy cadence of the Deep South – Louisiana, I guessed.

'Come in, won't you?'

I followed him, a Hindu trailing an elephant, into his office. It was large and well windowed but no more elegantly turned out than the waiting room. The walls were sheathed with the same false oak and were devoid of decoration save for a large wooden crucifix above the desk, a Formica-and-steel rectangle that looked like government surplus. The ceiling was low, perforated white squares suspended in a grid of aluminum. There was a door behind the desk.

I sat in one of a trio of vinyl upholstered chairs. He settled himself in a swivel chair that groaned in protest, laced his fingers together and leaned forward across the desk, which now looked like a child's miniature.

'I trust Tim has given you a comprehensive tour and has answered all of your questions.'

'He was very helpful.'

'Good,' he drawled, giving the word three syllables. 'He's a very capable young man. I handpick our staff.' He squinted. 'Just as I handpick all volunteers. We want only the best for our children.'

He sat back and rested his hands on his belly.

'I'm extremely pleased that a man of your stature would consider joining us, Doctor. We've never had a child psychologist in the Gentlemen's Brigade. Tim tells me you're retired.'

He gazed at me jovially. It was clear I was expected to explain myself.

'Yes. That's true.'

'Hmm.' He scratched behind one ear, still smiling. Waiting. I smiled back.

'You know,' he finally said, 'when Tim mentioned your visit I thought your name was familiar. But I couldn't place it. Then it came to me, just a few moments ago. You ran that program for those children who were the victims of that day-care scandal, didn't you?'

'Yes.'

'Wonderful work. How are they doing, the children?'

'Quite well.'

'You — retired soon after the program was over, did you?'

'Yes.'

The enormous head shook sadly.

'Tragic affair. The man killed himself, if I recall.'

'He did.'

'Doubly tragic. The little ones abused like that and a man's life wasted with no chance of salvation. Or,' he smiled, 'to use a more secular term, with no chance of rehabilitation. They're one and the same, salvation and rehabilitation, don't you think, Doctor?'

'I can see similarity in the two concepts.'

'Certainly. It depends upon one's perspective. I confess,' he sighed, 'that I find it difficult, at times, to divorce myself from my religious training when dealing with issues of human relations. I must struggle to do so, of course, in view of our society's abhorrence of even a minimal liaison between church and state.'

He wasn't protesting. The broad face was suffused with calm, nourished by the sweet fruit of martyrdom. He looked at peace with himself, as content as a hippo sunning in a mudhole.

'Do you think the man — the one who killed himself — could have been rehabilitated?' he asked me.

'It's hard to say. I didn't know him. The statistics on treatment of lifelong pedophiles aren't encouraging.'

'Statistics.' He played with the word, letting it roll slowly off his tongue. He enjoyed the sound of his own voice.

'Statistics are cold numbers, aren't they? With no consideration for the individual. And, Tim informs me, on a mathematical level, statistics have no relevance for an individual. Is that correct?'

'That's true.'

'When folks quote statistics, it reminds me of the joke about the Okie – Okie jokes were fashionable before your time – woman who had borne ten children with relative equanimity but who became very agitated upon learning she was pregnant with the eleventh. Her doctor asked her why, after having gone through the travails of pregnancy, labor and delivery ten times, she was suddenly so distraught. And she told him she had read that every eleventh child born in Oklahoma was an Indian, and durned if she was going to raise a redskin!'

He laughed, the belly heaving, the eyes black slits. His glasses slid down his nose and he righted them.

'That, Doctor, sums up my view of statistics. You know, most of the children at La Casa were statistics prior to their coming here – doctor numbers in the Dependency Court files, codes for the DPSS caseworkers to catalog, scores on IQ tests. And those numbers said they were beyond hope. But we take them and we work strenuously to transform those numbers into little *individuals*. I don't care about a child's IQ score, I want to help him claim his birthright as a human being – opportunity, basic health and welfare, and, if you'll permit a clerical lapse, a *soul*. For there is a soul in every single one of those children, even the ones functioning at a vegetative level.'

'I agree that it's good not to be limited by numbers.' His man, Kruger, had been pretty handy with statistics when they served his purpose and I was willing to bet La Casa made use of a computer or two to churn out the right numbers when the occasion called for it.

'Our work is effecting change. It's an alchemy of sorts. Which is why suicide – any suicide – saddens me deeply. For all men are capable of salvation. That man was a quitter, in the ultimate sense. But of course,' he lowered his voice, 'the quitter has become the archetype of modern man, hasn't he, Doctor? It has become fashionable to throw up one's hands after the merest travesty of effort. Everyone wants quick and easy solutions.'

Including, no doubt, those who retired at thirty-two.

'There are miracles happening every day, right on these grounds. Children who've been given up on gain a new sense of themselves. A youngster who is incontinent learns to control his bowels.' He paused, like a politician after an applause line. 'So-called retarded children learn to read and write. Small miracles, perhaps, when measured against a man walking on the moon, or perhaps not.' His eyebrows arched, the thick lips parted to reveal widely spaced, horsey teeth. 'Of course, Doctor, if you find the word miracle unduly sectarian, we can substitute *success*. That is a word the average American can relate to. Success.'

Coming from someone else it could have been a cheap throwaway oration worthy of a Sunday morning Jesus-huckster. But McCaffrey was good and his words carried the conviction of one ordained to carry out a sacred mission.

'May I ask,' he inquired pleasantly, 'why you retired?'

'I wanted a change of pace, Reverend. Time to sort out my values.'

'I understand. Reflection can be profoundly valuable.

211

However, I trust you won't absent yourself from your profession for too long. We need good people in your field.'

He was still preaching, but now mixing it with an ego massage. I understood why the corporate honchos loved him.

'In fact I have begun to miss working with children, which is why I called you.'

'Excellent, excellent. Psychology's loss will be our gain. You worked at Western Pediatric, didn't you? I seem to remember that from the paper.'

'There and in private practice.'

'A first-rate hospital. We send many of our children there when the need for medical attention arises. I'm acquainted with several of the physicians on staff and many of them have been quite generous – giving of themselves.'

'Those are busy men, Reverend; you must be quite persuasive.'

'Not really. However, I do recognize the existence of a basic human need to *give*, an altruistic drive, if you will. I know this flies in the face of the modern psychologies which limit the notion of drive to self-gratification, but I'm convinced I'm right. Altruism is as basic as hunger and thirst. You, for example, satisfied your own altruistic need within the scope of your chosen profession. But when you stopped working, the hunger returned. And here,' he spread his arms, 'you are.'

He opened a drawer of the desk, took out a brochure, and handed it to me. It was glossy and well done, as polished as the quarterly report of an industrial conglomerate.

'On page six you'll see a partial list of our board.'

I found it. For a partial list it was long, running the height of the page in small print. And impressive. It included two county supervisors, a member of the city council, the Mayor, judges, philanthropists, entertainment biggies, attorneys, businessmen, and plenty of MDs, some of whose names I recognized. Like L. Willard Towle.

'Those are all busy men, Doctor. And yet they find the time for our children. Because we know how to tap that inner resource, that well-spring of altruism.'

I flipped through the pages. There was a letter of endorsement from the governor, lots of photographs of children having fun, and even more pictures of McCaffrey. His looming bulk appeared pinstriped on the Donahue show, in tuxedo at a Music Center benefit, in a jogging suit with a group of his young charges at the victory line of the Special Olympics. McCaffrey with TV personalities, civil rights leaders, country singers and bank presidents.

Midway through the brochure I found a shot of McCaffrey in a room I recognized as the lecture hall at Western Pediatric. Next to him, white hair gleaming, was Towle. On the other side was a small man, froggy, squat, grim even as he smiled. The guy with Peter Lorre eyes whose photograph I'd seen in Towle's office. The caption beneath the photo identified him as the Honorable Edwin G. Hayden, supervising judge of the Dependency Court. The occasion was McCaffrey's address to the medical staff on 'Child Welfare: Past, Present and Future.'

'Is Dr Towle very involved in La Casa?' I asked.

'He serves on our board and is one of our rotating physicians. Do you know him?'

'We've met. Casually. I know him by reputation.'

'Yes, an authority on behavioral pediatrics. We find his services invaluable.'

'I'm sure you do.'

He spent the next quarter-hour showing me his book, a soft-covered locally printed volume of saccharine clichés and first-rate graphics. I bought a copy, for fifteen bucks, after he gave me a more sophisticated version of the pitch for cash Kruger had thrown my way. The bargain basement ambience of the office lent credibility to the spiel. Besides, I was OD'ed on positive thinking and it seemed a small price to pay for respite.

He took the three five-dollar bills, folded them and placed them conspicuously in a collection box atop the desk. The receptacle was papered with a drawing of a solemn-looking child with eyes that rivaled Melody Quinn's in size, luminosity and the ability to project a sense of inner hurt.

He stood, thanked me for coming, and took my hand in both of his. 'I hope we see more of you, Doctor. Soon.'

It was my turn to smile.

'Plan on it, Reverend.'

Grandma was ready for me as I stepped into the waiting room, with a sheaf of stapled booklets and two sharpened number two pencils.

'You can fill these out right here, Doctor Delaware,' she said sweetly.

I looked at my watch.

'Gee, it's much later than I thought. I'll have to take a raincheck.'

'But—' She became flustered.

'How about you give them to me to take home? I'll fill them out and mail them back to you.'

'Oh no, I couldn't do that! These are psychological tests!' She clutched the papers to her breast. 'The rules are that you must fill them out here.'

'Well, then, I'll just have to come back.' I started to leave.

'Wait. Let me ask someone. I'll ask Reverend Gus if it's—'

'He told me he was going to retire for a period of meditation. I don't think he wants to be disturbed.'

'Oh.' She was disoriented. 'I must ask someone. You wait right here, Doctor, and I'll find Tim.'

'Sure.'

When she was gone I slipped out the door, unnoticed.

The sun had almost set. It was that transitional time of day when the diurnal palette is slowly scraped dry, colors falling aside to reveal a wash of gray, that ambiguous segment of twilight when everything looks just a little bit fuzzy around the edges.

I walked toward my car unsettled. I'd spent three hours at La Casa and had learned little other than that the Reverend Augustus McCaffrey was a shrewd old boy with overactive charisma glands. He'd taken the time to check me out and wanted me to know it. But only a paranoiac could rightfully see anything ominous in that. He was showing off, displaying how well informed and prepared he was. The same went for his advertising the abundance of friends in high places. It was psychological muscle-flexing. Power respected power, strength gravitated to strength. The more connections McCaffrey could show, the more he was going to get. And that was the way to big bucks. That, and collection boxes illustrated with sad-eyed waifs.

I had the key in the door of the Seville, facing the campus of the institution. It looked empty and still, like a well-run farm after the work's all done. Probably dinner time, with the kids in the cafeteria, the counselors watching, and the Reverend Gus delivering an eloquent benediction.

I felt foolish.

I was about to open the door when I caught a glimpse of a flurry of movement near the forestlike Grove, several hundred feet in the distance. It was hard to be certain, but I though I saw a struggle, heard the sound of muffled cries.

I put the car keys back in my pocket and let the copy of McCaffrey's book drop to the gravel. There was no one else in sight, except for the guard in the booth at the entrance and his attention was focused in the opposite direction. I needed to get closer without being seen. Carefully I made my way down the hill upon which the parking lot sat, staying in the shadow of buildings whenever I could. The shapes in the distance were moving, but slowly.

I pressed myself against the flamingo-pink wall of the southernmost dormitory, as far as I could go without abandoning cover. The ground was moist and mushy, the air rotten with fumes given off by a nearby trash dumpster. Someone had tried to write FUCK in the pink paint, but the corrugated metal was a hostile surface and it came out chicken scratches.

The sounds were clearer and louder now, and they were definitely cries of distress – animal cries, bleating and plaintive.

I made out three silhouettes, two large, one much smaller. The small one seemed to be walking on air.

I inched closer, peering around the corner. The three figures passed before me, perhaps thirty feet away moving along the southern border of the institution. They walked across the concrete of the pool deck and came under the illumination of a yellow anti-bug light affixed to the eave of the poolhouse.

It was then that I saw them clearly, flash frozen in the lemon light.

The small figure was Rodney and he'd appeared suspended because he was being carried in the firm grip of Halstead, the coach, and Tim Kruger. They grasped him under the arms so that his feet dangled inches from the ground.

They were strong men but the boy was giving them a struggle. He squirmed and kicked like a ferret in a trap, opened his mouth and let out a wordless moan. Halstead clamped a hairy hand over the mouth but the child managed to wrench free and scream again. Halstead stifled him once more and it went on that way as they retreated out of the light and my line of vision, the alternating sounds of cries and muted grunts a crazy trumpet solo that grew faint then faded away.

Then it was silent and I was alone, back to the wall, bathed in sweat, clothes clammy and sticking to me. I wanted to perform some heroic act, to break out of the deadening inertia that had settled around my ankles like quick-drying cement.

But I couldn't save anybody. I was a man out of his element. If I followed them there'd be rational explanations for everything and a herd of guards to quickly turn me out, taking careful note of my face so that the gates of La Casa would never again open before it.

I couldn't afford that, just yet.

So I stood, up against the wall, rooted in the ghost-town stillness, feeling sick and helpless. I clenched my fists until they hurt and listened to the dry urgent sound of my own breathing like the scraping of boots against alley stones.

I forced the image of the struggling boy out of my mind.

When I was sure it was safe I sneaked back to my car.

217

17

THE FIRST TIME I called, at 8 A.M., nobody answered. A half-hour later the University of Oregon was open for business.

'Good morning, Education.'

'Good morning. This is Dr Gene Adler calling from Los Angeles. I'm with the Department of Psychiatry at Western Pediatric Medical Center in Los Angeles. We're currently recruiting for a counseling position. One of our applicants has listed on his resumé the fact that he received a master's degree in counseling education from your department. As part of our routine credentials check I was wondering if you could verify that for me.'

'I'll switch you to Marianne, in transcripts.'

Marianne had a warm, friendly voice but when I repeated my story for her she told me, firmly, that a written request would be necessary.

'That's fine with me,' I said, 'but that will take time. The job for which this individual has applied is being competitively sought by many people. We were planning to make a decision within twenty-four hours. It's just a formality – verification of records – but our liability insurance stipulates that we have to do it. If you'd like I can have the applicant call you to release the information. It's in his best interests.'

'Well . . . I suppose it'll be all right. All you want to know

218

is if this person received a degree, right? Nothing more personal than that?'

'That's correct.'

'Who's the applicant?'

'A gentleman named Timothy Kruger. His records list an MA four years ago.'

'One moment.'

She was gone for ten minutes, and when she returned to the phone she sounded upset.

'Well, Doctor, your formality has turned out to be of some value. There is no record of a degree being granted to a person of that name in the last ten years. We do have a record of a Timothy Jay Kruger attending one semester of graduate school four years ago, but his major wasn't in counseling, it was in secondary teaching, and he left after that single semester.'

'I see. That's quite disturbing. Any indication of why he left?'

'None. Does that really matter now?'

'No, I suppose not – you're absolutely certain about this? I wouldn't want to jeopardize Mr Kruger's career—'

'There's no doubt whatsoever.' She sounded offended. 'I checked and double-checked, Doctor, and then I asked the head of the department, Dr Gowdy, and he was positive no Timothy Kruger graduated from here.'

'Well, that settles it, doesn't it? And it certainly casts a new light on Mr Kruger. Could you check one more thing?'

'What's that?'

'Mr Kruger also listed a BA in psychology from Jedson College in Washington State. Would your records contain that kind of information as well?'

'It would be on his application to graduate school. We should have transcripts, but I don't see why you need to—'

'Marianne, I'm going to have to report this to the State Board of Behavioral Science examiners, because state licensure is involved. I want to know all the facts.'

'I see. Let me check.'

This time she was back in a moment.

'I've got his transcript from Jedson here, Doctor. He did receive a BA but it wasn't in psychology.'

'What was it in?'

She laughed.

'Dramatic arts. Acting.'

I called the school where Raquel Ochoa taught and had her pulled out of class. Despite that, she seemed pleased to hear from me.

'Hi. How's the investigation going?'

'We're getting closer,' I lied. 'That's what I called you about. Did Elena keep a diary or any kind of records around the apartment?'

'No. Neither of us were diary writers. Never had been.'

'No notebooks, tapes, anything?'

'The only tapes I saw were music – she had a tape deck in her new car – and some cassettes Handler gave her to help her relax. For sleep. Why?'

I ignored the question.

'Where are her personal effects?'

'You should know that. The police had them. I suppose they gave them back to her mother. What's going on? Have you found out something?'

'Nothing definite. Nothing I can talk about. We're trying to fit things together.'

'I don't care how you do it, just catch him and punish him. The monster.'

I dredged up a rancid lump of false confidence and smeared it all over my voice. 'We will.'

'I know you will.'

Her faith made me uneasy.

'Raquel, I'm away from the files. Do you have her mother's home address handy?'

'Sure.' She gave it to me.

'Thanks.'

'Are you planning on visiting Elena's family?'

'I thought it would be helpful to talk to them in person.'

There was silence on the other end. Then she spoke.

'They're good people. But they may shut you out.'

'It's happened before.'

She laughed.

'I think you'd do better if I went with you. I'm like a member of the family.'

'It's no hassle for you?'

'No. I want to help. When do you want to go?'

'This afternoon.'

'Fine. I'll get off early. Tell them I'm not feeling well. Pick me up at two thirty. Here's my address.'

She lived in a modest West LA neighborhood not far from where the Santa Monica and San Diego Freeways merged in blissful union, an area of crackerbox apartment buildings populated by singles who couldn't afford the Marina.

She was visible a block away, waiting by the curb, dressed

in a pigeon-blood crepe blouse, blue denim skirt and tooled western boots.

She got in the car, crossed a pair of unstockinged brown legs and smiled.

'Hi.'

'Hi. Thanks for doing this.'

'I told you, this is something I want to do. I want to feel useful.'

I drove north, toward Sunset. There was jazz on the radio, something free form and atonal, with saxophone solos that sounded like police sirens and drums like a heart in arrest.

'Change it, if you'd like.'

She pushed some buttons, fiddled with the dial, and found a mellow rock station. Someone was singing about lost love and old movies and tying it all together.

'What do you want to know from them?' she asked, settling back.

'If Elena told them anything about her work – specifically the child who died. Anything about Handler.'

There were lots of questions in her eyes but she kept them there.

'Talking about Handler will be especially touchy. The family didn't like the idea of her going out with a man who was so much older. And,' she hesitated, 'an Anglo, to boot. In situations like that the tendency is to deny the whole thing, not even to acknowledge it. It's cultural.'

'To some extent it's human.'

'To some extent, maybe. We Hispanics do it more. Part of it is Catholicism. The rest is our Indian blood. How can you survive in some of the desolate regions we've lived in without denying reality? You smile, and pretend it's lush and fertile and there's plenty of water and food, and the desert doesn't seem so bad.'

'Any suggestions how I might get around the denial?'

'I don't know.' She sat with her hands folded in her lap, a proper schoolgirl. 'I think I'd better start the talking. Cruz – Elena's mom – always liked me. Maybe I can get through. But don't expect miracles.'

She had little to worry about on that account.

Echo Park is a chunk of Latin America transported to the dusty, hilly streets that, buttressed by crumbling concrete embankments on either side of Sunset Boulevard, rise between Hollywood and downtown. The streets have names like Macbeth and Macduff, Bonnybrae and Laguna, but are anything but poetic. They climb to the south and dip down into the Union District ghetto. To the north they climb, feeding into the tiny lake-centered park that gives the area its name, continue through arid trails, get lost in an incongruous wilderness that looks down upon Dodger Stadium, and Elysian Park, home of the Los Angeles Police Academy.

Sunset changes when it leaves Hollywood and enters Echo Park. The porno theatres and by-the-hour motels yield to *botánicas* and *bodegas*, outlets for Discos Latinos, an infinite array of food stands – taco joints, Peruvian seafood parlors, fast-food franchises – and first-rate Latino restaurants, beauty shops with windows guarded by styrofoam skulls wearing blond Dynel wigs, Cuban bakeries, storefront medical and legal clinics, bars and social clubs. Like many poor areas, the Echo Park part of Sunset is continually clogged with foot traffic.

The Seville cut a slow swath through the afternoon mob. There was a mood on the boulevard as urgent and sizzling as the molten lard spitting forth from the fryers of the food stands. There were homeboys sporting homemade tattoos, fifteen-year-old mothers wheeling fat babies in rickety strollers that threatened to fall apart at every curb, rummies, pushers, starched-collared immigration lawyers, cleaning women on shore leave, grandmothers, flower vendors, a never-ending stream of brown-eyed children.

'It's very weird,' said Raquel, 'coming back here. In a fancy car.'

'How long have you been gone?'

'A thousand years.'

She didn't seem to want to say more so I dropped it. At Fairbanks Place she told me to turn left. The Gutierrez home was at the end of an alley-sized twister that peaked, then turned into a dirt road just above the foothills. A quarter mile further and we'd have been the only humans in the world.

I'd noticed that she had a habit of biting herself – lips, fingers, knuckles – when she was nervous. And she was gnawing at her thumb right now. I wondered what kind of hunger it satisfied.

I drove cautiously – there was scarcely room for a single vehicle – passing young men in T-shirts working on old cars with the dedication of priests before a shrine, children sucking candy-coated fingers. Long ago, the street had been planted with elms that had grown huge. Their roots buckled the sidewalk and weeds grew in the cracks. Branches scraped the roof of the car. An old woman with inflamed legs wrapped in rags pushed a shopping cart full of memories up an incline worthy of San Francisco. Graffiti scarred every free inch of space, proclaiming the immortality of Little Willie Chacon, the Echo Parque Skulls, Los Conquistadores, the Lemoyne Boys and the tongue of Maria Paula Bonilla.

'There.' She pointed to a cottagelike frame house painted light green and roofed with brown tarpaper. The front yard was dry and brown but rimmed with hopeful beds of red geraniums and clusters of orange and yellow poppies that looked like all-day suckers. There was rock trim at the base of the house and a portico over the entry that shadowed a sagging wooden porch upon which a man sat.

'That's Rafael, the older brother. On the porch.'

I found a parking space next to a Chevy on blocks. I turned the wheels to the curb and locked them in place. We got out of the car, dust spiraling at our heels.

'Rafael!' she called and waved. The man on the porch took a moment to lift his gaze, then he raised his hand — feebly, it seemed.

'I used to live right around the corner,' she said, making it sound like a confession. She led me up a dozen steps and through an open iron gate.

The man on the porch hadn't risen. He stared at us with apprehension and curiosity and something else that I couldn't identify. He was pale and thin to the point of being gaunt, with the same curious mixture of Hispanic features and fair coloring as his dead sister. His lips were bloodless, his eyes heavily lidded. He looked like the victim of some systemic disease. He wore a long-sleeved white shirt with the sleeves rolled up just below the elbows. It bloused out around his waist, several sizes too large. His trousers were black and looked as if they'd once belonged to a fat man's suit. His shoes were bubble-toed oxfords, cracked at the tips, worn unlaced with the tongues protruding and revealing thick white socks. His hair was short and combed straight back.

He was in his mid-twenties but he had an old man's face, a weary, wary mask.

Raquel went to him and kissed him lightly on the top of his head. He looked up at her but was unmoved.

'H'lo, Rocky.'

'Rafael, how are you?'

'OK.' He nodded his head and it looked for a moment as if it would roll off his neck. He let his eyes settle on me; he was having trouble focusing.

Raquel bit her lip.

'We came by to see you and Andy and your mom. This is Alex Delaware. He works with the police. He's involved in investigating Elena's – case.'

His face registered alarm, his hand tightened around the arm of the chair. Then, as if responding to a stage direction to relax, he grinned at me, slumped lower, winked.

'Yeah,' he said.

I held out my hand. He looked at it, puzzled, recognized it as a long lost friend, and extended his own thin claw.

His arm was pitifully undernourished, a bundle of sticks held together by a sallow paper wrapper. As our fingers touched his sleeve rode up and I saw the track marks. There were lots of them. Most looked old – lumpy charcoal smudges – but a few were freshly pink. One, in particular, was no antique, sporting a pinpoint of blood at its center.

His handshake was moist and tenuous. I let go and the arm fell limply to his side.

'Hey, man,' he said, barely audible. 'Good to meetja.' He turned away, lost in his own timeless dream-hell. For the first time I heard the oldies music coming from a cheap transistor radio on the floor beside his chair. The puny plastic box crackled with static. The sound reproduction was atrocious, the music had the chalky quality of notes filtered through a mile of mud. Rafael had his head thrown back, enraptured. To him it was the Celestial Choir transmitting directly to his temporal lobes.

'Rafael,' she smiled.

He looked at her, smiled, nodded off and was gone.

She stared at him, tears in her eyes. I moved toward her and she turned away in shame and rage.

'Goddammit.'

'How long has he been shooting up?'

'Years. But I thought he'd quit. The last I'd heard he'd quit.' She raised her hand to her mouth, swayed, as if ready to fall. I got in position to catch her but she righted herself. 'He got hooked in Vietnam. Came home with a heavy habit. Elena spent lots of time and money trying to help him get off. A dozen times he tried, and each time he slipped back. But he'd been off it for over a year. Elena was so happy about it. He got a job as a boxboy at the Lucky's on Alvarado.'

She faced me, nostrils flaring, eyes floating like black lilies in a salty pond, lips quivering like harp-strings.

'Everything is falling apart.'

She grasped the newel post on the porch rail for support. I came behind her.

'I'm sorry.'

'He was always the sensitive one. Quiet, never dating, no friends. He got beat up a lot. When their dad died he tried to take over, to be the man of the house. Tradition says the

227

oldest son should do that. But it didn't work. Nobody took him seriously. They laughed. We all did. So he gave up, as if he'd failed some final test. He dropped out of school, stayed home and read comic books and watched TV all day – just stared at the screen. When the army said they wanted him he seemed glad. Cruz cried to see him go, but he was happy . . .'

I looked at him, sitting so low he was almost parallel with the ground. Swallowed up by junkie-slumber. His mouth was open and he snored loudly. The radio played 'Daddy's Home.'

Raquel hazarded another look at him, then whipped her head away, disgusted. She wore an expression of noble suffering, an Aztec virgin steeling herself for the ultimate sacrifice.

I put my hands on her shoulders and she leaned back in my arms. She stayed there, tense and unyielding, allowing herself a miser's ration of tears.

'This is a hell of a start,' she said. Inhaling deeply, she let out her breath in a breeze of wintergreen. She wiped her eyes and turned around. 'You must think all I do is weep. Come on, let's go inside.'

She pulled the screen door open and it slapped sharply against the wood siding of the house.

We stepped into a small front room furnished with old but cared-for relics. It was warm and dark, the windows shut tight and masked by yellowing parchment shades – a room unaccustomed to visitors. Faded lace curtains were tied back from the window frames and matching lace coverlets shielded the arms of the chairs – a sofa and loveseat set upholstered in dark green crushed velvet, the worn spots shiny and the color of jungle parrots, two wicker rockers. A painting of the two dead Kennedy brothers in black velvet hung over the mantel. Carvings in wood and Mexican onyx sat atop lace-covered end tables. There were two floor lamps with beaded shades, a plaster Jesus in agony hanging on the whitewashed wall next to a still life of a straw basket of oranges. Family portraits in ornate frames covered another wall and there was a large graduation picture of Elena suspended high above those. A spider crawled in the space where wall met ceiling.

A door to the right revealed a sliver of white tile. Raquel walked to the sliver and peeked in.

'Señora Cruz?'

The doorway widened and a small, heavy woman appeared, dish-towel in hand. She wore a blue print dress, unbelted, and her gray-black hair was tied back in a bun, held in place by a mock tortoiseshell comb. Silver earrings dangled from her ears and salmon spots of rouge punctuated her cheekbones. Her skin had the delicate, baby-soft look common in old women who had once been beautiful.

'Raquelita!'

She put her towel down, came out, and the two women embraced for a long moment.

When she saw me over Raquel's shoulder, she smiled. But her face closed up as tight as a pawnbroker's safe. She pulled away and gave a small bow.

'Señor,' she said, with too much deference, and looked at Raquel, arching one eyebrow.

'Señora Gutierrez.'

Raquel spoke to her in rapid Spanish. I caught the words 'Elena,' 'policía,' and 'doctor.' She ended it with a question.

The older woman listened politely, then shook her head.

'No.' Some things are the same in any language.

Raquel turned to me. 'She says she knows nothing more than what she told the police the first time.'

'Can you ask her about the Nemeth boy? They didn't ask her about that.'

She turned to speak, then stopped.

'Why don't we take it slowly? It would help if we ate. Let her be a hostess, let her give to us.'

I was genuinely hungry and told her so. She relayed the message to Mrs Gutierrez, who nodded and returned to her kitchen.

'Let's sit down,' Raquel said.

I took the loveseat. She tucked herself into a corner of the sofa.

The señora came back with cookies and fruit and hot coffee. She asked Raquel something.

'She'd like to know if this is substantial enough or would you like some homemade *chorizo*?'

'Please tell her this is wonderful. However if you think my accepting *chorizo* would help things along, I'll oblige.'

Raquel spoke again. A few moments later I was facing a platter of the spicy sausage, rice, refried beans and salad with lemon-oil dressing.

'*Muchas gracias, señora.*' I dug in.

I couldn't understand much of what they were saying, but it sounded and looked like small talk. The two women touched each other a lot, patting hands, stroking cheeks. They smiled, and seemed to forget my presence.

Then suddenly the wind shifted and the laughter turned to tears. Mrs Gutierrez ran out of the room, seeking the refuge of her kitchen.

Raquel shook her head.

'We were talking about the old times, when Elena and I were little girls. How we used to play secretary in the bushes, pretend we had typewriters and desks out there. It became difficult for her.'

I pushed my plate aside.

'Do you think we should go?' I asked.

'Let's wait a while.' She poured me more coffee and filled a cup for herself. 'It would be more respectful.'

Through the screen door I could see the top of Rafael's fair head above the rim of the chair. His arm had fallen, so that the fingernails scraped the ground. He was beyond pleasure or pain.

'Did she talk about him?' I asked.

'No. As I told you, it's easier to deny.'

'But how can he sit there, shooting up, right in front of her, with no pretense?'

'She used to cry a lot about it. After a while you accept the fact that things aren't going to turn out the way you want them to. She's had plenty of training in it, believe me. If you asked her about him she'd say he was sick. Just as if he had a cold, or the measles. It's just a matter of finding the right cure. Have you heard of the *curanderos*?'

'The folk doctors? Yes. Lots of the Hispanic patients at the hospital used them along with conventional medicine.'

'Do you know how they operate? By caring. In our culture the cold, distant professional is regarded as someone who simply doesn't care, who is just as likely to deliver the *mal ojo* – the evil eye – as he is to cure. The *curandero*, on the other hand, has little training or technology at his disposal – a few snake powders, maybe. But he cares. He lives in the community, he is warm, and familiar, has tremendous rapport. In a way, he's a folk psychologist more than a folk doctor. That's why I suggested you eat – to establish a personal link. I told her you were a caring person. Otherwise she'd say nothing. She'd be polite, lady-like – Cruz is from the old school – but she'd shut you out just the same.' She sipped at her coffee.

'That's why the police learned nothing when they came here, why they seldom do in Echo Park, or East LA, or San Fernando. They're too professional. No matter how well meaning they may be, we see them as Anglo robots. You do care, Alex, don't you?'

'I do.'

She touched my knee.

'Cruz took Rafael to a *curandero* years ago, when he first started dropping out. The man looked into his eyes and said they were empty. He told her it was an illness of the soul, not of the body. That the boy should be given to the church, as a priest or monk, so that he could find a useful role for himself.'

'Not bad advice.'

She sipped her coffee. 'No. Some of them are very sophisticated. They live by their wits. Maybe it would have prevented the addiction if she'd followed through. Who knows? But she couldn't give him up. I wouldn't be surprised if she blames herself for what he's become. For everything.'

The door to the kitchen opened. Mrs Gutierrez came out wearing a black band around her arm and a new face that was more than just fresh makeup. A face hardened to withstand the acid bath of interrogation.

She sat down next to Raquel and whispered to her in Spanish.

'She says you may ask any questions you'd like.'

I nodded with what I hoped was obvious gratitude.

'Please tell the señora that I express my sorrow at her tragic loss and also let her know that I greatly appreciate her taking the time during her period of grief to talk to me.'

The older woman listened to the translation and acknowledged me with a quick movement of her head.

'Ask her, Raquel, if Elena ever talked about her work. Especially during the last year.'

As Raquel spoke a nostalgic smile spread across the older woman's face.

'She says only to complain that teachers did not get paid enough. That the hours were long and the children could get difficult.'

'Any particular children?'

A whispered conference.

'No child in particular. The señora reminds you that Elena was a special kind of teacher who helped children with problems in learning. All the children had difficulties.'

I wondered to myself if there'd been a connection between growing up with a brother like Rafael and the dead girl's choice of specialty.

'Did she speak at all about the child who was killed. The Nemeth boy?'

Upon hearing the question Mrs Gutierrez nodded, sadly, then spoke.

'She mentioned it once or twice. She said she was very sad about it. That it was a tragedy,' Raquel translated.

'Nothing else?'

'It would be rude to pursue it, Alex.'

'OK. Try this. Did Elena seem to have more money than usual recently? Did she buy expensive gifts for anyone in the family?'

'No. She says Elena always complained about not having enough money. She was a girl who liked to have good things. Pretty things. One minute.' She listened to the older woman, nodding affirmation. 'This wasn't always possible, as the family was never rich. Even when her husband was alive. But Elena worked very hard. She bought herself things. Sometimes on credit, but she always made her payments. Nothing was repossessed. She was a girl to make a mother proud.'

I prepared myself for more tears, but there were none. The grieving mother looked at me with a cold, dark expression of challenge. I dare you, she was saying, to besmirch the memory of my little girl.

I looked away.

'Do you think I can ask her about Handler now?'

Before Raquel could answer, Mrs Gutierrez spit. She gesticulated with both hands, raised her voice and uttered what had to be a string of curses. She ended the diatribe by spitting again.

'Need I translate?' asked Raquel.

'Don't bother.' I made a mental search for a new line of questioning. Normally, my approach would have been to start off with small talk, casual banter, and subtly switch to direct questions. I was dissatisfied with the crude way I was handling this interview, but working with a translator was like doing surgery wearing garden gloves.

'Ask her if there is anything else she can tell me that might help us find the man who – you phrase it.'

The old woman listened and answered vehemently.

'She says there is nothing. That the world has become a crazy place, full of demons. That a demon must have done this to Elena.'

'*Muchas gracias, señora.* Ask her if I might have a look at Elena's personal effects.'

Raquel asked her and the mother deliberated. She looked me over from head to toe, sighed, and got up.

'*Venga,*' she said, and led me to the rear of the house.

The flotsam and jetsam of Elena Gutierrez's twenty-eight years had been stored in cardboard boxes and stuck in a corner of what passed, in the tiny house, as a service porch. There was a windowed door with a view of the backyard. An apricot tree grew there, gnarled and deformed, spreading its fruit-laden branches across the rotting roof of a single car garage.

Across the hall was a small bedroom with two beds, the domicile of the brothers. From where I knelt I could see a maple dresser and shelves constructed of unfinished planks resting on cinder blocks. The shelves held a cheap stereo and a modest record collection. A carton of Marlboros and a pile of paperbacks shared the top of the dresser. One of the beds was neatly made, the other a jumble of tangled sheets. Between them was a single pine end table holding a lamp with a plastic base, an ashtray, and a copy of a Spanish girlie magazine.

Feeling like a Peeping Tom, I pulled the first box close and began my excursion in pop archeology.

By the time I'd gone through three boxes I'd succumbed to an indigo mood. My hands were filthy with dust, my mind filled with images of the dead girl. There'd been nothing of substance, just the broken shards that surface at any prolonged dig. Clothing smelling of girl, half-empty bottles of cosmetics – reminders that someone had once tried to make her eyelashes look thick and lush, to give her hair that Clairol shine, to cover her blemishes and gloss her lips and smell good in all the right places. Scraps of paper with reminders to pick up eggs at Vons and wine at Vendôme and other cryptograms, laundry receipts, gasoline credit-card stubs, books – lots of them, mostly biographies and poetry, souvenirs – a miniature ukelele from Hawaii, an ashtray from a hotel in Palm Springs, ski boots, an almost-full disk of birth control pills, old lesson plans, memos from the principal, children's drawings – none by a boy named Nemeth.

It was too much like graverobbing for my taste. I understood, more than ever, why Milo drank too much.

There were two boxes to go. I went at them, working faster, and was almost done when the roar of a motorcycle filled the air, then died. The back door opened, footsteps sounded in the foyer.

'What the fuck—'

He was nineteen or twenty, short and powerfully built, wearing a sweat-soaked brown tank top that showed every muscle, grease-stained khaki pants and work boots coated with grime. His hair was thick and shaggy. It hung to his shoulders and was held in place by a thonged leather headband. He had fine, almost delicate features that he'd tried to camouflage by growing a mustache and beard. The mustache was black and luxuriant. It dropped over his lips and glistened like sable fur. The beard was a skimpy triangle of down on his chin. He looked like a kid playing Pancho Villa in the school play.

There was a ring of keys hanging from his belt and the

keys jingled when he came toward me. His hands were balled up into grimy fists and he smelled of motor oil.

I showed him my LAPD badge. He swore, but stopped.

'Listen man, you guys were here last week. We told you we had nothin'—' He stopped and looked down at the contents of the cardboard box strewn on the floor. 'Shit, you went through all that stuff already. I just packed it up, man, gettin' it ready for the Goodwill.'

'Just a recheck,' I said amiably.

'Yeah, man, why don't you dudes learn to get it right in the first fuckin' place, OK?'

'I'll be through in a moment.'

'You're through now, man. Out.'

I stood.

'Give me a few minutes to wrap it up.'

'Out, man.' He crooked his thumb toward the back door.

'I'm trying to investigate the death of your sister, Andy. It wouldn't hurt you to cooperate.'

He took a step closer. There were grease smudges on his forehead, and under his eyes.

'Don't "Andy" me, dude. This is my place and it's *Mr* Gutierrez. And don't give me that shit about investigating. You guys aren't never gonna catch the dude who did it to Elena 'cause you don't really give a fuck. Come bustin' into a home and going through personal stuff and treatin' us like peasants, man. You go out on the street and find the dude, man. This was Beverly Hills, he'd already 'a' been caught, he do this to some rich guy's daughter.'

His voice broke and he shut up to hide it.

'Mr Gutierrez,' I said softly, 'cooperation from family can be very helpful in these—'

'Hey, man, I told you, this family don't know nothing about this. You think we know what kind of crazy asshole do something like that? You think people around here act like that, man?'

He squinted at my badge, reading it with effort, moving his lips. He mouthed the word 'consultant' a couple of times before getting it.

'Aw, man, I don't believe it. You're not even a real cop. Fucking consultant, they send around here. What's PhD, man?'

'Doctorate in psychology.'

'You a shrink, man – fuckin' headshrinker they send aroun' here, think someone's crazy here! You think someone in this family is crazy, man? Do you?'

He was breathing on me now. His eyes were soft and brown, long-lashed and dreamy as a girl's. Eyes like that could make you doubt yourself, could lead a guy to get into some heavy macho posturing.

I thought the family had plenty of problems but I didn't answer his question.

'What the fuck you doin' here, psychin' us out, man?'

He sprayed me with spittle as he spoke. A balloon of anger expanded in my gut. Automatically my body assumed a defensive karate stance.

'It's not like that, I can explain. Or are you determined to be pig-headed?'

I regretted the words even as they left my mouth.

'Pig – goddammit man, you're the pig!' His voice rose an octave and he grabbed the lapel of my jacket.

I was ready but I didn't move. He's in mourning, I kept telling myself. He's not responsible.

I met his gaze and he backed off. Both of us would have welcomed an excuse to duke it out. So much for civilization.

'Get out, man. Now!'

'Antonio!'

Mrs Gutierrez had come into the hallway. Raquel was visible behind her. Seeing her I felt suddenly ashamed. I'd done a great job of screwing up a sensitive situation. The brilliant psychologist . . .

'Mom, did you let this dude in?'

Mrs Gutierrez apologized to me with her eyes and spoke to her son in Spanish. He seemed to wilt under mama's wagging finger and dark looks.

'Mom, I told you before, they don't give a—' He stopped, continued in Spanish. It sounded like he was defending himself, the machismo slowly rendered impotent.

They went back and forth for a while. Then he started in on Raquel. She gave it right back to him: 'The man is trying to help you, Andy. Why don't you help him instead of chasing him away?'

'I don't need nobody's help. We're gonna take care of ourselves the way we always did.'

She sighed.

'Shit!' He went into his room, came out with a pack of Marlboros and made a big deal out of lighting one and jamming it into his mouth. He disappeared, momentarily, behind a blue cloud, then the eyes flashed once again, moving from me to his mother, to Raquel, and back to me. He pulled his key ring from his belt and held the keys sandwiched between his fingers, impromptu brass knuckles.

'I'm leaving now, dude. But when I get back you fucking well better be gone.'

239

He kicked the door open and jogged out. We heard th
thunder of the motorcycle starting and the diminishing
scream of the machine as it sped away.

Mrs Gutierrez hung her head and said something to
Raquel.

'She asks your forgiveness for Andy's rudeness. He's beer
very upset since Elena's death. He's working two jobs and
under a lot of pressure.'

I held a hand up to stop the apology.

'There's no need to explain. I only hope I haven't caused
the señora needless troubles.'

Translation was superfluous. The look on the mother's
face was eloquent.

I rummaged through the last two boxes with little enthusiasm and came up with no new insights. The sour taste of
the confrontation with Andy lingered. I experienced the kine
of shame you feel upon digging too deep, seeing and hearing
more than you need or want to. Like a child walking in or
his parents' lovemaking or a hiker kicking aside a rock only
to catch a glimpse of something slimy on the underside.

I'd seen families like the Gutierrezes' before; I'd known
scores of Rafaels and Andys. It was a pattern: The slob and
the superkid, playing out their roles with depressing
predictability. One unable to cope, the other trying to take
charge of everything. The slob, getting others to take care
of him, shirking his responsibilities, coasting through life
but feeling like – a slob. The superkid, competent, compulsive, working two jobs, even three when the situation called
for it, making up for the slob's lack of accomplishment,
earning the admiration of the family, refusing to stoop under

240

the weight of his burden, keeping his rage under wraps — but not always.

I wondered what role Elena had played when she was alive. Had she been the peacemaker, the go-between? Getting caught in the crossfire between slob and superkid could be hazardous to one's health.

I repacked her things as neatly as I could.

When we stepped onto the porch Rafael was still stuporous. The sound of the Seville starting up jolted him awake, and he blinked rapidly, as if coming out of a bad dream, stood with effort, and wiped his nose with his sleeve. He looked in our direction, puzzled. Raquel turned away from him, a tourist avoiding a leprous beggar. As I pulled away I saw a spark of recognition brighten his doped-up countenance, then more bewilderment.

The approaching darkness had dimmed the activity level on Sunset but there was still plenty of life on the streets. Car horns honked, raucous laughter rose above the exhaust fumes and mariachi music blared from the open doors of the bars. Traces of neon appeared and lights flickered in the foothills.

'I really blew it,' I said.

'No, you can't blame yourself.' In the mood she was in, boosting me took effort. I appreciated that effort and told her so.

'I mean it, Alex. You were very sensitive with Cruz — I can see why you were a successful psychologist. She liked you.'

'It obviously doesn't run in the family.'

She was silent for a few blocks.

'Andy's a nice boy — he never joined the gangs, took lots

of punishment because of it. He expects a lot out of himself. Everything's on his shoulders, now.'

'With all that weight why add a two-ton chip?'

'You're right. He makes more problems for himself – don't we all? He's only eighteen. Maybe he'll grow up.'

'I keep wondering if there was some way I could have handled it better.' I recounted the details of my exchange with the boy.

'The pigheaded crack didn't help things, but it didn't make a difference. He came in ready to fight. When Latin men get that way there's little you can do. Add alcohol to that and you can see why we pack the emergency rooms with knifing victims every Saturday night.'

I thought of Elena Gutierrez and Morton Handler. They'd never made it to the emergency room. I allowed myself a short ride on that train of thought then skidded to a stop and dumped the thoughts in a dark depot somewhere in the south of my subconscious.

I looked over at Raquel. She sat stiffly in the soft leather, refusing to give herself over to comfort. Her body was still but her hands played nervously with the fabric of her skirt.

'Are you hungry?' I asked. When in doubt, stick to basics.

'No. If you want you can stop for yourself.'

'I can still taste the *chorizo*.'

'You can take me home, then.'

When I got to her apartment it was dark and the streets were empty.

'Thanks for coming with me.'

'I hope it was helpful.'

'Without you it would have been disastrous.'

'Thank you.' She smiled and leaned over. It started out

as a kiss on the cheek but one or both of us moved and it turned into a kiss on the lips. Then a tentative nibble, nurtured with heat and want, that matured quickly into a gasping, ravenous adult bite. We moved closer simultaneously, her arms easing around my neck, my hands in her hair, on her face, at the small of her back. Our mouths opened and our tongues danced a slow waltz. We breathed heavily, squirming, struggling to get closer.

We necked like two teenagers for endless minutes. I undid a button of her blouse. She made a throaty sound, caught my lower lip between her teeth, licked my ear. My hand slithered around to the hot silk of her back, working with a mind of its own, undoing the clasp of her brassiere, cupping around her breast. The nipple, pebble-hard and moist, nestled against my palm. She lowered one hand, slender fingers tugging at my fly.

I was the one who stopped it.

'What's the matter?'

There's nothing you can say in a situation like that that doesn't sound like a cliché or totally idiotic, or both. I opted for both.

'I'm sorry. Don't take it personally.'

She threw herself upright, busied herself with buttoning, fastening, smoothing her hair.

'How else should I take it?'

'You're very desirable.'

'Very.'

'I'm attracted to you, dammit. I'd love to make love to you.'

'What is it, then?'

'A commitment.'

243

'You're not married, are you? You don't act married.'

'There are other commitments besides marriage.'

'I see.' She gathered up her purse and put her hand on the door handle. 'The person you're committed to, it would matter to her?'

'Yes. More important, it would matter to me.'

She burst out laughing, verging on hysteria.

'I'm sorry,' she said, catching her breath. 'It's so damned ironic. You think I do this often? This is the first time I've been interested in a guy in a long time. The nun cuts loose and comes face to face with a saint.'

She giggled. It sounded feverish, fragile, made me uneasy. I was weary of being on the receiving end of someone's – anyone's – frustration but I supposed she was entitled to her moment of cathartic stardom.

'I'm no saint, believe me.'

She touched my cheek with her fingers. It was like being raked with hot coals.

'No, you're just a nice guy, Delaware.'

'I don't feel like that, either.'

'I'm going to kiss you again,' she said, 'but it's going to stay chaste this time. The way it should have been in the first place.'

And she did.

18

THERE WERE two surprises waiting for me when I got home.

The first was Robin, in my ratty yellow bathrobe, stretched out on the leather sofa, drinking hot tea. A fire burned in the hearth and the stereo played the Eagles' 'Desperado.'

She was wearing a magazine photograph of Lassie around her neck like a miniature sandwich sign.

'Hello, darling,' she said.

I threw my jacket over a chair.

'Hi. What's with the dog?'

'Just my way of letting you know that I've been a bitch and I'm sorry.'

'You have nothing to be sorry for.' I removed the sign.

I sat beside her and took her hands in mine.

'I was rotten to you this morning, Alex, letting you leave like that. The moment the door closed I started missing you. You know how it is when you let your mind wander around – what if something happens to him, what if I never see him again – you go crazy. I couldn't work, couldn't be around machines in that state. The day was blown. I called you but I couldn't get through. So here I am.'

'Virtue has its rewards,' I muttered under my breath.

'What's that, sweetie?'

'Nothing.' Any recounting of my minor-league indiscretion would suffer in the retelling, emerging as either a boorish bathroom scribble – 'Yeah, I hopped a fast feel from another broad, honey' – or, worse, a confession.

I lay down beside her. We held each other, said nice things, talked baby talk, stroked each other. I was pumped up from the waist down, some of it a residue of the curbside session with Raquel, most of it belonging to the moment.

'There are two giant porterhouses in the refrigerator and a Caesar salad and burgundy and sourdough.' She whispered, tickling my nose with her pinkie.

'You're a very oral person,' I laughed.

'Is that neurotic, Doctor?'

'No. It's wonderful.'

'How about this? And this?'

The robe fell open. She kneeled above me, letting it slide down her shoulders. Backlit by the glow of the fire, she looked like a piece of glorious, golden statuary.

'Come on, sweetie,' she coaxed, 'get out of those clothes.' And she took the matter into her own hands.

'I do love you,' she said later. 'Even if you are catatonic.'

I refused to budge, and lay spreadeagled on the floor.

'I'm cold.'

She covered me, stood and stretched, and laughed with pleasure.

'How can you jump around afterwards?' I groaned.

'Women are stronger than men,' she said gaily, and proceeded to dance around the room, humming, stretching more so that the muscles of her calves ascended in the slender columns of her legs like bubbles rising in a carpenter's level. Her eyes reflected orange Halloween light. When she moved a shudder went through me.

'Keep jiggling like that and I'll show you who's stronger.'

'Later, big boy.' She teased me with her foot and leaped away from my grabbing paws with fluid agility.

By the time the steaks were ready Mrs Gutierrez's cuisine was a vague memory and I ate with gusto. We sat side by side in the breakfast nook, looking out through leaded glass as lights went on in the hills like the beacons of a distant search party. She rested her head on my shoulder. My arm went around her, my fingertips blindly traced the contours of her face. We took turns drinking from a single glass of wine.

'I love you,' I said.

'I love you too.' She kissed the underside of my chin. After several more sips:

'You were investigating those murders today, weren't you?'

'Yes.'

She fortified herself with a large swallow and refilled the glass.

'Don't worry,' she said. 'I'm not going to hassle you about it. I can't pretend I like it, but I won't try to control you.'

I hugged her by way of thanks.

'I mean, I wouldn't want you treating me that way, so I won't do it to you.' She was giving liberation the old school try, but worry remained suspended in her voice like a fly in amber.

'I'm watching out for myself.'

'I know you are,' she said, too quickly. 'You're a bright man. You can take care of yourself.'

She handed me the wine.

'If you want to talk about it, Alex, I'll listen.'

I hesitated.

'Tell me. I want to know what's going on.'

I gave her a rehash of the last two days, ending it with the confrontation with Andy Gutierrez, leaving out the ten turbulent minutes with Raquel.

She listened, troubled and attentive, digested it, and told me, 'I can see why you can't drop it. So many suspicious things, no connecting thread.'

She was right. It was reverse Gestalt, the whole so much less than the sum of its parts. A random assortment of musicians, sawing, blowing, thumping, yearning for a conductor. But who the hell was I to play Ormandy?

'When are you going to tell Milo?'

'I'm not. I spoke to him this morning and he basically told me to mind my own business, stay out of it.'

'But it's his job, Alex. He'll know what to do.'

'Honey, Milo will get bent out of shape if I tell him I visited La Casa.'

'But that poor child, the retarded one, isn't there something he could do about it?'

I shook my head.

'It's not enough. There'd be an explanation for it. Milo's got his suspicions – I'll bet they're stronger than he let on to me – but he's hemmed in by rules and procedures.'

'And you're not,' she said softly.

'Don't worry.'

'Don't worry, yourself. I'm not going to try to stop you. I meant what I said.'

I drank more wine. My throat had constricted and the cool liquid was astringently soothing.

She got up and stood behind me, putting her arms over my shoulders. It was a gesture of support not dissimilar from the one I'd offered Raquel just a few hours earlier. She reached down and played with the ridge of hair that vertically bisected my abdomen.

'I'm here for you, Alex, if you need me.'

'I always need you. But not to get involved in crap like this.'

'Whatever you need me for, I'm here.'

I rose out of the chair and drew her to me, kissing her neck, her ears, her eyes. She threw back her head and put my lips on the warm pulse at the base of her throat.

'Let's get into bed and snuggle,' she said.

I turned on the radio and tuned it to KKGO. Sonny Rollins was extracting a liquid sonata from his horn. I switched on a dim light and drew back the covers.

The second surprise of the evening lay there, a plain white envelope, business-size, unmarked and partially covered by the pillow.

'Was this here when you arrived?'

She'd taken off her robe. Now she held it to her breasts, seeking cover, as if the envelope were a living, breathing intruder.

'Could have been. I didn't go in the bedroom.'

I slit it open with my thumbnail and took out the single sheet of white paper folded inside. The page was devoid of date, address or any distinguishing logo. Just a white rectangle filled with lines of handwriting that slanted pessimistically downward. The penmanship, cramped and spidery, was familiar. I sat down on the edge of the bed and read.

Dear Doctor:

Here's hoping you sleep in your own bed in the near future so you have the opportunity to read this. I took the liberty of jimmying your rear door to get in and deliver this — you should get a better lock, by the way.

This afternoon I was relieved of my duties in the H-G case. El Capitán feels the case would benefit by the infusion of fresh blood — the tasteless choice of words was his, not mine. I have my doubts about his motivation, but I haven't exactly set any new detection records so I was in no position to debate it with him.

I must have looked pretty shattered by it, cause he got suddenly empathetic and suggested I take some R and R. In fact, he was very well versed in the details of my personnel file, knew that I'd accrued lots of vacation time and strongly urged me to use some of it.

At first I wasn't overjoyed at the idea, but I've since come to view it as an excellent one. I've found my place in the sun. A quaint little watering hole named Ahuacatlan, just north of Guadalajara. Some preliminary checking via long distance reveals that said burg is extremely well suited for someone of my recreational interests. Hunting and fishing, in particular.

I expect to be gone for two or three days. Phone contact is tenuous and undesirable — the natives

cherish privacy. Will call when I get back. Regards to
Stradivarius (Stradivariette?) and stay out of trouble.

All the best,
Milo

I gave it to Robin to read. She finished it and handed it back.

'What's he saying – that he was kicked off the case?'

'Yes. Probably because of outside pressure. But he's going
to Mexico to look into McCaffrey's background. Apparently
when he called down there he got enough over the phone
to make him want to pursue it.'

'He's going behind his captain's back.'

'He must feel it's worth it.' Milo was a brave man but no
martyr. He wanted his pension as much as the next guy.

'You were right then. About La Casa.' She got under the
covers and drew them up to her chin. She shivered, not from
the cold.

'Yes.' Never had being right seemed of such meager
solace.

The music from the radio peeked around corners and took
an unexpected pirouette. A drummer had joined Rollins, and
he slapped out a tropical tattoo on his tomtoms . . . I could
think only of cannibals and snake-encrusted vines. Shrunken
heads . . .

'Hold me.'

I got in beside her and kissed her and held her and tried
to act calm. But all the while my mind was elsewhere, lost on
some frozen piece of tundra, floating out to sea.

19

THE ENTRANCE LOBBY of Western Pediatric Medical Center was walled with marble slabs engraved with the names of long-dead benefactors. Inside, the lobby was filled with the injured, the ill and the doomed, all simmering in the endless wait that is as much a part of hospitals as are intravenous needles and bad food.

Mothers clutched bundles to their breasts, wails escaping from within the layers of blanket. Fathers chewed their nails, grappled with insurance forms and tried not to think about the loss of masculinity resulting from encounters with bureaucracy. Toddlers raced about, placing their hands on the marble, withdrawing them quickly at the cold and leaving behind grimy mementoes. A loudspeaker called out names and the chosen plodded to the admissions desk. A blue-haired lady in the green-and-white-striped uniform of a hospital volunteer sat behind the information counter, as baffled as those she was mandated to assist.

In a far corner of the lobby, children and grownups sat on plastic chairs and watched television. The TV was turned to a serial that took place in a hospital. The doctors and nurses on the screen wore spotless white, had coiffed hair, perfect faces, and teeth that radiated a mucoid sparkle as they conversed in slow, low, earnest tones about love, hate, anguish and death. The doctors and nurses who elbowed their way through the throng in the lobby were altogether more human – rumpled, harried, sleepy-eyed. Those entering rushed, responding to beepers and emergency phone calls. Those exiting did so with the alacrity of escaping prisoners, fearing last-minute calls back to the wards.

I wore my white coat and hospital badge and carried my briefcase as the automatic doors allowed me through and the sixtyish, red-nosed guard nodded as I passed:

'Morning, Doctor.'

I rode the elevator to the basement along with a despondent black couple in their thirties and their son, a withered, gray-skinned nine year old in a wheelchair. At the mezzanine we were joined by a lab tech, a fat girl carrying a basket of syringes, needles, rubber tubing and glass cylinders full of the ruby syrup of life. The parents of the boy in the wheelchair looked longingly at the blood; the child turned his head to the wall.

The ride ended with a bump. We were disgorged into a dingy yellow corridor. The other passengers turned right, toward the lab. I went the other way, came to a door marked 'Medical Records,' opened it and went in.

Nothing had changed since I'd left. I had to turn sideways to get through the narrow aisle carved into the floor-to-ceiling stacks of charts. No computer here, no high-tech attempt at organizing the tens of thousands of dog-eared manila files into a coherent system. Hospitals are conservative institutions, and Western Pediatric was the most stodgy of hospitals, welcoming progress the way a dog welcomes the mange.

At the end of the aisle was an unadorned gray wall. Just

in front of it sat a sleepy-looking Filipino girl, reading a glamor magazine.

'May I help you?'

'Yes. I'm Dr Delaware. I need to get hold of a chart of a patient of mine.'

'You could have your secretary call us, Doctor, and we'd send it to you.'

Sure. In two weeks.

'I appreciate that, but I need to look at it right now and my secretary's not here yet.'

'What's the patient's name?'

'Adams. Brian Adams.' The room was divided alphabetically. I picked a name that would take her to the far end of the A–K section.

'If you'll just fill out this form, I'll get it right for you.'

I filled out the form, falsifying with ease. She didn't bother to look at it and dropped it into a metal filebox. When she was gone, hidden between the stacks, I went to the L–Z side of the room, searched among the Ns and found what I was looking for. I slipped it into my briefcase and returned.

She came back minutes later.

'I've got three Brian Adamses, here, Doctor. Which one is it?'

I scanned the three and picked one at random.

'This is it.'

'If you sign this—' she held out a second form – 'I can let you have it on twenty-four-hour loan.'

'There'll be no need for that. I'll just examine it here.'

I made a show of looking scholarly, leafed through the medical history of Brian Adams, age eleven, admitted for a routine tonsillectomy five years previously, clucked my tongue, shook my head, jotted down some meaningless notes, and gave it back to her.

'Thanks. You've been most helpful.'

She didn't answer, having already returned to the world of cosmetic camouflage and clothing designed for the sado-intellectual set.

I found an empty conference room down the hall next to the morgue, locked the door from the inside and sat down to examine the final chronicles of Cary Nemeth.

The boy had spent the last twenty-two hours of his life in the Intensive Care Unit at Western Pediatric, not a second of it in a conscious state. From a medical point of view it was open and shut: Hopeless. The admitting intern had kept his notes factual and objective, labeling it Auto versus Pedestrian, in the quaint lexicon of medicine that makes tragedy sound like a sporting event.

He'd been brought in by ambulance, battered, crushed, skull shredded, all but his most rudimentary bodily functions gone. Yet thousands of dollars had been spent delaying the inevitable, and enough pages had been filled to create a medical chart the size of a textbook. I leafed through them: Nursing notes, with their compulsive accounting of intake and output, the child reduced to cubic centimeters of fluid and plumbing; ICU graphs, progress notes – that was a cruel joke – consultations from neurosurgeons, neurologists, nephrologists, radiologists, cardiologists; blood test, X-rays, scans, shunts, sutures, intravenous feedings, parenteral nutritional supplements, respiratory therapy, and, finally, the autopsy.

Stapled to the back inside cover was the sheriff's report,

another example of jargonistic reductionism. In this equally precious dialect, Cary Nemeth was V, for Victim.

V had been hit from behind while walking down Malibu Canyon Road just before midnight. He'd been barefoot, wearing pajamas – yellow, the report was careful to note. There were no skid marks, leading the reporting deputy to conclude that he'd been hit at full force. From the distance the body traveled, the estimated speed of the vehicle was between forty and fifty miles per hour.

The rest was paperwork, a cardboard snack from some downtown computer.

It was a depressing document. Nothing in it surprised me. Not even the fact that Cary Nemeth's private pediatrician of record, the physician who'd actually signed the death report, was Lionel Willard Towle, MD.

I left the chart stuck under a stack of X-ray plates and walked toward the elevator. Two eleven year olds had escaped from the ward and were waging a wheelchair drag race. They whooped by, IV tubing looping like lariats, and I had to swerve to avoid them.

I reached for the elevator button and heard my name called.

'H'lo, Alex!'

It was the medical director, chatting with a pair of interns. He dismissed them and walked my way.

'Hello, Henry.'

He'd put on a few pounds since I'd last seen him, jowls fighting the confines of his shirt collar. His complexion was unhealthily florid. Three cigars stuck out of his breast pocket.

'What a coincidence,' he said, giving me a soft hand. 'I was just about to call you.'

'Really? What about?'

'Let's talk in the office.'

He closed the door and scurried behind his desk.

'How've you been, son?'

'Just fine.' Dad.

'Good, good.' He took a cigar out of his pocket and made masturbatory motions up and down the cellophane wrapper. 'I'm not going to beat around the bush, Alex. You know that's not my way – always come right out and say what's on your mind is my philosophy. Let people know where you stand.'

'Please do.'

'Yes. Hmm. I'll come out and say it.' He leaned forward, either about to retch or preparing to impart some grave confidence. 'I've – we've received a complaint about your professional conduct.'

He sat back, pleasurably expectant, a boy waiting for a firecracker to explode.

'Will Towle?'

His eyebrows shot skyward. There were no fireworks up there, so they came back down again.

'You know?'

'Call it a good guess.'

'Yes, well, you're correct. He's up in arms about some hypnotizing you've done or some such nonsense.'

'He's full of shit, Henry.'

His fingers fumbled with the cellophane. I wondered how long it had been since he'd done surgery. 'I understand your point; however, Will Towle is an important man, not to be taken lightly. He's demanding an investigation, some kind of—'

257

'Witch hunt?'

'You're not making this any easier, young man.'

'I'm not beholden to Towle or anyone else. I'm retired, Henry, or have you forgotten that? Check the last time I received my salary.'

'That's not the point—'

'The point is, Henry, if Towle has a gripe against me, let him bring it up before the State Board. I'm prepared to swap accusations. I guarantee it will be an educational experience for all concerned.'

He smiled unctuously.

'I like you, Alex. I'm telling you this to warn you.'

'Warn me of what?'

'Will Towle's family has donated hundreds of thousands of dollars to this hospital. They may very well have paid for the chair you're sitting on.'

I stood up.

'Thanks for the warning.'

His little eyes hardened. The cigar snapped between his fingers, showering the desk with shreds of tobacco. He looked down at his lost pacifier and for a moment I thought he'd break into tears. He'd be great fun on the analyst's couch.

'You're not as independent as you think you are. There's the matter of your staff privileges.'

'Are you telling me that because Will Towle complained about me I'm in danger of losing my right to practice here?'

'I'm saying: Don't make waves. Call Will, make amends. He's not a bad fellow. In fact the two of you should have a lot in common. He's an expert in—'

'Behavioral Pediatrics. I know. Henry, I've heard his tune and we don't play in the same band.'

'Remember this, Alex – the status of psychologists on the medical staff has always been tenuous.'

An old speech came to mind. Something about the importance of the human factor and how it interfaced with modern medicine. I considered throwing it back in his face. Then I looked at his face and decided nothing could help it.

'Is that it?'

He had nothing to say. His type seldom does, when the conversation gets beyond platitudes, entendres, or threats.

'Good day, Doctor Delaware,' he said.

I left quietly, closing the door behind me.

I was down in the lobby, which had cleared of patients and was now filled with a group of visitors from some ladies' volunteer group. The ladies had old money and good breeding written all over their handsome faces – sorority girls grown up. They listened raptly as an administration lackey gave them a prefabricated spiel about how the hospital was in the forefront of medical and humanitarian progress for children, nodding their heads, trying not to show their anxiety.

The lackey prattled on about children being the resources of the future. All that came to my mind was young bones ground up as grist for someone's mill.

I turned and walked back to the elevator.

The third floor of the hospital housed the bulk of the administrative offices, which were shaped in an inverted T, paneled in dark wood, and carpeted in something the color and consistency of moss. The medical staff office was situated at the bottom of the stem of the T, in a glass-walled suite with a view of the Hollywood Hills. The elegant blonde behind the desk was someone I hadn't counted upon seeing, but I straightened my tie and went in.

She looked up, contemplated not recognizing me, then thought better of it and gave me a regal smile. She extended her hand with the imperious manner of someone who'd been at the same job long enough to harbor illusions of irreplaceability.

'Good morning, Alex.'

Her nails were long and thickly coated with mother-of-pearl polish, as if she'd plundered the depths of the ocean for the sake of vanity. I took the hand and handled it with the care it cried out for.

'Cora.'

'How nice to see you again. It's been a long time.'

'Yes it has.'

'Are you returning to us – I'd heard you resigned.'

'No, I'm not, and yes, I did.'

'Enjoying your freedom?' She favored me with another smile. Her hair looked blonder, coarser, her figure fuller, but still first-rate, packed into a chartreuse knit that would have intimidated someone of less heroic proportions.

'I am. And you?'

'Doing the same old thing,' she sighed.

'And doing it well, I'm sure.'

For a moment I thought the flattery was a mistake. Her face hardened and grew a few new wrinkles.

'We know,' I went on, 'who really keeps things together around here.'

'Oh, go on.' She flexed her hand like an abalone-tipped fan.

'It sure ain't the doctors.' I resisted calling her Ol' Buddy.

'Ain't that the truth. Amazing what twenty years of education won't give you in the way of common sense. I'm just a wage slave but I know which end is up.'

'I'm sure you could never be anyone's slave, Cora.'

'Well, I don't know.' Lashes as thick and dark as raven feathers lowered coquettishly.

She was in her early forties and under the merciless fluorescent lighting of the office every year showed. But she was well put together, with good features, one of those women who retain the form of youth but not the texture. Once, centuries ago, she'd seemed girlish, hearty and athletic, as we'd thrashed around the floor of the medical records office. It had been a one-shot deal, followed by mutual boycott. Now she was flirting, her memory cleansed by the passage of time.

'Have they been treating you OK?' I asked.

'As well as can be expected. You know how doctors are.' I grinned.

'I'm a fixture,' she said. 'If they ever move the office, they'll pick me up with the furniture.'

I looked up and down her body.

'I don't think anyone could mistake you for furniture.'

She laughed nervously and touched her hair self-consciously.

'Thanks.' Self-scrutiny became too unsettling and she put me in the spotlight.

'What brings you down here?'

'Tying up loose ends — a few unfinished charts, paperwork. I've been careless about answering my mail. I thought I received a notice about overdue staff dues.'

'I don't remember sending you one but it could have been one of the other girls. I was out for a month. Had surgery.'

261

'I'm sorry to hear that, Cora. Is everything all right?'

'Female troubles.' She smiled. 'They say I'm fine.' Her expression said that she thought 'they' were abject liars.

'I'm glad.'

We locked gazes. For just a moment she looked twenty, innocent and hopeful. She turned her back to me, as if wanting to preserve that image in my mind.

'Let me check your file.'

She got up and slid open the drawer of a black-lacquered file cabinet, and came up with a blue folder.

'No,' she said, 'you're all paid up. You'll be getting a notice for next year in a couple of months.'

'Thanks.'

'Don't mention it.'

She returned the folder.

'How about a cup of coffee?' I asked casually.

She looked at me, then at her watch.

'I'm not due for a break until ten, but what the hell, live it up, huh?'

'Right.'

'Let me go to the little girls' room and freshen up.' She fluffed her hair, picked up her purse and left the office to go into the lavatory across the hall.

When I saw the door shut after her I walked to the file cabinet. The drawer she'd opened was labeled. 'Staff A–G.' Two drawers down I found what I wanted. Into the old briefcase it went.

I was waiting by the door when she came out, flushed, pink and pretty, and smelling of patchouli. I extended my arm and she took it.

Over hospital coffee I listened to her talk. About her

divorce – a seven-year-old wound that wouldn't heal – the teenage daughter who was driving her crazy by doing exactly what she'd done as an adolescent, car troubles, the insensitivity of her superiors, the unfairness of life.

It was bizarre, getting to know for the first time a woman whose body I'd entered. In the scrambled word game of contemporary mating rituals, there was greater intimacy in her tales of woe than there had been in the opening of her thighs.

We parted friends.

'Come by again, Alex.'

'I will.'

I walked to the parking lot marveling at the ease with which I was able to slip on the cloak of duplicity. I'd always flattered myself with a self-assessment of integrity. But in the last three days I'd grown proficient at sneak-thievery, concealment of the truth, bald-faced lying and emotional whoring.

It must be the company I'd been keeping.

I drove to a cozy Italian place in West Hollywood. The restaurant had just opened and I was alone in my rear corner booth. I ordered veal in wine sauce, a side order of linguini with oil and garlic, and a Coors.

A shuffling waiter brought the beer. While I waited for the food I opened the briefcase and examined my plunder.

Towle's medical staff file was over forty pages long. Most of it consisted of Xeroxes of his diplomas, certificates and awards. His curriculum vitae was twenty pages of puffery, markedly devoid of scholarly publications – he'd coauthored one brief report while an intern, and nothing since – and filled with television and radio interviews, speeches to lay groups, volunteer service to La Casa and similar organizations. Yet he was a full clinical professor at the medical school. So much for academic rigor.

The waiter brought a salad and a basket of rolls. I picked up my napkin with one hand, started to return the file to the briefcase with the other, when something on the front page of the resumé caught my eye.

Under *college or university attended*, he'd listed Jedson College, Bellevue, Washington.

20

I GOT HOME, called the *LA Times*, and asked for Ned Biondi at the Metro desk. Biondi was a senior writer for the paper, a short, nervous character right out of *The Front Page*. I'd treated his teenage daughter for anorexia several years back. Biondi hadn't been able to come up with the money for treatment on a journalist's salary — compounded with a penchant for playing the wrong horse at Santa Anita — but the girl had been in trouble and I'd let it go. It had taken him a year and a half to clear his debt. His daughter had gotten straightened out after months of my chipping away at layers of self-hatred that were surprisingly ossified in someone seventeen years old. I remembered her clearly, a tall, dark youngster who wore jogging shorts and T-shirts that accentuated the skeletal conditions of her body; a girl ashen-faced and spindly legged who alternated between deep, dark spells of brooding silence and flights of hyperactivity during which she was ready to enter every category of Olympic competition on three hundred calories a day.

I'd gotten her admitted to Western Pediatric, where she'd stayed for three weeks. That, followed by months of psychotherapy, had finally gotten through to her, and allowed her to deal with the mother who was too beautiful, the brother who was too athletic, and the father who was too witty . . .

'Biondi.'

'Ned, this is Alex Delaware.'

It took a second for my name, minus title to register.

'Doctor! How are you?'

'I'm fine. How's Anne-Marie?'

'Very well. She's finishing up her second year at Wheaton – in Boston. She got As and a few Bs, but the Bs didn't panic her. She's still too rough on herself, but she seems to be adjusting well to the peaks and troughs of life, as you called them. Her weight is stable at a hundred and two.'

'Excellent. Give my regards when you speak to her.'

'I certainly will. It's nice of you to call.'

'Well actually there's more to this than professional follow-up.'

'Oh?' A foxy edge, the conditioned vigilance of one who pried open locked boxes for a living, came into his voice.

'I need a favor.'

'Name it.'

'I'm flying up north to Seattle tonight. I need to get into some transcripts at a small college near there. Jedson.'

'Hey, that's not what I expected. I thought you wanted a blurb about a book in the Sunday edition or something. This sounds serious.'

'It is.'

'Jedson. I know it. Anne-Marie was going to apply there – we figured a small place would be less pressure for her – but it was fifty per cent more expensive than Wheaton, Reed, and Oberlin – and they're no giveaways themselves. What do you want with their transcripts?'

'I can't say.'

'Doctor.' He laughed. 'Pardon the expression, but you're

prick-teasing. I'm a professional snoop. Dangle something weird in front of me I get a hard-on.'

'What makes you think anything's weird?'

'Doctors running around trying to get into files is weird. Usually it's the shrinks who get broken into, if my memory serves me correctly.'

'I can't go into it now, Ned.'

'I'm good with a secret, Doc.'

'No. Not yet. Trust me. You did before.'

'Below the belt, Doc.'

'I know. And I wouldn't gut-punch you if it wasn't important. I need your help. I may be onto something, maybe not. If I am you'll be the first to hear about it.'

'Something big?'

I thought about it for a moment.

'Could be.'

'OK,' he sighed, 'what do you want me to do?'

'I'm giving your name as a reference. If anyone calls you, back up my story.'

'What's the story?'

He listened.

'It seems harmless enough. Of course,' he added cheerfully, 'if you get found out I'll probably be out of a job.'

'I'll be careful.'

'Yeah. What the hell, I'm getting ready for the gold watch, anyway.' There was a pause as if he were fantasizing life after retirement. Apparently he didn't like what he saw, because when he came back on the line, there was verve in his voice and he offered a reporter's priapic lament.

'I'm gonna go nuts wondering about this. You sure you don't want to give me a hint about what you're up to?'

'I can't, Ned.'

'OK, OK. Go spin your yarn and keep me in mind if you knit a sweater.'

'I will. Thanks.'

'Oh, hell, don't thank me, I still feel crummy about taking all that time to pay you. I look at my baby now and I see a pink-cheeked, smiling young lady, a beauty. She's still a little too thin for my taste, but she's not a walking corpse like before. She's normal, at least as far as I can tell. She can smile now. I owe you, Doctor.'

'Stay well, Ned.'

'You too.'

I hung up. Biondi's words of gratitude made me entertain a moment's doubt about my own retirement. Then I thought of bloody bodies and doubt got up and took a seat in the rear of the hearse.

It took several false starts and stops to reach the right person at Jedson College.

'Public relations, Ms Dopplemeier.'

'Ms Dopplemeier, this is Alex Delaware. I'm a writer with the *Los Angeles Times*.'

'What can I do for you, Mr Delaware?'

'I'm doing a feature on the small colleges of the West, concentrating on institutions that are not well known but academically excellent nonetheless. Claremont, Occidental, Reed, etcetera. We'd like to include Jedson in the piece.'

'Oh, really?' She sounded surprised, as if it was the first time anyone had labeled Jedson academically excellent. 'That would be very nice, Mr Delaware. I'd be happy to talk to you right now and answer any questions you might have.'

'That wasn't exactly what I had in mind. I'm aiming for a more personal approach. My editor is less interested in statistics than in color. The tenor of the story is that small colleges offer a degree of personal contact and – intimacy – that is missing from the larger universities.'

'How true.'

'I'm actually visiting the campuses, chatting with staff and students – it's an impression piece.'

'I understand exactly what you mean. You want to come across with a voice that's human.'

'Exactly. That's a marvelous way of putting it.'

'I did two years at a trade paper in New Jersey before coming to Jedson.' Within the soul of every flack there lurks a journalistic homunculus, chafing to be released to proclaim 'Scoop!' to the ears of the world.

'Ah, a kindred soul.'

'Well, I've left it, but I do think of going back from time to time.'

'It's no way to get rich, but it does keep me hopping, Ms Dopplemeier.'

'Margaret.'

'Margaret. I'm planning to fly up tonight and wondered if I might come by tomorrow and pay you a visit.'

'Let me check.' I heard paper rustling. 'How about at eleven?'

'Fine.'

'Is there anything you'd like me to do by way of preparation?'

'One thing we're looking at is what happens to graduates of small colleges. I'd be interested in hearing about some of your notable alumni. Doctors, lawyers, that sort of thing.'

'I haven't had a chance to thoroughly acquaint myself with the alumni roster – I've only been here for a few months. But I'll ask around and find out who can help you.'

'I'd appreciate that.'

'Where can I reach you if I need to?'

'I'll be in transit most of the time. You can leave any message with my colleague at the *Times*, Edward Biondi.' I gave her Ned's number.

'Very good. It's all set for tomorrow at eleven. The college is in Bellevue, just outside of Seattle. Do you know where that is?'

'On the east shore of Lake Washington?' Years back I'd been a guest lecturer at the University of Washington and had visited my host's home in Bellevue. I remembered it as an upper-middle-class bedroom community of aggressively contemporary homes, straight-edge lawns and low-rise shopping centers occupied by gourmet shops, antique galleries and high-priced haberdasheries.

'That's correct. If you're coming from downtown take I–5 to 520 which turns into the Evergreen Point Floating Bridge. Drive all the way across the bridge to the east shore, turn south at Fairweather and continue along the coastline. Jedson is on Meydenbauer Bay, right next to the yacht club. I'm on the first floor of Crespi Hall. Will you be staying for lunch?'

'I can't say for sure. It depends upon how my time is running.' And what I find.

'I'll have something prepared for you, just in case.'

'That's very kind of you, Margaret.'

'Anything for a fellow journalist, Alex.'

My next call was to Robin. It took her nine rings to answer.

270

'Hi.' She was out of breath. 'I had the big saw going, didn't hear you. What's up?'

'I'm going out of town for a couple of days.'

'Tahiti, without me?'

'Nothing quite so romantic. Seattle.'

'Oh. Detective work?'

'Call it biographical research.' I told her about Towle's having attended Jedson.

'You're really going after this guy.'

'He's going after me. When I was at WP this morning Henry Bork grabbed me in the hall, trundled me off to his office and delivered a not-so-subtle version of the old arm twist. Seems Towle's been questioning my ethics in public. He keeps cropping up, like toadstools after a flood. He and Kruger share an alma mater and it makes me want to know more about the ivy-covered halls of Jedson.'

'Let me come up with you.'

'No. It's going to be all business. I'll take you on a real vacation, after this is all over.'

'The thought of you going up there all alone depresses me. It's dreary this time of year.'

'I'll be fine. You just take care of yourself and get some work done. I'll call you when I get settled.'

'You're sure you don't want me to come along?'

'You know I love your company, but there'll be no time for sight-seeing. You'd be miserable.'

'All right,' she said reluctantly. 'I'll miss you.'

'I'll miss you too. I love you. Take care.'

'The same goes for you. Love you, sweetie. Bye bye.'

'Bye.'

* * *

I took a 9 P.M. flight out of LAX and landed at Sea-Tac Airport at 11.25. I picked up a rented Nova at a Hertz desk. It was no Seville but it did have an FM radio that someone had left on a classical station. A Bach organ fugue in a minor key unraveled out of the dash speaker and I didn't cut it off: The music matched my mood. I confirmed my reservation at the Westin, drove away from the airport, connected to the Interstate highway and headed north toward downtown Seattle.

The sky was as cold and hard as a handgun. Minutes after I hit the blacktop the gun proved to be loaded: It fired a blast of thunder and the water started coming down. Soon it was one of those angry Northwest torrents that transforms a highway into miles of drive-thru car wash.

'Welcome to the Pacific Northwest,' I said out loud.

Pine, spruce and fir grew in opaque stands on both sides of the road. Starlit billboards advertised rustic motels and diners offering logger's breakfasts. Except for semis groaning under loads of timber I was the road's sole traveler. I thought to myself how nice it would be to be heading for a mountain cabin, Robin at my side, with a trunkload of fishing gear and provisions. I felt a sudden pang of loneliness and longed for human contact.

I reached downtown shortly after midnight. The Westin rose like a giant steel-and-glass test tube amid the darkened laboratory of the city. My seventh-floor room was decent, with a view of Puget Sound and the harbor to the west, Lake Washington and the islands to the east. I kicked off my shoes and stretched out on the bed, tired, but too jumpy for sleep.

I caught the sign-off edition of the news on a local station.

The anchor man was wooden-jawed and shifty-eyed, and reported the day's events impersonally. He lent identical emphasis to an account of mass murder in Ohio and the hockey scores. I cut him off in midsentence, turned off the lights, stripped down in darkness and stared at the harbor lights until I fell asleep.

21

A THOUSAND YARDS of rain forest shielded the Jedson campus from the coastal road. The forest yielded to twin stone columns engraved with Roman numerals that marked the origin of a cobbled drive running through the center of the college. The drive terminated in a circular turn-around punctuated by a pockmarked sundial under a towering pine.

At first glance, Jedson resembled one of those small colleges back East that specialize in looking like dwarf Harvards. The buildings were fashioned of weathered brick and embellished with stone and marble cornices, slate and copper roofing – designed in an era when labor was cheap and intricate moldings, expansive arches, gargoyles and goddesses the order of the day. Even the ivy looked authentic, tumbling from slate peaks, sucking the brick, trimmed topiary-fashion to bypass recessed, leaded windows.

The campus was small, perhaps half a square mile, and filled with tree-shaded knolls, imposing stands of oak, pine, willow, elm and paper birch, and clearings inlaid with marble and bordered by stone benches and bronze monuments. All very traditional until you looked to the west and saw manicured lawns dipping down to the dock and the private harbor beyond. The slips were occupied by streamlined, teak-decked cruisers, fifty-foot craft and larger, topped with sonar and radar screens and clutches of antennae: Clearly twentieth-century, obviously West Coast.

The rain had lifted and a triangle of light peeked out from under the charcoal folds of the sky. A few knots out of the harbor an armada of sailboats sliced through water that looked like tin foil. The boats were rehearsing some type of ceremony, for they each rounded the same buoy marker and unfurled outrageously colored spinnakers – oranges, purples, scarlets and greens, like the tail-feathers of a covey of tropical birds.

There was a lucite-encased map on a stand and I consulted it to locate Crespi Hall. The students passing by seemed a quiet lot. For the most part they were apple-cheeked and flaxen-haired, their eye color traversing the spectrum from light blue to dark blue. Their hairstyles were expensively executed but seemed to date from the Eisenhower age. Trousers were cuffed, pennies shined prettily from the tops of loafers and there were enough alligators on shirts to choke the Everglades. A eugenicist would have been proud to observe the straight backs, robust physiques and stiff-lipped self-assurance of those to the manor born. I felt as if I'd died and gone to Aryan Heaven.

Crespi was a three-story rhomboid fronted by Ionic columns of varicose-veined white marble. The public relations office was hidden behind a mahogany door labeled in gold stencil. When I opened it, the door creaked.

Margaret Dopplemeier was one of those tall, rawboned women predestined for spinsterhood. She'd tried to couch an ungainly body in a tentlike suit of brown tweed, but the angles and corners showed through. She had a big-jawed face, uncompromising lips, and reddish-brown hair cut in an incongruously girlish bob. Her office was hardly larger than the interior of my car – public relations was obviously not a prime concern for the elders of Jedson – and she had to squeeze between the edge of her desk and the wall to get up to greet me. It was a maneuver that would have looked clumsy performed by Pavlova and Margaret Dopplemeier turned it into a lurching stumble. I felt sorry for her but made sure not to show it: She was in her midthirties and by that age women like her have learned to cherish self-reliance. It's as good a way as any of coping with solitude.

'Hello, you must be Alex.'

'I am. Pleased to meet you, Margaret.' Her hand was thick, hard and chafed – from too much wringing or too much washing, I couldn't be sure.

'Please sit down.'

I took a slat-backed chair and sat in it uncomfortably.

'Coffee?'

'Please. With cream.'

There was a table with a hot plate to the back of her desk. She poured coffee into a mug and gave it to me.

'Have you decided about lunch?'

The prospect of looking across the table at her for an extra hour didn't thrill me. It wasn't her plainness, nor her stern face. She looked ready to tell me her life story and I was in no mood to fill my head with extraneous material. I declined.

'How about a snack, then?'

She brought forth a tray of cheese and crackers, looking uncomfortable in the role of hostess. I wondered why she'd gravitated toward PR Library science would have seemed more fitting. Then the thought occurred to me that public relations at Jedson was probably akin to library work, a desk job involving lots of clipping and mailing and very little face-to-face contact.

'Thank you.' I was hungry and the cheese was good.

'Well.' She looked around her desk, found a pair of eyeglasses, and put them on. Behind the glass her eyes grew larger and somehow softer. 'You want to get a feel for Jedson.'

'That's right – the flavor of the place.'

'It's quite a unique place. I'm from Wisconsin myself, went to school at Madison, with forty thousand students. There are only two thousand here. Everyone knows everyone else.'

'Kind of like one big family.' I took out a pen and notepad.

'Yes.' At the word family her mouth pursed. 'You might say that.' She shuffled some papers and began reciting:

'Jedson College was founded by Josiah T. Jedson, a Scottish immigrant who made his fortune in mining and railroads in 1858. That's three years before the University of Washington was founded, so we're really the old school in town. Jedson's intention was to endow an institution of higher learning where traditional values coexisted side by side with education in the basic arts and sciences. To this day, primary funding for the college comes from an annuity from the Jedson Foundation, although other sources of income are existent.'

'I've heard tuition is rather high.'

'Tuition,' she frowned, 'is twelve thousand dollars a year, plus housing, registration and miscellaneous fees.'

I whistled.

'Do you give scholarships?'

'A small number of scholarships for deserving students are given each year, but there is no extensive program of financial aid.'

'Then there's no interest in attracting students from a wide socio-economic range.'

'Not particularly, no.'

She took off her glasses, put her prepared material aside and stared at me myopically.

'I would hope we don't get into that particular line of questioning.'

'Why is that, Margaret?'

She moved her lips, trying on several unspoken words for size, rejecting them all. Finally she said: 'I thought this was going to be an impression piece. Something positive.'

'It will be. I was simply curious.' I had touched a nerve – not that it did me any good, for upsetting my source of information was the last thing I needed. But something about the upper-class smugness of the place was irritating me and bringing out the bad boy.

'I see.' She put her glasses back on and picked up her papers, scanned them and pursed her lips. 'Alex,' she said, 'can I speak to you off the record – one writer to another?'

'Sure.' I closed the notepad and put the pen in my jacket pocket.

'I don't know how to put this.' She played with one tweed lapel, twisting the coarse cloth then smoothing it. 'This story, your visit – neither are particularly welcomed by the administration. As you may be able to tell from the grandeur of our surroundings, public relations is not avidly sought by Jedson College. After I spoke to you yesterday I told my superiors about your coming, thinking they'd be more than pleased. In fact, just the opposite was true. I wasn't exactly given a pat on the back.'

She pouted, as if recalling a particularly painful spanking.

'I didn't intend to get you in trouble, Margaret.'

'There was no way to know. As I told you, I'm new here. They do things differently. It's another way of life – quiet, conservative. There's a timeless quality to the place.'

'How,' I asked, 'does a college attract enrolment without attracting attention?'

She chewed her lip.

'I really don't want to get into it.'

'Margaret, it's off the record. Don't stonewall me.'

'It's not important,' she insisted, but her bosom heaved and conflict showed in the flat, magnified eyes. I played on that conflict.

'Then what's the fuss? We writers need to be open with one another. There are enough censors out there.'

She thought about that for a long time. The tug-of-war was evident on her face and I couldn't help but feel rotten.

'I don't want to leave here,' she finally said. 'I have a nice apartment with a view of the lake, my cats and my books. I don't want to lose – everything. I don't want to have to pack up and move back to the Midwest. To miles of flatland with no mountains, no way of establishing one's perspective. Do you understand?'

Her manner and tone were brittle – I knew that manner, for I'd seen it in countless therapy patients, just before the defenses came tumbling down. She wanted to let go and I was going to help her, manipulative bastard that I was . . .

'Do you understand what I'm saying?' she was asking.

And I heard myself answer, so smooth, so sweet:

'Of course I do.'

'Anything I tell you has to be confidential. Not for print.'

'I promise. I'm a feature writer. I have no aspirations of becoming Woodward or Bernstein.'

A faint smile appeared on the large, bland features.

'You don't? I did, once upon a time. After four years on the Madison student paper I thought I was going to turn journalism on its ear. I went for one solid year with no writing job – I did waitressing. I hated it. Then I worked for a dog magazine, writing cutesy-poo press releases on poodles and schnauzers. They brought the little beasts into the office for photographs and they fouled the carpet. It stunk. When that folded I spent two years covering union meetings and polka parties in New Jersey and that finally squeezed all the illusions out of me. Now all I want is peace.'

Again the glasses came off. She closed her eyes and massaged her temples.

'When you get down to it, that's what all of us want,' I said.

She opened her eyes and squinted in my direction. From the way she strained I must have been a blur. I tried to look like a trustworthy blur.

She popped two pieces of cheese into her mouth and ground them to dust with lantern jaws.

'I don't know that any of it is relevant to your story,' she said. 'Especially if it's a puff piece you're after.'

I forced a laugh.

'Now that you've got me interested, don't leave me dangling.'

She smiled. 'One writer to another?'

'One writer to another.'

'Oh,' she sighed, 'I suppose it's no biggie.

'In the first place,' she told me, between mouthfuls of cheese, 'no, Jedson College is not interested in attracting outsiders, period. It's a college, but in name and formal status only. What Jedson College really is – functionally – is a *holding pen*. A place for the privileged class to stash their children for four years before the boys enter Daddy's business and the girls marry the boys and turn into Suzy Homemaker and join the Junior League. The boys major in business or economics, the girls in art history and home economics. The gentleman's C is the common goal. Being too smart is frowned upon. Some of the brighter ones do go on to law school or medical school. But when they finish their training they return to the fold.'

She sounded bitter, a wallflower describing last year's prom.

'The average household income of the families that send their kids here is over a hundred thousand dollars a year. Think of that, Alex. Everyone is rich. Did you see the harbor?'

I nodded.

'Those floating toys belong to students.' She paused, as if she still couldn't believe it. 'The parking lot looks like the Monte Carlo Grand Prix. These kids wear cashmere and suede for horsing around.'

One of her raw, coarse hands found the other and caressed it. She looked from wall to wall of the tiny room as if searching for hidden listening devices. I wondered what she was so nervous about. So Jedson was a school for rich kids. Stanford had started out that way too and might have ended up similarly stagnant if someone hadn't figured out that not letting in smart Jews and Asians and other people with funny names and high IQs would lead to eventual academic entropy.

'There's no crime in being rich,' I said.

'It's not just that. It's the utter mindlessness that goes along with it. I was at Madison during the sixties. There was a sense of social awareness. Activism. We were working to end the war. Now it's the anti-nukes movement. The university can be a greenhouse for the conscience. Here, nothing grows.'

I envisioned her fifteen years back, dressed in khakis and sweatshirt, marching and mouthing slogans. Radicalism had fought a losing battle with survival, eroded by too much of nothing. But she could still take an occasional hit of nostalgia . . .

'It's especially hard on the faculty,' she was saying. 'Not the Old Guard. The Young Turks – they actually call themselves that. They come here because of the job crunch, with their typical academic idealism and liberal views and last two, maybe three years. It's intellectually stultifying – not to mention the frustration of earning fifteen thousand dollars a year when the student's wardrobes cost more than that.'

'You sound as if you have first-hand knowledge.'

'I do. There was – a man. A good friend of mine. He came here to teach philosophy. He was brilliant, a Princeton graduate, a genuine scholar. It ate him up. He talked to me about it, told me what it was like to stand up in front of a class and lecture on Kierkegaard and Sartre and see thirty pairs of vacant blue eyes staring back, *Übermensch U*. he called it. He left last year.'

She looked pained. I changed the subject.

'You mentioned the Old Guard. Who are they?'

'Jedson graduates who actually develop an interest in something other than making money. They go on to earn advanced degrees in humanities – something totally useless like history or sociology or literature – and then come crawling back here to teach. Jedson takes care of its own.'

'I'd imagine they find it easier to relate to the students, coming from the same background.'

'They must. They stay on. Most of them are older – there haven't been too many returning scholars lately. The Old Guard may be shrinking. Some are quite decent, really. I get the feeling they were always outcasts – the misfits. Even the privileged castes have those, I suppose.'

The look on her face bespoke firsthand experience with the pain of social rejection. She may have sensed she was in danger of crossing the boundary from social commentary to psychological striptease, for she drew back, put on her glasses and smiled sourly.

'How's that for public relations?'

'For someone new you've certainly got a handle on the place.'

'Some of it I've seen for myself. Some I learned.'

'From your friend the scholar?'

'Yes.' She stopped and picked up an oversized imitation leather handbag. It didn't take her long to find what she was looking for.

'This is Lee,' she said, and handed me a snapshot of herself and a man several inches shorter than she. The man was balding, with tufts of thick, dark, curling hair over each ear, a bushy dark mustache and rimless round spectacles. He wore a faded blue work shirt and jeans and high-laced hiking boots. Margaret Dopplemeier was dressed in a serape that accentuated her size, baggy cords and flat sandals. She had her arm around him, and looked maternal and childishly dependent at the same time. 'He's in New Mexico now, working on his book. In solitude, he says.'

I gave her back the photo.

'Writers often need that.'

'Yes. We've gone round and round about that.' She put her keepsake back, made a move toward the cheese and then retracted her hand, as if she'd suddenly lost her appetite.

I let a silent moment pass, then performed a lateral arabesque away from her personal life.

'What you're saying is fascinating, Margaret. Jedson is set up with all the enrolment it needs – it's a self-perpetuating system.'

The word 'system' can be a psychological catalyst for anyone who's flirted with the Left. It got her going again.

'Absolutely. The percentage of students whose parents are also Jedson graduates is unbelievably high. I'll bet that the two thousand students come from no more than five to seven hundred families. The same surnames keep cropping up when I compile lists. That's why when you called it a family before I was taken aback. I wondered how much you knew.'

'Nothing until I came here.'

'Yes. I've said too much, haven't I?'

'In a closed system,' I persisted, 'publicity is the last thing the establishment wants.'

'Of course. Jedson is an anachronism. It survives the twentieth century by staying small and keeping out of the headlines. My instructions were to wine you, dine you, see that you took a nice little stroll around the campus, then escort you off the grounds with little or nothing to write about. The Trustees of Jedson don't want exposure in the *Los Angeles Times*. They don't want issues like affirmative action or equal opportunity enrolment to rear their ugly heads.'

'I appreciate your honesty, Margaret.'

For a moment I thought she was going to cry.

'Don't make it sound as if I'm some kind of saint. I'm not and I know it. My talking to you was spineless. Deceitful. The people here aren't evil, I have no right to expose them. They've been good to me. But I get so weary of putting up a front, of attending quaint little teas with women who can talk all day about china patterns and place settings – they give a class here in place settings, do you believe that?'

She looked at her hands as if unable to envision them holding anything as delicate as china.

'My job is pretense, Alex. I'm a glorified mailing service. But I'll not leave,' she insisted, debating an unseen adversary. 'Not yet. Not at this point in my life. I wake up and see the lake. I have my books and a good stereo. I can pick fresh blackberries not far from here. I eat them in the morning with cream.'

I said nothing.

'Will you betray me?' she asked.

'Of course not, Margaret.'

'Then go. Forget about including Jedson in your story. There's nothing here for an outsider.'

'I can't.'

She sat straight in her chair.

'Why not?' There was terror and anger in her voice, something decidedly menacing in her eyes. I could understand her lover's flight to solitude. I was certain the mental deadness of Jedson's student body wasn't the only thing he'd been escaping.

I had nothing to offer her that would keep our lines of communication open, other than the truth and the chance to be a coconspirator. I took a deep breath and told her the real reason for my visit.

When I was through she wore the same possessive-dependent look I'd seen in her photograph. I wanted to back away, but my chair was inches from the door.

'It's funny,' she said, 'I should feel exploited, used. But I don't. You have an honest face. Even your lies sound righteous.'

'I'm no more righteous than you are. I simply want to get some facts. Help me.'

'I was a member of SDS, you know. The police were pigs to me in those days.'

'These aren't those days, I'm not a policeman, and we're not talking about abstract theory and the polemics of revolution. This is triple murder, Margaret, child abuse, maybe more. Not political assassinations. Innocent people hacked into bloody gobbets, mashed into human garbage. Children run down on lonely canyon roads.'

She shuddered, turned away, ran an unpolished fingernail along the top of a tooth, then faced me again.

'And you think one of them – a Jedsonite – was responsible for all of that?' The very idea was delicious to her.

'I think two of them had some involvement in it.'

'Why are you doing this? You say you're a psychiatrist.'

'Psychologist.'

'Whatever. What's in it for you?'

'Nothing. Nothing you'd believe.'

'Try me.'

'I want to see justice done. It's been eating at me.'

'I believe you,' she said softly.

She was gone for twenty minutes and when she returned it was with an armful of oversized volumes bound in dark blue Morocco leather.

'These are the yearbooks, if your estimates of their ages are correct. I'm going to leave you with them and search for the alumni files. Lock yourself in when I'm gone and don't answer the door. I'll knock three times, then twice. That will be our signal.'

'Roger.'

'Ha.' She laughed, and for the first time looked almost attractive.

Timothy Kruger had lied about being a poor boy at Jedson. His family had donated a couple of buildings and even a casual reading of the book made it obvious the Krugers were Very Important. The part about his athletic prowess, though, was true. He'd lettered in track, baseball and Greco-Roman wrestling. In his yearbook pictures he resembled the man I'd spoken to days before. There were shots of him jumping hurdles, throwing the javelin, and later on, in a section on drama, in the roles of Hamlet and Petruchio. The impression I got was that of a big man on campus. I wondered how he'd ended up at La Casa de los Niños operating under a phony credential.

L. Willard Towle's photo showed him to have been a Tab

Hunter-type blond in his youth. Notations under his name mentioned presidency of the Pre-Med Club and the Biology Honor Society, as well as captain of the crew team. There was also an asterisk that led to a footnote advising the reader to turn to the last page of the book. I obeyed the instructions and came to a black-bordered photograph – the same picture I'd seen in Towle's office, of his wife and son against a backdrop of lake and mountains. There was an inscription beneath the photo:

In Memoriam
Lilah Hutchison Towle
1930–1951

Lionel Willard Towle, Jr
1949–1951

Under the inscription were four lines of verse.

How swiftly doth the night move
To dash our hopes and dim our dreams;
But even in the darkest night
The ray of peace yet beams.

It was signed 'S.'

I was rereading the poem when Margaret Dopplemeier's coded knock sounded on the door. I slid open the latch and she came in holding a manila envelope. She locked the door, went behind her desk, opened the packet and shook out two three-by-five index cards.

'These are straight out of the sacred alumni file.' She

glanced at one and handed it to me. 'Here's your doctor.'

Towle's name was at the top, written out in elegant script. There were several entries under it, in different hands and different colors of ink. Most of them took the form of abbreviations and numeric codes.

'Can you explain it to me?'

She came around and sat down next to me, took the card and studied it.

'There's nothing mysterious about any of it. The abbreviations are meant to save space. The five digits after the name are the alumnus code, for mailing, filing, that kind of thing. After that you've got the number 3, which means he's the third member of his family to attend Jedson. the *med* is self-explanatory – it's an occupation code, and the *F:med* means medicine is also the family's primary business. If it were shipping, it would say *shp*, banking, *bnk*, and so on. *B:51* is the year he received his bachelor's degree. *M:J, 148793* indicates that he married another Jedson student and her alumnus code is cross-referenced. Here's something interesting – there's a small *d* in parentheses after the wife's code, which means she's deceased, and the date of death is 6/17/51 – she died when he was still a student here. Did you know that?'

'I did. Would there be any way of finding out more about that?' She thought for a moment.

'We could check the local papers for that week, for an obituary or funeral notice.'

'What about the student paper?'

'The *Spartan* is a rag,' she said scornfully, 'but I suppose it would cover something like that. Back issues are stored in the library, on the other side of campus. We can go there later. Do you think it's relevant?'

She was flushed, girlish, given over totally to our little intrigue.

'It just could be, Margaret. I want to know everything I can about these people.'

'Van der Graaf,' she said.

'What's that?'

'Professor Van der Graaf, from the history department. He's the oldest of the Old Guard, been around Jedson longer than anyone I know of. On top of that he's a great gossip. I sat next to him at a garden party and the sweet old thing told me all sorts of tidbits – who was sleeping with whom, faculty dirt and the like.'

'They let him get away with it?'

'He's close to ninety, rolling in family money, unmarried with no heirs. They're just waiting for him to croak and leave it all to their college. He's been emeritus from way back. Keeps an office on campus, sequesters himself there pretending to write books. I wouldn't be surprised if he sleeps there. He knows more about Jedson than anybody.'

'Do you think he'd talk to me?'

'If he was in the right mood. In fact I thought of him when you told me over the phone that you wanted to find out about illustrious alumni. But I figured it was too risky leaving him alone with a reporter. You never know what he's going to do or say.'

She giggled, enjoying the old man's ability to rebel from a position of power.

'Of course now that I know what you want,' she continued, 'he'd be perfect. You'd need some kind of story about why you wanted to talk about Towle, but I don't imagine that would be very difficult for someone as artful as you.'

'How about this: I'm a reporter for *Medical World News*. Call me Bill Roberts. Dr Towle's been elected President of the Academy of Pediatrics and I'm doing a background story on him.'

'Sounds good. I'll call him now.'

She reached for the phone and I took another look at Towle's alumnus card. The only information she hadn't covered was a column of dated entries under the heading $ – donations to Jedson, I assumed. They averaged ten thousand dollars a year. Towle was a faithful son.

'Professor Van der Graaf,' she was saying, 'this is Margaret Dopplemeier from Public Relations. I've been fine, thank you, and yourself? Very good – oh, I'm sure we can work that out, Professor.' She covered the receiver with her hand and winked at me, mouthing the words 'good mood.' 'I didn't know you liked pizza, Professor. No. No, I don't like anchovies either. Yes, I do like Duesenbergs. I know you do . . . Yes, I know. The rain was coming down in sheets, Professor. Yes, I would. Yes, when the weather clears up. With the top down. I'll bring the pizza.'

She flirted with Van der Graaf for five more minutes and finally broached the subject of my visit. She listened, gave me the OK sign with thumb and forefinger and went back to flirting. I picked up Kruger's card.

He was the fifth member of his family to attend Jedson and his degree was listed as having been granted five years previously. There was no mention of current position – the family was recorded as being active in *stl*, and *rl-est*. No mention of matrimony was present, nor had he donated money to the school. There was however an interesting cross-reference. Under *REL-F*: It said Towle. Finally, the three letters DLT were written in large, block characters at the bottom of the card.

Margaret got off the phone.

'He'll see you. As long as I come along, and quote: Give me a brisk massage, young lady. You'll be prolonging the years of a living fossil, unquote. The old lecher,' she added affectionately.

I asked her about Towle's name on Kruger's card.

'*REL-F* – related family. Apparently your two subjects are cousins of some sort.'

'Why isn't that listed on Towle's card as well?'

'The heading was probably added after he graduated. Rather than go back and mark each card they simply used it on the new ones. *DLT*, though, is more interesting. He's been deleted from the file.'

'Why's that?'

'I don't know. It doesn't say. It never would. Some transgression. With his family background it had to be something big. Something that made the school want to wash its hands of him.' She looked up at me. 'This is getting interesting, isn't it?'

'Very.'

She put the cards back in the envelope and locked it in her desk.

'I'll take you to Van der Graaf now.'

22

A GILDED CAGE of an elevator took us to the fifth floor of a domed building on the west side of the campus. It relaxed its jaws and let us out into a silent rotunda, wainscoted in marble and veneered with dust. The ceiling was concave plaster upon which a now-faded mural of cherubs blowing bugles had been painted: We were inside the shell of the dome. The walls were stone and gave off an odor of rotting paper. A stationary diamond-paned window separated two oak doors. One was labeled MAP ROOM and looked as if it hadn't been opened in generations. The other was blank.

Margaret knocked on the unadorned door and, when no answer was forthcoming, pushed it open. The room it revealed was high-ceilinged and spacious, with cathedral windows that afforded a view of the harbor. Every free inch of wall space was taken up by bookshelves crammed haphazardly with ragged volumes. Those books that hadn't found a resting place in the shelves sat in precariously balanced stacks on the floor. In the center of the room was a trestle table piled high with manuscripts and still more books. A globe on a wheeled stand and an ancient claw-footed desk were pushed into the corner. A McDonald's take-out box and a couple of crumpled, greasy napkins sat atop the desk.

'Professor?' said Margaret. To me: 'I wonder where he's gone.'

'Peek-a-boo!' The sound came from somewhere behind the trestle table.

Margaret jumped and her purse flew out of her hands. The contents spilled on the floor.

A gnarled head peeked around the curled edges of a pile of yellowed paper.

'Sorry to startle you, dear.' The head came into view, thrown back in silent laughter.

'Professor,' said Margaret, 'shame on you.' She bent to retrieve the scattered debris.

He came out from behind the table looking sheepish. Until that point I'd thought he was sitting. But when the head didn't rise in my sight I realized he'd been standing all along.

He was four feet and a few inches tall. His body was of conventional size but it was bent at the waist, the spine twisted in an S, the deformed back burdened with a hump the size of a tightly packed knapsack. His head seemed too large for his frame, a wrinkled egg topped by a fringe of wispy white hair. When he moved he resembled a drowsy scorpion.

He wore an expression of mock contrition but the twinkle in the rheumy blue eyes said far more than did the down-turned, lipless mouth.

'Can I help you, dear?' His voice was dry and cultured.

Margaret gathered the last personal effects from the floor and put them in her purse.

'No, thank you, Professor. I've got it all.' She caught her breath and tried to look composed.

'Will you still come with me on our pizza picnic?'

'Only if you behave yourself.'

He put his hands together, as if in prayer.

'I promise, dear,' he said.

'All right. Professor, this is Bill Roberts, the journalist I spoke to you about. Bill, Professor Garth Van der Graaf.'

'Hello, Professor.'

He looked up at me from under sleepy lids.

'You don't look like Clark Kent,' he said.

'I beg your pardon.'

'Aren't newspaper reporters supposed to look like Clark Kent?'

'I wasn't aware of that specific union regulation.'

'I was interviewed by a reporter after the War – the big one. Number two – pardon the scatological entendre. He wanted to know what place the war would have in history. *He* looked like Clark Kent.' He ran one hand over his liver-spotted scalp. 'Don't you have a pair of glasses or something, young man?'

'I'm sorry, but my eyes are quite healthy.'

He turned his back to me and walked to one of the bookshelves. There was a queer, reptilian grace to his movements, the stunted body seeming to travel sideways while actually moving forward. He climbed slowly up a footstool, reached up and grabbed a leatherbound volume, climbed down and returned.

'Look,' he said, opening the book which I now saw was a looseleaf binder containing a collection of comic books. 'This is who I mean.' A shaky finger pointed to a picture of the *Daily Planet*'s star reporter entering a phone booth. 'Clark Kent. *That's* a reporter.'

'I'm sure Mr Roberts knows who Clark Kent is, Professor.'

'Then let him come back when he looks more like him and I'll talk to him,' the old man snapped.

Margaret and I exchanged helpless looks. She started to say something and Van der Graaf threw back his head and let out an arid cackle.

'April Fool!' He laughed lustily at his own wit, the merriment dissolving into a phlegmy fit of coughing.

'Oh, Professor!' Margaret scolded.

They went at each other again, verbally jousting. I began to suspect that their relationship was well established. I stood on the sidelines feeling like an unwilling spectator at a freak show.

'Admit it, dear,' he was saying, 'I had you fooled!' He stamped his foot with glee. 'You thought I'd gone totally senile!'

'You're no more senile than I,' she replied. 'You're simply a naughty boy!'

My hopes of getting reliable information from the shrunken hunchback were diminishing by the moment. I cleared my throat.

They stopped and stared at me. A bubble of saliva had collected in the corner of Van der Graaf's puckered mouth. His hands vibrated with a faint palsy. Margaret towered over him, legs akimbo.

'Now I want you to cooperate with Mr Roberts,' she said sternly.

Van der Graaf gave me a dirty look.

'Oh, all right,' he whined. 'But only if you drive me around the lake in my Doosie.'

'I said I would.'

'I have a thirty-seven Duesenberg,' he explained to me.

'Magnificent chariot. Four hundred snorting stallions under a gleaming ruby bonnet. Chromium pipes. Consumes petroleum with ravenous abandon. I can no longer drive it. Maggie, here, is a large wench. Under my tutelage she could handle it. But she refuses.'

'Professor Van der Graaf, there was a good reason why I turned you down. It was raining and I didn't want to get behind the wheel of a car worth two hundred thousand dollars in hazardous weather.'

'Pshaw. I took that baby from here to Sonoma in forty-four. It thrives on meteorological adversity.'

'All right. I'll drive you. Tomorrow, if I get a good report on your behavior from Mr Roberts.'

'I'm the professor. I do the grading.'

She ignored him.

'I have to go to the library, Mr Roberts. Can you find your way back to my office?'

'Certainly.'

'I'll see you when you're through, then. Goodbye, Professor.'

'Tomorrow at one. Rain or shine,' he called after her.

When the door had closed he invited me to sit.

'I'll stand, myself. Can't find a chair that fits me. When I was a boy Father called in carpenters and woodcarvers, trying to come up with some way to seat me comfortably. To no avail. They did produce some fascinating abstract sculpture, however.' He laughed, and held on to the trestle table for support. 'I've stood most of my life. In the end it probably was beneficial. I've got legs like pig iron. My circulation's as good as that of a man half my age.'

I sat in a leather armchair. We were at eye level.

'That Maggie,' he said. 'Such a sad girl. I flirt with her, try to cheer her up. She seems so lonely most of the time.' He rummaged among the papers and pulled out a flask.

'Irish whiskey. You'll find two glasses in the top right drawer of the desk. Kindly retrieve them and give them to me.'

I found the glasses, which looked none too clean. Van der Graaf filled them each with an inch of whiskey, without spilling a drop.

'Here.'

I watched him sip his drink and followed suit.

'Do you think she could be a virgin? Is such a thing possible in this day and age?' He approached the question as if it were an epistemological puzzle.

'I really couldn't say, Professor. I only just met her an hour ago.'

'I can't conceive of it, virginity in a woman her age. Yet the notion of those milkmaid's thighs wrapped around a pair of rutting buttocks is equally preposterous.' He drank more whiskey, contemplated Margaret Dopplemeier's sex life in silence, and stared off into space.

Finally he said: 'You're a patient young man. A rare quality.'

I nodded.

'I figure you'll come around when you're ready, Professor.'

'Yes, I do confess to a fair amount of childish behavior. It's a perquisite of my age and station. Do you know how long it's been since I taught a class or wrote a scholarly paper?'

'Quite a while, I imagine.'

'Over two decades. Since then I've been up here engaged in long solitary stretches of allegedly deep thought – actually I loaf. And yet, I'm an honored Professor Emeritus. Don't you think it's an absurd system that tolerates such nonsense?'

'Perhaps there's a feeling that you've earned the right to retirement with honor.'

'Bah!' He waved his hand. 'That sounds too much like death. Retirement with honor and maggots gnawing at one's toes. I'll confess to you, young man, that I never earned anything. I wrote sixty-seven papers in learned journals, all but five utter garbage. I coedited three books that no one ever read, and, in general, pursued a life of a spoiled wastrel. It's been wonderful.'

He finished his whiskey and put the glass down on the table with a thump.

'They keep me around here because I've got millions of dollars in a tax-free trust fund set up for me by Father and they hope I'll bequeath it all to them.' He smiled crookedly. 'I may or may not. Perhaps I should will it all to some Negro organization, or something equally outrageous. A group fighting for the rights of lesbians, perhaps. Is there such a cabal?'

'I'm sure there must be.'

'Yes. In California, no doubt. Speaking of which, you want to know about Willie Towle from Los Angeles, do you?'

I repeated the story about *Medical World News*.

'All right,' he sighed, 'if you insist, I'll try to help you. God knows why anyone would be interested in Willie Towle, for a duller boy never set foot on this campus. When I found out he became a physician, I was amazed. I never thought him intellectually capable of anything quite that advanced. Of course the family is firmly rooted in medicine – one of the Towles was Grant's personal surgeon during the Civil War – there's a morsel for your article – and I imagine getting Willie admitted to medical school was no particular challenge.'

'He's turned out to be quite a successful doctor.'

'That *doesn't* surprise me. There are different types of success. One requires a combination of personality traits that Willie did indeed possess: Perseverance, lack of imagination, innate conservatism. Of course, a good, straight body and a conventionally attractive face don't hurt, either. I'll wager he hasn't climbed the ranks by virtue of being a profound scientific thinker or innovative researcher. His strengths are of a more mundane nature, are they not?'

'He has a reputation as a fine doctor,' I insisted. 'His patients have only good things to say about him.'

'Tells them exactly what they want to hear, no doubt. Willie was always good at that. Very popular, president of this and that. He was my student in a course on European civilization, and he was a charmer. Yes, Professor, no, Professor. Always there to hold out my chair for me – Lord, how I detested that. Not to mention the fact that I rarely sat.' He grimaced at the recollection. 'Yes, there was a certain banal charm there. People like that in their doctors. I believe it's called bedside manner. Of course his essay exams were most telling, revealing his true substance. Predictable, accurate but not illuminating, grammatical without being literate.' He paused. 'This isn't the kind of information you were expecting, is it?'

I smiled. 'Not exactly.'

'You can't print this, can you?' He seemed disappointed.

'No. I'm afraid the article is meant to be laudatory.'

'Hale and hearty blah-blah stuff – in the vernacular, bull-shit, eh? How boring. Doesn't it bore you to have to write such drivel?'

'At times. It pays the bills.'

'Yes. How arrogant of me not to take that into consideration. I've never had to pay bills. My bankers do that for me. I've always had far more money than I know what to do with. It leads one to incredible ignorance. It's a common fault of the indolent rich. We're unbelievably ignorant. And inbred. It brings about psychological as well as physical aberrations.' He smiled, reached around with one arm, and tapped his hunch. 'This entire campus is a haven for the offspring of the indolent, ignorant, inbred rich. Including your Doctor Willie Towle. He descends from one of the most rarefied environments you will ever find. Did you know that?'

'Being a doctor's son?'

'No, no.' He dismissed me as if I were an especially stupid pupil. 'He's one of the Two Hundred – you haven't heard of them?'

'No.'

'Go into the bottom drawer of my desk and pull out the old map of Seattle.'

I did what I was told. The map was folded under several back issues of *Playboy*.

'Give it to me,' he said impatiently. He opened it and spread it on the table. 'Look here.'

I stood over him. His finger pointed to a spot at the north

end of the Sound. To a tiny island shaped like a diamond.

'Brindamoor Island. Three square miles of innately unappealing terrain upon which are situated two hundred mansions and estates to rival any found in the United States. Josiah Jedson built his first home there – a Gothic monstrosity, it was – and others of his ilk mimicked him. I have cousins who reside there – most of us are related in one way or the other – though Father built *our* home on the mainland, in Windermere.'

'It's barely noticeable.'

The island was a speck in the Pacific.

'And meant to be that way, my boy. In many of the older maps the island isn't even labeled. Of course there's no land access. The ferry makes one round-trip from the harbor when the weather and tides permit. It's not unusual for a week or two to elapse without the trip being completed. Some of the residents own private airplanes and have landing strips on their properties. Most are content to remain in splendid isolation.'

'And Dr Towle grew up there?'

'He most certainly did. I believe the ancestral digs have been sold. He was an only son and when he moved to California there seemed no reason to hold on to it – most of the homes are far larger than homes have a right to be. Architectural dinosaurs. Frightfully expensive to maintain – even the Two Hundred have to budget nowadays. Not all had ancestors as clever as Father.'

He patted his midriff in self-congratulation.

'Do you feel growing up in that kind of isolation had any effect on Dr Towle?'

'Now you sound like a psychologist, young man.'

302

I smiled.

'In answer to your question: Most certainly. The children of the Two Hundred were an insufferably snobbish lot – and to merit that designation at Jedson College requires extraordinary chauvinism. They were clannish, self-centered, spoiled, and not overly bright. Many had deformed siblings with chronic physical or mental problems – my remark about inbreeding was meant in all seriousness – and seemed to have been left callous and indifferent by the experience, rather than the opposite.'

'You're using the past tense. Don't they exist today?'

'There are amazingly few young ones left. They get a taste of the outside world and are reluctant to return to Brindamoor – it really is quite bleak, despite the indoor tennis courts and one pathetic excuse for a country club.'

To stay in character I had to defend Towle.

'Professor, I don't know Doctor Towle well, but he's very well spoken of. I've met him and he seems to be a forceful man, of strong character. Isn't it possible that growing up in the type of environment you describe Brindamoor to be could increase one's individuality?'

The old man looked at me with contempt.

'Rubbish! I understand you have to pretty up his image, but you'll get nothing but the truth from me. There wasn't an individual in the bunch from Brindamoor. Young man, solitude is the nectar of individuality. Our Willie Towle had no taste for it.'

'Why do you say that?'

'I cannot recall ever seeing him alone. He palled around with two other dullards from the island. The three of them pranced around like little dictators. The Three Heads of

State they were called behind their backs – pretentious, puffed-up boys. Willie, Stu and Eddy.'

'Stu and Eddy?'

'Yes, yes, that's what I said. Stuart Hickle and Edwin Hayden.'

At the mention of those names I gave an involuntary start. I struggled to neutralize my expression, hoping the old man hadn't noticed the reaction. Happily, he appeared oblivious, as he lectured in that parched voice:

'. . . and Hickle was a sickly, pimple-faced rotter with a spooky disposition, not a word out of him that wasn't censored by the other two. Hayden was a mean-spirited little sneak. I caught him cheating on an exam and he attempted to bribe me out of failing him by offering to procure for me an Indian prostitute of supposedly exotic talents – can you imagine such gall, as if I were unable to fend for myself in affairs of lust! Of course I failed him and wrote a sharp letter to his parents. Got no reply – no doubt they never read it, off on some European jaunt. Do you know what became of him?' he ended rhetorically.

'No,' I lied.

'He's now a judge – in Los Angeles. In fact, I believe all three of them, the glorious Heads, moved to Los Angeles. Hickle's some kind of chemist – wanted to be a doctor, just like Willie, and I believe he actually did begin medical school. But he was too stupid to pull through.'

'A judge,' he repeated. 'What does that say about our judicial system?'

The information was pouring in fast and, like a pauper suddenly discovering a sizeable inheritance, I wasn't sure how to deal with it. I wanted to shed my cover and wring

304

every last bit of information out of the old man, but there was the case – and my promises to Margaret – to think about.

'I'm a nasty old bugger, am I not?' cackled Van der Graaf.

'You seem very perceptive, Professor.'

'Oh, do I?' He smiled craftily. 'Any other tidbits I can toss your way?'

'I know Dr Towle lost his wife and child several years back. What can you tell me about that?'

He stared at me, then refilled his glass and sipped. 'All part of your story?'

'All part of fleshing out the portrait,' I said. It sounded feeble.

'Ah, yes, fleshing it out. Of course. Well, it was a tragedy, no two ways about it, and your doctor was rather young to be dealing with it. He was married during his sophomore year to a lovely girl from a good Portland family. Lovely, but outside his circle – the Two Hundred tended to marry each other. The engagement came as a bit of a surprise. Six months later the girl gave birth to a son and that mystery was cleared up.

'For a while the trio seemed to be breaking up – Hickle and Hayden slinked off by themselves as Willie attended to the duties of a married man. Then the wife and child were killed and the Heads were reunited. I suppose it's natural that a man will seek the comfort of friends in the wake of such a loss.'

'How did it happen?'

He peered into his glass and downed the last few drops.

'The girl – the mother – was taking the child to the hospital. He'd woken up with the croup or some such ailment. The nearest emergency facility was at the Children's

Orthopedic Hospital, at the University. It was in the early morning hours, still dark. Her car went over the Evergreen Bridge and plunged into the lake. It was daybreak before it was found.'

'Where was Dr Towle?'

'Studying. Burning the midnight oil. Of course this caused him to be guilt-stricken, absolutely wretched. No doubt he blamed himself for not having been there and been drowned himself. You know the type of self-flagellation embraced by the bereaved.'

'A tragic affair.'

'Oh yes. She was a lovely girl.'

'Dr Towle keeps her picture in his office.'

'A sentimentalist, is he?'

'I suppose.' I drank some whiskey. 'After the tragedy he began seeing more of his friends?'

'Yes. Though as I hear you use the term I realize something. In my concept of friendship there is implied a bond of affection, some degree of mutual admiration. Those three always looked so grim when they were together – they didn't seem to enjoy each other's company. I never knew what the link between them was, but it did exist. Willie went away to medical school and Stuart tagged along. Edwin Hayden attended law school at the same university. They settled in the same city. No doubt you'll be contacting the other two in order to obtain *laudatory* quotes for your article. If there is an article.'

I struggled to remain calm.

'What do you mean?'

'Oh, I think you know what I mean, my boy. I'm not going to ask you to present identification confirming you're

306

who you say you are — it wouldn't prove a thing anyway — because you seem like a pleasant, intelligent young man and how many visitors to whom I can blab do you think I receive? Enough said.'

'I appreciate that, Professor.'

'And well you should. I trust you have your reasons for wanting to ask me about Willie. Undoubtedly they're boring and I've no wish to know them. Have I been helpful?'

'You've been more than helpful.' I filled our glasses and we shared another drink, no conversation passing between us.

'Would you be willing to be a bit more helpful?' I asked.

'That depends.'

'Dr Towle has a nephew. Timothy Kruger. I wonder if there's anything you could tell me about him.'

Van der Graaf raised his drink to his lips with trembling hands. His face clouded.

'Kruger.' He said the name as if it were an epithet.

'Yes.'

'Cousin. Distant cousin, not nephew.'

'Cousin, then.'

'Kruger. An old family. Prussians, every one of them. Power brokers. A powerful family.' His mellifluousness was gone and he spat out the words with mechanical intonation. 'Prussians.'

He took a few steps. The arachnid stagger ceased abruptly and he let his hands drop to his sides.

'This must be a police matter,' he said.

'Why do you say that?'

His face blackened with anger and he raised one fist in the air, a prophet of doom.

'Don't trifle with me, young man! If it has something to do with Timothy Kruger there's little else it could be!'

'It is part of a criminal investigation. I can't go into details.'

'Oh, can't you? I've wagged my tongue at you without demanding to know your true intentions. A moment ago I judged them to be boring. Now I've changed my mind.'

'What is it about the Kruger name that scares you so much, Professor?'

'Evil,' he said. 'Evil frightens me. You say your questions are part of a criminal investigation. How do I know what side you're on?'

'I'm working with the police. But I'm not a policeman.'

'I won't tolerate riddles! Either be truthful or be gone!'

I considered the choice.

'Margaret Dopplemeier,' I said. 'I don't want her to lose her job because of anything I tell you.'

'Maggie?' he snorted. 'Don't worry about her, I've no intention of letting on the fact that she led you to me. She's a sad girl, needs intrigue to spice up her life. I've spoken enough to her to know that she clings longingly to the Conspiracy Theory of Life. Dangle one before her – she'll go for it like a trout for a lure. Kennedy assassinations, Unidentified Flying Objects, cancer, tooth decay – all the result of a grand collusion of anonymous demons. No doubt you recognized that and exploited it.'

He made it sound Machiavellian. I didn't dispute it.

'No,' he said. 'I've no interest in crushing Maggie. She's been a friend. Apart from that, my loyalties to this institution are far from blind. I detest certain aspects of this place – my true home, if you will.'

'Such as the Krugers?'

'Such as the environment that allows Krugers and their ilk to flourish.'

He tottered, the too-large head lolling on its misshapen base.

'The choice is yours, young man. Put up or shut up.'

I put up.

'Nothing in your story surprises me,' he said. 'I didn't know of Stuart Hickle's death nor of his sexual proclivities, but neither are shocking. He was a bad poet, Dr Delaware, very bad – and nothing is beyond a bad poet.'

I recalled the verse at the bottom of Lilah Towle's yearbook obituary. It was clear who 'S' was.

'When you mentioned Timothy I became alarmed, because I didn't know if you were in the employ of the Krugers. The badge you showed me is well and fine, but such trinkets are easily counterfeited.'

'Call Detective Delano Hardy at West Los Angeles Police Division. He'll tell you what side I'm on.' I hoped he wouldn't take me up on it – who knew how Hardy would react?

He looked at me thoughtfully. 'No, that won't be necessary. You're a dreadful liar. I believe I can intuitively tell when you're telling the truth.'

'Thank you.'

'You're welcome. A compliment was intended.'

'Tell me about Timothy Kruger,' I said.

He stood blinking, gnomelike, a concoction of a Hollywood special-effects lab.

'The first thing I'd like to emphasize is that the evil of

the Krugers has nothing to do with wealth. They would be evil paupers – I imagine they were, at one time. If that sounds defensive, it is.'

'I understand.'

'The very wealthy are not evil, Bolshevist propaganda to the contrary. They are a harmless lot – overly sheltered, reticent, destined for extinction.' He took a step backward as if retreating from his own prediction.

I waited.

'Timothy Kruger,' he finally said, 'is a murderer, plain and simple. The fact that he was never arrested, tried or convicted does nothing to diminish his guilt in my eyes. The story goes back seven – no, eight years. There was a student here, a farm boy from Idaho. Sharp as a tack, built like Adonis. His name was Saxon. Jeffrey Saxon. He came here to study, the first of his family to finish high school, dreaming of becoming a writer.

'He was accepted on an athletic scholarship – crew, baseball, football, wrestling – and managed to excel in all of those while maintaining an A average. He majored in history and I was his faculty advisor, though by that time I wasn't teaching any more. We had many chats, up here in this room. The boy was a pleasure to converse with. He had an enthusiasm for life, a thirst for knowledge.'

A tear collected in the corner of one drooping, blue eye.

'Excuse me.' The old man pulled out a linen handkerchief and dabbed his cheek. 'Dusty in here, must get the custodial staff to clean.' He sipped his whiskey and when he spoke his voice was enfeebled by memories.

'Jeffrey Saxon had the curious, searching nature of a true scholar, Dr Delaware. I recall the first time he came up here

310

and saw all the books. Like a child let loose in a toy store. I lent him my finest antiquarian volumes – everything from the London edition of Josephus' *Chronicles* to anthropologic treatises. He devoured them. "For God's sake, Professor," he'd say, "it would take several lifetimes to learn even a fraction of what there is to know." That's the mark of an intellectual, in my view, becoming cognizant of one's own insignificance in relation to the accumulated mass of human knowledge.

'The others, of course, thought him a rube, a hick. They made fun of his clothes, his manner, his lack of sophistication. He spoke to me about it – I'd become a kind of surrogate grandfather I suppose – and I reassured him that he was meant for more noble company than what Jedson had to offer. In fact I'd encouraged him to put in for a transfer to an Eastern school – Yale, Princeton – where he could achieve significant intellectual growth. With his grades and a letter from me, he might have made it. But he never got a chance.

'He became attached to a young lady, one of the Two Hundred, pretty enough, but vapid. This in itself, was no error, as the heart and the gonads must be satisfied. The mistake was in choosing a female already coveted by another.'

'By Tim Kruger?'

Van der Graaf nodded painfully.

'This is difficult for me, Doctor. It brings back so much.'

'If it's too difficult for you, Professor, I can leave now and come back some other time.'

'No, no. That would serve no purpose.' He took a deep breath. 'It comes down to a smarmy soap opera of a tale.

Jeffrey and Kruger were interested in the same girl, they had words in public. Tempers flared, but it seemed to pass. Jeffrey visited me and vented his spleen. I played amateur psychologist – professors so often are required to provide emotional support to their students and I confess I did a fine job of it. I urged him to forget the girl, knowing her type, understanding full well that Jeffrey would be the loser in any battle of wills. The young of Jedson are homing pigeons, as predictable as their ancestors, reverting to type. The girl was meant to mate with one of her own. There were better things, finer things, awaiting Jeffrey, an entire lifetime of opportunity and adventure.

'He wouldn't listen. He was like a knight of old, imbued with the nobility of his mission. Conquer the Black Jouster, rescue the fair maiden. Total rubbish – but he was an innocent. *An innocent.*'

Van der Graaf paused, out of breath. His face had turned a sickly greenish shade of pale and I feared for his health.

'Perhaps we should stop for the moment,' I suggested. 'I can return tomorrow.'

'Absolutely not! I'll not be left here in solitary confinement with a poisonous lump lodged in my craw!' He cleared his throat. 'I'll be on with it – you sit there and pay close attention.'

'All right, Professor.'

'Now then, where was I – ah, Jeffrey as a White Knight. Foolish boy. The enmity between him and Timothy Kruger continued and festered. Jeffrey was ostracized by all the others – Kruger was a campus luminary, socially established. I became Jeffrey's sole source of support. Our conversations changed. No longer were they cerebral exchanges. Now I was conducting psychotherapy on a full-time basis – an activity with which I was most uncomfortable, but I felt I couldn't abandon the boy. I was all he had.

'It culminated in a wrestling match. Both the boys were Greco-Roman wrestlers. They agreed to meet, late at night, in the empty gymnasium, just the two of them for a grudge match. I'm no wrestler myself, for obvious reasons, but I do know that the sport is highly structured, replete with regulations, the criteria for victory clearly drawn. Jeffrey liked it for that reason – he was highly self-disciplined for one so young. He walked into that gym alive and left on a stretcher, neck and spine snapped, alive in only the most vegetative sense of the word. Three days later he died.'

'And his death was ruled an accident,' I said softly.

'That was the official story. Kruger said the two of them had gotten involved in a complicated series of holds and in the ensuing tangle of torsos, arms and legs, Jeffrey had been injured. And who could dispute it – accidents do occur in wrestling matches. At worst it seemed a case of two immature men behaving in an irresponsible manner. But to those of us who knew Timothy, who understood the depth of the rivalry between them, that was far from a satisfactory explanation. The college was eager to hush it up, the police all too happy to oblige – why go up against the Kruger millions when there are hundreds of poor people committing crimes?

'I attended Jeffrey's funeral – flew to Idaho. Before I left I ran into Timothy on campus. Looking back I see he must have sought me out.' Van der Graaf's mouth tightened, the wrinkles deepening as if controlled by some internal drawstring. 'He approached me near the Founder's statue. "I hear you're traveling, Professor," he said. "Yes," I replied, "I'm

313

flying to Boise tonight." "To attend the last rites for your young charge?" he asked. There was a look of utter innocence on his face, feigned innocence – he was an actor, for God's sake, he could manipulate his features at will.

'"What's it to you?" I replied. He bent to the ground, picked up a dry oak twig and sporting an arrogant smirk – the same smirk one can see in photographs of Nazi concentration camp guards tormenting their victims – snapped the twig between his fingers, and let it drop to the ground. Then he laughed.

'I've never in my life been so close to committing murder, Doctor Delaware. Had I been younger, stronger, properly armed, I would have done it. As it was, I simply stood there, for once in my life at a loss for words. "Have a nice trip," he said, and, still smirking, backed away. My heart pounded so, I was assaulted with a spell of dizziness, but fought to maintain my equilibrium. When he was out of eyesight I broke down and sobbed.'

A long moment passed between us.

When he appeared sufficiently composed I asked him:

'Does Margaret know about this? About Kruger?'

He nodded.

'I've spoken of it to her. She's my friend.'

So the awkward publicist was more spider than fly after all. The insight cheered me for some reason.

'One more thing – the girl. The one they were fighting over. What became of her?'

'What do you expect?' He sneered, some of the old vitriol returning to his voice. 'She shunned Kruger – most of the others did. They were afraid of him. She attended Jedson for three more undistinguished years, married an

314

investment banker and moved to Spokane. No doubt she's a proper hausfrau, shuttling the kiddies to school, brunching at the club, boffing the delivery boy.'

'The spoils of battle,' I said.

He shook his head. 'Such a waste.'

I looked at my watch. I'd been up in the dome for a little over an hour, but it seemed longer. Van der Graaf had unloaded a truckful of sewage during that time, but he was a historian, and that's what they're trained to do. I felt tired and tense, and I longed for fresh air.

'Professor,' I said. 'I don't know how to thank you.'

'Putting the information to good use would be a step in the right direction.' The blue eyes shone like twin gaslights. 'Snap some twigs of your own.'

'I'll do my best.' I got up.

'I trust you can see yourself out.'

I did.

When I was halfway across the rotunda I heard him cry out: 'Remind Maggie of our pizza picnic!'

His words echoed against the smooth, cold stone.

23

AMONG CERTAIN PRIMITIVE TRIBES, there exists the belief that when one vanquishes an enemy it is not enough to destroy all evidence of corporeal life: The soul must be vanquished as well. That belief is at the root of the various forms of cannibalism that have been known to exist – and still exist – in many regions of the world. You are what you eat. Devour your victim's heart, and you encompass his very being. Grind his penis to dust and swallow the dust, and you've co-opted his manhood.

I thought of Timothy Kruger – of the boy he'd killed and how he'd assumed the identity of a struggling scholarship student when describing himself to me – and visions of lip-smacking, bone-crunching savagery intruded upon the idyllic verdancy of the Jedson campus. I was still struggling to erase those visions when I climbed the marble steps of Crespi Hall.

Margaret Dopplemeier responded to my coded knock with a 'Wait one second!' and an open door. She let me in and locked the door.

'Did you find Van der Graaf helpful?' she asked airily.

'He told me everything. About Jeffrey Saxon and Tim Kruger and the fact that you were his confidante.'

She blushed.

'You can't expect me to feel guilty for deceiving you when you did the same to me,' she said.

'I don't,' I assured her, 'I just wanted you to know that he trusted me and told me everything. I know you couldn't until he did.'

'I'm glad you understand,' she said primly.

'Thank you for leading me to him.'

'It was my pleasure, Alex. Just put the information to good use.'

It was the second time in ten minutes that I'd received that mandate. Add to that a similar order from Raquel Ochoa and it made for a heavy load.

'I will. Do you have the clipping?'

'Here.' She handed me the photocopy. The death of Lilah Towle and 'Little Willie' had made the front page, sharing space with a report on fraternity hijinks and a reprint of an Associated Press report on the dangers of 'mariwuana reefers.' I started to read but the copy was blurred and barely legible. Margaret saw me straining.

'The original was rubbed out.'

'It's OK.' I skimmed the article long enough to see that it was consistent with Van der Graaf's recollection.

'Here's another story, several days later — about the funeral. This one's better.'

I took it from her and examined it. By now the Towle affair was on page six, a social register item. The account of the ceremony was maudlin and full of dropped names. A photograph at the bottom caught my eye.

Towle led the mourners' procession, haggard and grim, hands folded in front of him. To one side was a younger, still toadlike Edwin Hayden. To the other, slightly to the rear, was a towering figure. There was no mistaking the identity of the mourner.

The kinky hair was black, the face bloated and shiny. The heavy framed eyeglasses I'd seen a few days before were replaced by gold-rimmed, round spectacles resting low on the meaty nose.

It was the Reverend Augustus McCaffrey in younger days.

I folded both papers and slipped them in my jacket pocket.

'Call Van der Graaf,' I said.

'He's an old man. Don't you think you've questioned him enou—'

'Just call him,' I cut her off. 'If you don't I'll run back there myself.'

She winced at my abruptness, but dialed the phone.

When the connection was made she said, 'Sorry to bother you, Professor. It's *him* again.' She listened, shot me an unhappy look and handed me the receiver, holding it at arm's length.

'Thank you,' I said sweetly. Into the phone: 'Professor, I need to ask you about another student. It's important.'

'Go on. I've only Miss November of 1973 occupying my attention. Who is it?'

'Augustus McCaffrey – was he a friend of Towle, too?'

There was silence on the other end of the line and then the sound of laughter.

'Oh, dear me! That's a laugh! Gus McCaffrey, a Jedson student! And him touched by the tar brush!' He laughed some more and it was a while before he caught his breath. 'Mary Mother of God, no, man. He was no *student* here!'

'I've got a photograph in front of me showing him at the Towle funeral—'

'Be that as it may, he was no student. Gus McCaffrey was – I believe they call themselves maintenance engineers today – Gus was a janitor. He swept the dormitories, took out the trash, that kind of thing.'

'What was he doing at the funeral? It looks like he's right behind Towle, ready to catch him if he falls.'

'No surprise. He was originally an employee of the Hickle family – they had one of the largest homes on Brindamoor. Family retainers can grow quite close to their masters – I believe Stuart brought him over to Jedson when he began college here. He did eventually attain some kind of rank within the custodial staff – supervising janitor or something similar. Leaving Brindamoor may very well have been an excellent opportunity for him. What's big Gus doing today?'

'He's a minister – the head of that children's home I told you about.'

'I see. Taking out the Lord's trash, so to speak.'

'So to speak. Can you tell me anything about him.'

'I honestly can't, I'm afraid. I had no contact with the nonacademic employees – there's a tendency to pretend they're invisible that's acquired over time. He was a big brute of a fellow, that I do recall. Slovenly, seemed quite strong, may very well have been bright – your information certainly points in that direction, and I'm no social Darwinist with a need to dispute it. But that is really all I can tell you. I'm sorry.'

'Don't be. One last thing – where can I get a map of Brindamoor Island?'

'There's none that I know of outside the County Hall of Records – wait, a student of mine did an undergraduate thesis on the history of the place, complete with residential map. I don't have a copy but I believe it would be stored in the library, in the thesis section. The student's name was – let me think – Church? No, it was something else of a clerical nature – Chaplain. Gretchen Chaplain. Look under C, you should find it.'

'Thanks again, Professor. Goodbye.'

'Goodbye.'

Margaret Dopplemeier sat at her desk, glaring at me.

'I'm sorry for being rude,' I said. 'It was important.'

'All right,' she said. 'I just thought you could have been a little more polite in view of what I've done for you.' The possessive look slithered into her eyes like a python into a lagoon.

'You're right. I should have. I won't trouble you further.' I stood up. 'Thanks so much for everything.' I held out my hand, and when she reluctantly extended hers, I took it. 'You've really made a big difference.'

'That's good to know. How long will you be staying?'

Gently I broke the handclasp.

'Not long.' I backed away, smiled at her, finally got my hand on the knob and pushed. 'All the best, Margaret. Enjoy your blackberries.'

She started to say something, then thought better of it. I left her standing behind her desk, a circle of pink tongue-tip visible in the corner of her unattractive mouth, searching for a taste of something.

The library was properly austere and very respectably stocked with books and journals for a college the size of Jedson. The main room was a marble cathedral draped in heavy red velvet and lit by oversized windows placed ten feet apart. It was filled with oak reading tables, green-shaded lamps, leather chairs. All that was missing were people to read the august volumes that papered the walls.

The librarian was an effete young man with close-cropped hair and a pencil mustache. His shirt was red plaid, his tie a yellow knit. He sat behind his reference table reading a recent copy of *Artforum*. When I asked him where the thesis section was, he looked up with the astonished expression of a hermit observing the penetration of his lair.

'There,' he said, languidly, and pointed to a spot at the south end of the room.

There was an oak card catalog and I found Gretchen Chaplain's thesis listed in it. The title of her magnum opus had been *Brindamoor Island: Its History and Geography*.

Theses by Frederick Chalmers and O. Winston Chastain were present, but Gretchen's rightful place between them was unfilled. I checked and doublechecked the Library of Congress number but that was a fruitless ritual: The Brindamoor study was gone.

I went back to Plaid Shirt and had to clear my throat twice before he tore himself away from a piece on Billy Al Bengston.

'Yes?'

'I'm looking for a specific thesis and can't seem to find it.'

'Have you checked the card file to make sure it's listed?'

'The card's there but the thesis isn't.'

'How unfortunate. I would guess it's been checked out.'

'Could you check for me, please?'

He sighed and took too long to raise himself out of his chair. 'What's the author's name?'

I gave him all the necessary information and he went behind the checkout counter with an injured look. I followed him.

'Brindamoor Island – dreary place. Why would you want to know about *that*?'

'I'm a visiting professor form UCLA and it's part of my research. I didn't know an explanation was necessary.'

'Oh, it's not,' he said, quickly, and buried his nose in a stack of cards. He lifted out a portion of the cards and shuffled them like a Vegas pro. 'Here,' he said, 'that thesis was checked out six months ago – my, it's overdue, isn't it?'

I took the card. Scant attention had been paid to Gretchen's masterpiece. Prior to its last withdrawal a half year ago, the last time it had been checked out was in 1954, by Gretchen herself. Probably wanted to show it to her kids – Mummy was once quite a scholar, little ones . . .

'Sometimes we get behind on checking on overdue notices. I'll get right on this, Professor. Who checked it out last?'

I looked at the signature and told him. As the name left my mouth my brain processed the information. By the time the two words had dissolved I knew my mission wouldn't be complete without a trip to the island.

24

THE FERRY TO Brindamoor Island made its morning trip at seven thirty.

When the wake-up call from the desk came in at six it found me showered, shaved and tensely bright-eyed. The rain had started again shortly after midnight, pounding the glass walls on the suite. It had roused me for a dream-like instant during which I was certain I'd heard the sound of cavalry hooves stampeding down the corridor, and had gone back to sleep anyway. Now it continued to come down, the city below awash and out of focus, as if viewed from inside a dirty aquarium.

I dressed in heavy slacks, leather jacket, wool turtleneck, and took along the only raincoat I had: An unlined poplin doublebreasted affair that was fine for Southern California but of uncertain utility in the present surroundings. I caught a quick breakfast of smoked salmon, bagels, juice and coffee and made it to the docks at ten after seven.

I was among the first to queue up at the entrance to the auto bay. The line moved and I drove down a ramp into the womb of the ferry behind a VW bus with Save the Whale stickers on the rear bumper. I obeyed the gesticulations of a crewman dressed in dayglo orange overalls and parked two inches from the slick, white wall of the bay. An ascent of two flights brought me on deck. I walked past a gift shop, tobacconist and snack bar, all closed, and a blackened room furnished wall to wall with video games. A waiter played Pac Man in solitude, devouring dots with brow-furrowing concentration.

I found a seat with a view at the stern, folded my raincoat across my lap and settled back for the one-hour ride.

The ship was virtually empty. My few fellow passengers were young and dressed for work: Hired help from the mainland commuting to their assigned posts at the manors of Brindamoor. The return trip, no doubt, would be filled with commuters of another class: Lawyers, bankers, other financial types, on their way to downtown offices and paneled boardrooms.

The ocean pitched and rolled, frothing in response to the surface winds that drag-raced along its surface. There were smaller craft at sea, mostly fishing boats, tugs and scows, and they danced in command, curtsying and dipping. For all the ferry moved it might have been a toy model on a shelf.

A group of six young men in their late teens came aboard and sat down ten feet away. Blond, bearded in varying degrees of shagginess, dressed in rumpled khakis and dirt-grayed jeans, they passed around a thermos full of something that wasn't coffee, joked, smoked, put their feet up on chairs and emitted a collective guffaw that sounded like a beery laugh track. One of them noticed me and held up the thermos.

'Swig, my man?' he offered.

I smiled and shook my head.

He shrugged, turned away and the party started up again.

The ferry's horn sounded, the rumble of its engines rever-
berating through the floorboards, and we started to move.

Halfway through the trip I walked over to where the six
young drinkers sat, now slumped. Three of them slept,
snooring open-mouthed, one was reading an obscene comic
book, and two, including the one who'd offered me the drink,
sat smoking, hypnotized by the glowing ends of their cigarettes.

'Excuse me.'

The two smokers looked up. The reader paid no attention.

'Yeah?' The generous one smiled. He was missing half of
his front teeth: Bad oral hygiene or a quick temper. 'Sorry,
man, we got no more Campbell's soup.' He picked up the
thermos and shook it. 'Ain't that right, Dougie?'

His companion, a fat boy with drooping mustaches and
muttonchop sideburns, laughed and nodded his head.

'Yeah, no more soup. Chicken noodle. Ninety proof.'

From where I was standing the whole bunch of them
smelled like a distillery.

'That's all right. I appreciate the offer. I was just wondering
if you could give me some information about Brindamoor.'

Both boys looked puzzled, as if they'd never thought of
themselves as having any information to give.

'What do you want to know? Place is a drag,' said
Generous.

'Fuckin-A.' Fat Boy nodded assent.

'I'm trying to find a certain house on the island, can't seem
to get hold of a map.'

'That's 'cause there ain't any. People there like to hide from
the rest of the world. They got private cops ready to roust
you for spittin' the wrong way. Me 'n' Doug and the rest of

these jokers go over to do groundswork on the golf course, pickin' up crap and litter and stuff. Finish the day and head straight back for the boat, man. We want to keep our jobs, we stick to that – exactly.'

'Yeah,' said the fat one. 'No shootin' for the local beaver, no partyin'. Workin' people been doin' it for years and years – my dad worked Brindamoor before he got in the union, and I'm just doin' it until he gets me in. Then, fuck those hermits. He told me they had a song for it, back in those days: Heft and tote, then float on the boat.' He laughed and slapped his buddy on the back.

'What you interested in findin'?' Generous lit another cigarette and placed it in the snaggled gap where his upper incisors should have been.

'The Hickle house.'

'You related to them?' Doug asked. His eyes were the color of the sea, bloodshot and suddenly dull with worry, wondering if I was someone who could turn his words against him.

'No. I'm an architect. Just doing a little sightseeing. I was told the Hickle house would be of interest. Supposed to be the biggest one on the island.'

'Man,' he said, 'they're all big. You could fit my whole fuckin' neighborhood in one of them.'

'Architect, huh?' Generous's face brightened with interest. 'How much school it take to do that?'

'Five years of college.'

'Forget it,' the fat one kidded him. 'You're an airhead, Harm. You got to learn how to read and write first.'

'Fuck you!' said his friend, good-naturedly. To me: 'I worked construction last summer. Architecture's probly pretty interestin'.'

'It is. I do mostly private houses. Always looking for new ideas.'

'Yeah, hey, right. Gotta keep it interestin'.'

'Aw, man,' chided Dougie. 'We don't do nothing interestin'. Clean up goddam garbage – hell, man, there's fun going on there at that club, 'cause last week Matt 'n' me found a couple of used rubbers out by hole number eleven – and we're missin' it, Harm.'

'I don't need those people for my fun,' said the generous one. 'You want to know about houses, mister, let's ask Ray.' He turned and leaned across one sleeping boy to elbow the one with the comic book, who'd kept his nose buried in his reading and hadn't looked up once. When he did, his face had the glazed look of someone very stupid or very stoned.

'Huh?'

'Ray, you dumbshit, man wants to know about the Hickle house.'

The boy blinked, uncomprehending.

'Ray's been droppin' too much acid out in the woods. Just can't seem to shake himself out of it.' Harm grinned, his tonsils visible. 'C'mon, man, where's the Hickle place?'

'Hickle,' Ray said. 'My old man used to work there – spooky place he said. Weird. I think it's on Charlemagne. The old man used to—'

'All right, man.' Harm shoved Ray's head down and he returned to his comic book. 'They got strange names for streets on the island, Mister. Charlemagne, Alexander, Suleiman.'

Conquerors. The little joke of the very rich was evidently lost on those who were its intended butt.

'Charlemagne is an inland road. You go just past the main

drag, past the market, a quarter mile – look hard because the street signs are usually covered by trees – and turn, lemme see, turn right, that's Charlemagne. After that you'd best ask around.'

'Much obliged.' I reached in and pulled out my wallet. 'Here's for your trouble,' I said, taking out a five.

Harm held out his hand – in protest, not collection. 'Forget it, mister. We didn't do nothin'.'

Doug, the fat boy, gave him an angry look and grunted.

'Up yours, Dougie,' said the boy with the missing teeth. 'We didn't do nothin' for the man's money.' Despite his unkempt hair and the war zone of a mouth, he had intelligence and a certain dignity. He was the kind of kid I wouldn't mind having at my side when the going got rough.

'Let me buy you a round, then.'

'Nah,' said Harm. 'We can't drink no more, mister. Got to hit the course in half an hour. Be slick as snot on a day like this. Bubble Butt here, drink any more, he could fall and bounce down and crush the rest of us.'

'Fuck you, Harm,' said Doug, without heart.

I put the money back. 'Thanks much.'

'Think nothin' of it. You build some houses that don't need union help, you want reliable construction muscle, remember Harmon Lundquist. I'm in the book.'

'I will.'

Ten minutes before the boat reached shore the island emerged from behind a dressing screen of rain and fog, an oblong, squat, gray chunk of rock. Except for the coiffure of trees that covered most of its outer edges, it could have been Alcatraz.

I went down to the auto bay, got behind the wheel of the Nova and was ready when the man in orange waved us down the ramp. The scene outside might have been lifted off the streets of London. There were enough black topcoats, black umbrellas, and black hats to fill Piccadilly. Pink hands held briefcases and the morning's *Wall Street Journal*. Eyes stared straight ahead. Lips set grimly. When the gate at the foot of the gangway opened they moved in procession, each man in his place, every shiny black shoe rising and falling in response to an unseen drummer. A squadron of perfect gentlemen. A gentlemen's brigade . . .

Just beyond Brindamoor Harbor was a small town square built around an enormous towering elm and rimmed with shops: A bank with smoked glass windows, a brokerage house, three or four expensive looking clothiers with conservatively dressed, faceless mannequins in their windows, a grocer, a butcher, a dry cleaner's that also housed the local post office, a book store, two restaurants – one French, the other Italian – a gift shop, and a jewelers. All the stores were closed, the streets empty and, except for a flock of pigeons convening under the elm, devoid of life.

I followed Harm's directions and found Charlemagne Lane with no trouble. A thousand yards out of the square the road narrowed and darkened, shadowed by walls of fern, devil ivy and shrub maple. The green was broken by an occasional gate – wrought iron or redwood, the former usually backed by steel plating. There were no mailboxes on the road, no public display of names. The estates seemed to be spaced several acres apart. A few times I caught a glimpse of the properties behind the gates: Lots of rolling lawns, sloping drives paved with brick and stone, the houses imposing and grand – Tudor, Regency, Colonial – the driveways stabling Rolls Royces, Mercedes and Cadillac limousines, as well as their more utilitarian four-wheeled cousins – stationwagons paneled with phony wood, Volvos, compacts. Once or twice I saw gardeners laboring in the rain, their power mowers sputtering and belching.

The road continued for another half-mile, the properties growing larger, the houses set back further from the gates. It came to an abrupt halt at a thicket of cypress. There was no gate, no visible means of entry, just the forestlike growth of thirty-foot trees, and for a moment I thought I'd been misled.

I put on my raincoat, pulled up the collar and got out. The ground was thick with pine needles and wet leaves. I walked to the thicket and peered through the branches. Twenty feet ahead, almost totally hidden by the overgrowth of tangled limbs and dripping vegetation, was a short stone pathway leading to a wooden gate. The trees had been planted to block the entry; from the size of them they were at least twenty years old. Discounting the possibility that someone had taken the trouble to transplant a score of full grown cypress to the site, I decided it had been a long time since the normal human business of living had taken place here.

I pushed my way to the gate and tried it. Nailed shut. I took a good look at it – two slabs of tongued-and-grooved redwood hinged to brick posts. The posts connected to chain link fencing piled high with thorny spirals. No sign of electricity or barbed wire. I found a foothold on a wet rock, slipped a couple of times and finally managed to scale the gate.

I landed on another world. Acres of wasteland spread before me; what had once been a formal lawn was now a swamp of weeds, dead grass and broken rock. The ground had sunk in several places, creating pools of water that stagnated and provided oases for the mosquitoes and gnats that hovered overhead. Once-noble trees had been reduced to jagged stumps and felled, rotten hulls crawling with fungus. Rusted auto parts, old tires and discarded cans and bottles were scattered throughout what was now a sodden trash dump. Rain fell on metal and made a hollow, clanging sound.

I walked up a pathway paved in herringbone brick, choked with weeds and covered by slimy moss. In the places where the roots had pushed through, the bricks stuck out of the ground like loose teeth in a broken jaw. I kicked aside a drowned field mouse and slogged toward the former residence of the Hickle clan.

The house was massive, a three-story structure of hand-hewn stone that had blackened with age. I couldn't imagine it as ever being beautiful but doubtless it had once been grand: A brooding, slate-roofed mansion trimmed with gingerbread, festooned with eaves and gables and girdled by wide stone porches. There was rusted wrought-iron furniture on the front porch, a nine-foot-high cathedral door and a weather vane at the highest peak in the shape of a witch riding a broomstick. The old crone twirled in the wind, safely above the desolation.

I climbed the stairs to the front entry. Weeds had grown clear up to the door, which was nailed shut. The windows were similarly boarded and bolted tight. In spite of its size – perhaps because of it – the house seemed pathetic, a forgotten dowager, abandoned to the point where she no longer cared how she looked and sentenced to a fate of decaying in silence.

I forced my way through a makeshift barrier of rotting boards that had been stacked in front of the porte-cochere.

The house was at least a hundred and fifty feet long and it took me a while to check each window on the ground floor: All were sealed.

The rear property was another three acres of swamp. A four-car garage, designed as a miniature of the house, was inaccessible – nailed and fastened. A fifty-foot swimming pool was empty save for several inches of muddy water in which floated a host of organic debris. The remains of a grape arbor and trellised rose garden were evident only as a jumble of peeling wood and cracked stone supporting a bird's nest of lifeless twigs. Stone benches and statues slanted and pitched on broken bases, Pompeii in the wake of Vesuvius.

The rain began to come down harder and colder. I put my hands in the pocket of my raincoat, by now soaked through, and looked for shelter. It would take tools – hammer and crowbar – to get into the house or the garage, and there were no large trees that could be trusted not to topple at any moment. I was out in the open like a bum caught in a blitz.

I saw a flash of light and braced myself for an electric storm. None came and the light flashed again. The heavy downpour made it difficult to see but the third time the light appeared I was able to draw a bead on it and walk in its direction. Several squishy footsteps later I could see it had come from a glass greenhouse at the rear of the estate, just beyond the bombed-out arbor. The panes were opaque with dirt, some of which ran in brown trickles, but they appeared intact. I ran toward it, following the light that flickered, danced, disappeared, then flickered again.

The door to the greenhouse was closed but it opened silently to the prompting of my hand. Inside it was warm, steamy and sour with the aroma of decomposition. Waist-high wooden tables ran along both sides of the glass room; between them was a walkway floored with woodchips, peat, mulch and topsoil. A collection of tools – pitchforks, rakes, spades, hoes – stood in one corner.

Upon the tables were pots of gorgeously flowering plants: Orchids, bromeliads, blue hydrangea, begonias of every hue, scarlet and white impatiens – all in full bloom and spilling abundantly from their terracotta houses. A wooden beam into which metal hooks had been embedded was suspended above the tables. Hanging from the hooks were fuchsias dripping purple, ferns, spider plants, creeping charlies, more begonias. It was the Garden of Eden in the Great Void.

The room was dim, and it reverberated with the sound of the rain assaulting the glass roof. The light that had drawn me appeared again, brighter and closer. I made out a shape at the other end of the greenhouse, a figure in yellow slicker and hood holding a flashlight. The figure shone the flashlight on plants, picking up a leaf here, a flower there, examining the soil, pinching off a dry branch, setting aside a ripe blossom.

'Hello,' I said.

The figure whirled and the flashlight beam washed over my face. I squinted in the glare and brought my hand up to shield my eyes.

The figure came closer.

'Who are you?' demanded a voice, high and scared.

'Alex Delaware.'

The beam lowered. I started to take a step.

'Stay right there!'

I put my foot down.

The hood was pulled back. The face it revealed was round, pale, flat, utterly Asian, female but not feminine. The eyes were two razor cuts in the parchment skin, the mouth an unsmiling hyphen.

'Hello, Mrs Hickle.'

'How do you know me – what do you want?' There was toughness diluted by fear in the voice, the toughness of the successful fugitive who knows vigilance must never cease.

'I just thought I'd pay you a visit.'

'I don't want visitors. I don't know you.'

'Don't you? Alex Delaware – doesn't the name mean anything to you?'

She didn't bother to lie, just said nothing.

'It was my office darling Stuart chose for his last big scene – or maybe it was chosen for him.'

'I don't know what you're talking about. I don't want your company.' Her English was clipped and slightly accented.

'Why don't you call the butler and have me ejected?'

Her jaws worked; white fingers tightened around the flashlight.

'You refuse to leave?'

'It's wet and cold outside. I'd appreciate the chance to dry off.'

'Then you'll go?'

'Then I stay and we talk awhile. About your late husband and some of his good buddies.'

'Stuart's dead. There's nothing to talk about.'

'I think there's plenty. Lots of questions.'

She put down the flashlight and folded her arms in front of her. There was defiance in the gesture. Any trace of fear had faded and her demeanor was one of irritation at being disturbed. It puzzled me – she was a lone woman accosted by a stranger in a deserted place but there was no panic.

'Last chance,' she said.

'I'm not interested in blowing your cover. Just let me—'

She clicked her tongue against the roof of her mouth.

A large shadow materialized into something living and breathing.

I saw what it was and my bowels went weak.

'This is Otto. He doesn't like strangers.'

He was the largest dog I'd ever seen, a Great Dane the size of a healthy pony, colored like a Dalmatian – white dappled with gray-black splotches. One ear was partially shredded. His maws were black and wet with saliva, hanging loose in that half-smile, half-snarl so characteristic of attack dogs, revealing pearly-white fangs and a tongue the size of a hot-water bag. His eyes were piggy and too small for his head. They reflected orange pinpoints of light as they scanned me.

I must have moved, because his ears perked. He panted and looked up at his mistress. She cooed at him. He panted faster and gave her hand a fast swipe with the pink slab of tongue.

'Hi there, big fella,' I said. The words came out strangled. His jaws opened wider in a growling yawn.

I backed away and the dog arched his neck forward. He was a muscular beast, from head to quivering haunch.

'Now maybe I don't want you to go,' said Kim Hickle.

I backed away further. Otto exhaled and made a sound that came from deep in his belly.

'I told you I won't give you away.'

'So you say.'

I took two more steps backward. Baby steps. Playing a deranged version of Simon Says. The dog moved closer.

'I just wanted to be alone,' she said. 'Nobody to bother

me. Me and Otto.' She looked lovingly at the great brute. 'You found out. You bother me. How did you find me?'

'You left your name in a library file at Jedson College.'

'So you hunted me.'

'No. It was an accident, finding the card. It's not you I'm after.'

She clicked her tongue again and Otto came a few feet closer. His malevolent leer loomed larger. I could smell him, rank and eager.

'First you, now others will follow. Asking questions. Blaming me, saying I'm bad. I'm not bad. I'm a good woman, good for children. I was a good wife to a sick man, not a sick woman.'

'I know,' I soothed. 'It wasn't your fault.'

Another click. The dog moved within springing distance. She had him controlled, like a radio-operated toy. Start, Otto. Stop, Otto, Kill, Otto . . .

'No. Not my fault.'

I stepped back. Otto followed me, stalking, one paw scraping the ground, the shorthairs rising.

'I'll go,' I said. 'We don't have to talk. It's not that important. You deserve your privacy.' I was rambling, stalling for time, my eyes on the tools in the corner. Mentally, I measured the distance to the pitchfork, covertly rehearsing the move I might have to make.

'I gave you a chance. You didn't take it. Now it's too late.'

She clicked twice and the dog sprang, coming at me in a blur of snarling darkness. I saw the forepaws raised in the air, the wet, hungry, gnashing mouth, the orange eyes zeroed on their target, all in a fraction of a second. Still within that second, I feinted to the right, sank to my knees and lunged

336

for the pitchfork. My fingers closed around wood and I snatched it and jabbed upward.

He came down on me, a ton of coiled monster, crushing the breath from my chest, the paws and teeth scraping and snapping. Something went through cloth, then leather, then skin. Pain took hold of my arm from elbow to shoulder, piercing and sickening. The handle of the pitchfork slipped from my grasp. I shielded my face with one sleeve, as Otto nuzzled at me with his wet nose, trying to get those buzz-saw jaws around my neck. I twisted away, reached out blindly for the pitchfork, got hold of it, lost it and found it again. I landed a knuckle punch on the crown of his skull. It was like pummeling armor plate. He reared up on his hind legs, roaring with rage and bore down. I turned the pitchfork prong-upwards. He lunged, throwing his full weight down on me. My legs bent and my back hit the dirt. The air went out of me and I fought for consciousness, swallowed up in churning fur and struggling to keep the fork between us.

Then he whinnied shrilly; at the same time I felt the pitchfork hit bone, scrape and slide as I twisted the handle, full of hate. The prongs went into him like a warm knife into butter.

We embraced, the dog's tongue on my ear, his mouth slavering, open in agony, an inch from carving out a chunk of my face. I put all of my strength behind the pitchfork, pushing and twisting, vaguely aware of the sound of a woman screaming. He cried out like a puppy. The prongs went in a final inch and then could sink no deeper. His eyes opened wide with injured pride, blinked spasmodically, then closed. The huge body shuddered convulsively atop me. A tide of blood shot out of his mouth, splashing across my nose, lips and chin. I gagged on the warm, salty muck. Life passed out of him and I struggled to roll free.

The whole thing had taken less than half a minute.

Kim Hickle looked at the dead dog, then at me, and made a run for the door. I pulled myself to standing position, yanked the pitchfork out of the barrel chest and blocked her way.

'Get back,' I gasped. I moved the pitchfork and droplets of gore flew through the air. She froze.

The greenhouse was silent. The rain had stopped. The silence was broken by a low, rumbling noise: Bubbles of gas escaping from the big dog's corpse. A mound of feces followed, running down the limp legs and mingling with the mulch.

She watched it and started to cry. Then she went limp and sat on the floor with the hopeless, stuporous look of a refugee.

I jammed the pitchfork into the ground and used it to lean on. It took me a full minute to catch my breath, another two or three to check for damages.

The raincoat was ruined, torn and blood-soaked. With some effort I got it off and let it fall to the ground. One arm of the leather jacket was shredded. I slipped out of it, too, and rolled up the sleeve of the turtleneck. I inspected my bicep. The layers of clothing had prevented it from being worse but it wasn't pretty: Three puncture wounds that had already begun to swell, surrounded by a maze of abrasions. The arm felt stiff and sore. I bent it and nothing felt broken. The same went for my ribs and my other limbs, although my entire body floated just above agony. I stretched carefully, using a limbering routine I'd learned from Jaroslav. It made me feel a little better.

'Did Otto have his shots?' I asked.

She didn't answer. I repeated the question, punctuating it with a grasp of the pitchfork handle.

'Yes. I have the papers.'

'I want to see them.'

'It's true. You can believe me.'

'You just tried to get that monster to rip out my throat. Right now your credibility isn't high.'

She looked at the dead animal and went into a meditative away. She seemed to be one who was used to waiting. I was in no mood for a battle of endurance.

'You've got two choices, Mrs Hickle. One, cooperate and I'll leave you to your little Walden. Or, you can make it hard for me and I'll see that your story makes page one of the *LA Times* Metro section. Think of it: Molester's widow finds refuge in abandoned homesite. Poetic, isn't it? Ten to one the wire services pick it up.'

'What do you want from me?'

'Answers to questions. I've no reason – or desire – to hurt you.'

'You're really the one whose office Stuart – died in?'

'Yes. Who else were you expecing?'

'No one,' she said too quickly.

'Towle? Hayden? McCaffrey?'

At the mention of each name her face registered pain sequentially, as if her bones were being broken in stages.

'I'm not with them. But I want to know more about them.'

She raised herself to a squat, stood, and picked up the bloodied raincoat. Carefully she placed it over the dog's still form.

'I'll talk to you,' she said.

25

THERE WAS an entrance to the four-car garage that had eluded me: At ground level, hidden behind an untrimmed blue spruce, was a window covered with chicken-coop wire mesh. She kneeled, played with a couple of strategic strands and the mesh came loose. A push, a wriggle and she was inside. I followed. I was much larger and it wasn't easy. My injured arm brushed against the pane and I had to hold my breath to stop from crying out as I squeezed through.

A half-jump brought me to a narrow room that had originally been a root cellar. It was damp and dark, the walls lined with shallow wooden shelving, the floor of poured concrete painted red. There was a wooden shutter above the window, held in place by an eye and hook. She unfastened it and it slammed shut. There was a second of darkness during which I braced myself for something devious. Instead came the pleasing pungence of kerosene, reminiscent of teenage love by the light of the campfire, and smoky illumination. She tilted the slats of the shutter so that additional light came in but visibility from the outside was obscured.

My eyes adjusted to the light and the details came into focus: A thin pallet and bedroll lay on the floor. The kerosene lamp, a hot plate, a can of Sterno and a packet of plastic utensils shared space on a rickety wooden table that had been painted and repainted so many times it looked like soft sculpture. There was a utility sink in one corner and above it a rack holding an empty jam jar, a toothbrush, toothpowder, safety razor and a bar of laundry soap. Most of the remaining floor space was taken up by wooden milk cartons of a type I hadn't seen since childhood. The boxes had tube-shaped hand holes on two sides and bore the imprint of 'Farmer Del's Dairy, Tacoma, Wash – Our Butter Is Best, Put It to the Test.' Below the slogan was a picture of a bored-looking heifer and a phone number with a two-letter prefix. She'd stacked the cartons three-high in places. The contents of some of them were visible – packets of freeze-dried food, canned goods, paper towels, folded clothing. Three pairs of shoes, all rubber-soled and sturdy, were lined up neatly against the wall. There were metal hooks hammered into a raw wood support beam. She hung her slicker on one of them and sat down on a straight-backed chair of unfinished pine. I settled myself on an overturned milk carton.

We looked at each other.

In the absence of competing stimuli the pain in my arm took over. I winced, and she saw it.

She got up, soaked a paper towel in warm water, came over and swabbed the wound. She poked around in one of the boxes and found sterile gauze, adhesive tape and hydrogen peroxide. Tending to me like Florence Nightingale, she bandaged the arm. The craziness of the situation wasn't lost on me – minutes ago she'd tried to kill me, now she clucked maternally and smoothed down the tape. I stayed karate-wary, expecting her to revert at any moment to murderous rage, to dig her fingers into the inflamed flesh and take advantage of the blinding pain to jab me in the eye.

341

But when she was finished she returned to her seat.

'The papers,' I reminded her.

More poking around. But quick. She knew exactly where everything was. A sheaf of papers bound with a thick rubber band found its way into my hand. There were veterinarian's bills, rabies vaccination records, Kennel Club registration – the dog's full name had been Otto Klaus Von Schulderheis out of Stuttgart-Munsch and Sigourn-Daffodil. Quaint. There were also diplomas from two obedience schools in LA and a certificate stating that Otto had been trained as an attack dog for defensive purposes only. I handed the papers back to her.

'Thank you,' she said.

We sat across from one another, pleasant as school chums. I took a good look at her and tried to work up some genuine animosity. What I saw was a sad-looking Oriental woman in her forties, her hair chopped Chinadoll short, sallow, frail, homely in baggy work clothes and shabby as a churchmouse. She sat, hands in lap, docile. The hatred wouldn't come.

'How long have you been living here?'

'Six months. Since Stuart's death.'

'Why live like this – why not open up the house?'

'I thought this would be better for hiding. All I want is to be alone.'

She didn't make much of a Garbo.

'Hiding from whom?'

She looked at the floor.

'Come on. I won't hurt you.'

'The others. The other sick ones.'

'Names.'

'The ones you mentioned and others.' She spit out a half-dozen other names I didn't recognize.

'Let's be specific. By sick you mean child molesters – all those men are child molesters?'

'Yes, yes. I didn't know it. Stuart told me later, when he was in prison. They volunteered at a children's home, took the kids to their houses. Did sick things with them.'

'And at your school, too.'

'No! That was only Stuart. The others never came to the school. Only at the children's home.'

'La Casa de los Niños. Your husband was a member of the Gentlemen's Brigade.'

'Yes. He told me he was doing it to help children. His friends recruited him, he said. The judge, the doctor, the others. I thought it was so nice of him – we didn't have children of our own – I was proud of him. I never knew what he was really doing – just like I didn't know about what he did at the school.'

I said nothing.

'I know what you're thinking – what they all thought. That I knew all along. How could I not know what my own husband was doing in my own house? You blame me as much as you blame Stuart. I tell you, I didn't know!'

Her arms went out beseechingly, the hands saffron talons. I noticed that the nails had been gnawed to the quick. There was a desperate, feral look on her face.

'I did not know,' she repeated, turning it into a self-punishing mantra. 'I did not know. He was my husband but I did not know!'

She was in need of absolution but I didn't feel like a father confessor. I stayed tight-lipped and observed her with forced detachment.

'You must understand the kind of marriage Stuart and I had to see how he could have been doing all of those things without my knowledge.'

My silence said, convince me.

She bowed her head and began.

'We met in Seoul,' she said, 'shortly after the war. My father had been a professor of linguistics. Our family was prosperous, but we had ties to the socialists and the KCIA killed them all. They went on rampages after the war, murdering intellectuals, anyone who wasn't a blind slave to the regime. Everything we owned was confiscated or destroyed. I was hidden, given to friends the day before KCIA thugs broke into the house and slit the throats of everyone – family, servants, even the animals. Things got worse, the government clamped down harder. The family that took me in grew frightened and I was turned out to the street. I was fifteen years old, but very small, very skinny, looking twelve. I begged, ate scraps. I – I sold myself. I had to. To survive.'

She stopped, looked past me, gathered her strength and continued.

When Stuart found me I was feverish, infested with lice and venereal disease, covered with sores. It was at night. I was huddled under newspapers in an alley at the back of a café where the GIs went to eat and drink and find bar girls. I knew it was good to wait in such places because Americans threw away enough food to feed entire families. I was so sick I could barely move, but I waited for hours, forcing myself to stay awake so the cats wouldn't get my dinner first. The restaurant closed shortly after midnight. The soldiers came out, loud, drunk, staggering through the alley. Then Stuart, by himself, sober. Later I found out he never drank alcohol. I tried to keep quiet but my pain made me cry out. He heard, came over, so big, a giant in uniform, bending over me saying "Don't worry, little girl." He picked me up in his arms and took me to his apartment. He had lots of money, enough to rent his own place off base. The GIs were on R and R, celebrating, making lots of unwanted babies. Stuart had nothing to do with those kinds of things. He used his place to write poetry. To fiddle with his cameras. To be alone.'

She seemed to lose track of time and space, and staring absently at the dark wooden walls.

'He took you to his place,' I prompted.

'For five weeks he nursed me. He brought doctors, bought medicine. Fed me, bathed me, sat at my bedside reading comic books – I loved American comic books because my father had always brought them home to me from his travels. Little Orphan Annie. Terry and the Pirates. Dagwood. Blondie. He read them all to me, in a soft, gentle voice. He was different from any man I'd ever met. Thin, quiet, like a teacher, with those eyeglasses that made his eyes look so big, like a big bird.

'By the sixth week I was well. He came into bed and made love to me. I know now it was part of the sickness – he must have thought I was a child, that must have excited him. But I felt like a woman. Over the years as I became a woman, when I was clearly no longer a child, he lost interest in me. He used to like to dress me up in little girl's things – I'm small, I could fit into them. But when I grew up, saw the world outside, I would have nothing to do with that. I asserted myself and he withdrew. Maybe that was when he started to act out his sickness. Maybe,' she said in a wounded voice, 'it was my fault. For not satisfying him.'

'No. He was a troubled man. You don't have to bear that responsibility,' I said, not with total sincerity. I didn't want it all to deteriorate into a wet session of self-recrimination.

'I don't know. Even now it seems so unreal. The papers, the stories about him. About us. He was such a kind man, gentle, quiet.'

I'd heard similar pictures painted of other child molesters. Often they were exceptionally mild-mannered men, with a natural ability to gain rapport with their young victims. But of course it had to be that way: Kids won't flock to an unshaven ogre in a soiled trenchcoat. They *will* be drawn to Uncle Wally who's so much nicer than mean old Mom and Dad and all the other grownups who don't *understand*. To Uncle Wally with his magic tricks and neat collection of baseball cards and really terrific toys at his house and mopeds and video recorders, and cameras and neat, weird books . . .

'You must understand how much I loved him,' she was saying. 'He saved my life. He was American. He was rich. He said he loved me too. "My little geisha" he called me. I'd laugh and tell him "No, I'm Korean, you silly. The Japanese are pigs!" He'd smile and call me his little geisha again.

We lived together in Seoul for four months. I waited for him to get off-base on leave, cooked for him, cleaned, brought him his slippers. Was his wife. When his discharge papers came, he told me he was taking me back to the States. I was in heaven. Of course his family – there was only a mother and some elderly aunts – would have nothing to do with me.

Stuart didn't care. He had money of his own, trust funds from his father. We traveled together to Los Angeles. He said he'd gone to school there – he did go to medical school, but flunked out. He took a job as a medical technician. He didn't need to work, it was a job that didn't pay much, but he liked it, said it kept him busy. He liked the machines – the meters and the test tubes – he was always a tinkerer. Gave me his entire paycheck, as if it was petty cash, told me to spend it on myself.

'We lived together that way for three years. I wanted marriage, but couldn't ask. It took me a while to get used to American ways, to women not being just property, to having rights. I pushed it when I wanted children. Stuart was indifferent to the idea, but he went along with it. We married. I tried to get pregnant but couldn't. I saw doctors, at UCLA, Stanford, Mayo. They all said there was too much scarring. I'd been so sick in Korea, it shouldn't have surprised me, but I didn't want to believe it. Looking back now, I know it was a good thing we did not have any little ones. At the time, after I finally accepted it, I became depressed. Very withdrawn, not eating. Eventually Stuart couldn't ignore it any longer. He suggested I go to school. If I loved children I could work with them, become a teacher. He may have had his own motives, but he seemed concerned for me – whenever I was sick or low he was at his best.

'I enrolled in junior college, then college, and learned so much. I was a good student,' she recalled, smiling. 'Very motivated. For the first time I was out in the world, with other people – until then I'd *been* Stuart's little geisha. Now I began to think for myself. At the same time he drifted away from me. There was no anger, no resentment that he put into words. He simply spent more time with his cameras and his bird books – he used to like to read books and magazines on nature, though he never hiked or walked. An armchair bird lover. An armchair man.

'We became two distant cousins living in the same house. Neither of us cared, we were busy. I studied every spare moment, by now I knew I wanted to go beyond the bachelor's and get a credential in early childhood. We went our own ways. There were weeks when we never saw each other. There was no communication, no marriage. But no divorce either – what would have been the point? There were no fights. It was live and let live. My new friends, my college friends, told me I was liberated, I should be happy to have a husband who didn't bother me. When I became lonely I went deeper into my studies.

'I finished the credential and they gave me field placements at local preschools. I liked working with the little ones but I thought I could run a better school than those I had seen. I told Stuart, he said sure, anything to keep me happy, out of his way. We bought a big house in Brentwood – there always seemed to be money for anything – and I started Kim's Korner. It was a wonderful place, a wonderful time. I finally stopped mourning not having children of my own. Then he—'

She stopped, covered her face with her hands and rocked back and forth.

I got up and put a hand on her shoulder.

'Please don't do that. It's not right. I tried to have Otto kill you.' She lifted her face, dry and unlined. 'Do you understand that? I wanted him to *kill* you. Now you are being kind and understanding. It makes me feel worse.'

I removed the hand and sat back down.

'Why the need for Otto, why the fear?'

'I thought you were sent by the ones who killed Stuart.'

'The official verdict was that he killed himself.'

She shook her head.

'No. He didn't commit suicide. They said he was depressed. It was a lie. Of course when he was first arrested, he was very low. Humiliated and guilty. But he bounced out of it. That was Stuart's way. He could block out reality as easily as exposing a roll of film. Poof, and the image is gone. The day before he was arraigned we spoke on the phone. He was in high spirits. To hear him talk, the arrest was the best thing that ever happened to him – to us. He'd been ill, now he would get help. We'd start all over again, as soon as he got out of the hospital. I could even get another school, in another city. He suggested Seattle and talked of our reclaiming the family mansion – that was how I got the idea to come here.

'I knew it would never happen. By then I'd decided to leave him. But I went along with the fantasies, saying, yes dear, certainly, Stuart. Later we had other conversations and it was the same thing. Life was going to be better than ever. He was not talking like a man about to blow his brains out.'

'It's not that simple. People often kill themselves right after an upswing in mood. The suicide season is spring, you know.'

'Perhaps. But I know Stuart and I know he didn't kill himself. He was too shallow to let something like the arrest bother him for a long time. He could deny anything. He denied me for all those years, denied our marriage – that's why he could do those things without my knowing about them. We were strangers.'

'But you know him well enough to be sure he didn't commit suicide.'

'Yes,' she insisted. 'That story about the false phone call to you, the picked locks. That kind of scheming isn't – wasn't Stuart. For all his sickness he was naïve, almost simple. He wasn't a planner.'

'It took planning to get those children down in the cellar.'

'You don't have to believe me. I don't care. He's done his damage. Now he's dead. And I'm in a cellar of my own.'

Her smile was pitiful.

The lamp sputtered. She got up to adjust the wick and add more kerosene. When she sat back down I asked her: 'Who killed him and why?'

'The others. His so-called friends. So he wouldn't expose them. And he would have. During our last visits he'd hint around. Say things like, "I'm not the only sick one, Kimmy" or "Things aren't what they seem with the Gentlemen." I knew he wanted me to ask him, to help him spill it out. But I didn't. I was still in shock over losing the school, wrapped in my own shame, I didn't want to hear about more perversions. I cut him off, changed the subject. But after he died it came back to me and I put it all together.'

'Did he mention anyone by name as being sick?'

'No. But what else could he have meant? They'd come to pick him up, parking their big soft cars in the driveway, dressed in those sport jackets with the Casa insignia. When he'd leave with them he'd be excited. His hands trembling. He'd come back in the early hours of the morning, exhausted. Or the next day. Isn't it obvious what they were doing?'

'You haven't told anyone of your suspicions?'

'Who would believe me? Those men are powerful –
doctors, lawyers, executives, that horrid little Judge Hayden.
I wouldn't stand a chance, the wife of a molester. To the
public I'm as guilty as Stuart. And there's no evidence –
look what they did to him to shut him up. I had to run.'

'Did Stuart ever mention knowing McCaffrey from
Washington?'

'No. Did he?'

'Yes. What about a child named Cary Nemeth. Did his
name come up?'

'No.'

'Elena Gutierrez? Morton Handler – Doctor Morton
Handler?'

'No.'

'Maurice Bruno?'

She shook her head. 'No. Who are these people?'

'Victims.'

'Violated like the others?'

'The ultimate violation. Dead. Murdered.'

'Oh my God.' She put her hands to her face.

Telling her story had made her sweat. Strands of black
hair stuck to her forehead. 'So it continues,' she said mourn-
fully.

'That's why I'm here. To put an end to it. What else can
you tell me that would help?'

'Nothing. I've told you everything. They killed him.
They're evil men, hiding their ugly secret under a cloak of
respectability. I ran to escape them.'

I looked around the dingy room.

'How long can you continue this way?'

'Forever, if no one gives me away. The island is secluded,

351

this property is hidden. When I have to go to the mainland to shop I dress like a cleaning maid. No one notices me. I stockpile as much as possible to avoid making too many trips. The last one was over a month ago. I live simply. The flowers are my one extravagance. I planted them from seed packets and bulbs. They occupy my time, with watering, feeding, pruning, re-potting. The days go by quickly.'

'How safe can you be – Towle and Hayden have roots here.'

'I know. But their families haven't lived here for a generation. I checked. I even went by their old homes. There are new faces, new names. There's no reason for them to look for me here. Not unless you give them one.'

'I won't.'

'On my next trip I'll buy a gun. I'll be prepared for them if they come. I'll escape and go somewhere else. I'm used to it. The memory of Seoul returns in my dreams. It keeps me watchful. I'm sorry to hear about the other murders, but I don't want to know about them. There's nothing that I can do.'

I got up and she helped me on with my jacket.

'The funny thing is,' she said, 'this estate probably belongs to me. As does the Brentwood property and the rest of the Hickle fortune. I'm Stuart's sole heir – we wrote our wills several years ago. He never discussed finances with me so I don't know how much he left, but it has to be considerable. There were bearer bonds, other pieces of real estate all up and down the coast. In theory I'm a rich woman. Do I look it?'

'There's no way to get in touch with the executors of his will?'

'The executor is a partner in Edwin Hayden's law firm. For all I know he's one of *them*. I can do without wealth when all it means is a fancy funeral.'

She used her chair to climb out of the window. I followed her. We walked in the direction of the big, black house.

'You worked with the children from my school. How are they doing?'

'Very well. The prognosis is good. They're amazingly resilient.'

'That's good.'

A few steps later:

'And the parents – did they hate me?'

'Some. Others were surprisingly loyal and defended you. It created a schism in the group. They worked it out.'

'I'm glad. I think about them often.'

She accompanied me to the edge of the swamp that fronted the mansion.

'I'll let you go the rest of the way by yourself. How does the arm feel?'

'Stiff, but nothing serious. I'll survive.'

I held out my hand and she took it.

'Good luck,' she said.

'Same to you.'

I walked through weeds and mud, chilled and tired. When I turned around to look she was gone.

I stayed in the ferry's dining room drinking coffee for much of the return trip to the mainland, going over what I'd learned. When I got back to the hotel I called Milo at the station, was told he wasn't there and tried his home number. Rick Silverman answered.

'Hi, Alex. There's static. Is this long distance?'

'It is. Seattle. Is Milo back yet?'

'No. I expect him tomorrow. He went to Mexico on a supposed vacation but it sounds like work to me.'

'It is. He's looking into the background of a guy named McCaffrey.'

'I know. The minister with the children's home. He said you turned him on to it.'

'I may have sparked his interest but when I spoke to him about it he brushed me off. Did he mention what led him to make the trip?'

'Let me see – I recall his saying he phoned the police down there – it's some small town, I forget the name – and they jerked him around. They implied they had something juicy for him but that he'd have to come up with some bucks to get it. It surprised me – I thought cops cooperated with each other – but he said that's the way they always are.'

'That's it?'

'That's it. He invited me to come along but it didn't work out well with my schedule – I had a twenty-four-hour shift coming up and it would have required too much trading with the other guys.'

'Have you heard from him since he left?'

'Just a postcard from the airport at Guadalajara. An old peasant pulling a burro next to a Saguaro cactus that looked plastic. Very classy stuff. He wrote "Wish you were here" on it.'

I laughed.

'If he does call, tell him to give me a ring. I've got some more information for him.'

'Will do. Anything specific?'

'No. Just have him call.'

'OK.'

'Thanks. Look forward to meeting you some day, Rick.'

'Likewise. Maybe when he gets back and wraps things up.'

'Sounds good.'

I got out of my clothes and examined the arm. There was some oozing, but nothing bad. Kim Hickle had done a good patchup job. I did a half-hour of limbering exercises and a bit of karate, then soaked in a hot bath for forty-five minutes while reading the throwaway guide to Seattle the hotel had furnished.

I called Robin, got no answer, dressed and went for dinner. I remembered a place from my previous visit, a cedar-paneled room overlooking Lake Union, where they barbecued salmon over alder wood. I found it, using my memory and a map, arrived early enough to get a table with a view, and proceeded to put away a large salad with Roquefort, a beautiful coral-colored chinook fillet, potatoes, beans, a basket of hot cornbread and two Coors. I topped it off with homemade blackberry ice cream and coffee and, with a full belly, watched the sun go down over the lake.

I browsed a couple of bookstores in the University District, found nothing exciting or uplifting, and drove back to the hotel. There was an Oriental imports shop in the lobby, still open. I went in, bought a green cloisonné necklace for Robin and rode the elevator back up to my room. At nine I called her again. This time she answered.

'Alex! I was hoping it was you.'

'How are you, doll? I called you a couple of hours ago.'

'I went out for dinner. By my lonesome. Ate an omelet

355

in a corner of the Cafe Pelican all by myself. Isn't that a pathetic image?'

'I supped alone, too, my lady.'

'How sad. Come home soon, Alex. I miss you.'

'I miss you too.'

'Was the trip productive?'

'Very.' I filled her in on the details, careful to exclude my encounter with Otto.

'You're really on to something. Don't you feel strange, uncovering all those secrets?'

'Not really, but I'm not looking at it from the outside.'

'I am, and believe me, it's freaky, Alex. I'll just be glad when Milo gets back and he can take over.'

'Yes. How are things going with you?'

'Nothing nearly as exciting. One thing new. This morning I got a call from the head of a new feminist group – it's a kind of a women's chamber of commerce. I fixed this woman's banjo, she came down to pick it up and we got to talking. This was a couple of months ago. Anyway, she called and invited me to give a lecture to their group next week. The topic's something like The Female Artisan in Contemporary Society subtitle Creativity Meets the Business World.'

'That's fantastic. I'll be sure to be there listening if they let me in.'

'Don't you dare! I'm scared enough as it is. Alex, I've never given a speech before – I'm absolutely petrified.'

'Don't worry. You know what you're talking about, you're bright and articulate, they'll love you.'

'So you say.'

'So I say. Listen, if you're really nervous I'll do a little hypnosis with you. To help you relax. It'll be a piece of cake.'

'You think hypnosis will help?'

'Sure. With your imagination and creativity you'll be a terrific subject.'

'I've heard you talk about it, how you used to do it with patients, but I never thought of asking you to do it with me.'

'Usually, darling, we find other ways to occupy our time together.'

'Hypnosis,' she said. 'Now I've got something else to worry about.'

'Don't worry. It's harmless.'

'Totally?'

'Yes. Totally, in your case. The only time you run into a problem is when the subject has major emotional conflicts or deep-seated problems. In those cases hypnosis can dredge up primal memories. You get a stress reaction, some terror. But even that can be helpful. The trained psychotherapist uses the anxiety constructively, to help the patient work it through.'

'And that couldn't happen to me?'

'Certainly not. I guarantee it. You're the most normal person I've ever met.'

'Ha. You've been retired too long!'

'I challenge you to come up with one single symptom of psychopathology.'

'How about extreme horniness, hearing your voice and wanting to be able to touch you and grab you and put you in me?'

'Hmmm. Sounds serious.'

357

'Then come on back and do something about it, Doctor.'

'I'll be back tomorrow. Treatment will commence immediately.'

'What time?'

'The plane lands at ten – a half-hour after that.'

'Damn, I forgot – I have to go to Santa Barbara tomorrow morning. My aunt's sick, in the ICU at Cottage Hospital. It's a family thing, I have to be there. If you came in earlier we could have breakfast before I leave.'

'I'm taking the earliest flight, hon.'

'I suppose I could postpone it, show up later.'

'Visit your aunt. We'll have dinner.'

'It might be a late dinner.'

'Drive straight to my place and we'll take it from there.'

'All right. I'll try to make it by eight.'

'That's great. Speedy recovery to your aunt. I love you.'

'Love you too. Take care.'

26

SOMETHING BOTHERED ME the next morning. The troubled feeling persisted during the ride to Sea-Tac and up the ramp to the plane. I couldn't get a handle on what it was that lurked in a bottom drawer of my mind, that lingered through the serving of the plastic food, the forced smiles of the flight attendants, the copilot's bad jokes. The harder I tried to bring it to the forefront of my consciousness the further back it sank. I felt the impatience and frustration of a child encountering Chinese finger puzzle for the first time. So I decided to just ride with it, sit back and wait and see if it came to me on its own.

It wasn't until shortly before landing that it did. What had stuck in my head was last night's conversation with Robin. She'd asked me about the dangers of hypnosis and I'd given her a speech about it being harmless unless the experience stirred up latent conflicts. *Dredged up primal memories* had been my exact words. Dredge up primal memories and the reaction is often terror...

I was stuffed with tension as the landing wheels touched down. Once free, I jogged through and out of the airport, picked up the Seville in the overnight lot, paid a considerable ransom to get it out the gate and headed east on Century Boulevard. Caltrans, in its infinite wisdom, had chosen to set up construction in the middle of the road during the morning rush in and out of LAX and, caught in a jam, I cooked in the Cadillac for the mile to the San Diego Freeway on-ramp. I took the freeway north, connected to Santa Monica West, and exited just before Pacific Coast Highway. A drive down Ocean and a few turns brought me to the Palisades and the place where Morton Handler and Elena Gutierrez had lost their lives.

The door to Bonita Quinn's apartment was open. I heard cursing from within and entered. A man was standing in the front room kicking the floral sofa and muttering under his breath. He was in his forties, curly-haired, flabby and putty-colored with discouraged eyes and a steel-wool goatee separating his first chin from his second. He wore black slacks and a light blue nylon shirt that clung to every tuck and roll of his gelatinous torso. One hand held a cigarette and flicked ashes onto the carpet. The other groped for treasure behind a meaty ear. He kicked the couch again, looked up, saw me and waved the smoking hand around the tiny room.

'OK, you can get to work.'

'Doing what?'

'Loading this shit outta here – aren't you the mover—' he looked at me again, this time with sharpened eyes. 'No, you don't look like a mover. Excuse me.' He threw back his shoulders. 'What can I do for you?'

'I'm looking for Bonita Quinn and her daughter.'

'You and me both.'

'She's gone?'

'Three friggin' days. With who knows how many rent checks. I've got tenants complaining their calls weren't answered, repairs that haven't been done. I call her, no answer. So I come down here myself and find she's been gone for three days, left all this junk, hightailed it. I never had a good feeling about her. You do someone a favor, you get shafted. Happens every time.'

He inhaled his cigarette, coughed and sucked again. There was yellow around the irises of his eyes; gray, unhealthy flesh pouched the wary orbs. He looked like a man recuperating from a coronary or just about to have one.

'What are you, collection agency?'

'I'm one of her daughter's doctors.'

'Oh yeah? Don't tell me about doctors. It's one of you that got me into this in the first place.'

'Towle?'

His eyebrows rose. 'Yeah? You from his office? Cause if you are, I got plenty—'

'No. I just know him.'

'Then you know he's a nag. Gets into stuff he has no business getting into. My wife hears me say this, she'll kill me. She loves the guy. Says he's terrific with the kids, so who am I to argue, right? What kind of doctor are you, anyway?'

'Psychologist.'

'The kid had problems, huh? Wouldn't surprise me. She looked a little iffy, if you know what I mean.' He held out his hand, tilted it like the wing of a glider.

'You said Dr Towle got you into the mess with Bonita Quinn?'

'That's right. I met the guy once or twice, maybe. I don't know him from Adam. One day he calls me out of the clear blue and asks me if I could give a job to a patient of his. He heard there was an opening for a manager in this place, and could I help this lady out. I say does this person have experience – we're talking multiple units here, not some duplex. He says no, but she can learn, she's got a kid, needs the money. I say, listen, Doc, this particular building is singles-oriented, the job's not right for someone with a kid. The manager's place is too small.' He looked at me scowling. 'Would you stick a kid in a hole like this?'

'No.'

'Me neither. You don't have to be a doctor to see it's not fit. I tell Towle this. I explain it to him. I say, Doc, this job is meant for a single person. Usually I get a student from UCLA to do it – they don't need a lot of space. I've got other buildings, I tell him. In Van Nuys, a couple in Canoga Park, more family-oriented. Let me call my man in the Valley, have him check it out, I'll see if I can help this person.

'Towle says, no, it has to be this building. The kid's already enrolled in school in this neighborhood, to move her would be traumatic, he's a doctor, he knows this to be a fact. I say, but Doc, you can't have kids making noise in a place like this. The tenants are mostly singles, some like to sleep late. He says I guarantee you this kid is well behaved, she makes no noise. I think to myself this kid makes no noise, there's gotta be something wrong with her – now *you* show up and it makes sense.

'I try to put him off, but he presses me. He's a nag. My wife loves him, she'll kill me if I get him pissed off, so I say OK. He makes an appointment for me to meet this lady, shows up with the Quinn broad and the kid. I was surprised. I gave it a little thought the night before, figured he was humping this broad, that's why the Albert Schweitzer routine. I expected something classy, with curves. One of those aspiring actress types, you know what I mean? He's older, but he's a classy-looking guy, right? So in he walks with her and the kid and they look like a pair outta the Dust Bowl, real hicks. The mother is scared outta her skull, she's smoking more than me, which is a feat – the kid's, like I told you, a little iffy, just stares into space, though I'll grant you she's quiet. Didn't make a sound. I had my doubts she could handle the job, but what could I do, I already committed myself. I hired her. She did OK. She was a hard worker, but she learned very slowly. No complaints about the kid, though. Anyway, she stays for a few months, then she flies the coop leaving me with this junk and she's probably got five grand worth of rent checks. I have to go back and trace 'em and have the tenants put stops on 'em and write new ones. I gotta clean this place, hire someone new. Let me tell you, no more Mister Nice Guy for Marty. For doctors or anyone else.'

He folded his arms over his chest.

'You have no idea where she went?' I asked.

'I did, would I be standing here jawing with you?'

He went into the bedroom. It was as bleak as I remembered it.

'Look at this. How can people raise kids like this? I got three, each has his own room, they got TVs, bookshelves, Pac Mans, all that stuff. How can a kid's mind grow in a place like this?'

'If you hear from her or find out where she is, would you please call me?' I took out an old business card, crossed out the number and wrote my home phone number on it.

He glanced at it, and put it in his pocket. Running one finger along the top of the dresser he came up with a digit cloaked with dust kittys. He flung the dust away. 'Yecch. I hate dirt. I like things to be clean, know what I mean? My apartments are always clean – I pay extra for the best cleaning service. It's important tenants should feel healthy in a place.'

'You'll call me?'

'Sure, sure. You do the same for me, too, OK? I wouldn't mind finding Miss Bonita, get my checks back, give her a piece of my mind.' He fished in his pocket, pulled out an alligator billfold and from it produced a pearl-gray business card that said M and M Properties, Commercial and Residential, Marduk I. Minassian, President, followed by a Century City address.

'Thanks, Mr Minassian.'

'Marty.'

He continued probing and inspecting, opening drawers and shaking his head, bending to look under the bed Bonita Quinn had shared with her daughter. He found something under there, stood up, looked at it and tossed it in a metal wastebasket where it landed with a clang.

'What a mess.'

I looked in the basket, saw what he had discarded, and pulled it out.

It was the shrunken head Melody had shown me the day we'd spent together at the beach. I held it in my palm and the rhinestone eyes glared back, glossy and evil. Most of the synthetic hair had come loose but a few black strands stuck out of the top of the snarling face.

'That's junk,' said Minassian. 'It's dirty. Throw it away.'

I closed my hand over the child's keepsake, more sure than ever that the hypothesis I'd developed on the plane was

ight. And that I had to move fast. I put the shrunken head
n my pocket, smiled at Minassian, and left.

'Hey!' he called after me. And then he muttered something that sounded like 'Crazy doctors!'

I retraced my route, got back on the freeway and headed
East, driving like a demon and hoping the Highway Patrol
wouldn't spot me. I had my LAPD consultant badge in my
pocket but I doubted it would help. Even police consultants
aren't supposed to weave in and out of traffic going eighty
miles an hour.

I was lucky. Traffic was light, the guardians of the asphalt
were nowhere to be seen, and I made it to the Silver Lake
exit just before one. Five minutes later I was walking up the
steps to the Gutierrez home. The orange and yellow poppies
drooped, thirsty. The porch was empty. It creaked as I stepped
onto it.

I knocked on the door. Cruz Gutierrez answered, knit-
ting needles and bright pink yarn in her hands. She didn't
seem surprised to see me.

'*Sí señor?*'

'I need your help, señora.'

'*No hablo inglés.*'

'Please. I know you understand enough to help.'

The dark, round face was impassive.

'Señora, the life of a child is at stake.' That was optimism
speaking. '*Una niña.* Seven years old – *siete años.* She's in
danger. She could be killed. *Muerta* – like Elena.'

I let that sink in. Liver-spotted hands tightened around
the blue needles. She looked away.

'Like the other child – the Nemeth boy. Elena's student.

He didn't die in an accident, did he? Elena knew that. She died because of that knowledge.'

She put her hand on the door and started to close it. I blocked it with the heel of my palm.

'I feel for your loss, señora, but if Elena's death is to take on meaning, it can be through preventing more killing. Through stopping the deaths of others. Please.'

Her hands started shaking. The needles rattled like chopsticks in the grasp of a spastic. She dropped them and the ball of yarn. I bent and retrieved them.

'Here.'

She took them, held them to her bosom.

'Come in, please,' she said, in English that was barely accented.

I was too edgy to want to sit but when she motioned me to the green velvet sofa I settled in it. She sat across from me as if awaiting sentence.

'First,' I said, 'you must understand that darkening Elena's memory is the last thing I want to do. If other lives were not at stake I wouldn't be here at all.'

'I understand,' she said.

'The money – is it here?'

She nodded, got up, left the room and came back minutes later with a cigar box.

'Take.' She gave me the box as if it held something alive and dangerous.

The bills were in large denominations – twenties, fifties, hundreds – neatly rolled and held together by thick rubber bands. I made a cursory count. There was at least fifty thousand dollars in the box, probably a good deal more.

'Take it,' I said.

'No, no. I don't want. Black money.'

'Just keep it here, until I come back for it. Does anyone else know about it – either of your sons?'

'No.' She shook her head adamantly. 'Rafael know he take it and buy the dope. No. Only me.'

'How long have you had it here?'

'Elena, she bring it over the day before she was killed.' The mother's eyes filled with tears. 'I say, what is this, where you get this. She say, can't tell you, Mama. Jus' keep it for me. I come back for it. She never come back.' She pulled a lace-trimmed handkerchief from up her sleeve and dabbed at her eyes.

'Please. Take it back. Hide it again.'

'Only a little while, señor, OK? Black money. Bad eye. *Mal ojo.*'

'I'll come back for it if that's what you want.'

She took the box, disappeared again, and returned shortly.

'You're sure Rafael didn't know?'

'I sure. He know, it would all be gone.'

That made sense. Junkies weren't known for being able to hold on to their nickels and dimes, let alone a small fortune.

'Another question, señora. Raquel told me that Elena had in her possession certain tapes – recorded tapes. Of music, and of relaxation exercises given to her by Dr Handler. When I went through her things I found no such tapes. Do you know anything about that?'

'I don't know. This is the truth.'

'Has anyone been through those boxes before I got here?'

'No. Only Rafael an' Antonio, they look for books, things to read. The *policia* take boxes first. Nothin' else.'

'Where are your sons, now?'

She stood up, suddenly agitated.

'Don' hurt. They good boys. They don' know nothin'.'

'I won't. I just want to talk to them.'

She looked to one side, at the wall covered with family portraits. At her three children, young, innocent and smiling; the boys with short hair, slicked and parted, and open-necked white shirts; the girl in a frilly blouse between them. At the graduation picture: Elena in mortarboard and gown, wearing a look of eagerness and confidence, ready to take on the world with her brains and her charm and her looks. At the somber-tinted photo of her long-dead husband, stiff and solemn in starched collar and gray serge suit, a workingman unaccustomed to the fuss and fiddling that went with having one's countenance recorded for posterity.

She looked at the pictures and her lips moved, almost imperceptibly. Like a general surveying a smoldering battle-field, she conducted a silent body count.

'Andy working,' she said, and gave me the address of a garage on Figueroa.

'And Rafael?'

'Rafael I don' know. He say he go look for work.'

She and I both knew where he was. But I'd opened enough wounds for one day, so I kept my mouth shut, except to thank her.

I found him after a half-hour's cruising up and down Sunset and in and out of several side streets. He was walking south on Alvarado, if you could call the stumbling, self-absorbed lurch that propeled him headfirst, feet following, a walk. He stayed close to buildings, veering toward the street when people or objects got in his way, quickly returning to the shadow of awnings. It was close to eighty but he wore a long-sleeved flannel shirt hanging loose over khakis and buttoned to the neck. On his feet were high-topped sneakers; the laces on one of them had come loose. He looked even thinner than I remembered.

I drove slowly, staying in the right lane, out of his field of vision, and keeping pace with him. Once he passed a group of middle-aged men, merchants. They pointed at him behind his back, shook their heads and frowned. He was oblivious to them, cut off from the external world. He pointed with his face, like a setter homing in on a scent. His nose ran continuously and he wiped it with his sleeve. His eyes shifted from side to side as his body kept moving. He ran his tongue over his lips, slapped his thin thighs in a steady tattoo, pursed his lips as if in song, bobbed his head up and down. He was making a concentrated effort at looking cool but he fooled no one. Like a drunk working hard at coming across sober his mannerisms were exaggerated, unnatural and lacking spontaneity. They produced the opposite effect: He appeared to be a hungry jackal on the prowl, desperate, gnawed upon from within and hurting all over. His skin was glossy with sweat, pale and ghostly. People got out of his way as he boogied toward them.

I sped up and drove two blocks before pulling to the curb and parking near an alley behind a three-story building that housed a Latin grocery on the ground floor and apartments on the upper two.

A quick look shot backward confirmed that he was still coming.

I got out of the car and ducked into the alley, which stunk of rotting produce and urine. Empty and broken wine bottles littered the pavement. A hundred feet away was a loading dock, unattended, its steel doors closed and bolted. A dozen vehicles were illegally parked on both sides; exit from the alley was blocked by a half-ton pickup left perpendicular to the walls. Somewhere off in the distance a mariachi band played 'Cielito Lindo'. A cat screeched. Horns honked out on the boulevard. A baby cried.

I peeked my head out and retracted it. He was half a block away. I got ready for him. When he began crossing the alley I said in a stage whisper: 'Hey, man. I got what you need.'

That stopped him. He looked at me with great love, thinking he'd found salvation. It threw him off when I grabbed him by his scrawny arm and pulled him into the alley. I dragged him several feet until we'd found cover behind an old Chevy with peeling paint and two flat tires. I slammed him against the wall. His hands went up protectively. I pushed them down and pinioned both of them with one of my own. He struggled but he had no strength. It was like tussling with a toddler.

'Whadyou want, man?'

'Answers, Rafael. Remember me? I visited you a few days ago. With Raquel.'

'Hey, yeah, sure,' he said, but there was only confusion in the watery hazel eyes. Snot ran down one nostril and into his mouth. He let it sit there a while before reaching up with his tongue and trying to flick it away. 'Yeah, I remember, man. With Raquel, sure, man.' He looked up and down the alley.

'You remember, then, that I'm investigating your sister's murder.'

'Oh, yeah, sure. Elena. Bad stuff, man.' He said it without

feeling. His sister had been sliced up and all he could think of was that he needed a packet of white powder that could be transformed into his own special type of milk. I'd read dozens of tomes on addiction, but it was there, in that alley, that the true power of the needle became clear to me.

'She had tapes, Rafael. Where are they?'

'Hey, man, I don't know shit about tapes.' He struggled to break loose. I slammed him against the wall again. 'Oh, man, I'm hurting, just let me go fix myself up and then I talk to you about tapes. OK, man?'

'No. I want to know now, Rafael. Where are the tapes?'

'I don't know, man, I told you that!' He was whining like a three year old, snotfaced and growing more frantic with each passing second.

'I think you do and I want to know.'

He bounced in my grasp, clattering like a sack of loose bones.

'Lemme go, motherfucker!' he gasped.

'Your sister was murdered, Rafael. Turned into hamburger. I saw pictures of what she looked like. Whoever did it to her took their time. It hurt her. And you're willing to deal with them.'

'I don't know what you're talkin' about, man.'

More struggling, another slam against the wall. He sagged this time, closed his eyes and for a moment I thought I'd knocked him out. But he opened them, licked his lips and gave a dry, hacking cough.

'You were off the stuff, Rafael. Then you started shooting up again. Right after Elena's death. Where'd you get the dough? How much did you sell her out for?'

'I don't know nothin'.' He shook spastically. 'Lemme go. I don't know nothin'.'

'Your own sister,' I said. 'And you sold out to her murderers for the price of a fix.'

'Pu*leeze*, mister. Lemme go.'

'Not until you talk. I don't have time to waste time with you. I want to know where those tapes are. You don't tell me soon I'll take you home with me, tie you up and let you go cold turkey in the corner. Imagine that – think how bad you hurt now, Rafael. Think how much worse it's going to get.'

He crumpled.

'I gave them to some dude,' he stuttered.

'For how much?'

'Not money, man. Stuff. He gave me stuff. Enough for a week's fixing. Good stuff. Now lemme go. I gotta appointment.'

'Who was the guy?'

'Just some dude. Anglo. Like you.'

'What did he look like?'

'I don't know, man, I can't think straight.'

'The corner, Rafael. Tied up.'

'Twenty-five, six. Short. Built good, solid. Real straight-lookin'. Light hair, over the forehead, OK?'

He'd described Tim Kruger.

'Why did he say he wanted the tapes?'

'He dint say, man, I dint ask. He had good stuff, you unnerstand?'

'Didn't you wonder? Your sister was dead and you didn't wonder why some stranger would give you smack for her tapes?'

'Hey, man, I dint wonder, I don' wonder. I don' think. I just go flyin'. I gotta go flyin' now. I'm hurtin', man. Lemme go.'

'Did your brother know about this?'

'No! He kill me, man. You hurt me, but he *kill* me, you unnerstand? Don' tell him!'

'What was on the tapes, Rafael?'

'I dunno. I don' listen, man!'

On principle I refused to believe him.

'The corner. Tied up. Bone dry.'

'Jus' some kid talkin', man, I swear that's it. I dint hear the whole thing, but when he offered me the stuff for them I took a listen before I gave them to the dude. Some kid talkin' to my sister. She's listenin' and sayin' tell me more and he's talkin'.'

'About what?'

'I don' know man. It started to get heavy, the kid's cryin', Elena's cryin', I switched it off. I don' wanna know.'

'What were they crying about, Rafael?'

'I don't know, man, something about how somebody hurt the kid, Elena's askin' him if they hurt him, he's sayin' yes, she's cryin', then the kid's cryin', too.'

'What else?'

'That's it.'

I throttled him just hard enough to rattle his teeth.

'You wan' me to make somethin' up, I can do it, man, but that's all I know!'

He cried out, snuffling and sucking for air.

I held him at arm's length, then let go. He looked at me unbelievingly, slithered against the wall, found a space between the Chevy and a rusted Dodge van. Staring at me, he wiped his nose, passed between the two cars and made a run for freedom.

* * *

I drove to a gas station at Virgil and Sunset, filled up, and used the pay phone to call La Casa de los Niños. The receptionist with the upbeat voice answered. Slipping into a drawl I asked her for Kruger.

'Mr Kruger isn't in, today, sir. He'll be in tomorrow.'

'Oh yeah, that's right! He told me he'd be off the day I got in.'

'Would you care to leave a message, sir?'

'Heck no. I'm an old friend from school. Tim and I go way back. I just blew in on a business trip – I'm selling tool and die, Becker Machine Works, San Antonio, Texas – and I was supposed to look old Tim up. He gave me his number at home but I must have lost it. Do you have it?'

'I'm sorry, sir, we're not supposed to give out personal information.'

'I can dig that. But like I say, Tim and me are tight. Why don't you call him at home, tell him old Jeff Saxon's on the line, ready to drop in but stuck without the address.'

A clatter of ringing phones sounded in the background.

'One moment, sir.'

When she returned I asked her:

'You call him yet, ma'am?'

'No – I – it's rather busy right now, Mr . . .'

'Saxon. Jeff Saxon. You call old Tim and tell him old Jeff Saxon's in town to see him, I guarantee you he'll be—'

'Why don't I just give you the number?' She recited seven digits, the first two of which signified a beach cities location.

'Thank you much, I believe Tim told me he lived near the beach – that far from the airport?'

'Mr Kruger lives in Santa Monica. It's about a twenty-minute ride.'

'Hey, that's not bad – maybe I'll just drop in on him, kind of a surprise, what do you think?'

'Sir, I have to—'

'You wouldn't happen to have the address? I tell you, it's been one hell of a day, what with the airline losing my sample case and I've got two meetings tomorrow. I think I packed the address book in the suitcase, but now I can't be sure and—'

'Here's the address, sir.'

'Thank you much, ma'am. You've been very helpful. And you have a nice voice.'

'Thank you, sir.'

'You free tonight?'

'I'm sorry, sir, no.'

'Fellow's gotta try, right?'

'Yes, sir. Goodbye, sir.'

I'd been driving north for a good five minutes before I heard the buzzing. I realized, then, that the sound had been with me since I'd pulled out of the gas station. The rearview mirror revealed a motorcycle several lengths back, bouncing in the distance like a fly on a hot windshield. The driver twisted the handle accelerator and the fly grew like a monster in a Japanese horror flick.

He was two lengths behind, and gaining. As he approached I got a look at him, jeans, boots, black leather jacket, black helmet with full-face tinted sun visor that completely masked his features.

He rode my tail for several blocks. I changed lanes. Instead of passing, he hung back, allowing a Ford full of nuns to come between us. A half mile past Lexington the nuns turned off. I steered sharply toward the curb and came to a sudden stop in front of a Pup 'n' Taco. The motorcycle sped by. I waited until he'd disappeared, told myself I was being paranoid, and got out of the Seville. I looked for him, didn't see him, bought a Coke, got behind the wheel and reentered the boulevard.

I'd turned east on Temple headed for the Hollywood Freeway when I heard him again. Verifying his presence in the mirror caused me to miss the on ramp, and I stayed on Temple, dipping under the bridge created by the overpass. The motorcycle stayed with me. I gave the Seville gas and ran a red light. He maintained his position, buzzing and spitting. The next intersection was filled with pedestrians and I had to stop.

I kept a watch on him through the side mirror. He rolled toward me, three feet away, now two, approaching on the driver's side. One hand went inside the leather jacket. A young mother wheeled a small child in a stroller, passing directly in front of my bumper. The child wailed, the mother chewed gum, heavy legged, moving oh so slowly. Something metallic came into the hand in the mirror. The motorcycle was just behind me, almost flush with the driver's window. I saw the gun now, an ugly little snub-nosed affair, easy to conceal in a large palm. I raced my engine. The gum-chewing young matron wasn't impressed. She seemed to move in slow motion, indolently working her jaws, the child now screaming at the top of his lungs. The light remained red but its catercornered cousin had turned amber. The longest light in the history of traffic engineering . . . how long could an amber light last?

The snout of the revolver pressed against the glass,

directly in line with my left temple. A black hole miles long wrapped in a concentric halo of silver. The mother still dragged her heavy body lazily across the intersection, her heel in line with my right front tire, unaware that the man in the green Cadillac was going to be blown away any second. The finger on the trigger blanched. The mother stepped clear by an inch. I twisted the steering wheel to the left, pressed down hard on the accelerator and shot diagonally across the intersection into the path of the ongoing traffic. I gunned the engine, laid a long patch of rubber, heard a Delphic chorus of curses, shouts, honking horns and squealing brakes, and shot up the first side street, narrowly missing a head-on collision with a Water and Power van coming from the opposite direction.

The street was narrow and winding, and pocked with potholes. The Seville was no sports car and I had to fight its slack steering system to maintain speed and control around the turns. I climbed, bounced down hard, and swooped steeply down a hill. A boulevard stop at the bottom was clear. I sped through. Three blocks of level turf at seventy miles an hour and the buzz was back, growing louder. The motorcycle, so much easier to maneuver, was catching up fast.

The road came to an end at a cracked masonry wall. Left or right? Decisions, decisions, with the adrenaline shooting through every corpuscle, the buzz now a roar, my hands sweaty, slipping off the wheel. I looked in the mirror, saw one hand come off the bars and aim the gun at my tires. I chose left and floored the Seville, putting my body into it. The road rose, scaling empty streets, higher, spiraling into the smog, a roller coaster of a street planned by a berserk engineer. The motorcyclist kept riding up on my rear, raking his gun hand off the bars whenever he could, striving for steady aim . . .

I swerved continuously, dancing out of his sights, but the narrowness of the street gave me little leeway. I knew I had to avoid slipping unconsciously into a regular rhythm – back and forth, back and forth, a gasoline-fueled metronome – for to do so would be to offer an easy target. I drove erratically, crazily, jerking the wheel, slowing down, speeding up, careening against the curb, losing a hubcap that spun off like a chromium Frisbee. It was a direct assault on my axle and I didn't know how long it could last.

We continued to climb. A view of Sunset below appeared around a corner. We were back in Echo Park, on the south side of the boulevard. The road hit its peak. A shot whizzed by so close that the Seville's windows vibrated. I swerved and a second shot went far afield.

The terrain changed as the altitude rose, thinning from residential blocks of frame houses to progressively emptier stretches of dusty lots, with here and there a decrepit shack. No more telephone poles, no cars, no signs of human habitation . . . perfect for an afternoon killing.

We began to race downhill and I saw with horror that I was heading full-speed into a dead end, mere yards from slamming into a pile of dirt at the mouth of an empty construction site. There was no escape – the roar terminated at the site and was additionally blocked by piles of cinder block, stacks of drywall, lumber and more mounds of excavated dirt. A goddam *box canyon*. If the impact of smashing nose-first into the dirt didn't kill me, I'd be imbedded, tires spinning hopelessly, as immobile as parsley in aspic, a perfect, passive target . . .

The man on the motorcycle must have harbored similar thoughts in that same instant, for he engaged in a quick series of confident actions. He removed his gun hand from the bars, slowed, and came around to the left, ready to be at my side when my escape came to an end.

I made the only move left for me: I jammed on the brakes. The Seville convulsed, skidded violently, spun and rocked on its bearings, threatening to capsize. I needed the skid to continue, so I steered away from it. The car spun like a rotor blade.

Then a sudden impact threw me across the seat.

My front end had gone out of control and collided with the cycle as it came out of a spin with full torque behind it. The lighter vehicle bounced off the car, caromed and sailed through the air in a wide arc over the hill of earth. I watched as man and machine parted ways, the cycle climbing, stunt-like, falling, its rider thrown loose, flying higher, a scarecrow cut free from its stake, then falling too, landing unseen.

The Seville stopped spinning and its engine died. I pulled myself up. My sore arm had been knocked against the passenger door panel and it hummed with pain. No sign of movement came from the site. I got out quietly, crouched behind the car and waited there as my head cleared and my breathing slowed. Still nothing. I spied a two-by-four several feet away, snatched it, hefted it like a stave and circled the mound of dirt, staying low to the ground. Creeping onto the site I saw that a partial foundation had been laid – a right angle of concrete from which corrugated steel rods protruded like flowerless stalks. The remains of the motorcycle were visible immediately, a rubbish heap of seared metal and shattered windshield.

It took several more minutes of poking amid the rubble to find the body. It had landed in a ditch at the junction of the two cement arms, a spot where the earth was etched with caterpillar tread marks, next to a broken fiberglass shower stall and half-concealed by molding sheets of insulation.

The opaque helmet was still in place but it had offered no protection from the steel rod that stuck out through a large, jagged hole in the rider's throat. The shaft extended just below the Adam's apple; it had created a good-sized exit wound coming through. Blood seeped from the hole, turning muddy in the dirt. The trachea was visible, still pink, but deflated, leaking fluid. A fleck of gore tipped the rod.

I knelt and undid the helmet strap, and tried to pull off the headpiece. The neck had bent unnaturally upon being pierced and it proved a difficult task. As I struggled I felt steel scrape against vertebrae, cartilage and gristle. My belly quaked with nausea. I heaved and turned away to vomit in the dirt.

With a bitter taste in my mouth and eyes brimming with tears, breathing hard and loud, I returned to the grisly chore. The helmet finally came loose and the bare skull flopped to the ground. I stared down into the lifeless, bearded face of Jim Halstead, the coach at La Casa de Los Niños. His lips were drawn back in death, cast in a permanent sneer. The force of landing after his final free fall had snapped his jaws down upon his tongue, and the severed tip rested on the hairy chin like some fleshy, parasitic grub. His eyes were open and rolled backward, the whites flooded with blood. He cried crimson tears.

I looked away from him and saw the sun hit something shiny several feet to the right. I walked to it, found the gun

nd examined it – a chrome-plated .38. I took it and tucked
t in the waistband of my trousers.

The ground at my feet radiated heat and the stench of
omething burning. Congealed tar. Toxic waste. Bio-
ndegradable garbage. Polyvinyl vegetation. A bluejay had
anded on Halstead's face. It pecked at his eyes.

I found a dusty drop cloth peppered with specks of dried
ement. The bird fled at my approach. I covered the body
vith the cloth, weighted down the corners with large stones
nd left him that way.

27

THE ADDRESS the receptionist had given me for Tim Kruger matched the oversized steel numbers on the face of a bone-white highrise on Ocean, just a mile or so from where the Handler–Gutierrez murders had taken place.

The entry hall was a crypt of marble floors and mirrors, furnished with a single white cotton sofa and two rubber plants in wicker canisters. The upper half of one wall was given over to rows of alphabetically arranged brass mail-boxes. It didn't take long to locate Kruger's apartment on the twelfth floor. I took a short silent ride on an elevator padded with gray batting and exited into a corridor floored in royal-blue plush and paper with grass-cloth.

Kruger's place was located in the northwest corner of the building. I knocked on the royal-blue door.

He opened it, dressed in jogging shorts and a Casa de los Niños T-shirt, shiny with perspiration and smelling as if he'd been exercising. He saw me, stifled his surprise and said 'Hello, Doctor' in a stagey voice. Then he noticed the gun in my hand and the stolid face turned ugly.

'What the—'

'Just get in,' I said.

He backed into the apartment and I followed. It was a small place, low ceilings sprayed with plaster cottage cheese and starred with glitter. The walls and carpet were beige. There was little furniture and what was there looked rented. A wall of glass offering a panoramic view of Santa Monica Bay saved it from being a cell. There was no artwork on the walls, except for a single, framed wrestling poster from Hungary. A tiny convenience kitchen was off on one side, a foyer to the other.

Athletic equipment filled a good portion of the living room – snow skis and boots, a pair of waxed wooden oars, several sets of tennis rackets, running shoes, a mountaineer's backpack, a football, a basketball, a bow and quiver of arrows. A beige-painted brick mantel was topped by a dozen trophies.

'You're an active boy, Tim.'

'What the hell do you want?' The yellow-brown eyes moved around like pachinko balls.

'Where's the little girl – Melody Quinn?'

'I don't know what you're talking about. Put that thing away.'

'You know damn well where she is. You and your fellow murderers abducted her three days ago because she's a witness to your dirty work. Have you killed her too?'

'I'm no killer. I don't know any kid named Quinn. You're crazy.'

'No killer? Jeffrey Saxon might not agree.'

His mouth dropped open, then shut abruptly.

'You left a trail, Tim. Pretty arrogant to think no one would find it.'

'Who the hell are you, anyway?'

'I'm who I said I was. A better question is who are *you*? A rich boy who can't seem to stay out of trouble? A guy who enjoys snapping twigs at hunchbacks and waiting for the tears? Or just an amateur actor whose best bit is an impression of Jack the Ripper?'

'Don't try to pin that on me!' He rolled his hands into fists.

'Hands up.' I waved the gun.

He obeyed very slowly, straightening his thick, brown arms and lifting them above his head. It drew my attention upward, and away from his feet. That enabled him to make his move.

The kick came at me like a boomerang, catching the underside of my wrist and numbing the fingers. The gun flew from my grasp and landed on the carpet with a thud. We both leaped for it and ended in a tangle on the floor, punching, kicking, gouging. I was oblivious to pain and seething with fury. I wanted to destroy him.

He was an iron man. It was like fighting an outboard motor. I clawed at his abdomen, but couldn't find an inch of extra flesh. I elbowed him in the ribs. It knocked him backward, but he rebounded as if on springs and landed a punch to the jaw that threw me off-balance long enough for him to get me in a headlock, then hold me skilfully at bay so that my arms were ineffective.

He grunted and increased the pressure. My head felt ready to burst. My vision blurred. I struck at him helplessly. With a strange kind of delicacy he danced out of reach, squeezing me tighter. Then he started pulling my head back. A little more and I knew my neck would snap. I experienced a sudden kinship with Jeffrey Saxon, drew upon a reserve of strength and brought my heel down hard on his instep. He cried out and reflexively let go, then tried to renew the lock, but it was too late. I landed a kick that snapped his head to the side and followed it with a series of rapid straightarm punches to the lower belly. When he doubled over I chopped down on the place where his head joined his neck. He sank to his knees, but I didn't take any chances – he was strong and skilled. Another kick to the face. Now he was down. I placed one foot under bridge of his nose. One quick forward motion and splinters of bone would lobotomize him. It turned out to be an unnecessary precaution. He was out.

I found a coil of thick nylon rope in the mountaineer's pack and trussed him as he lay on his abdomen, feet drawn up behind him, bound and secured to another piece of rope that similarly raised his arms. I checked the knots, drew them tight and dragged him clear of any weapon. I retrieved the .38, kept it in one hand, went into his kitchen and soaked a towel in cold water.

When several minutes of slapping him with the towel elicited no more than a half-conscious groan, I made another trip to the kitchen, pulled a Dutch oven out of a dish drainer, filled it with water and dumped the contents on his head. That brought him around.

'Oh, Jesus,' he moaned. He tried those first struggles that all prisoners attempt, gnashed his teeth, finally realized his predicament and sank back down, gasping.

I prodded the back of one leg with the muzzle of the .38.

'You like sports, Tim. That's fortunate because they'll let you exercise in prison. Without exercise the time can go very slowly. But I'm going to ask you questions and if you don't give me satisfactory answers I'm going to maim you, bit by bit. First I'll shoot you right here.' I pressed cold steel into warm flesh. 'After that your leg might be good for getting you on the john. Then I'll do the same to the other leg. From there to fingers, wrists, elbows. You'll do your time as a vegetable, Tim.'

I listened to myself talk, hearing a stranger. To this day I don't know if I would have followed through on the threat. I never had to find out.

'What do you want?' His speech came out in spurts, constricted with fear and hampered by the uncomfortable position.

'Where's Melody Quinn?'

'At La Casa.'

'Where at La Casa?'

'The storage rooms. Near the forest.'

'Those cinder block buildings – the ones you avoided discussing when you gave me the tour?'

'Uh-huh. Yes.'

'Which one? There were four.'

'The last one – furthest from the front.'

A spreading stain darkened the carpet at my feet. He'd wet himself.

'Jesus,' he said.

'Let's keep going, Tim. You're doing fine.'

He nodded, seemingly eager for praise.

'Is she still alive?'

'Yes. As far as I know. Cousin Will – Doctor Towle wanted to keep her alive. Gus and the judge agreed. I don't know for how long.'

'What about her mother?'

He closed his eyes and said nothing.

'Talk, Tim, or your leg goes.'

'She's dead. The guy they sent to get the kid and her did it. They buried her in the Meadow.'

I remembered the stretch of field at the north side of La Casa. *We're planning to plant a vegetable garden this summer* he'd told me . . .

'Who is he?'

'Some crazy guy. A gimp – kind of paralyzed on one side. Gus called him Earl.'

It wasn't the name I expected but the description was right.

'Why'd he do it?'

'Leave as few loose ends as possible.'

'On McCaffrey's orders?'

He was silent. I exerted pressure on the gun. High thigh quivered.

'Yeah. On his orders. Earl doesn't operate on his own.'

'Where is this Earl character now?'

More hesitation. Without thinking I flicked the tip of the .38 over his kneecap. His eyes widened with surprise and hurt. Tears ran out of them.

'Oh, God!'

'Don't get religious. Just talk.'

'He's gone – dead. Gus had Halstead rip him off. After they buried the woman. He was filling the grave and Halstead hit him with the shovel, pushed him in with her and covered them both with dirt. He and Gus were laughing about it later. Halstead said when he hit Earl on the head it gave off a hollow sound. They used to talk like that, behind the guy's back – call him the gimp, damaged goods . . .'

'Mean guy, that Halstead.'

'Yeah. He is.' Kruger's visage brightened, eager to please. 'He's after you too. You were snooping around. Gus didn't know how much the kid told you. I'm tipping you off, man, watch your—'

'Thanks, pal, but Halstead's no threat anymore. To anyone.'

He looked up at me. I answered the unspoken question with a quick nod.

'Jesus,' he said, broken.

I didn't give him time to reflect.

'Why'd you kill Handler and Gutierrez?'

'I told you, I *didn't*. That was Halstead and Earl. Gus told 'em to make it look like a sex thing. Halstead told me later Earl was a natural for the job – carved 'em up like he enjoyed it. Really went to town on the teacher. Halstead held her and Earl used the knife.'

Two men, maybe three, Melody had said.

'You were there, too, Tim.'

'No. Yeah. I – I drove them there. With the headlights out. It was a dark night, no moon, no stars. I circled the parking lot, then figured I might get noticed, so I drove around in the Palisades and came back. They still weren't through – I remember wondering what was taking them so long. I left again, drove around some more, came back and they were just coming out. They wore black, like demons. I could see the blood, even against the black. They smelled of blood. It was all over them, dark, like the clothing, but a different texture – you know, shiny. Wet.'

Dark men. Two, maybe three.

He stopped.

'That's not the end of the story, Tim.'

'That's it. They undressed in the car, stuffed the knife in a duffel bag. We burned it in one of the canyons – the clothes, bag, everything. Dumped whatever was left off the Malibu pier.' He paused again, out of breath. 'I didn't kill anybody.'

'Did they say anything in the car?'

'Halstead was stone silent. It bothered me, how freaked-out he looked, because he's a mean one – that story about getting a knife pulled on him by a kid is bullshit. He was kicked out of Manual Arts for beating up a couple of students pretty badly. Before that he was booted out of the marines. He loved violence. But whatever happened in that apartment got to him – he was silent, man.'

'How about Earl?'

'Earl was – different – like he *dug* it, you know? He was licking his lips and rocking back and forth like an autistic kid. Jabbering, saying "Sonofabitch" over and over. Weird. Crazy. Finally Halstead told him to shut the fuck up and he yelled something back – in Spanish. The guy spoke a lot in Spanish. Halstead yelled back and I thought the two of them were going to tear each other up right there. It was like driving around with two caged beasts. I calmed them down, used Gus's name – that always worked for Earl. I couldn't wait to get away from them that night. Prototypical psychopaths, both of them.'

'Save the scholarly stuff and tell me how you killed Bruno.'

He looked at me with renewed fear.

'You know everything, don't you.'

'What I don't you're going to fill in.' I waved the gun in the air. '*Bruno.*'

'We – they did that the night after doing the doctor and the teacher. Halstead didn't want Earl along but Gus insisted. Said two men on the job was better. I had the feeling he played them off against each other. I wasn't there at all. Halstead drove and did the killing. He used a baseball bat from the athletic supplies bin. I was there when he came back and told Gus about it. They found the salesman eating dinner, beat him to death right there at the table. Earl ate the rest of the meal.'

Two murders pinned on two dead men. Very neat. It stunk and I told him so.

'That's the way it was. I'm not saying I'm totally innocent. I knew what they were going to do when I drove them to the shrink's place. I gave them the key. But I didn't do any of the killing.'

'How'd you get the key?'

'Cousin Will gave it to me. I don't know where he got it.'

'All right. We've talked about who. Now tell me why all the butchery.'

'I assumed you knew—'

'Don't assume a goddam thing.'

'OK, OK. It's the Brigade. It's a cover for child molesters. The shrink and the girl found out and they were blackmailing him. Stupid of them to think they could get away with it.'

I remembered the pictures Milo'd shown me that first day. They'd paid far too high a price for their stupidity.

I chased the bloody images from my mind and returned to Kruger.

'Are all the Gentlemen perverts?'

'No. Only about a quarter. The rest are straight-arrows. It makes it easier to conceal, sneaking the perverts in among them.'

'And the kids never talk?'

'Not until – we pick the ones that the pervs take home

with care, mostly those who can't talk back. Retarded, or they don't know English, severely CP. Gus likes orphans because they don't have family ties, no one looks out for them.'

'Was Rodney one of the chosen ones?'

'Uh-huh.'

'Did his fear of the doctor have something to do with that?'

'Yeah. One of the weirdos got a little rough with him. A surgeon. Gus warns them to go easy. He doesn't want the kids actually *hurt* – spoiled merchandise isn't worth as much. But it doesn't always work out. Those guys aren't normal, you know.'

'I know.' Anger and disgust made it hard to see straight. Kicking his head in would have been primally satisfying, but it was a pleasure I was going to have to deny myself . . .

'I'm not one of them,' he was insisting, sounding almost as if he'd convinced himself. 'I think it's disgusting, actually.'

I bent down and grabbed him by the throat.

'You went along with it, asshole!'

His face purpled, the butterscotch eyes bulging. I let go of his head. It dropped to the floor. He landed on his nose and it started to bleed. He writhed in confinement.

'Don't say it. You were just following orders.'

'You don't understand!' he sobbed. Real tears mixed with the mustache of blood on his upper lip creating a momentary illusion of harelip. But for his degree in drama I might have been impressed. 'Gus took me in when the rest of them – my so-called friends and family, everyone – blackballed me for the Saxon thing. You can think what you want but that wasn't murder. It was — an accident. Saxon was no innocent victim. He wanted to kill *me* — that's the truth.'

'He's in no position to state his case.'

'Shit! No one believed me. Except Gus. He knew what it could be like at that place. They all thought I was a washout — shame of the family and all that crap. He gave me responsibility. And I lived up to his expectations — I showed my stuff, showed you don't need a degree. Everything was perfect, I ran La Casa as smooth as—'

'You're a terrific stormtrooper, Tim. Right now I want answers.'

'Ask,' he said weakly.

'How long has the Brigade been a cover for child molesters?'

'From the beginning.'

'Just like in Mexico?'

'Just like. Down there, to hear him tell it — the police knew all about it. All he had to do was grease a few palms. They let him bring in rich businessmen from Acapulco — Japanese, lots of Arabs — to play with the kids. The place was called Father Augustino's Christian Home — whatever that is in Spanish. It went good for a long time until a new police commissioner, some religious nut, took over and didn't like it. Gus claims the guy ripped him off for thousands in payoff then double-crossed him and shut the place down anyway. He moved up here and set up camp. Brought Crazy Earl with him.'

'Earl was his boy in Mexico?'

'Yup. I figure he did the shitwork. Followed Gus like a lap dog. The guy spoke Spanish like a beaner — I mean the accent was fine but what he said was gibberish —

we're talking brain damage, man. A robot with the screws loose.'

'McCaffrey had him killed anyway.'

Kruger gave the closest approximation to a shrug the ropes would allow.

'You have to know Gus. He's cold. Loves power. Get in his way and you're done. Those suckers didn't have a chance.'

'How did he get set up so fast in LA?'

'Connections.'

'Cousin Willie?'

He hesitated. I prodded him with the .38.

'Him. Judge Hayden. Some others. One seemed to lead to another. Each one knew at least one other closet sicko. Amazing how many of those guys there are. Cousin Will was a surprise to me, 'cause I knew him really well. Always seemed such a priss, holier than thou. My folks held him up as an example to follow – fine, upstanding Cousin Doctor.' He laughed hoarsely. 'And the guy's a kiddy boffer.' More laughter. 'Though I can't say I actually saw him take a kid home – I set up the schedules and I never set him up with anything. All I *know* he did was patch injured kids up whenever we called. Still, he must be as sick as the rest, why else would he be kissing up to Gus?'

I ignored the question and asked one of my own.

'How long was the blackmail going on?'

'A few months. Like I told you we screened the kids, to make sure they wouldn't talk. One time we blew it. There was this one boy, an orphan, just perfect. Everyone thought he was mute. Jesus, he never talked to *us*. We had speech and hearing tests – the government pays for all of that –

and everything came back no speech. We were sure, and we were wrong. The kid talked all right. He told the teacher plenty. She freaked out and reported it to Cousin Will – he was the kid's pediatrician. She didn't know he was involved in it himself. He told Gus.'

And Gus had him killed. Cary Nemeth.

'Then what?'

'I – do we have to talk about it?'

'We goddamn as hell do! How did it happen?'

'They ran him down with a truck. They took him out of bed in the middle of the night, must have been close to midnight. Nothing's out there at that hour. Put him on the road, walking. In his pajamas. I remember the pajamas. Yellow, with baseballs and mitts all over. I – I could have tried to stop it but it wouldn't have made a difference. The kid knew, he had to go. Simple as that. They would have done it later and probably me, too. It was wrong to do that to a little kid. Cold-blooded. I started to say something. Gus squeezed my arm. Told me to shut up. I wanted to scream. The kid was walking on the road, all alone, half-asleep, like he was dreaming. I kept quiet. Halstead got into the truck, drove it a ways down the road. I could hear him revving it up, from around the bend. He came back speeding, head-lights on high beam. Hit the kid from behind – he never knew what happened, he was half asleep.'

He stopped talking, panting, and closed his eyes.

'Gus talked about doing the teacher right then and there but he decided to wait, see if she'd told anyone else. He had Halstead follow her. He staked out her place. She wasn't there. Just her roommate. Halstead wanted to kidnap *her*, beat it out of *her*, see if she knew anything. Then he saw the teacher come back with some guy – it was Handler – to pick up her stuff. Like she was moving in with him. Halstead reported it back to Gus. Now it was getting complicated. They kept watching the two of them and finally saw them meet with Bruno. We knew Bruno – he'd volunteered at La Casa, seemed like a great guy. Very outgoing. The kids loved him. It was clear, at that point, that he'd been a spy. Now it was three mouths that had to be closed.

'The calls came a few days later. It was Bruno, disguising his voice, but we knew it was him. Saying he had tapes of the Nemeth kid telling all. He even played a few seconds over the phone. They were amateurs, they didn't know Gus had them from day one, right in the crosshairs. It was pathetic.'

Pathetic *was* the word for the scenario. Take one nice girl. Elena Gutierrez, up from the barrio, attractive, vibrant. A little materialistic, but warm-hearted. A gifted teacher. Depressed about her job, burned out, she seeks help, enters therapy with Morton Handler, MD, psychopath cum psychiatrist. Ends up going to bed with Handler but continues to tell him her problems – one major one being the kid who never talked before who's suddenly opening up and telling her terrible things about strange men doing bad things to him. He opens up to Miss Gutierrez because she's warm and understanding. A real talent for drawing them out, Raquel Ochoa had said. A talent for working with the ones who didn't respond to anyone else. A talent that cost Elena her life. Because what was human tragedy to her smelled profitable to Morton Handler. Nasty things in high places – what could be juicier?

Of course Handler thinks these things but he keeps them

to himself. After all, maybe the kid is making it all up. Maybe Elena is overreacting – you know women, especially Latin women – so he tells her to keep listening, emphasizes what a good job she's doing, what a source of support she is for the child. Bides his time.

Shouldn't I report this to someone? She asks him. Wait, dear, be cautious, until you know more. But the child is crying out for help, the bad men are still coming for him . . . Elena takes it upon herself to call Cary's doctor. And thus signs his death warrant.

When Elena hears of the child's death, she suspects the awful truth; she falls apart. Handler shoves tranquilizers down her throat, calms her down. All the while his psychopathic mind is going click click click, because now he *knows* there's money to be made.

Enter Maurice Bruno: Fellow psychopath, former patient, new buddy. A real smoothie. Handler recruits him and offers him a cut of the yield if he infiltrates the Gentlemen's Brigade and finds out as much as he can. Names, places, dates. Elena wants to call the police. Handler quiets her down with more pills and more talk. The police are ineffectual, my darling. They won't do anything about it. I know from experience. Slowly, gradually, he gets her to go along with the blackmail scheme. This is the real way to punish them, he assures her. Hit them where it hurts. She listens, so unsure, so confused. Something seems so wrong about profiting from the death of a helpless little boy, but then again, nothing will bring him back, and Morton seems to know what he's talking about. He's very persuasive and besides, there's that Datsun 280ZX she's always wanted, and those outfits she saw last week at Neiman-Marcus. She could never afford them on

hat the damned school pays her. And who the hell ever
d anything for her, anyway? *Look out for number one* Morton
ways says, and maybe he's got a point there . . .

'Earl and Halstead looked for the tapes,' Kruger was
ying, 'after they tied them up. They tortured them to get
em to tell where they kept them but neither of them talked.
alstead complained to Gus that he could have gotten it out
 them but Earl went to work too fast with the knife.
andler passed out when he cut his throat, the girl freaked
ut totally, screaming, they had to jam something in her
outh. She choked, then Earl finished her, played with her.'

'But you finally found the tapes, didn't you, Timmy?'

'Yes. She'd kept them at her mother's. I got them from
er junkie brother. Used smack as a bribe.'

'Tell me more.'

'That's it. They tried to put the squeeze on Gus. He paid
em once or twice – big amounts 'cause I saw large rolls
f bills – but it was just to give them false confidence. They
ever had a chance from the start. We never got the money
ack, but I don't think it mattered. It was a drop in the
ucket. Besides, money doesn't seem to turn Gus on. He
ves simply, eats cheap. There's big bucks rolling in every
ay. From the government – state and federal Private dona-
ons. Not to mention the thousands the pervs pay him for
eir jollies. He stashes some away but I've never seen him
 anything extravagant. It's power he's after, not bread.'

'Where are the tapes?'

'I gave them to Gus.'

'Come on.'

'I gave them to him. He sent me on an errand and I de-
vered.'

'That's a strong-looking knee. Pity to pulverize it to bor
meal.' I stepped on the back of his leg and bore down.
forced his head up, had to hurt.

'Stop! OK. I made a copy. I had to. For leverage. Wh.
if Gus wanted me out of the way one day? I mean I w:
his golden boy now but you could never know, right?'

'Where are they?'

'In my bedroom. Taped to the bottom of the mattress.

'Don't go away.' I released my foot.

He gnashed his teeth like a netted shark.

I found three unmarked cassettes where he said they'd b
pocketed them and returned.

'Tell me some names. Of the molesters in the Brigade.

He recited like a kid delivering his confirmation speec
Automatic. Nervous. Overly rehearsed.

'Any more?'

'Isn't that enough?'

He had a point. He'd mentioned a well-known filr
director, a deputy DA, a political biggie – a behind-the
scenes man who managed to stay in front – corporat
attorneys. Doctors. Bankers. Real estate honchos. Men whos
names usually got in print when they donated something c
won an award for humanitarian service. Men whose name
on a campaign endorsement roster brought in votes. Ne
Biondi would have enough to turn LA society on its ear fo
quite some time.

'You're not going to forget all of this when the police as
you about it, are you, Tim?'

'No! Why should I? Maybe cooperating can buy m
out?'

'You're not getting out. Accept it. But at least,' I addec

398

you won't end up fertilizing McCaffrey's vegetable patch.'

He considered that. It must have been hard to count his blessings with the ropes biting into his wrists and ankles.

'Listen,' he said, 'I've helped you. Help me make a deal. 'll cooperate – I didn't kill anyone.'

The power he attributed to me was fictitious. I used it anyway.

'I'll do what I can,' I said magnanimously, 'but a lot of t's up to you. If the Quinn kid gets out of this healthy, I'll go to bat for you. If not, you're down the toilet.'

'Then get going, for God's sake! Get her out of there! I don't give her more than a day. Will put Gus off but it won't be for long. She'll have an accident. They'll never find the body. It's just a matter of time. Gus is sure she saw too much.'

'Tell me what I need to get her out of there safely.'

He looked away.

'I lied about where she is. It's not the furthest building, t's the one just before it. With the blue door. Metal door. There's a key in the pocket of my tan pants. Hanging in the closet in my room.'

I left him, fished it out and came back dangling the key.

'You're batting a thousand, Tim.'

'I'm being straight with you. Just help *me*.'

'Is anyone with her?'

'No. There's no need. Will has her on sedatives. Mostly he's out of it or sleeping. They send in someone to feed her, clean her up. She's strapped to the bed. The room's solid, concrete block. Only one way in – through the door. There's a single skylight window they keep open. Close it, anyone inside suffocates in forty-eight hours.'

399

'Could Will Towle get into La Casa without arousing suspicion?'

'Sure. Like I told you, he's on twenty-four-call for when the Gentlemen get too rough on the kids. Most of the time it's nothing serious — scrapes, lacerations. Sometimes the kids freak out, he gives them Valium or Mellaril, or a quick dose of Thorazine. Yeah, he could show up any time.'

'Good. You're going to call him. Tim. You're going to tell him he needs to make just such an emergency call. I want him entering La Casa a half-hour after dark — let's say seven thirty. Make sure he's on time. And alone. Make it sound convincing.'

'I could be more convincing if I could move around a little bit.'

'Work with what you've got. I have faith in you. Use your dramatic training. You were pretty good as Bill Roberts.'

'How'd you kn—'

'I didn't. Now I do. It was an educated guess. You're a trained actor, you were a natural for the part. Did your role include killing Hickle, too?'

'Ancient history,' he said. 'Yeah, I made the call. Setting it up in your office was Hayden's idea of a joke. He's a mean little mother. Sick sense of humor. But like I told you before, I didn't *kill* anybody. For the Hickle thing I wasn't even there. That was all Hayden and Cousin Will. They — and Gus — decided to shut him up — same old story, I guess. Hickle was a member of the Brigade, one of the originals. But he free-lanced with the kids at his wife's school.

'I remember after he got busted, the three of them were talking about it. Gus was ranting. "Damned stupid shithead!"

e was yelling, "I furnish that fool with enough hairless pussy
o keep him smiling for the rest of his life and he goes and
oes a dumbshit thing like this!" The way I figured it Hickle'd
lways been regarded as weak and stupid, easily influenced.
They bet that once he started confessing the school stuff he'd
pen his yap and bring it all down around them. They had to
ut him away.

'The way they did it was for Hayden to call him and tell
im he had good news. Hickle'd asked Hayden to pull strings
lowntown with the DA, which just goes to show you how
tupid he was. I mean at that time Hickle was page one. Just
knowing him was the kiss of death. But he called Hayden,
asked him anyway. Hayden faked it like he was going to try
o help. Couple days later he called him, said yeah, there
vas good news, he could help. They met at Hayden's house,
very hush-hush, no one around. From what I gather Will
lipped something in his tea – the guy didn't drink booze.
Something you could time precisely and that wore off, so
races were hard to find unless you were looking for some-
hing specifically. Will fixed the dosage – he's good at that.
When Hickle was out they moved him to your place. Hayden
icked the lock – he's good with his hands, does magic shows
or the kids at La Casa. Dresses up like a clown – Blimbo
he Clown – and does magic tricks.'

'Forget magic. Go on about Hickle.'

'That's it. They got him up there, faked the suicide. I don't
know who pulled the trigger. I wasn't there. The only reason
know anything about it is I did the Bill Roberts bit and a few
lays later Gus told me what it was all about. He was in one
of those dark moods when he talks like a megalomaniac. "Don't
hink your cousin the doctor is all that noble, my boy," he was

401

saying. "I can fry his ass and the asses of lots of noble men with one phone call." He gets that way – anti-rich, after he thinks back to how he was poor and all us rich folk mistreated him. That night, after they killed Hickle, we were sitting in his office. He was drinking gin and he started to reminisce about how he used to work for Mr Hickle – Hickle's father – from the time he was a little kid. He was an orphan and some agency basically sold him to the Hickles, like a slave. He said old Hickle had been a monster. Vicious temper, liked to kick the help around. He told me how he took it, kept his eye open, learned all the nasty family secrets – like Stuart's kinks, other stuff – saved it all up and used it to get off Brindamoor, to get the job at Jedson. I remember him smiling at me, half drunk, looking crazy. "I learned early," he said, "that knowledge is power." Then he talked about Earl, how the guy was damaged goods, but would do anything for him. "He'd eat my shit and call it caviar," he said. "That's power."'

Kruger had arched his back, picking his head up, stiffnecked, as he talked. Now exhausted, he sank back down.

'I guess,' he said, 'he's getting back at all of us.'

He lay in the ocher stain of dried urine, pitiful.

'Anything else you want to tell me, Tim?'

'I can't think of anything. You ask, I'll tell.'

I saw the tension travel up and down his bound limbs like a handcar on a twisted track and kept my distance.

There was a phone on the floor several feet away. I brought it near, stayed away from his arms and laid the speaker near his mouth. Holding the gun to his brow I punched in Towle's office number and stepped back.

'Make it good.'

He did. I would have been convinced. I hoped Towle was.

He signaled me the conversation was through by moving his eyes back and forth. I hung up and had him make a second call, to the security desk at La Casa to set up the doctor's visit.

'How was that?' he asked when he was through.

'Rave review.'

Oddly enough that seemed to please him.

'Tell me, Tim, how are your sinuses?'

The question didn't throw him. 'Great,' he blurted out, 'I'm never sick.' He said it with the bravado of the habitual athlete who believes exercise and firm muscles are guarantees of immortality.

'Good. Then this shouldn't bother you.' I crammed a towel into his mouth while he made enraged, muffled noises through the terry-cloth.

Carefully I dragged him to the bedroom, emptied the closet of anything that resembled a tool or weapon and shoved him inside, molding him to the confines of the tiny space.

'*If* I get out of La Casa with the kid and myself in good shape I'll tell the police where to find you. If I don't, you'll probably suffocate. Anything else you want to tell me?'

A shake of the head. Beseeching eyes. I closed the door and moved a heavy dresser in front of it. I replaced the gun in my waistband, closed all the windows in the apartment, drew the bedroom curtains and shut the bedroom door, blocking it with two chairs stood on end. I cut his phone line with a kitchen knife, drew the drapes so that the view of the ocean was erased and gave the place a final once-over. Satisfied, I walked out the door, slamming it tight.

28

THE SEVILLE was running, but shakily, as a result of the grand prix with Halstead. It was also too conspicuous for my purposes. I left it in a lot in Westwood Village, walked two blocks to a Budget Rent-A-Car and picked up a dark brown Japanese compact – one of those square little boxes of molded plastic papered with an allegedly metal shell. It took fifteen minutes to putt-putt through the traffic from one end of the village to the other. I pulled into the Bullocks garage, locked the gun in the glove compartment, locked the car and went shopping.

I bought a pair of jeans, thick socks, crepe-soled shoes, navy blue turtleneck and a windbreaker of the same dark hue. Everything in the store was tagged with plastic alarm clips and it took the salesgirl several minutes to liberate the garments after she'd taken my money.

'Wonderful world,' I muttered.

'You think this is bad, we have the expensive stuff – leather, furs – under lock and key. Otherwise they just waltz right out with it.'

We shared righteous sighs and, after being informed I was likely to be under surveillance, I decided not to change in the store's dressing room.

It was just past six and dark by the time I was back on

the street. Time enough to grab a steak sandwich, Greek salad, vanilla ice cream and lots of black coffee and watch the starless sky from the vantage point of a front table in a mom-and-pop eatery on West Pico. At six thirty I paid the tab and went into the restaurant's men's room to change. While slipping into my new duds I noticed a piece of folded paper on the floor. I picked it up. It was the copy of the Lilah Towle accident story given to me by Margaret Dopplemeier. I tried to read it again, with not much great success. I was able to make out something about the Coast Guard and high tides, but that was it. I put it back in the jacket pocket, straightened up and got ready to head for Malibu.

There was a pay phone at the back of the café, and I used it to call the West LA station. I thought of leaving a convoluted message for Milo, then thought better of it and asked for Delano Hardy. After being kept waiting for five minutes I was finally told he was out on a call. I left the convoluted message for him, paid the check, and headed for Malibu.

It was slow going but I'd constructed my schedule with that in mind. I reached Rambla Pacifica just before seven, and the county sign announcing La Casa de los Niños at ten after. The sky was empty and dark, like a drop down an endless well. A coyote howled from a distant gully. Nightbirds and bats flittered and squeaked. I switched off my headlights and navigated the next mile and a half by sense of touch. It wasn't all that difficult, but the little car resonated at every crack and bump in the road, and transmitted the shock waves directly though my skeletal system.

I came to a stop a half-mile before the La Casa turnoff. It was seven fifteen. There were no other vehicles on the road. Praying it stayed that way, I swung the car perpendicular to the road and blocked both lanes: Rear wheels facing the ravine that bordered the highway, front tires nosing the thick brush to the west. I sat in the darkened compartment, gun in hand, waiting.

At twenty-three after seven I heard the sound of an approaching engine. A minute later the Lincoln's square headlights came into view a quarter-mile up the road. I jumped out of the car, ran for cover in the brush and crouched, holding my breath.

He saw the empty car late and had to screech to a stop. He left his motor running, the lights on, and walked into the beam, cursing. The white hair gleamed silver. He wore a charcoal double-breasted blazer over a white open-necked shirt, along with black flannel pants and black-and-white golf shoes with tassels. Not a crease, not a wrinkle.

He ran a hand alongside the flank of the little car, touched the hood, grunted, and leaned through the open driver's door.

It was then that I sprang silently on crepe and put the gun in the small of his back.

As a matter of taste and principle I hate firearms. My father loved them, collected them. First there were the Lugers he brought home as World War II mementos. Then the deer rifles, the shotguns, automatic pistols picked up in pawn shops, an old rusted Colt .45, nasty-looking Italian pistols with long snouts and engraved butts, blue steel .22s. Lovingly polished and displayed in the den, behind the glass of a cherrywood case. Most of them loaded, the old man toying with them while watching TV. Calling me over to show off the details of construction, the niceties of ornamentation; talk of chamber velocity, core, bore, muzzle, grip. The smell of machine oil. The odor of burnt matches that permeated his hands. As a small child I'd have nightmares of the guns leaving their perches, like pets slipping out of their cages, taking on instincts of their own, barking and snarling . . .

One time he had a fight with my mother, a loud and nasty one. In anger he went to the case and snatched at the first thing he put his hands on — a Luger: Teutonically efficient. He pointed it at her. I could see it now: She screaming 'Harry!' he realizing what he was doing; horrified, dropping the gun as if it were a venomous sea creature; reaching out to her, stuttering apologies. He never did it again, but the memory changed him, them — and me, five years old, standing, blanket in hand, half-hidden by the door, watching. Since then I've hated guns. But at that moment I loved the feel of the .38 as it dented Towle's blazer.

'Get in the car,' I whispered. 'Sit behind the wheel and don't move or I'll blow your guts out.'

He obeyed. Quickly I ran to the passenger side and in beside him.

'You,' he said.

'Start the engine.' I put the gun in his side, rougher than I had to be.

The little car coughed to life.

'Pull it to the side of the road, so that the driver's door is right up against that rock. Then turn off the engine and throw the key out the window.' He did as he was told, the noble profile steady.

I got out and ordered him to do likewise. The way I'd had him park, the exit from the driver's side was blocked by

407

forty feet of granite. He slid out the passenger's side and stood motionless and stoic at the edge of the empty road.

'Hands up.'

He gave me a superior look and complied.

'This is outrageous,' he said.

'Use one hand to remove your car keys. Toss them *gently* on the ground over there.' I pointed to a spot fifteen feet away. Keeping the gun trained on him, I scooped them up.

'Walk to your car, get in on the driver's side. Put both hands on the wheel where I can see them.'

I followed him to the Lincoln. I got in the back, right behind him, and placed the tip of the gun in the hollow at the base of his skull.

'You know your anatomy,' I said softly. 'One bullet to the medulla oblongata and the lights go out forever.'

He said nothing.

'You've done a fine job of mucking up your life and the lives of plenty of others. Now it's coming down on you. What I'm offering you is a chance for partial redemption. Save a life for once, instead of destroying it.'

'I've saved many lives in my day. I'm a physician.'

'I know, you're a saintly healer. Where were you when it came to saving Cary Nemeth?'

A dry, croaking sound came from deep inside of him. But he maintained his composure.

'You know everything, I suppose.'

'Just about. Cousin Tim can be talkative when the circumstances are right.' I gave him a few examples of what I knew. He was unmoved, stoic, hands melded to the wheel, a white-haired mannikin set up for display.

'You knew my name before we met,' I said, 'from the

Hickle thing. When I called you invited me to the office. To see how much Melody had told me. It didn't make sense to me then, a busy pediatrician taking the time to sit and chat face-to-face. Anything we spoke about could have been discussed over the phone. You wanted to sound me out. Then you tried to block me.'

'You had a reputation as a persistent young man,' he said. 'Things were piling up.'

'Things? Don't you mean bodies?'

'There's no need to be melodramatic.' He talked like a Disneyland android: Flat, without inflection, devoid of self-doubt.

'I'm not trying to be. It's just that multiple murder still gets to me. The Nemeth boy. Handler. Elena Gutierrez. Morry Bruno. Now, Bonita Quinn and good old Ronnie Lee.'

At the mention of the last name he gave a small, but noticeable start.

'Ronnie Lee's death bother you, in particular?'

'I'm not familiar with that name. That's all.'

'Ronnie Lee Quinn. Bonita's ex. Melody's father. *R. L.* A blond fellow, tall, crazy-looking, with a bad left side. Hemiparesis. With McCaffrey's southern accent it may have sounded like he was calling him Earl.'

'Ah,' he said, pleased that things made sense once again, 'Earl. Disgusting fellow. Unwashed. I remember meeting him once or twice.'

'Piss-poor protoplasm, right?'

'If you will.'

'He was one of McCaffrey's bad guys from Mexico, brought back to do a dirty job or two. Probably wanted to see his kid, so McCaffrey found her and Bonita for him.

Then it dawned on him how she could fit in. She was a bright one, Bonita, wasn't she? Probably thought you were Santa Claus when you got her the job managing Minassian's building.'

'She was appreciative,' said Towle.

'You were doing her a big favor. You set her up so you could have access to Handler's apartment. She's the manager, she gets a master key. Then the next time she's in the office for Melody's checkup, she "loses" her purse. It's easy to do, the lady's a scatterbrain. She didn't *have it together*. That's what your office girl told me. Always losing things. Meanwhile you lift the key and McCaffrey's monsters can get in whenever they want – look for tapes, do a little slashing and hacking. No sweat off poor Bonita's back, except when she becomes expendable and ends up as food for next season's zucchini crop. A dull woman. More piss-poor protoplasm.'

'It wasn't supposed to happen that way. That wasn't in the plan.'

'You know how it is, the best-laid plans and all that.'

'You're a sarcastic young man. I hope you aren't that way with your patients.'

'Ronnie Lee finishes off Bonita – he may have done it because McCaffrey told him to, or perhaps it was just settling an old score. But now McCaffrey has to get rid of Ronnie Lee, too, because fiend that he is, even he may baulk at watching his own daughter die.'

'You're very bright, Alex,' he said. 'But the sarcasm really is an unattractive trait.'

'Thanks for the advice. I know you're an expert on bedside manner.'

'As a matter of fact, I am. I pride myself on it. Obtain

early rapport with the child and family no matter how disparate your background may be from theirs. That's the first step in delivering good care. It's what I instruct the first-year students when I proctor the pediatric section of Introduction to Clinical Medicine.'

'Fascinating.'

'The students give me excellent ratings on my teaching. I'm an excellent teacher.'

I exerted forward pressure with the .38. His silver hair parted but he didn't flinch. I smelled his hair tonic, cloves and lime.

'Start the car and pull it to the side of the road. Just behind that giant eucalyptus.'

The Lincoln rumbled and rolled, then stopped.

'Turn off the engine.'

'Don't be rude,' he said. 'There's no need to try to intimidate me.'

'Turn it off, Will.'

'*Doctor* Towle.'

'Doctor Towle.'

The engine quieted.

'Is it necessary to keep that thing at the back of my head?'

'I'll ask the questions.'

'It seems needless – superfluous. This isn't some cheap Western movie.'

'It's worse. The blood is real and nobody gets up and walks away when the smoke clears.'

'More melodrama. Mellow drama. Strange phrase.'

'Stop playing around,' I said angrily.

'Playing? Are we playing? I thought only children played. Jump rope, Hopscotch.' His voice rose in pitch.

411

'Grownups play too,' I said. 'Nasty games.'

'Games. Games help the child maintain ego integrity. I read that somewhere – Erikson? Piaget?'

Either Kruger wasn't the only actor in the family or something was happening that I hadn't been prepared for . . .

'Anna Freud,' I whispered.

'Yes. Anna. Fine woman. Would have loved to meet her, but both of us so busy . . . Pity . . . The ego must maintain integrity. At all costs.' He was silent for a minute, then: 'These seats need cleaning. I see spots on the leather. They make a good leather cleaner now . . . I saw it at the car wash.'

'Melody Quinn,' I said, trying to reel him back in. 'We need to save her.'

'Melody. Pretty girl. A pretty girl is like a melody. Pretty little child. Almost familiar . . .'

I talked to him but he kept fading away. Minute by minute he regressed, the rambling growing progressively more incoherent and out of context, so that at his worst, he was emitting word salad. He seemed to be suffering, the aristocratic face crowded with pain. Every few minutes he repeated the phrase, 'The ego must maintain integrity,' as if it was a catechism.

I needed him to get into La Casa but in his present state he was useless. I started to panic. His hands remained on the steering wheel but they trembled.

'Pills,' he said.

'Where?'

'Pocket . . .'

'Go ahead,' I said, not without suspicion, 'reach in and get them. The pills and nothing else. Don't take too many.'

'No . . . two pills . . . recommended dosage . . . never more . . . nevermore . . . quoth the raven . . . nevermore . . .'

'Get them.'

I kept the gun trained on him. He lowered one hand and drew out a vial not unlike the one that had held Melody's Ritalin. Carefully he shook out two white tablets, closed the vial and put it down.

'Water?' he asked, childlike.

'Take them dry.'

'I shall . . . nuisance.'

He swallowed the pills.

Kruger had been right. He *was* good at adjusting dosages. Within twelve minutes on my watch he was looking and sounding much better. I thought of the strain he underwent each day maintaining himself in the public eye. No doubt talking about the murders had hastened the deterioration.

'Silly of me to miss . . . the afternoon dose. Never forget.'

I observed him with morbid fascination, watching the changes in his speech and behavior as the psychoactive chemicals took hold of his central nervous system, making note of the gradually increasing attention span, the diminishing non sequiturs, the restoration of adult conversational patterns. It was like peering into a microscope and watching a primitive organism mitose into something far more complex.

When the drug was still in its initial stage he said:

'I've done many . . . bad things. Gus had me do bad things. Very wrong for a . . . man of my stature. For someone of my breeding.'

I let it pass.

Eventually he was lucid. Alert, seemingly undamaged.

'What is it, Thorazine?' I asked him.

'A variant. I've managed my own pharmacologic care fo
some time now. Tried a number of the phenothiazines . .
Thorazine was good but it made me too drowsy. Couldn'
have that while conducting physicals . . . Wouldn't want t
drop a baby. No, nothing like that. Dreadful, drop an infant
This is a new agent, far superior to the others. Experimenta
Sent to me by the manufacturer. Just write away for samples
use MD after the name, no need to justify or explain. They'r
more than happy to oblige . . . I have a healthy supply. Mus
take the afternoon dose, though, or everything gets confuse
– that's what happened, isn't it?'

'Yes. How long does it take for kick in?'

'In a man my size twenty to twenty-five minutes – remark
able, isn't it? Pop, down the hatch, wait, and the picture tube
regains clarity. Life is so much more bearable. Things hur
so much less. Even now I feel it working, like muddy water
turning crystalline. Where were we?'

'We were talking about the nasty games McCaffrey'
perverts play with little children.'

'I'm not one of those,' he said quickly.

'I know. But you helped those perverts molest hundred
of children, gave time and money to McCaffrey, set u
Handler and Gutierrez and Hickle. You overdosed Melody
Quinn to keep her mouth shut. Why?'

'It's all over, isn't it?' he asked, sounding relieved.

'Yes.'

'They'll take away my license to practice medicine.'

'Definitely. Don't you think that's best?'

'I suppose so,' he said reluctantly. 'I still feel there's plenty
left in me, plenty of good work to be done.'

'You'll have your chance,' I reassured him, realizing that the pills were less than perfect. 'They'll send you some place for the rest of your life where you'll experience little in the way of stress. No paperwork, no billing, none of the hassles of medical practice. No Gus McCaffrey telling you what to do, how to run your life. Just you – and you'll look and feel fine because they'll let you continue to take your pills – and help other people. People in need of help. You're a healer, you'll be able to help them.'

'I'll be able to help,' he repeated.

'Absolutely.'

'One human being to another. Unencumbered.'

'Yes.'

'I have a good bedside manner. When I'm well. When I'm not well things get confused and things hurt – even ideas hurt, thoughts can be painful. I'm not at my best, when that happens. But when I'm functioning well I can't be beat for helping people.'

'I know that, Doctor. I know your reputation.'

McCaffrey had spoken to me of an innate drive toward altruism. I knew whose buttons he'd been pushing with that one.

'I'm beholden to Gus,' he said, 'not due to any unusual sexual proclivity. That's his link with the others – with Stuart and Eddy. Since we'd been boys I'd known of their – strange ways. We all grew up in an isolated place, a strange place. We were cultivated, like orchids. Private lessons for this and that, having to look appropriate, act appropriately. Sometimes I wonder if that refined atmosphere didn't do us more harm than good. Look how we turned out, I, with my spells – I know there are labels for it these days, but I

415

prefer to avoid them – Stuart and Eddy with their strange sexual habits.

'They started fooling with each other one summer, when we were nine or ten. Then with other children. Smaller children, much smaller. I didn't think much of it except to know that I wasn't interested in it. The way we were raised, right or wrong didn't seem as relevant as – appropriate and inappropriate. "That's not appropriate, Willie," Father would say. I imagine had Stuart or Eddy's fathers caught them with the little ones, that would have been their description of the entire affair: *Inappropriate*. Like using the wrong fork at dinner.'

His description of coming of age on Brindamoor was strikingly like the one Van der Graaf had given me. At that moment he seemed akin to the fancy goldfish in the tank at Oomasa: Beautiful, showy, cultivated by mutation and centuries of inbreeding, raised in a protected environment. But ultimately stunted and unadaptable to the realities of life.

'In that sense, the sexual one,' he said, 'I was quite normal. I married, fathered a child, a son. I performed quite adequately. Stuart and Eddy continued as my chums, going about their perverted ways. It was live and let live. They never mentioned my – spells. I let them be. Stuart was really a fine fellow, not overly bright, but well meaning. It was a pity he had to . . . Except for that one kink, he was a good boy. Eddy was, is different. A sense of humor but a mean one. A nasty streak runs through him. He is habitually caustic and sarcastic – that's why I'm sensitive to that type of thing. Perhaps it's because of his size . . .'

'Your tie to McCaffrey,' I prompted.

'Small men often get that way. You're — I can't see you now, but I recall you as being medium-sized. Is that correct?'

'I'm five-eleven,' I said wearily.

'That's medium-sized. I've always been large. Father was large. It's just as Mendel predicted — long peas, short peas — fascinating field, genetics, isn't it?'

'Doctor—'

'I've wondered about the genetic impact on many traits. Intellect, for example. The liberal dogma would have us believe that environment makes the largest contribution to intelligence. It's an egalitarian premise, but reality doesn't bear it out. Long peas, short peas. Smart parents, smart children. Stupid parents, stupid children. I, myself, am a heterozygote. Father was brilliant. Mother was an Irish beauty, but very simple. She lived in a world where that combination served to create the perfect hostess. Father's showpiece.'

'Your tie to McCaffrey,' I said sharply.

'My tie? Oh nothing more serious than life and death.'

He laughed. It was the first time I'd heard his laugh and I hoped it would be the last. It was a vacant discordant note, a blatant musical error screaming out in the middle of a symphony.

'I lived with Lilah and Willie Junior on the third floor of the Jedson dormitory. Stuart and Eddy shared a room on the first. As a married student I was given larger quarters — really a nice little apartment, when you got down to it. Two bedrooms, bath, living room, small kitchen. But no library, no study, so I did my reading at the kitchen table. Lilah had made it a cheerful place — bunting, trim, curtains, womanly types of things. Willie Junior was a little over two at the time, I remember. It was my senior year. I'd been having trouble with some of the premedical courses – physics, organic chemistry. I've never been a brilliant person. However, if I apply myself and keep my attention span steady I can do quite well. I desperately wanted to get into medical school on my own merits. My father and his father before him were doctors, all had been brilliant students. The joke, behind my back, was that I'd inherited my mother's brains as well as her looks – they didn't think I heard but I did. I wanted so much to show them that I could succeed on my own merits, not because I was Adolf Towle's son.

'The night it happened Willie Junior had been feeling poorly, unable to sleep. He'd been screaming and crying out, Lilah was frazzled. I ignored her requests for help, plunging myself into my studies, trying to shut out everything else. I had to bring my science grades up. It was imperative. The more anxious I got, the less able I was to pay attention. I tried to deal with it by embracing a kind of tunnel vision.

'Lilah had always been patient with me, but that night she became furious, started to come unglued. I looked up, saw her coming at me, her hands – she had tiny hands, a delicate woman – rolled up into fists, mouth open – I suppose she was screaming – eyes full of hatred. She seemed to me a bird of prey, about to swoop down and pick at my bones. I pushed her away with my arm. She fell, tumbling back, hit her head on the corner of a bureau – a hideous piece, an antique her mother had given her – and lay there, simply lay there.

'I can see the whole thing clearly now, as if it had just happened yesterday. Lilah lies there, motionless. I rise out of my chair, dreamlike, everything is swaying, everything

418

is confusing. A small shape coming at me from the right, like a mouse, a rat. I swat it away. But it's not a rat, no, no. It's Willie Junior, coming back at me, crying for his mother, hitting me. Only dimly aware of his presence I strike out at him again, catch him on the side of his head. Too hard. He falls, lands, lies still. Unmoving. A large bruise masks the side of his face . . . My wife, my child, dead at my hands. I prepare to find my razor, cut my wrists, be done with it.

'Then Gus's voice is at my back. He stands in the doorway, huge, obese, sweaty, in work clothes, broom in hand. The janitor, cleaning the dormitories at night. I smell him – ammonia, body odor, cleaning fluids. He's heard the noise and has come to check. He looks at me, a long hard look, then at the bodies. He kneels over them, feels for a pulse. "They're dead," he tells me in a flat voice. For a second I think he's smiling and I'm ready to pounce on him, to attempt a third murder. Then the smile becomes a frown. He's thinking. "Sit down," he commands me. I'm not used to being ordered around by one of his class but I'm weak and sick with grief, my knees are buckling, everything's unraveling . . . I turn away from Lilah and Willie Junior, sit, put my face in my hands. Start to cry. I begin to grow more confused . . . A spell is coming on. Everything is starting to hurt. I have no pills, not like I'll have years later, when I'm a doctor. Now I'm merely a premedical student, powerless, hurting.

'Gus makes a telephone call. Minutes later my friends Stuart and Eddy appear in the room, like characters walking onstage in the midst of a dreadful play . . . The three of them talk among themselves, sometimes looking at me, muttering. Stuart comes to me first. He places a hand on my shoulder. "We know it was an accident, Will," he says. "We know it wasn't your fault." I start to argue with him but the words stick in my throat ... The spells make it so hard to talk, so painful ... I shake my head. Stuart comforts me, tells me everything will be all right. They will take care of everything. He rejoins Gus and Eddy.

'They wrap the bodies in a blanket, tell me not to leave the room. At the last moment they decide Stuart should stay with me. Gus and Eddy leave with the bodies. Stuart gives me coffee. I cry. I cry myself to sleep. Later that evening they return and tell me the story I'm to report to the police. They rehearse me, such good friends. I do a fine job. They tell me so. I feel some sense of relief at that. At least there is something I'm good at. Play-acting. That's what a bedside manner is, after all. Give the audience what it clamors for ... My first audience is made up of the police. Then an officer of the Coast Guard – a family friend. They've found Lilah's car. Her body is macerated and bloated, I needn't identify it if it's too much of an ordeal. Scraps of Willie Junior's clothing have been found clinging to her hands. His body has drifted away. The tides, explains the officer. They'll continue to search ... I break down and ready myself for the next show, the well-wishers, the press ...'

The tides, I thought, the Coast Guard. Something there ...

'Several months later I'm accepted at the medical school,' Towle was saying. 'I move to Los Angeles. Stuart comes with me, though we both know he'll never be able to finish. Eddy goes to law school in Los Angeles. The Heads are reunited – that's what they called us. The Three Heads of State.

'We go about our new lives, there is never a mention of

the favor they've done for me. Of that night. However they are far more open than ever before about their sexual perversions, leaving nasty photographs where I can see them, not bothering to hide or conceal anything. They know I'm powerless to say a thing, even should I find a ten year old in my bed. A rotten mutual interdependence now binds us.

'Gus has disappeared. Years later, when I'm a doctor, on my way to prominence, the bedside manner fully developed, he appears at my office after the patients have all gone home. Further fattened, well dressed, no longer a janitor. Now, he jokes, he's a man of God. He shows me the mail-order divinity degree. And he's come to ask a few favors from me. To *cash in some old IOUs* is the way he puts it. I paid him that evening and I've been paying him, in one way or another, ever since.'

'It's time to stop paying,' I said. 'Let's not sacrifice Melody Quinn to him.'

'The child is doomed, as things stand. I urged Gus to put it off. Her accident. Told him it was by no means evident that she'd seen or heard anything. But he won't be delayed much longer. What's one more life to a man like that?' He paused. 'Does she really pose a danger to him?'

'Not really. She sat at the window and saw shadows of men.' One of whom she'd recognized as her father – she didn't know him but she had a picture. On the day I hypnotized her, right after the session, she went into a spontaneous discussion of him. She showed me the picture and a trinket he'd given her. When she had the night terrors I should have figured it out. I thought the hypnosis hadn't evoked anything in her. It had. It had brought back memories of her father, of seeing him lurking outside her window, entering Handler's place. She knew something bad had happened in the apartment. She knew her daddy had done something terrible. She suppressed it. And it came back in her sleep.

It had started coming together for me when I'd seen the clue she'd left behind when Ronnie Lee had come by and abducted her and her mother. A shrunken head, precious until now, a symbol of Daddy. For her to have abandoned it meant she'd kissed him off, had come to grips with the fact that Daddy was a bad man, come back, not to visit, but to hurt. Perhaps she'd watched him manhandle Bonita, or maybe it was the rough, uncaring way he'd spoken to her. Whatever it had been, the child had known.

Looking back it seemed so logical, but at the time the associations had been remote.

'It's ironic,' Towle was saying. 'I prescribed Ritalin to control her behavior and it was that same prescription that caused her insomnia, that led her to be awake at the wrong time.'

'Ironic,' I said. 'Now let's go in there and get her out. You're going to help me. When it's over I'll see to it that you're cared for properly.'

He didn't say anything. Simply sat straight in the seat, working hard at looking noble.

'Are you requesting my help?'

'I am, Doctor.'

'Request granted.'

29

I LAY on the floor of the Lincoln, covered by a blanket.

'My gun is pointed at your spine,' I told him. 'I don't expect any trouble but we haven't known each other long enough for trust to be worth much.'

'I understand,' he said. 'I'm not offended.'

He drove to the La Casa access road, turned left and steered smoothly and slowly to the chain link barrier. He identified himself to the voice on the squawk box and was let in. A brief stop at the guardhouse, an exchange of pleasantries, plenty of 'Doctor, Sirs' from the guard and we were in.

He drove to the far end of the parking lot.

'Park away from the light,' I whispered.

The car came to a halt.

'It's clear now,' he said.

I crawled from under the blanket, got out of the car and motioned him to follow. We walked up the path, side by side. Counselors passed us in pairs, greeted him with deference and moved on. I tried to look like his associate.

La Casa was peaceful at night. Camp songs filtered through the trees. 'A Hundred Bottles of Beer.' 'Oh Susanna.' Children's voices. An off-key guitar. Microphoned adult commands. Mosquitoes and moths vied for space around mushroom lights imbedded in the foliage at our feet.

The sweet smell of jasmine and oleander in the air. An occasional whiff of brine from the ocean, so close but unseen. To the right the open gray-green expanse of the Meadow. A pleasant enough graveyard . . . The Grove, dark as fudge, a piney refuge . . .

We passed the pool, taking care not to slip on the wet cement. Towle moved like an old warrior heading into his last battle, chin up, arms at his side, marching. I kept the .38 within easy reach.

We made it to the bunkers unnoticed.

'That one,' I said. 'With the blue door.'

Down the ramp. A hard twist of the key and we were in.

The building was divided into two rooms. The one in the front was empty except for a single folding chair pushed under an aluminum bridge table. The walls were of unpainted block and smelled of mildew. The floors were cold slab concrete, as was the ceiling. A square black wound of skylight marked the ceiling's center. The only light came from a single, unadorned bulb.

She was in the back, on an army cot, covered with a coarse olive drab blanket and restrained with leather straps across her ankles and chest. Her arms were pinioned under the blanket. She breathed slowly, mouth open, sleeping, head to one side, her pale, tear-streaked skin translucent in the semi-darkness. Wisps of hair hung loosely around her face. Tiny, vulnerable, lost.

At the foot of the cot was a plastic tray holding an uneaten, congealed fried egg, limp French fries, shriveled brown-tipped lettuce and an open wax container of milk.

'Untie her.' I pointed the gun.

Towle bent over her, working in the dimness to unfasten the straps.

'What do you have her on?'

'Valium, high dose. Thorazine on top of that.'

Dr Towle's magic elixir.

He got the restraints loose and peeled back the blanket. She was wearing dirty jeans and a red-and-white striped T-shirt with Snoopy on the front. He lifted the shirt and palpated her abdomen, took her pulse, felt her forehead: Played doctor.

'She looks thin, but otherwise healthy,' he pronounced.

'Wrap her back up. Can you carry her?'

'Certainly,' he replied, miffed that I could doubt his strength.

'All right then, let's go.'

He gathered her up in his arms, looking for all the world like the Great White Father. The child let out a sigh, a shudder, and clung to him.

'Keep her totally covered once we get outside.'

I began a half-turn. A soft, musical voice at my back drawled:

'Don't move, Doctor Delaware, or you'll lose your fucking head.'

I stood still.

'Put the young one down, Will. Take his gun.'

Towle looked at me blankly. I shrugged. He placed Melody on the the cot gently and covered her. I handed him the .38.

'Against the wall with your hands up, Doctor. Search him, Will.'

Towle patted me down.

'Turn around.'

McCaffrey stood there grinning, filling the opening

425

between the two rooms, a .357 magnum in one hand, a Polaroid camera in the other. He wore an iridescent lime-green jump-suit decorated with a score of snap-pockets and buckles, and matching lime patent leather shoes. In the dim light his complexion reflected greenly as well.

'Task, tsk, Willie. What mischief are we up to tonight?'

The great physician hung his head and shuffled nervously.

'Not feeling loquacious tonight, Willie? That's all right. We'll talk later.' The colorless eyes narrowed. 'Right now there's business to attend to.'

'Is this your idea of altruism?' I looked at Melody's limp form.

'Shut up!' he snapped. To Towle: 'Remove the child's clothing.'

'Gus – I – why?'

'Just do as I say, Willie.'

'No more, Gus,' Towle pleaded. 'We've done enough.'

'No, you idiot. We haven't done enough at all. This smart-ass here has the potential to cause us – you *and* me – lots of trouble. I made plans to eliminate him, but apparently I'll have to do the job myself.'

'Plans,' I sneered. 'Halstead's rotting in a vacant lot with a spike in his throat. He was a bumbler, like all of your slaves.'

McCaffrey pursed his thick lips.

'I'm warning you,' he said.

'That's your specialty, isn't it?' I continued, playing for time. I saw his massive silhouette shift as he tried to keep me in his sights. But the darkness made it difficult as did Towle's body, which had gotten between us as he fidgeted under his master's glare. 'You have a knack for finding bumblers and losers, emotional cripples, misfits. The same knack flies have or locating shit. You zero in on their open wounds, sink your fangs into them, suck them dry.'

'How literary,' he replied in a lilting voice, obviously fighting to maintain control. We were in close quarters and impulsiveness could prove hazardous.

'Her clothes, Will,' he said. 'Take them all off.'

'Gus—'

'Do it, you sniveling piece of turd!'

Towle raised his arm in front of his face like a child warding off a blow. When none was forthcoming he moved toward the child.

'You're a doctor,' I said. 'A respected physician. Don't listen to him—'

Fast, faster than I thought possible, McCaffrey stepped forward in the clearing Towle had created. He slashed with one elephantine sleeve and raked the side of my head with his gun. I fell to the floor, my face exploding with pain, hands protecting myself from further assault, blood running between my fingers.

'Now you stay there, sir, and keep your fucking mouth shut.'

Towle removed Melody's T-shirt. Her chest was concave and white, the ribs twin grilles of gray-blue shadow.

'Now the pants. The panties. Everything.'

'Why are we doing this, Gus?' Towle wanted to know. To my ears, which were far from perfect, one being ripped and bloody, the other filled with watery echoes, his speech sounded slurred. I wondered if stress could break through the biochemical barrier he'd erected around his damaged mind.

'Why?' McCaffrey laughed. 'You're not used to seeing this type of thing firsthand, are you, Willie? You've had a

sanitized role up until now, enjoying the luxury of distance
Well, no matter, I'll explain it to you.'

He raised an eyebrow at Towle contemptuously, looked
down at me and laughed again. The sound reverberated
painfully in my injured skull. The blood continued to run down
my face. My head felt mushy, loose on its stalk. I began to
grow nauseated and dizzy, and the floor rose up at me. Terror
gripped me as I wondered if he'd hit me hard enough to cause
brain damage. I knew what a subdural hematoma could do to
the fragile gray jelly that made life worth living ... Crazily,
fighting for strength and clarity, I pictured my brain in an
anatomist's tray, pinioned and splayed, and tried to localize
the site of the injury. The gun had smashed against my left
side – the dominant hemisphere, for I am right-handed ... that
was bad. The dominant side controlled logical processes:
Reasoning, analysis, deduction – the stuff to which I'd grown
addicted over thirty-three years. I thought about losing all of
that, of fading into dimness and confusion, then remembered
two-year-old Willie Junior, struck down in much the same
way. He'd lost it all ... which might have been merciful. For
had he survived, the damage would have been great. Left
side/right side ... the tides ...

'We're going to put on a little stage play, Willie,' McCaffrey
lectured. 'I'll be the producer and director. You'll be my assistant, helping me with the props.' He swung the camera in an
arc. 'The stars of the show will be little Melody and our
friend Doctor Alex Delaware. The name of the play will be
– "Death of a Shrink," subtitled "Caught in the Act." A
morality play.'

'Gus—'

'The plot is as follows: Doctor Delaware, our erstwhile

llain, is well known as a caring, sensitive child psycholo-
st. However, unbeknownst to his colleagues and his
tients, his choice of profession did not arise out of any
eat sense of – altruism. No, Doctor Delaware has chosen
become a kiddy shrink to be closer to the kiddies. To be
le to fondle and abuse their genitals. In short, a deviate,
opportunist, the lowest of the low. An evil and gravely
ck man.' He paused to look down on me, chuckling,
eathing hard. Despite the chill, he was sweating, his glasses
ding low on his nose. The top of his kinky head was a
lo of moisture. I looked at the .38 in Towle's hand, and
easured the distance between it and the spot where I lay.
cCaffrey saw me, shook his head, and mouthed the word
, showing me his teeth.

'With these same depraved motivations in mind, Doctor
elaware applies for membership in the Gentlemen's Brigade.
e visits La Casa. We show him around. We screen him and
ir tests reveal him to be unsuitable for inclusion into our
onorable fraternity. We reject him. Furious and frustrated at
eing denied a lifetime supply of hairless pussy and tiny little
icks, he simmers.'

He stopped the narration and made loud slurping noises.
elody stirred in her sleep.

'He simmers,' he repeated. 'Stews in his own juices.
inally, at the height of his sick rage, he breaks into La Casa
ne night and roams the grounds until he finds a victim. A
oor orphan girl, defenseless, alone in her dormitory because
ie is sick in bed with the flu. The madman loses control.
apes her, virtually tears her apart – the autopsy will show
ncommon savagery. Will. Takes pictures of the ghastly deed.
hideous crime. As the child cries out, screaming for her

life, we – you and me, Will – happen to be passing by. W
rush to her aid, but it is too late. The child has succumbed

'We take in the carnage before us with horror and disgus
Delaware, discovered, rises up against us, gun in hand
Heroically we wrestle him to the ground, struggle for th
weapon and in the process the murderer is fatally wounded
The good guys win, and there is peace in the valley.'

'Amen,' I said.

He ignored me.

'Not bad, eh, Will?'

'Gus, it won't work.' Towle stepped between us again
'He knows everything – the teacher and the Nemet
boy—'

'Quiet. It will work. The past is the best predictor of th
future. We have succeeded before, we will continue t
triumph.'

'Gus—'

'Silence! I'm not asking you, I'm telling you. Strip her!'

I propped myself on my elbows and spoke through aching
swollen jaws, struggling to make sense out of what I wa
saying even as I told it.

'How about another script? This one's called *The Big Lie*
It's about a man who thinks he's murdered his wife and chil
and sells out his entire life to a blackmailer.'

'Shut up.' McCaffrey advanced on me. Towle blocked hi
way, aiming the .38 at the half-acre of green-clad fat. It wa
a Mexican standoff.

'I want to hear what he has to say, Gus. Things are confusin
me. Things hurt. I want him to explain . . .'

'Think,' I said, talking as fast as the pain allowed. 'Di
you ever check Willie Junior's body for signs of life? Nc

He did. *He* told you your boy was dead. That you'd killed him. But was the body ever found? Did you ever actually see the body?'

Towle's face tightened with concentration. He was slipping, losing his grip on reality, digging his nails in, fighting to hold on.

'I — I don't know. Willie was dead. They told me. The ides . . .'

'Maybe. But think: It was a golden opportunity. Lilah's death wouldn't have brought a charge greater than involuntary manslaughter. Domestic violence wasn't even taken seriously in those days. With the lawyers your family would have hired, you might have gotten off with probation. But two deaths — especially with one a child — would have been impossible to brush off. He needed you to believe Junior was dead to be able to hook you.'

'Will,' said McCaffrey, threateningly.

'I don't know — such a long time . . .'

'Think! Did you hit him hard enough to kill him? Maybe not. Use your brain. It's a good one. You remembered before.'

'I used to have a good brain,' he muttered.

'You still do! Remember. You hit little Willie on the side of the head. What side?'

'Don't know—'

'Will, it's all lies. He's trying to poison your mind.' McCaffrey looked for a way to silence me. But Towle's gun rose and nudged the spot where a normal person would have had a heart.

'What side, Doctor?' I demanded.

'I'm right-handed,' he answered, as if discovering the fact

431

for the first time. 'I use my right hand. I hit him with my right hand . . . I see it . . . He's coming at me from his bedroom. Crying for Mommy. Coming from the right, throwing herself at me. I – hit him – on his right side. The right side.'

The pain in my head turned the act of talking into torture, but I bore down.

'Yes. Exactly. Think! What if McCaffrey hoaxed you – you didn't *kill* Willie. You injured him, but he survived. What kind of damage, what kind of symptoms, could be caused by trauma to the right hemisphere in a developing child?'

'Right hemisphere cerebral damage – the right brain controls the left side,' he recited. 'Right brain damage causes left-side dysfunction.'

'Perfect,' I urged him on. 'A severe blow to the right brain could bring about left-side hemiparesis. *A bad left side.*'

'Earl . . .'

'Yes. The body was never found because the child never died. McCaffrey felt his pulse, found one, saw you in shock over what you'd done and exploited your guilt. He wrapped up both bodies, with a little help from your buddies. Lilah was put behind the wheel of the car and dumped off the Evergreen Bridge. McCaffrey took the child. Probably got him some kind of medical help, but not the best, because a reputable doctor would have had to report the incident to the police. After the funeral he disappeared. Those were *your* words. He disappeared because he had to. He had the child with him. He took him to Mexico, who knows where, renamed him, changed him from your son into the kind of person someone raised by a monster would turn out to be. He made him his *robot*.'

'Earl . . . Willie Junior.' Towle's brows knitted.

'Ridiculous! Out of the way, Will! I order it!'

'It's the truth,' I said through the pounding in my head. Tonight, before you took your pills, you said Melody looked vaguely familiar. Turn carefully – don't let *him* out of your sight – and take a look at her. Tell me why.'

Towle backed away, kept the gun on McCaffrey, took a short look at Melody, and then a longer one.

'She looks,' he said, softly, 'like Lilah.'

'Her grandmother.'

'I couldn't know—'

Of course he couldn't. The Quinns were poor, illiterate, the dregs of society. Piss-poor protoplasm. His views on the genetic superiority of the upper class would have prevented him from even fantasizing a connection between them and his bloodline. Now his defenses were down and the insights were hitting his consciousness like drops of acid – each point of contact raising psychic wounds. His son a murderer, a man conditioned to be a night-hunting beast. Dead. His daughter-in-law, intellectually limited, a helpless, pathetic creature. Dead. His granddaughter, the child on whom he'd plied his trade and medicated into stupor. Alive. But not for long.

'He wants to murder her. To tear her apart. You heard him. The autopsy will show *uncommon savagery*.'

Towle turned on the man in green.

'Gus—' he sobbed.

'Now, now, Will,' said McCaffrey soothingly. Then he blew Towle away with the .357. The bullet entered his abdomen and exited through his back in a fine spray of blood, skin and cashmere. He slammed backward, landing at the side of the cot. The report of the big gun echoed through the concrete room. A thunderstorm. The child awoke and began screaming.

McCaffrey pointed the gun at her, reflexively. I threw myself

433

at him and kicked his wrist, knocking the gun loose. It sailed backward, into the front room. He howled, rabid. I kicked him again, in the shin. His leg felt like a side of beef. He backed into the front room, wanting the gun. I went after him. He lunged, his bulk rolling. I used both hands to hit him in the lower back. My fists sank into his softness. He barely budged. His hand was inches from the magnum. I kicked it away, then used my foot to smash his ribs with little effect. He was too damned big and too damned tall to be able to get a facial punch in. I went for his legs and thighs, and tripped him.

He came crashing down, a felled redwood, taking me with him. Snarling, cursing, drooling, he rolled on top of me and got his hands around my throat. He panted his sour breath on me, the lumpy face crimson, the fish eyes swallowed by fleshy folds, squeezing. I fought to get out from under him but couldn't move. I experienced the panic of the sudden paralytic. He squeezed tighter. I pushed up helplessly.

His face darkened. With effort, I thought. Crimson to maroon to red-black, then a splash of color. The kinky hair exploding. The blood bright and fresh, pouring out of his nose, his ears, his mouth. The eyes opening wide, blinking furiously. A look of great insult on the grotesque face. Gargling noises from the jowl-wrapped gullet. Needles and triangles of broken glass raining down upon us. His inert carcass a shield from the rain.

The skylight was an open wound now. A face peered down. Black, serious. Delano Hardy. Something else black: The nose of a rifle.

'Hold on, Consultant,' he said. 'We're coming to get you.'

* * *

434

'Your face looks uglier than mine,' Milo said when he'd pulled McCaffrey off me.

'Yeah,' I said, struggling to articulate through a mouth that felt as if I'd sucked on razor blades, 'but mine will look better in a couple of days.'

He grinned.

'The kid seems OK,' said Hardy from the back room. He came out with Melody in his arms. She was shivering. 'Scared but unharmed, as the papers say.'

Milo helped me to my feet. I walked to her and stroked her hair.

'It's going to be all right, sweetheart.' Funny how clichés seem to find their niche during rough times.

'Alex,' she said. She smiled. 'You look funny.'

I squeezed her hand and she closed her eyes. Sweet dreams.

In the ambulance Milo kicked his shoes off and sat, yoga style, by the side of my stretcher.

'My hero,' I said. It came out *Mmmm mirrow*.

'This one's going to be good for a *long* time, pal. Free use of the Caddy on demand, cash loans with no interest, gratis therapy.'

'In other words,' I fought to enunciate through swollen jaws, 'business as usual.'

He laughed, patted my arm and told me to shut up. The ambulance attendant agreed.

'The man may need wires,' he said. 'He shouldn't talk.'

I started to protest.

'Shh!' said the attendant.

A half-mile later Milo looked at me and shook his head.

'You are one lucky turkey, friend. I got into town an hour and a half ago and got Rick's note to call you. I call your place. Robin was there, sans you, worried. You had a dinner date at seven, but no you. She says it's not like compulsive old you to be late, please could I do something. She also filled me in on your jaunts – you've been a busy little bee in my absence, haven't you? I call in to the station – on a vacation day, I might add – and get this schitzy message about Kruger written in Del Hardy's fine cursive scrawl; also something about he's going to La Casa. I went to Kruger's, got through your barricade, found him trussed, scared shitless. He was a wreck, spilled his guts without being asked – amazing what a little sensory deprivation will do, huh? I beep Del, catch him in his car on Pacific Coast Highway – which is still full of traffic at this hour, what with producers and starlets going home – make believe it's code three and siren it all the way along the side of the road. The pros take over and the rest is goddamn history.'

'I didn't want a full-scale raid.' I forced out the words, in agony. 'Didn't want anything to happen to the kid—'

'Please shut up, sir,' said the attendant.

'Shush,' said Milo, gently. 'You did a great job. Thanks. OK? Don't do it again. Turkey.'

The ambulance came to a halt at Santa Monica Hospital's Emergency Room. I knew the place because I'd given a series of lectures to the staff on the psychological aspects of trauma in children. There'd be no lecture tonight.

'You OK?' Milo asked.

'Um-hmm.'

'OK. I'll let the white coats take over. Gotta go and arrest a judge.'

30

ROBIN TOOK one look at me, jaws wired shut, eyes blackened, and burst into tears. She hugged me, fussed over me and sat by my side feeding me soup and soda. That lasted for a day. Then she got in touch with her anger and let me have it for being so crazy to put my life on the line. I was in no position to defend myself. She tried not speaking to me for six hours, then relented and things started to get back to normal.

When I could talk I called Raquel Ochoa.

'Hi,' she said. 'You sound funny.'

I told her the story, keeping it brief because of the pain. She said nothing for a moment, then softly:

'There *were* monsters.'

'Yes.'

The silence between us was uncomfortable.

'You're a man of principle,' she said, finally.

'Thank you.'

'Alex – that evening – us. I don't regret it. It got me thinking. Made me realize I have to go out and find something – someone – for myself.'

'Don't settle for less than the best.'

'I – thanks. Take care of yourself. Mend fast.'

'I'll work on it. Goodbye.'

'Goodbye.'

My next call was to Ned Biondi, who rushed over that afternoon and interviewed me until the nurses kicked him out. I read his stories for days. He had it all down – McCaffrey's Mexico days, the Hickle murder, the Gentlemen's Brigade, the suicide of Edwin Hayden the night he was arrested. The judge had shot himself in the mouth while dressing to go to the station with Milo. It seemed fitting in light of what he'd done to Hickle, and Biondi didn't miss the chance to wax philosophical.

I phoned Olivia Brickerman and asked her to take care of Melody. Two days later she found an older, childless couple up in Bakersfield, people she knew and trusted, with lots of patience and five acres for running. Nearby was a gifted child psychologist, a woman I'd known from graduate school, with experience in stress and bereavement. To them would be entrusted the task of helping the little girl piece her life together.

Six weeks after the fall of La Casa de los Niños, Robin and I met Milo and Rick Silverman for dinner at a quiet, elegant seafood place in Bel Air.

My friend's amour turned out to be a guy who could have walked out of a cigarette ad – six feet tall, broad-shouldered, narrow-hipped, masculine, handsome face overlaid with just a touch of crag, head of tight bronze curls, matching bristle mustache. He wore a tailored black silk suit, black-and-white striped shirt and a black knit tie.

'Lucky Milo,' Robin whispered as they joined our table.

Next to him, Milo looked baggier than ever, though he'd tried to spruce himself up, his hair slicked down like that of a kid in church.

Milo made the introductions. We ordered drinks and got acquainted. Rick was quiet and reserved, with nervous, surgical hands that had to be holding something – a glass, a fork, a stirrer. He and Milo exchanged loving glances. Once I saw them touch hands, for just a second. As the evening progressed he opened up and talked about his work, about what he liked and didn't like about being a doctor. The food came. The others had lobster and steak. I had to content myself with soufflé. We chatted, the evening went well.

After the dishes had been cleared away, before the pastry cart and the brandy, Rick's beeper went off. He excused himself and went to the phone.

'If you gentlemen don't mind, I'll make a stop in the ladies' room.' Robin patted her mouth with her napkin and rose. I followed her sway until she disappeared.

Milo and I looked at each other. He picked a piece of fish off his tie.

'Hello, friend,' I said.

'Hello.'

'He's a nice guy, Rick. I like him.'

'I want this one to last. It's hard, the way we live.'

'You look happy.'

'We are. Different in lots of ways, but we also have a lot in common. He's getting a Porsche 928,' he said with a laugh.

'Congratulations. You're a good-lifer now.'

'All comes to he who waits.'

I motioned the waiter over and we ordered fresh drinks. When they came I said: 'Milo, there's something I've been wanting to talk to you about. About the case.'

He took a long swallow of scotch.

'What about?'

'Hayden.'

His face grew grave.

'You're my shrink – so that this conversation is confidential?'

'Better than that. I'm your friend.'

'OK,' he sighed. 'Ask what I know you're going to ask.'

'The suicide. It doesn't make sense on two grounds. First, the kind of guy he was. I got the same picture from everyone. An arrogant, nasty, sarcastic little bastard. Loved himself. Not a trace of self-doubt. That kind don't kill themselves. They search for ways to shift the blame to others, they weasel out of things. Second, you're a pro. How could you get so sloppy as to let him do it?'

'The story I told Internal Affairs was that he was a judge. I treated him with deference. I let him get dressed. In his study. They bought it.'

'Tell me about it. Please.'

He looked around the restaurant. The tables nearby were empty. Rick and Robin were still gone. He gulped down the rest of his drink.

'I went for him right after I left you. Must have been after ten by then. He lived in one of those huge English Tudor palaces in Hancock Park. Old money. Big lawn. Bentley in the driveway. Topiary. A doorbell out of a Karloff flick.

'He answered the door, a little wimp of a guy, maybe five-four. Strange eyes. Spooky. He was wearing a silk dressing gown, holding a brandy in one hand. I told him what I'd come for. It didn't faze him.

'He was very proper, distant, as if what I was there for

had nothing to do with him. I followed him inside the house. Lots of family portraits. Moldings around the ceilings, chandeliers – I want you to get the flavor of this. Lord of the Manor. Led me to his study in the back. The requisite oak panels, wall-to-wall leather-covered books, the kind people collect but never read. A fireplace with two porcelain grayhounds, carved desk, blah blah blah.

'I pat him down, find a .22, take it. "It's for protection at night, officer," he tells me. "You never know who'll come knocking at your door." He's laughing, Alex, I swear I couldn't believe it. The guy's life is crashing down around him, he's going to hit the front page as a kiddy-diddler and he's laughing.

'I read him his rights, go into the spiel, he looks bored. Sits down at his desk, like I'm there for a favor. Then he starts talking to me. Laughing in my face. "How amusing," he says, "that they send you, the *faggot cop*, after me in a case like this. You of all people should understand." He goes on like that for a while, smirking, implying, then coming right out and saying it. That we're birds of a feather. Partners in crime. Perverts. I'm standing there listening to this and getting hotter and hotter. He laughs some more and I see that's what he wants, to stay in control of the situation. So cool down, smile back. Whistle. He starts telling me the things they did to the kids, like it's supposed to arouse me. Like we're buddies at a stag party. My stomach is turning and he's putting us in the same boat.

'As he talks, he comes into focus, psychological focus. It's like I can see behind the spooky eyes, into his brain. And all I see is dark and bad. Nothing good in there. Nothing good can come from this guy. He's a washout. I'm judging the judge. I'm prophesying. Meanwhile he's going on about the parties they used to have with the kids, how much he's going to miss them.'

He stopped and cleared his throat. Took my drink and finished it.

'I'm still looking through him, into his future. And I know what's going to happen. I look around that big room. I know the kind of money behind this guy. He'll get a Not Guilty by Reason, they'll cart him off to some country club. Eventually he'll buy his way out and start all over again. So I make a decision. Right there on the spot.

'I walk around behind him, grab his scrawny little head and tilt it back. I take out the .22 and jam it in his mouth. He's struggling, but he's an old wimp. It's like holding down an insect, a goddamn bug. I position him – I've seen enough forensic reports to know what it should look like. I say "Nighty-night, Your Honor," and pull the trigger. The rest you know. OK?'

'OK.'

'Now how about another drink? I'm thirsty as hell.'